OTHER BOOKS BY JUDITH RICHARDS

Summer Lightning

Seminole Summer

The Sounds of Silence

Too Blue to Fly

THELONIOUS RISING

THELONIOUS RISING

BY JUDITH RICHARDS

Little Rock, Arkansas
2014

This is a work of fiction. All characters, organizations and events portrayed in this novel are either products of the author's imagination or are used fictitiously.

THELONIOUS RISING
by Judith Richards

www.RiversEdgeMedia.com

Published by River's Edge Media, LLC
100 Morgan Keegan Drive, Ste. 305
Little Rock, AR 72202

Edited by Robin Miura
Cover design by Gable White

Manufactured in the United States of America.

ISBN-13: 978-1-940595-04-7

Printed in the United States of America.

This book is dedicated to two great artists, and my longtime friends, Don and Martha Andrews.

PROLOGUE

Over the hot tropical waters of West Africa a fitful breeze flung salt spray in the faces of fishermen. Storms are common in the Atlantic between June and November. Most weather disturbances falter and die, no sooner born than ended.

Wind blowing from the east six miles high may collide with wind blowing from the opposite direction, creating a shear that will decapitate a storm and rip it apart before an eye can solidify. Warm waters fuel a hurricane, but cold ocean currents can destroy the system before it gains strength.

For the moment, this particular disturbance has no name. Meteorologists say she is a tropical depression that should be watched, but five days east of Florida, with gale force winds, she is worthy of no more than a warning to seafaring ships. When winds reach hurricane force, they will dignify her with a name: Katrina.

{CHAPTER ONE}

Nine-year-old Thelonious Monk DeCay stood at his opened bedroom window and listened to the coo of mourning doves in the willows. From Holy Cross Church came the toll of a bell announcing early Mass. He had two more weeks before the start of home schooling. Labor Day meant fewer tourists coming to New Orleans and the end of summer freedom.

Sitting on the floor behind him, his best friend used Superglue to attach metal beer caps to the soles of his oxfords. "Monk, if you don't hurry, we'll lose our corner." Percy Brown blew on the glue to hasten drying. "I'm about too big for these shoes," he said. "I hate to give them up. They're the best taps I ever had."

They were going to dance for tourists in the Quarter.

Beyond a levee along the Mississippi River, a ship's horn gave warning to boats approaching from the Inner Harbor Navigational Canal. The sound thrummed in the marrow of Monk's bones and hushed the doves.

"Monk, damn it, get dressed!"

Grandmama heard Percy swear and yelled from the kitchen. "No cussing, Percy Brown. It shows you're ignorant."

"Yes ma'am, Miss James."

"And don't call my grandson Monk. His name is Thelonious."

"Yes ma'am, Miss James."

Three weeks after he was born, his father named him Monk because his mother had failed to do so. Thelonious Monk, was his choice, Grandmama said, a famous jazz pianist and composer born in Rocky Mount, North Carolina, and raised in New York City. "A genius," Grandmama had told Monk. "I shared a stage with him twice, and he admired my style." In an old trunk, she had a picture of the musician that appeared on the cover of *Time* magazine published February 28, 1964.

"Thelonious Monk started playing piano when he was your age," Grandmama said. "He's the man who invented bebop."

It was a term Monk did not know.

Reciting his successes, Grandmama said, "Eleven years after he died, he was honored with a Grammy Lifetime Achievement Award. You're named for a brilliant man, Thelonious. Make your namesake proud and practice the piano."

Thelonious was a mouthful, and everybody called him Monk when Grandmama wasn't around.

Getting dressed to go perform, Monk used rope for a belt. His trousers were intentionally tattered and too short. A ragamuffin image was part of their act. The stage was Jackson Square, passersby their audience.

"Come eat, boys," Grandmama called.

Prompted by a poke of Percy's finger, Monk said, "We don't have time, Grandmama."

"You can't dance all day without fuel for the body. Potato pancakes are ready. Take off those taps coming across my linoleum, Percy."

Not that anyone would notice if he didn't. The worn linoleum had been there longer than Monk had been living with Grandmama, which was since his mother died six years ago.

The ship's horn moaned again, and above the levee Monk saw the mast of a seagoing vessel glide by.

"I expect you to look after Thelonious," Grandmama glared at Percy. She said the same thing every morning.

"I will, Miss James."

She turned from the range and the floor creaked under her weight. She scooped fritters onto plates. Percy added Tabasco. Monk took his plain.

"Stay out the way of gang boys and their badness. Get your elbows off the table, Percy."

"Yes ma'am."

Percy ate quickly and stood up to leave.

"What do you say, Percy?" Grandmama prompted.

"I say thank you for breakfast, Miss James." He moved toward the door and Monk rose to follow.

"Ah-ah-ah!" Grandmama grabbed his arm and stuck out an ebony cheek to get a kiss. Then she said, "Want a kiss, Percy?"

"No ma'am. I got one to home."

Monk hung his shoes around his neck tied together by laces. He patted his pocket to be sure his harmonica was there, grabbed a floppy straw hat, and then ran to overtake Percy out by the street.

Percy pushed the wheel and Monk trotted alongside until they crossed the canal bridge where bicycling was forbidden. Then Monk climbed on the handlebars and Percy peddled. Four miles to go.

The air was warm on Monk's face. He clamped the hat to his head with one hand, careful not to get his toes in the spokes of the bicycle. Suburban smells gave way to city scents of burnt rubber and automobile fumes. They passed dark dens where zydeco pulsed from opened doorways. In another building half a block farther, the recorded music of Fats Domino lured customers into a bar where men drank beer for breakfast and played bourré.

Percy maneuvered around abandoned cars and over broken curbing. He took back alleys and side streets to avoid the hangout of thugs who charged a fee to let them pass. From the Lower Ninth Ward they went through Bywater and Faubourg Marigny to the Quarter.

"Got your come money?" Percy spoke over Monk's shoulder.

"I got it." He kept four one-dollar bills to sweeten the pot.

When tourists saw paper money in a hat, they tended to donate in kind. Loose change invited more coins.

At age thirteen, Percy was four years older than Monk, taller, stronger, and more nearly the color of Grandmama's dark complexion than Monk's cinnamon tan. Percy was a better dancer and played a mean bone. Tourists enjoyed him but held onto their money, and that's where Monk came in.

He couldn't blow the mouth harp as well as Percy, and he certainly couldn't make sparks fly with his homemade taps. But he was small and looked younger than his nine years. Percy taught him to "sell" the act. Grinning and thrashing, tapping and whooping, sucking and blowing the M. Hohner Marine Band harmonica Monk played while Percy kept time with slaps and claps.

They were a team in holey clothes, wearing scuffed shoes and twine bound trousers. When they were home practicing together, Grandmama sat on the back steps and coached them. She knew show business. "Yelp and holler," Grandmama tutored. "Knee-slap and clickety-clack with those taps. If people laugh out loud, they'll part with their money."

There were days when they made fifty or sixty dollars.

Percy hit a pothole and Monk was nearly unseated. "Sorry, Monk."

It hurt his tailbone, but Monk said, "I'm okay."

Sooner or later every visitor to New Orleans ended up in Vieux Carré, known to the world as the French Quarter. Monk enjoyed walking past window displays of Mardi Gras masks and vulgar bumper stickers. In the evening, hawkers stood on the banquette tempting passersby with descriptions of floorshows inside. But for now, the bawdy houses had not begun to open. Monk was seldom here at night because Grandmama expected him home before dark, and anyway, cops chased him off. At sundown Bourbon Street closed to motor traffic and only pedestrians were allowed. At that point, the Quarter was not for children.

Someday when he was a grown man, Monk planned to explore those forbidden places that Grandmama called dens of iniquity. Percy had already been inside. He'd been everywhere. One of his aunts ran a voodoo shop on Toulouse, half a block off Bourbon. If the police caught Percy wandering, he told them he was going to see his aunt and they let him through. A second aunt was a bishop at the Blessed Baby Jesus Spiritual Church. In her company Percy was allowed to be present, because where the bishop went was God's will. His aunt, Bishop Beulah, once saved a naked stripper who was halfway up a rubbing pole when she got the calling and went into rapture right there on the stage. Percy was a witness.

Bicycling through gathering tourists, Percy predicted, "Going to be good crowds today. Be hot, but good crowds."

The Quarter was a magical place. Street musicians produced energetic melodies from guitars, accordions, and homemade percussions. Clowns and robotic mimes performed on every corner. Newly washed streets smelled faintly of garbage, but overriding that came the odor of beignets and coffee from Café Du Monde. Lucky Dog vendors pushed their carts up and down nearby streets offering steamed wieners. Restaurants served Cajun and French foods that contributed exotic aromas of baked fish with garlic sauce and crawfish étouffée. Over it all wafted the malty smell of spilled beer.

Rising from the center of the square, General Andrew Jackson sat astride a rearing horse, his hat held high as though to acknowledge cheers from a grateful population. In 1814 he defeated the British and saved the city during the Battle of New Orleans. The square was named in his honor.

Monk knew these things because the historian, Quinton Toussaint, had told him.

"There's the old queer now," Percy sneered.

"Don't call him that, Percy. He's our friend."

"He ain't my friend, Monk. You're the one he wants to do."

"He doesn't do anything."

"One of these days he might."

Quinton wore green seersucker trousers, a ruffled canary yellow shirt, and his hat was decorated with long feathers dyed the colors of Mardis Gras, purple, green, and gold. When he saw them coming, he stood up. At the age of eighty-two, he was ten years older than Grandmama, but whereas her weight made Grandmama move slowly, Quinton was thin and spry.

"There you are, boys! I thought I'd have to trip the terpsichore in your absence this morning." Monk didn't always understand what he said. Quinton's voice was high tenor, and he spoke with a lilting delivery as though about to sing every sentence.

"Miss James made us eat breakfast before Monk could leave," Percy explained.

"As indeed she should," Quinton said. "May I help with your shoes, Monk?"

"I got them."

Percy was ready, testing his new taps with a heel, toe, and slide. Monk envied the crisp clicks and sparks he created.

Quinton spoke to passing strangers. "They'll be performing shortly. The best act in New Orleans." He pronounced the name of the city, Nawlins.

Monk placed his straw hat on the pavement, positioned dollar bills for best effect, and stepped away ready to dance.

They began with body slaps and toe taps, building a rhythm that made people pause to listen. Monk blew full-mouth on his harmonica, suck-n-blow, suck-n-blow, followed by handclaps and steady taps, holding the cadence. Then Percy yielded the rhythm and tongued his harp down to a single quavering note, with a double tongue beat. A melody established, the music gathered listeners; Monk jumped into motion, tapping, grinning, and slapping his chest in time to Percy's harmony.

"Do it like the Spirit's on you," Percy counseled. He'd learned that from his aunt Bishop Beulah. "Move where the Spirit says go!"

Tap-a-dap, heel and toe, long slide; Quinton wailed and people laughed. Money fell into the hat. Percy joined Monk and side-by-side they moved in unison, clippity-tap-clippity-clap. Quinton howled again and stepped forward to drop a five-dollar bill in the hat. He'd get it back later. It was seed money to get the folks going.

Sidle-slide, leg slap, chest thump, hip bump, Monk dropped back and blew chords on the harmonica. Percy did his stuff. He was smooth and fluid, a polished professional. Tap-a-dap, slap his heel, tap-a-dap, Quinton Toussaint squealed; tap-a-dap, and now Monk took over. His best moves were really the easy ones, but crowds liked them. He twisted his mouth to show concentration, feet flying, taps singing; Percy on the mouth harp hit every other note, a-one-and-two, and-a-one-and-two.

Suddenly, Monk twirled, flashed a grin and looked at the spectators one after another; they smiled and laughed.

Clickety-clack; slap his back, slap and clap, clickety-clack.

Quinton whooped.

People applauded.

Horses along the curb stood in harness, ready to pull coaches filled with touring customers. Whap and snap, the drivers joined in and now the audience: whap! Snap!

Monk was drenched with sweat. They both were. Whirling, spinning, arms thrown wide, then pulled in close to the ribs and moving as one, whap! A sudden clap. Whap, the taps. It couldn't get better than this.

It was in his genes, Grandmama said. His daddy was a jazzman who could play anything—percussion, brass, string, and piano. He passed his talent to the son. Monk's mother sang blues and gospel. Nobody ever struck a purer note, Grandmama had told him. Voice ran in the family. And Grandmama! Quinton Toussaint said she could've been world famous if she hadn't been sidetracked by tragedies in her life.

Quinton knew about Grandmama as he knew about everything else in Nawlins. He was a man who studied buildings, cultures, and events in the past. He loved all things ancient. But mostly, he loved music, especially jazz.

Whappity-whack, clickety-clack, sweat dripped from their noses and chins and soaked their shirts. This was more than street dancing. It was art. Move these boys from Jackson Square to New York City and they would mesmerize the crowds. That's what Quinton said. He named Central Park, Union Square, and the Village, anywhere they danced, they'd be stars, Quinton insisted.

"You can be nothing but what you are," he'd told Monk. "You have your grandmother's heart, the gift of talent from your parents; it's in your muscles and bones, Thelonious Monk. If it is your wish, someday you'll be on Broadway."

When Quinton said things like that, Monk saw Percy's jaw clamp tight, and resentment distorted his features. Percy's father mowed levees for the city, his mother kept accounts for a bookmaker. What Percy knew about music he had taught himself, and he did it by listening to CDs. It wasn't in his muscles and bones; he had to work for it.

"Jazz began in New Orleans," Quinton was fond of saying. "And Monk, you are the next link forged in a long line of creative musicians going back to your roots in Africa and the islands. God, I love you, boy. You thrill me to the core."

"Yeah," Percy observed, peddling home, "he loves you all right. Just be sure that's all he do."

Monk gave Grandmama half of the half he'd earned, and she said, "Y'all had a good day."

"Yes ma'am, we did."

She smoothed the currency on the kitchen table. He always gave her the newest and cleanest bills because she liked to stroke the money and count it several times.

"Twenty-two dollars, Thelonious. What would I do without you?"

They ate fried bologna for supper. The money laid there on the Formica tabletop so Grandmama could look at it now and then. "Isn't that something?" she'd say.

His legs ached from exertion. After his bath, Grandmama put him to bed. She rubbed his calves and thighs with homemade liniment, massaged his hips and back. A smell of camphor filled the room. All the while she talked about things he liked to hear.

"Your mama was a beautiful woman," Grandmama said. "Not fat like me."

"You're not fat, Grandmama."

"Blind at nine," she bent and kissed him on the hip.

"When folks knew your mama was going to sing at the Blessed Baby Jesus Spiritual Church, another body couldn't squeeze into a pew they'd be packed so tight."

Grandmama hummed "Amazing Grace" just the way Monk imagined his mother would've sung it. He could picture a congregation swaying side to side, lost in the pure notes that rose from his mother's throat.

"I once was lost, but now I'm found … " Grandmama crooned softly.

Then she said, "God had need of your mama, Thelonious."

"Yes ma'am."

"I speck God gets lonely, too."

"Yes ma'am."

He'd heard the stories countless times, but never tired of them. Grandmama sang again, how sweet the sound that saved a wretch like me …

Quinton Toussaint had told him that Grandmama stopped performing in public when Monk's mother died. She had a grandson to raise. At the time, Monk was only three.

"What made my mama die?" Monk asked Grandmama. She spoke of sickness that no doctor could cure, a disease that wouldn't turn loose.

The truth came from Quinton. Overdose, he'd said. Amazing grace, how sweet the sound that saved a wretch like me …

Grandmama pulled a sheet over his body. In the dark he heard a whirr of katydids in the willow, crickets under the house. He could track

Grandmama's movements by the creak of flooring as she walked down the hall to go wash dishes.

"Your mother was a tormented woman," the old historian had once confided to Monk. "Agony is bad for an artist, but good for art. Out of her angst came songs that wrenched the heart."

This was why Monk liked being with Quinton. He spoke of things Grandmama never mentioned.

"When your mother sang at Jazz Fest," Quinton said, "you couldn't get within fifty yards of the stage. If she and your daddy played a barrelhouse, news flashed around the Quarter like burning gas. There'd be so many people they couldn't get inside. Musicians came from other joints to stand in the street and listen. Your daddy could lay down some sounds on a piano."

"Talk about my daddy, Quinton."

"He was a handsome man. Educated. He could read sheet music he'd never seen without missing a note. He went to Juilliard in New York City, a very famous school, and might have ended up playing with a symphony if it hadn't been for jazz. Did you know that?"

"You told me."

"Bach, Beethoven, Rachmaninoff, he played everything. But jazz was his fever, and in that he was without equal. He was my friend, and I cared for him, as indeed I care for you, Monk."

In the musty hallway of Grandmama's house there was an autographed photo of Dean DeCay, playfully signed "Tooth." The nickname, applied by another musician, had stuck.

Grandmama called her corridor of photographs the rogue's gallery. There were pictures of Mahalia Jackson, Louis Armstrong, Duke Ellington, Professor Longhair, Dr. John, and the Neville Brothers.

Also on that wall there was a photograph of Monk's mother wearing a white dress, singing in a church choir. Many times Monk had stared at the image searching for his features in her face. Grandmama said he had his mother's eyes, but Monk couldn't tell; in the picture her eyes were closed, mouth open in mid-note.

On top of the upright piano in the living room there were framed pictures of Grandmama, heavyset even as a child. First she sang on Sunday, then she sang in bars, and finally she performed in auditoriums and theaters. She could sing anything, but she was known for gospel. "They kept telling me to go on a diet," she scoffed, "but I daren't do it. Look at lady opera singers. They blow your hair straight back and break a drinking glass when they do it. Those girls got balloons, and need 'em, to make sounds like they do."

Drifting off to sleep, Monk heard the trill of night callers. From the levee came a chorus of frogs.

Grandmama was in the kitchen humming, Amazing grace, how sweet the sound ...

As always, Monk had put his share of today's money in a tightly capped Mason jar, counting all of it again every time he added to the total. He had four hundred and eleven dollars so far.

Grandmama encouraged his savings. "That'll come handy someday when you go to college," she said. "Learning to hold money is one of the best lessons you can learn."

But Monk wasn't planning for college. He saved for a day when he could go in search of his father.

Grandmama said he was probably dead.

But Quinton disagreed. "Every jazzman in America would know if he died," Quinton said. "Oh, no. Tooth DeCay is alive."

{CHAPTER TWO}

Sunday morning, Monk wore a crisply starched green shirt and a red clip-on bow tie.

"Did you shine those shoes, Thelonious?" Grandmama called from her bedroom.

"Yes ma'am, with spit."

Actually, they were patent leather and required no shine. Grandmama meant, had he dusted and buffed them.

His trousers had a crease so sharp Grandmama said he cut grass walking across the lawn.

She looked in the bedroom door. "You are one handsome man," she said.

She wore a dark blue dress because that color slimmed her figure. Her hat was beige silk over a wire frame dome with matching cotton gloves.

"You're beautiful, Grandmama."

"Thank you, Thelonious."

They went out on the front stoop to wait for their ride. The musky smell of the river carried a faint scent of oil, like dribbled diesel on warm pavement. Above the levee a lone seagull looked lost, riding thermal currents so far north of the Gulf of Mexico.

"Grandmama, do you suppose birds are ever afraid of height?"

"If they were," she said, "they'd fly closer to ground."

A moment later she said, "Here comes Mr. Willy now," and she strained to stand up.

Willy Bouchard was a fruit and vegetable vendor in the Ninth Ward and Bywater. His pickup truck had signs down the sides, advertising melons, cucumbers, oranges, apples. He did what his daddy did before him, and his grandfather before that. Six days a week, driving through the ward, his gravelly voice announced the wares he had that day.

"Got squash! Fresh off the vine.
Creole raised and special prime—
Pears and apples and muscadines.
Straw-berries! Blue-berries!"

Mr. Willy was Percy Brown's uncle by marriage, the husband of Aunt Bishop Beulah. Every Sunday he was drafted to bring the faithful to Baby Jesus Spiritual Church. It was the one day of the week he shaved. Otherwise he wore graying whiskers. He was quick to grin and always bowed a bit and touched the brim of his hat when he spoke to a woman.

Over the rear of his truck a metal frame made out of galvanized water pipes supported sheets of plywood to keep produce shaded, so carrots wouldn't go limp and tomatoes get mushy. Every Sunday he removed boxes and baskets of fruits and vegetables from the back of his tan 1988 Ford pickup and put in two long benches. To help passengers get in and out, Mr. Willy had built a moveable set of steps. At each stop, he got out, put down the steps and helped the ladies aboard.

"Morning, Mr. Willy," Grandmama said. "How do the melons look this late in August?"

"Look good, Miss James. I be by with some next week."

"Save me one, Mr. Willy."

Monk was sandwiched between two portly bodies, facing Percy who was going through a similar crush on the opposite bench.

The slow drive to church could take thirty minutes or longer depending on the number of people Mr. Willy had to fetch. It gave the ladies plenty of time to catch up on neighborhood news.

"Your husband's not coming to church this morning, Lucille?" Grandmama questioned an acquaintance.

"They put him in jail last night, Miss James. He got to drinking like men sometime do. One thing led to another, and police say he disturbed the peace. They come around with chains and hauled off a mess of men from the Poland Home Social Club."

"Was there fighting?"

"No. Hadn't nobody complained about nothing. Police just come around and hauled them off. No women. Just men. I think they rounds up men just to get extra hands when they got a ditch to dig."

"It's slavery," another woman said. "I remember my daddy talking about how white folks took black men to sandbag levees when floods came years ago. Worked them under a gun, too."

"They been doing that since before the Civil War," the women agreed. "While he be in jail, if he got a dollar in his pocket, they'll be took it before they let him out, you can be sure of that."

"Police been stealing from poor folks longer than any of us lived," somebody commented.

"In school they teach chirren, if you got trouble, call the police."

"Yeah, do that," someone scoffed. "Call police and then you really got trouble."

Aunt Bishop Beulah was waiting at the church house door. She was sturdy like Grandmama with strong hands and ankles the size of fire hydrants. She had big lips and square teeth, two of which were capped with gold. When the Spirit came on her, she shouted the sermon with her mouth so wide, sitting in the front pew Monk could see that little dangly thing Grandmama called an epiglottis.

When the congregation assembled, Bishop Beulah stood at the podium and began: "How many times God got to say it to you?" she challenged the congregation. "How many times before you hear His message? That's what I'm talking about today."

Calls from the pulpit received replies from the audience. Women fanned their bosoms and flapped their blouses. Mothers stirred air around sleepy babies sweating on a pew.

"Today we're going to baptize Sister Julianne's daughter, Cherita," Aunt Bishop Beulah announced.

Sister Julianne was one of Monk's teachers in home schooling. There were times when he was so overcome by her beauty he had difficulty speaking. He was sure she thought him not quite bright. If she touched him, it seared the flesh and left him aquiver. In history class she had told them her ancestors came to Louisiana from French Acadia above the Canadian border. From them she inherited eyes so green and deep Monk was sure he might tumble into the cool bottomless pool of her gaze. When Sister Julianne smiled, it sucked air from his lungs. He loved her with no hope of ever saying so.

For her baptism, five-year-old Cherita wore a long pure white dress bound above the knees to keep water from billowing her skirt when she entered the liquid grave. After the dunking she emerged from the baptistery sputtering, a new person. She was met with shouts of praise and congratulations.

Cherita was one of six students who shared home schooling with Monk. She got piano lessons from Grandmama. In return, Cherita's mother, Julianne, taught English and history to other students in the home study group. Another teacher was Percy Brown's mama, whose subject was mathematics because she was good with numbers, keeping accounts like she did for bookmakers. At her home, Percy's mother taught computers to older boys like her son. Next year, Monk would be in that class, too.

Church today was boring. No one screamed impulsively. Nobody rolled on the floor in ecstatic convulsions. The Holy Spirit didn't come upon anybody, and there was no speaking in tongues.

"Give me a wit-ness!" Bishop Beulah hollered repeatedly. But nobody came forward.

After services, Aunt Bishop Beulah complained to Grandmama, "We didn't none of us sing with heart today. I prayed them up, but it didn't do any good."

"It's too hot, Beulah," Grandmama said. "Get us through August to when the weather turns cool and we'll be back to normal."

"Y'all still planning to start school after Labor Day?" Aunt Bishop Beulah inquired.

"Yes, we will," Grandmama said.

Percy and his younger brother, Benny, rode home in Mr. Willy's fruit and vegetable truck, this time sitting next to Monk. Benny's sleeve was slick from wiping his nose, and he kept lifting his lip to sniff. He was the darkest of the youngsters who came to home schooling.

"Let's go to the Quarter this afternoon, Percy," Monk suggested.

"I can't," Percy said. "Mama and Aunt Bishop Beulah are going over to help the Big Chief lay out a new suit. I got to practice anyway. Next

Mardi Gras I'll be a spy boy for the Soaring Eagles."

Envy took Monk's voice for a moment. Twice a year, at Mardi Gras and again on St. Joseph's, a spy boy ran ahead of the marching Big Chief and his procession. The spy boy's job was to watch for competing Mardi Gras Indian tribes, which he reported to the flag boy, who in turn advised the Big Chief. Spy boy was a position of honor.

"Let's go tomorrow then," Monk insisted.

"Monday, Tuesday, and Wednesday are lousy days, Monk."

"We could make a few dollars."

"Too hot to dance that hard for a few dollars," Percy said. "Let's wait until Thursday."

"Can I borrow your bike then?" Monk asked.

"I have to use it today."

The rest of the ride home was hot, dusty, and bumpy. Grandmama sat near the tailgate, eyes closed. Her body jiggled when the truck hit potholes.

"You got enough money to buy your own wheel," Percy said. "Why don't you do it?"

"Maybe I will," Monk agreed. But he knew he wouldn't. Grandmama would never let him go to the Quarter alone.

Behind the house, Grandmama kept a small garden where she raised tomatoes. Bending was difficult for her, so Monk did stoop work as she directed.

"Watch for hornworms, Thelonious."

"I am, Grandmama." When he found one, he dropped it into a cup of kerosene.

He liked the smell of newly turned soil, and it was a pleasure to watch things grow. In early March, they planted onions, garlic, and chili peppers to keep pests off the tomatoes. By late summer, basil, marigold, mint, and nasturtiums did the same job. Grandmama's plump, juicy tomatoes were summer money. She swapped her produce for Mr. Willy's fruits. She also traded with a neighbor who had laying hens. Another neighbor raised rabbits and Grandmama used their manure to fertilize the plot.

As Monk inspected plants, Grandmama sat in the shade on the porch with a glass of iced tea. She waved away gnats and swiggled ice cubes. "Thelonious, I see a tomato worm on that sprig to your left."

"No ma'am. That's a curled leaf. Grandmama, why did my daddy leave me?"

"Your mother died, Monk. Some things a man can't stand."

"Where did he go?"

"One place, then another."

Monk saw leaves with serrated edges, sure signs of a hornworm. He tracked it down and plucked it from under a leaf.

"Didn't he love me, Grandmama?"

"Of course he did. And he loved your mother. Lord knows she was crazy about him."

"Why didn't he write to me?" Monk asked.

"How much reading could a three-year-old do?"

"He could write to you, couldn't he?"

When he was about to get new information, Grandmama would pause to think before she spoke. He heard ice cubes tinkle in her glass. "Our side of the family never had much to do with your daddy's side," she said. "His people weren't happy when he married Elaine."

"I've learned to read. Why doesn't he write to me now?"

"I speck he's dead, Thelonious."

"Quinton doesn't think so."

"Quinton Toussaint? How you come by listening to him?"

"I see him at Jackson Square."

"Don't pay attention to that old man, Thelonious. He lives so far in the past he wouldn't know tomorrow if it showed up yesterday. Did Quinton say something to upset you?"

Monk choked with emotion. "Quinton said my daddy's not dead, Grandmama."

"I said I speck he's dead, Thelonious. I didn't say for sure. Thelonious, come here."

Grandmama took both his hands and kissed the dirty fingers. She pulled him onto her lap. She smelled of talcum powder and mint. "I love you," she said.

"I love you, Grandmama."

Doves stuttered in the willow, and soft breezes made the tree whisper a reply.

Grandmama kissed his forehead. "Let's make these creases go away. Bye-bye lines, don't furrow this sweet brow."

"Percy's got his mama and daddy," Monk said. "He's got aunts and uncles. Anytime I go to his house, kinfolks are crawling all over it. It's just you and me, Grandmama."

She chuckled and her breasts bobbed. "Looks like you have to make do with me by myself," she said.

That ended the conversation.

To learn more, he'd have to ask Quinton.

Monk rarely lied to Grandmama. He didn't have to. No matter what he did, she was very forgiving after the fact. It was before the fact that he had to fib.

Monday morning, barefoot, tap shoes draped around his neck, harmonica in pocket, he took his straw hat and went to Grandmama. She was still in bed. On hot days she moved only when necessary. Two fans blew across her body.

"Grandmama, I'm going to the Quarter."

"Where's Percy?"

"I'm meeting him across the canal bridge."

"Next time, have him come here to the house, so I can speak to him directly before y'all leave."

"I'll tell him to look after me," Monk preempted.

"Tell him he better. Y'all be careful, babe."

If he'd told her the truth, he wouldn't be going. Monk skipped out the back door into glaring sunshine. There wasn't a hint of breeze. Silken dust powdered leaves of trees and grass on the ground. A stray dog fell in step beside him, tongue lolling. They trotted along together until Monk reached the canal bridge, then the pup stopped and watched him go.

Cars drove by, tires sucking hot asphalt. He had to detour around several blocks where gang boys lounged on the street confronting younger boys and selling dope. Sweat glued the clothes to his body. Finally, he arrived at Jackson Square.

Percy was right; Monday was a bad day for tourists. People who came to town after the weekend were looking for a cut-rate hotel. They took pictures of one another and sat on benches feeding pigeons or watching other tourists. At the French Market they bought caps and T-shirts with slogans that told their friends they'd been to New Orleans. Families rode trolleys to the end of the line, sightseeing on the cheap. Audubon Park Zoo, Aquarium of the Americas, and gambling casinos pulled visitors away from Jackson Square.

Musicians and mimes played to a handful of people. Artists painted city scenes of iron lace and flowered balconies. Tarot readers predicted the future, and today few performers received contributions for their efforts.

Monk sat on a bench with Quinton. The historian smeared paste across his pink nose to prevent sunburn. He wore pink sunglasses. His shirt was pink. He glowed.

Monk watched overweight tourists window-shop as they strolled the banquettes.

"Where's Percy?" Quinton asked.

"He's practicing to be a spy boy for Big Chief of the Soaring Eagles in the Ninth Ward. He wants to be one of the Indians."

"Percy will be good at that," Quinton said.

"He might be," Monk said resentfully, but he knew it was true.

"Mardi Gras Indians got started in the days of slavery," Quinton noted. "The Indians and Black men saw themselves as brothers against the white devils. From the Indians, African captives learned about local herbs and remedies for strange new illnesses. Because Negroes had a friendly relationship with local tribes they wanted to emulate them."

A woman pushing a stroller paused with her children and stared at Quinton. Monk tried to see the man through her eyes. In addition to the sequined pink blouse, Quinton wore bright red trousers, and green Crocs with no socks. His nose was covered with zinc oxide and his feathered hat waved in a breeze.

"The Natchez tribe of Indians was famous for their spiritual knowledge, which wasn't far removed from what tribesmen had practiced in Africa," Quinton continued. "They both believed in power of the obeah and talisman. Spirits, charms, and hexes were things they shared in common. American Indians integrated runaway slaves into their tribes."

The woman and her children drew nearer. "Look at the clown, children." Quinton ignored them.

"There are many accounts of Indian nations giving sanctuary to escaped slaves," Quinton related. "The Seminole Wars in Florida came about because the U.S. Cavalry went down to recapture slaves being sheltered by tribes in the Everglades."

The lady tourist asked, "Are you a storyteller?"

"Yes ma'am, I am. Hyperbole is my middle name. Is there a tale you'd like to hear?"

"Does it cost anything?"

"As a part of the show," Quinton threw an arm around Monk, "my talented friend will do an amazing dance with appropriate hand claps and body slaps and a few chords on the harmonica. The total cost is one dollar."

"Will you accept Canadian?"

"Pearls, rubies, and diamonds, but no Canadian money," Quinton replied. "We have no way to exchange it."

The visitors moved on and the historian picked up his story where he left off.

"When Mardi Gras Indians go forth in their feathered suits today, it is a tribute to long dead allies from centuries past. Have you eaten, my boy?"

"Not yet."

"Talking about slaves made me think of Maspero's. Come along, lad. We'll continue this discussion over lunch."

Café Maspero had been a slave exchange where plantation owners once came to buy and sell human beings. Sitting where doomed captives had been on display, Monk could imagine the fear of kidnapped men and women put on the block for sale.

"Prospective buyers pinched the breast and buttocks of girls," Quinton recited. "They poked and pressed the pelvis, looking for healthy breeding stock."

Quinton divided a chopped sirloin sandwich and gave half to Monk. The meat was thick and dressing oozed over Monk's fingers. Quinton pushed a plate of French fried potatoes toward him. "Help yourself," he said.

"Quinton, you believe my daddy is alive?"

"Yes."

"Where do you think he might be?"

Quinton's blue eyes moved back and forth across Monk's face and he chewed his burger a long time. "Monk, if Tooth wanted to be found, you'd know where he is."

The thought shot pain through Monk's chest. "Why wouldn't he want me to find him?"

More chewing, endlessly. Quinton wiped his chin with a napkin. "Every man has demons, Monk. Sometimes a man hides from his past because memories are too painful to bear."

Behind them, a waitress dropped her tray and the clatter rebounded from the tiled floor to brick walls. Patrons hushed.

"You don't think he'd want to see me?" Monk asked.

Chewing, chewing, chewing. Quinton dabbed his lips. "I imagine any father would be curious about a son he hasn't seen for many years. Perhaps he wouldn't want you to see him, however."

"But, why?"

"Maybe because it would stir the sediment of memories long ago settled. He might dread questions he'd rather not answer. I'm guessing at all of this, I have no way of knowing."

"Sometimes I dream about him," Monk said. "I dream that I'm in some kind of trouble and he comes to help me."

Quinton sighed. "I imagine your father would have similar dreams in which he tried to reach you when you needed him."

He looked over the crowded room and changed the subject. "This building dates back to 1788 when Don Juan Paillet purchased the present site from Don Nerciso Alva. Paillet constructed a new building over existing ruins. Nothing here has changed much since then. The Paillet family owned the place for ninety years. It was also here that the pirate Jean Lafitte and his brother Pierre sold stolen goods to rich citizens. In this building Andrew Jackson planned the battle of New Orleans against the British."

Pedestrians walked past French doors that opened the café onto the street. Pigeons came in and pecked at food dropped on the floor.

"Over a period of time thousands of naked and terrified slaves were herded into a room upstairs where apartments are now," Quinton said. "They wept and trembled and waited to be sold. The bedlam then must've been louder than it is now."

Across the room, people shouted at one another. At the bar, a woman shrieked and men laughed. Voices created a jumble of noise. Monk could smell their bodies. Warm air came through the French doors. Humidity made the table sticky to touch. A horse-drawn carriage rattled past, and Monk heard the tour guide announce that this was the old slave exchange.

"The building was named for Pierre Maspero, who ran the exchange," Quinton said. "To English-speaking citizens this was 'Maspero's Exchange.' The French called it 'La Bourse de Maspero.'"

While Quinton paid the bill, Monk looked around at the brick walls, exposed beams of the high ceiling, and overhead fans that kept air moving. Their waitress was a girl only slightly older than Percy Brown. She had tattoos on her arms and legs; rings pierced her nose, lip and eyebrow. Monk thought she was pretty, but cluttered. Quinton had ordered a takeout sandwich.

He said, "Monk, are you going near Bourbon and Toulouse?"

"I can if you want me to."

Quinton gave him the sack. "This is lunch for our friend, Jon Latour. You know where to take it, don't you?"

"Yes sir."

"I'd deliver it myself," Quinton said, "but a publisher is here from Baton Rouge to discuss my new book. If I don't hurry, I'll be late. We're meeting at Galatoire's. There was a time when they wouldn't allow me in the place dressed as I am. But now I'm a published historian, therefore an accepted eccentric. Be careful going home, babe."

"Thanks for my lunch, Quinton."

Off the historian went, a bouncy lift in every step, feathers on his hat waving in the air above him.

Monk could feel rain coming. He draped the tap shoes around his neck, jammed the straw hat on his head, and hurried along St. Louis Street toward Bourbon.

Because of Quinton, Monk saw everything in a different light. Before the Louisiana Purchase in 1803, the French Quarter was the entire City of New Orleans. Local Indians called the area Chinchuba, which meant "alligator." It had been a swampy bog infested with snakes and mosquitoes, quick to flood and slow to drain.

“The precipitation from thirty-three states emptied into the Mississippi River,” Quinton liked to say. “In the spring when northern snows melted, the river overflowed and flooded the would-be city. Summers were unbearably hot and humid. The Indians must have thought Europeans were crazy when they chose to build homes in this sinking sodden soil.”

In those days travel and commerce were done mainly by waterways. “Therefore,” Quinton would say, “settlers began a battle with the river that has endured for three centuries, forever struggling to hold off muddy waters of the mighty Mississippi.”

Then Quinton would smile at Monk. “The dam story is a good one.”

“Yessir.”

“It’s a joke, Monk.”

“Yessir. I got it.”

{CHAPTER THREE}

The first time Monk heard about Jon Latour, he and Quinton Toussaint were ambling through the Quarter. The historian paused beside an ivy-covered wall and said, "Hello, Jon. This is my young friend, Thelonious Monk. He's the son of Tooth DeCay. You remember Tooth, the great jazzman who often played at Preservation Hall."

It was a perfectly normal conversation, except there was nobody there.

Quinton produced a sack of confections he'd bought from a candy kitchen near the French Market.

"There are no nuts in these chocolates," Quinton said to the wall. He pushed his offering through the ivy and when he withdrew his hand, the package was gone.

"I'll come by later with something for supper," Quinton had said. With that, he and Monk continued down the street.

"Who were you talking to?" Monk questioned.

"Jon Latour," Quinton said. "He has bad teeth. He can't eat candy with nuts. I wish he would go to a dentist, but that isn't going to happen."

Monk learned that it was Quinton's daily routine. He bought food and shoved it through the vines where somebody, or something, on the other side accepted it. Every time they made a delivery, Quinton revealed more about Monk to Jon, and more about Jon to Monk.

On another trip, Quinton said, "Monk's mother was Elaine DeCay, Jon. She was the blues singer who married Tooth DeCay. She died about six years ago. She had a lovely voice, and little wonder, her mother is Diane James the gospel singer."

Walking away, he explained to Monk. "I've known Jon all his life. When he was younger we spent time together, as do you and I. The current state of his mind did not happen overnight. Like an oyster creates a pearl with layers of nacre, dementia began with one tiny grain of irritation and a futile attempt to coat the troublesome grit. The next thing Jon knew, people dressed him in a backward coat with long sleeves and tried to fry his brain with electric shocks."

Departing from the drop site, Quinton had said, "Jon was always a good boy. He attended parochial school, went to confession on Saturday, and never missed Mass on the Sabbath until his mother died."

Now, by himself, with tap shoes slung around his neck by the laces, Monk carried food for Jon. He hurried along under darkening skies. A smattering of rain hit the street in huge wallops. Wind swirled trash in the gutter then died away to hot steamy stillness. Thunder grumbled.

When he reached the ivy-choked wall, he said, "Mr. Latour? Quinton Toussaint had to go to a meeting. He asked me to bring you a muffuletta."

The heavens rumbled and thunder echoed away to silence. A man and woman rushed by on their way to shelter. Down the street a garbage truck beeped a warning and backed up. Monk saw a small dog run into a doorway and cower, tail tucked between his legs.

"Mr. Latour, are you there?"

Monk parted the leaves of English ivy and peered through a hole in the wall. He saw a narrow walkway and at the far end a wrought-iron balcony overgrown with bougainvillea; the passage was littered with broken bottles, empty beer cans, and old newspapers.

He remembered something Quinton once said about Latour. "He's often there even when you don't see him. Like a strand of spider's silk adrift on the wind, he follows me as I walk along. If you take a breath, you might smell him."

And he did. It was an odor like wet laundry about to sour.

Standing at the wall, Monk said, "Mr. Latour, I don't want to drop this food and leave it. Rain will ruin the sandwich."

He thrust the muffuletta through the hole as far as he could reach and held it at arm's length. He felt a tug and released it.

He parted the ivy and peered through again. Nobody there.

Clouds roiled and lightning flashed. The percussion cracked sharply. Monk clutched his hat and ran.

A police car pulled up beside him. "Where you going, boy?"

Thinking quickly, Monk said, "To see my aunt."

"Who's your aunt?"

"Fiona, at the Voodoo Shop."

"Get along then," the cop said, and pulled away. Monk could see him looking back in his rear view mirror.

A tremendous clap of thunder hailed the rain and down it came as though poured from a bucket. In an instant he was drenched. He ran into the doorway of Fiona's Voodoo Shop.

Percy's aunt stood six feet tall before she put on high heel shoes. Grandmama described her as "willow-switch skinny," a physical condition Fiona attributed to potions she sold and spells she conjured.

She was a fearsome woman with piercing eyes accented by long false lashes and mascara. She wore a flowing red dress embroidered with signs of the zodiac. Her jangling earrings were made from bones of small animals and bits of silver strung together in a way that repelled evil spirits.

In glass display cases, alligator tooth jujus and voodoo dolls lay between imitation shrunken heads. There was jewelry from Haiti and Jamaica. A sign on the wall advertised personalized spells for specific problems. Another sign advised, "Oils, potions, and lotions are made with the freshest ingredients."

"You're dripping on my floor, Monk."

"I'm sorry, Miss Fiona."

"I was about to have a cup of tea," she said. "Will you join me?"

"Is it voodoo tea?"

"Orange pekoe and black."

"Will it put a hex on me?"

"No."

He declined, but she gave it to him anyway. They went through a beaded curtain into a small dimly lit room. Monk sat at a low table upon which there was a crystal ball and an incense burner. It was here that Fiona offered readings to her customers. Under glass on the tiny pentagon-shaped table was a list of suggested spells a customer might wish to order.

Pacify alienated ancestors and ask for their support in your efforts.

Get a new job, promotions, and raises.

Stay out of jail. (Be warned, if you commit a crime, we cannot remove your karma.)

Bring loved ones closer to you.

Return evil spells to those who have cast evil upon you.

"Can you do these things?" Monk asked.

"With prayer, yes."

"You have to pray?"

"Voodoo is a religion. Prayer is important."

Monk continued to read the list: Remove unwanted ghosts and spirits. Locate lost items. Increase virility and boost libido.

"Do you know Jon Latour, Miss Fiona?"

"I remember him from years ago. He is deceased."

Monk had intended to ask for help finding his father, but he now realized that Fiona didn't know everything. At this very minute Jon Latour was alive and eating a muffuletta only a couple of blocks away.

A tremendous clap of thunder shook the building and Monk flinched. "How will you get home?" Fiona inquired.

"Walk, I guess."

"Does your grandmother know you're here?"

He figured the truth now might save him from an inadvertent slip of her tongue later, so he said, "I snuck off to come dance for the tourists, Miss Fiona."

She laughed softly, and it was a tinkling sound like wind chimes. "My husband will be by to pick me up in an hour," she said. "We'll give you a ride home."

She looked into his cup. "Don't you like my tea?"

"I'm not very thirsty. But thank you."

She took the dishes through a second beaded curtain to the very rear of her shop. "Would you care for ginger snap cookies and a canned soft drink, Monk?"

"No, ma'am, thank you. I just ate lunch."

She laughed again, a ripple of pleasure that was pleasing to the ear and yet slightly unnerving.

"I won't tell your grandmother you were here," she offered.

"Thank you, Miss Fiona."

He spent the hour looking into display cases at dream-catcher sieves, southwest Indian medicine charms, and backwoods Louisiana dried skulls of possums and raccoons.

Riding home in the rear seat of Fiona's Cadillac, Monk listened to the adults talk. "Did you work today, Earl?"

"There be rain, woman, don't you see?"

Earl Thibodeaux described himself as "a full-blood-Cajun-coon-ass, and proud of it."

"Have you been drinking, Earl?" Fiona questioned her husband.

"I had four, maybe three buckets of beer."

"Did you fix that door in the garage?"

"Don't that another door, yeah?"

"I'm talking about the one the car goes through, Earl."

"I be do dat directly."

The windshield wipers swept back and forth leaving oily arcs across the glass. "Mr. Thibodeaux," Monk said, "let me out down the block from home, please."

"The rain be pouring, boy."

"That's all right. Let me out at the corner."

"And Earl," Fiona said, "we won't mention that we saw Monk in Vieux Carré."

"Ah-hah-yeah!" Earl said. "Dat boy been do bad?"

"Nothing of the kind," Fiona replied. "Simply don't mention it."

The man grinned in the rear view mirror and winked at Monk. "I won't say nothing, no," Earl said. "Be a secret me and you, right Monk?"

"Yes sir. Thank you."

As it turned out, Grandmama didn't ask about his trip to the Quarter.

It rained Tuesday and again Wednesday. Depressed over the loss of earning time, Monk sat on the back porch watching the garden get knocked to the ground in a cloudburst. Rain beat on the roof overhead and poured off the eave in a silvery screen.

Sister Julianne had come over to discuss the beginning of school with Grandmama. They were in the kitchen going over study plans. The daughter, Cherita, sat on the porch swing beside Monk, pumping one leg to maintain momentum.

"You be baptized?" Cherita asked.

"No."

"Go to hell if you don't." Her hair was braided in tight cornrows. The hem of her skirt was decorated with a parade of yellow ducklings that matched the tops of her socks. She wore yellow shoes.

"Now that you're baptized," Monk said, "do you feel different?"

"I don't think so."

"Did you feel cleaner after being dunked?"

"No."

"What was it like?" Monk questioned.

"Bishop Beulah pinched my nose so tight it hurt a little. I got strangled anyway when I opened my mouth just as she laid me back in the water."

"Did you see the Holy Spirit?"

"I saw little lights from squinching my eyes tight."

"If the Spirit didn't come to you, how do you know the baptism worked?" Monk asked.

"The Spirit came to me in a dream. He said get baptized because my time isn't long."

"What does that mean?

"I'm going to die, I reckon."

"Are you scared?"

"Not with Jesus holding my hand."

Monk had considered baptism for himself. Grandmama said do whatever he felt, but he didn't like the idea of coming up wet in front of the whole congregation.

Percy arrived on his bicycle rain soaked and barefoot. He slogged up onto the porch and sat on the floor. A puddle formed around him.

"Hey, Cherita."

"Hey you self, Percy."

"How did you like being baptized?"

"I got strangled wit' the water and I saw jabs of light from squinch eye."

"Did you see Jesus?"

"I didn't see nothing but jabs of light."

Percy stuck out his lower lip and blew a drop of water off the end of his nose. "I'm not going to do it, myself."

"Me either," Monk said.

"Go to hell then," Cherita warned.

"Uncle Earl uses one of Aunt Fiona's potions to keep him clean of sin no matter what he does," Percy said. "Which makes me remember, Monk. Where were you Monday?"

"What do you mean?"

"I came by looking for you. Miss James thought you were with me at Jackson Square."

Monk's stomach sank. He'd been caught in the lie.

He went into the kitchen. Sister Julianne didn't notice him standing against a wall waiting for a lull in conversation. He didn't want to reveal his deception in Sister Julianne's presence, so he stood quietly. She traced her plans for English lessons, conjugated verbs, appositives, and misplaced modifiers. Finally, Grandmama glanced up and without explanation he mouthed the words, "I'm sorry, Grandmama."

She stared at him and then nodded. She wasn't smiling.

Grandmama came to tuck him in bed. The rain had eased and the air cooled. "Did you wash your ears?" she asked.

"Yes ma'am."

"That's good, because I want you to hear what I have to say."

He knew what was coming.

"When you don't tell the truth," Grandmama said, "it means you don't trust me."

"That's not true, Grandmama."

"If you trusted me, you could say anything at all and know I'd try to understand."

"Yes ma'am."

"It hurt my feelings, Thelonious."

"I'm sorry."

"If you make up your mind to do something without my approval, say so outright and at least I'll know you trusted me enough to do that."

She bent over and kissed his forehead, the weight of her breast pressing him into the mattress.

"Grandmama, Cherita thinks she's going to die."

"She has a vivid imagination, Thelonious."

"She said it was going to happen soon."

"Don't none of us know when God will call." She kissed him again and then stood up.

"I love you, Grandmama. I won't lie again."

"Don't tell me that," Grandmama replied. "Say you'll try not to lie. There are times when truth won't do. Somebody axes how you feel, and you don't feel good and you know they don't care anyway—so what you going to say?"

"I say I'm fine."

"That's right. A policeman stops you on the street and axes do you have cash. You not going to say you do because he might take your money."

"Yes ma'am."

"But don't lie to the ones who love you, baby. And if you do lie, confess up quick and get it behind you."

After Grandmama left the room, he lay there in the dark thinking about Jon Latour. He wondered where the man slept during the heavy rains. Quinton said Latour heard voices, and that meant he was probably insane. But the faithful at Baby Jesus Spiritual Church heard voices and they weren't insane.

"Does Jon know he's crazy?" Monk had asked Quinton.

"He knows other people think he is. That's why he hides from society. He's afraid they'll lock him up and shoot electricity through his brain."

As they walked along that day, Quinton was quiet for a long time. Finally, he said, "Eventually Jon will need you to take my place."

"Me?" Monk stammered. "It can't be me. I'm going to find my father."

"And I have no doubt you will someday," Quinton said. "But sooner or later you'll come back here. No matter where you wander, or how far you go, you'll return to Nawlins. Native born always do."

In bed on his back, Monk threw off the sheet to capture a breeze. He heard rain dripping from the eave. Up at the canal a whistle blew to warn oncoming traffic that the drawbridge was about to open.

He wondered if his father was lying in the dark somewhere, thinking about him.

Monk had a bad taste in his mouth. Could a hex be caught just sitting beside a cup of orange pekoe and black tea?

He heard Grandmama creaking down the hallway. He pretended to be asleep. She came in, covered him with the sheet, and patted his bottom. She put her lips to his forehead and held them there for a long time. Her bosom pressed him down. He liked her bosom. It comforted him.

Before he knew it, he was asleep.

Thursday morning came clean and sunshined. Percy waited while Monk dressed.

"Did you take a bath, Thelonious?" Grandmama called from down the hall.

He did. Last night. But he said, "What for, Grandmama? I'll get hot and sweaty dancing."

"Fresh sweat smells better than yesterday's sweat."

They went through the usual routine: "Eat breakfast ... Percy, look out for Thelonious ... stay away from gang boys ..."

Then they were off. The sky was rain-swept, bright blue, and cloudless. The air smelled of oleander and damp pavement.

"Did you get in trouble for telling a lie?" Percy questioned.

"It hurt Grandmama's feelings. That was worse than a whipping."

"She ever beat you?"

"No."

Percy steadied the bike as Monk climbed onto the handlebars. "When my daddy gets mad he makes me bend over bare butt and tries to send me to the next parish with a paddle."

The bicycle lurched over uneven pavement and Monk held tight to his hat.

"Got your come money?" Percy asked.

"I got it. Watch the holes, Percy."

"Worst whipping I ever got was from my coon ass uncle Earl," Percy said. "I snuck out his Cadillac for a ride one night."

"You're lying, Percy! You didn't do that."

"Yeah, I did. Won't do it again I promise you. He began to whip me and I tried to survive it out without screaming. The longer I held quiet, the harder he hit me. I decided screaming wasn't a bad idea after all. That's the first time I ever prayed in that position.

"My aunt Fiona had fell asleep and when I cut loose yelling she woke up and made him stop. I'd have got away with taking the car except I left the radio on and the battery ran down, which he tended to notice right away."

People were already strolling through the French Market. Monk got off the bike and walked.

"Going to be a good day, Monk. Oops, there's the old queen."

"Percy, quit calling him that."

"Watch how his lips get pouty when he talks to you," Percy said. "Like he just said 'prune' and felt good doing it."

Quinton waved from afar, holding their place at the square.

Thinking of Jon Latour, Monk said, "Quinton looks after his friends."

"Maybe so, but watch his poochy lips."

Suddenly angry, Monk swung his tap shoes and Percy barely dodged the blow. "I want you to stop saying bad things about Quinton," Monk demanded. "Or I won't work with you anymore."

"Okay, Monk. To hell with it."

Monk stood, legs spread, face-on with the boy.

"I wouldn't let anybody talk about you that way, Percy, because you're my friend."

"All right," Percy said, "forget it."

When they approached Quinton, the old man held his arms wide. "My babes," he said. "How good to see you. May I help with your shoes, Monk?"

"No, thanks." Monk untied the laces to separate them.

Percy stood behind Quinton and pursed his lips. He pulled up his shirt and wiped his mouth as if that were his intention all along.

Quinton leaned close to Monk. "They've agreed to publish my book. It's an epistolary told in the words of people who shaped Jackson Square. I'm going to dedicate it to you and Jon Latour."

"Good, Quinton."

"Monk, something remarkable happened this morning. I took beignets to Jon, and he spoke to me. I can't remember the last time he said anything to me."

Startled, Monk said, "What did he say?"

"He said, tell Monk thank you for the sandwich."

"He said that? He said my name?"

"He did. He said tell Monk."

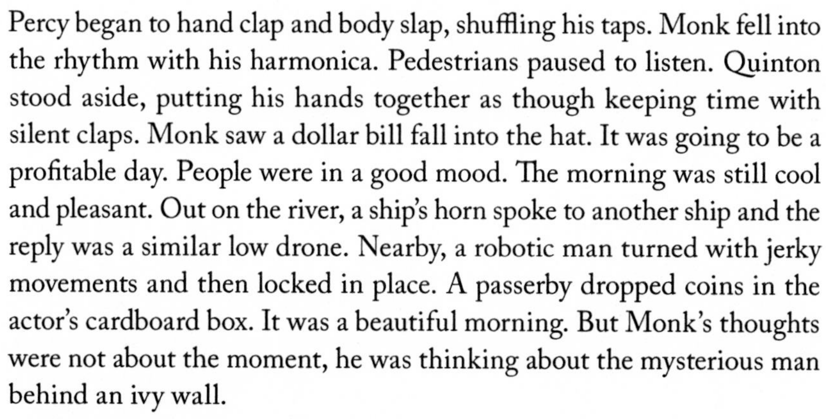

Percy began to hand clap and body slap, shuffling his taps. Monk fell into the rhythm with his harmonica. Pedestrians paused to listen. Quinton stood aside, putting his hands together as though keeping time with silent claps. Monk saw a dollar bill fall into the hat. It was going to be a profitable day. People were in a good mood. The morning was still cool and pleasant. Out on the river, a ship's horn spoke to another ship and the reply was a similar low drone. Nearby, a robotic man turned with jerky movements and then locked in place. A passerby dropped coins in the actor's cardboard box. It was a beautiful morning. But Monk's thoughts were not about the moment, he was thinking about the mysterious man behind an ivy wall.

Imagine that—Jon said his name.

{CHAPTER FOUR}

Getting money out of his savings jar, Monk dropped it and the glass shattered. Coins and dollar bills spilled across his bedroom floor. "Damn it!"

"Thelonious," Grandmama yelled from the kitchen, "you couldn't think of a better word than that?"

"It was the first one that came to mind, Grandmama."

"Then say nothing at all."

Grandmama said cussing was proof that a person wasn't educated enough to come up with a more acceptable expression. Swearing was like wearing a sign I am ignorant.

Looking at cash strewn across the floor, Percy said, "How much money did you have in that jar?"

"Four hundred thirty-four dollars."

"You saved that in one year?"

"This year and last. How much have you saved?"

"Nothing now," Percy said. "I had to loan it all to my coon ass uncle Earl because somebody stole the tires off his Cadillac."

"He'll pay you back won't he?"

"He says he will. Monk, you're so pokey. Let's go."

After a hurried breakfast and the usual instructions from Grandmama, they departed, Monk riding on the bicycle handlebars. The air felt restless, hot when still and cool when it blew. "You think it's going to rain, Percy?"

"TV said no. Hold on, Monk."

Monk lifted his rear end off the handlebars as Percy bumped the bike over a low curb and rode the banquette for a distance. An elderly man slouched on a bench holding a small quivering dog on his lap. Percy veered off the sidewalk to avoid a woman pushing a grocery cart filled with aluminum cans.

"I was going to use the money to upgrade my mama's computer," Percy explained. "She said we can go online if I help pay for it. That's what I was saving for."

Monk was looking forward to next year when he could join the class on computers. But for now, he knew nothing about it. He lifted his bottom again as they bumped off the walkway.

Percy crossed the street to dodge another cart filled with recyclables. Ahead of them a man on a bicycle carried huge plastic bags tied to his wheel and strapped on his back. He looked like a monstrous beetle moving slowly along. These were homeless people going to a reclamation center to sell junk.

"After we get online," Percy said, "My mama's going to get me a credit card. There's a store on the Internet called Amazon that sells music you can't find anywhere else: the Louis Armstrong Hot Fives, King Oliver's Creole Jazz Band, Jelly Roll Morton's Red Hot Peppers."

Monk couldn't imagine how a music store could be on Internet, like outer space, he thought.

Percy hit a pothole and Monk nearly toppled. "Damn it, Percy!"

Mimicking Grandmama, Percy said, "You can't think of a better word than that, Thelonious?"

They both laughed.

"Amazon has old-time music," Percy said. "Sonny Terry playing harmonica, with Brownie McGhee on guitar, things like that."

"Do you think they'd have my mama singing blues and my father playing jazz?"

"If it was ever put on a record I bet they would. Amazon has almost all the recorded music anybody ever made."

Percy stopped at the French Market. "Better get off and walk from here, Monk. It's too crowded to ride a wheel."

It was still early and already the Quarter teemed with pedestrians. An acrobatic group performed at the base of the levee near Café Du Monde.

Monk paused to watch them toss one another into the air.

"Monk, come on!"

Around the corner, artists displayed their paintings along a wrought iron fence that enclosed Jackson Square. Horse-drawn carriages loaded customers for tours of historic sites. It was a fabulous morning, and tourists were celebrating the end of summer.

"We're going to make money today," Monk predicted.

At their favorite site, Quinton held off a trio of musicians trying to set up equipment. "This area is reserved," the historian said. "Take your gear somewhere else."

"You don't own this space, old man."

"I've been on this corner for years, young man."

"Yeah? What do you do? Let's see your act."

As the dispute continued, Monk and Percy began to dance. Body slaps and hand claps and harmonica melody. People gathered around. Defeated, the intruding musicians gave up and went elsewhere. Quinton whooped and did a little dance step. Monk and Percy hit their heels on concrete and moved sideways in unison. The crowd applauded. Quinton passed around Monk's straw hat, "Show your approval!" he urged. "They deserve your generous support."

It promised to be a terrific day.

At the corner of Bourbon and Dumaine, the Clover Grill served breakfast twenty-four hours a day. The place was small and always crowded. When Quinton entered, the cook shouted, "Come in, Doctor! Where yat?" Monk was impressed with the title until he discovered bag ladies, hookers, and the homeless were all 'Doctor' to the cook.

Monk sat next to a window with a view of pedestrians on the street. It was easy to spot tourists. Most of them didn't have body art, and when they did it was different from that of residents at this end of Vieux Carré. French Quarter folks liked voodoo and Satanic symbols, Jesus on the cross, and dragons that twined round the arm.

"Order what you want, boys," Quinton offered.

A jukebox blasted so loud Monk had to read lips to understand. The cook came out to kiss somebody, male or female Monk couldn't say.

Between selections printed on the menu there were one-line comments that Monk had only recently understood after Percy explained them to him. You can beat our prices, but not our meat.

Quinton ran his finger down a list of ingredients and said, "Build your own omelet. Are you hungry, fellows?"

Monk read more quips on the menu. Our chili speaks for itself ... sooner or later. We may not be pretty, but we think we are.

"Pork chop or chicken fried steak and eggs," Quinton considered. "That sounds good, too."

Select members of our staff are available for private parties.

"What do you say, boys?" Quinton questioned. "What will it be?"

"Are you paying?" Percy asked.

"Yes, I'll pay."

"Why would you do that?"

Quinton ignored Percy's impolite question. "Monk, what do you want?"

"A waffle, please."

A waiter came to the table, thrust a hip to one side, and smirked. "Handsome company you're running with, Sweetie-Cue."

"Handsome and talented company, Merlin, and you're the cretin who stole my sterling silver King Louis sugar bowl last week."

"Did not steal," the waiter said. "I asked if I could borrow it, and you were too snockered to say no. I will return it at your next party."

"Bring back my creamer, too."

"Aloysius has that."

"Tell him to bring it back."

Quinton's expression softened. "Did you say waffle, Monk?"

On the menu, Monk read, No talking to yourself. Keep your hands on the table.

After the waiter left with their order, Percy sneered, "He's queer as a plucked duck."

"Ducks are not queer," Quinton said. "They just walk that way."

There was a lull in the din as the jukebox changed discs, and then it began to blast again.

"Quinton," Percy inquired, "do you have a credit card?"

"Why do you ask?"

"Monk wants to go online and order his mother and father's music CDs."

Embarrassed, Monk said, "Quinton, I didn't—"

Quinton raised a hand to hush him. "I have the money to pay," Monk blurted.

"He has to have a credit card to buy stuff online," Percy said. "He wants to order music, but I said, Monk, you need a credit card to buy online."

"I presume you're involved in this transaction, Percy?"

"I'll take him to the library and show him how to use the computer."

Their food arrived.

Monk ate his waffle and watched a heavily scribed woman with lavender hair. She wore a fishnet tank top, which exposed a red bra underneath. At her table sat a tall man wearing cowboy boots and a western style belt buckle the size of a saucer. She cuffed his shoulder with a fist, and he kissed the hand that hit him.

"Don't stare, Monk," Quinton said. "It isn't polite."

After eating, they strolled back toward Jackson Square. Quinton said, "In all the years we've known one another, you've never been to my house, have you, Monk?"

"No sir."

Quinton removed a business card from a snakeskin wallet and gave it to him. It read, Quinton Toussaint, Historian, with an address on Esplanade. "You pass my home when you come to the Quarter," he said. "We'll use my computer to find the music you want. Percy, you may come if you wish."

"Oh, no, thanks," Percy stepped away from them. "I'd only be in the way."

Riding home on the bicycle, Percy snickered behind Monk's ear. "Uh-huh, here it comes now," he said.

"What?"

"Nothing. Nothing at all."

Percy hit a pothole. Monk was fairly sure he'd done it on purpose.

Monk didn't want to give up making money on the weekend so he didn't go to Quinton's home right away. Friday had been the best day he and

Percy ever had. Saturday was nearly as good. Monk danced until his arms and legs felt heavy and Quinton's whoops sounded forced.

He collapsed on a bench next to Quinton and Percy. "Quinton, if it's all right I'll come by your house Monday."

"That's fine, Monk. Are you coming, too, Percy?"

"I might."

Surprised, Monk looked at him and Percy said, "I told Miss James I'd look after you."

"Percy," Quinton inquired, mildly, "why do you insult me?"

Percy stood up and moved away.

Watching him go, Quinton said. "He's jealous of you, Monk."

"I don't think so. He's better than I am at everything."

"Percy is older, therefore he has more experience. But you have something he lacks. Charisma."

"What's that?" Monk asked.

"Stage presence. Personality. Charm. When you smile, I see your mother looking at me."

"Grandmama says I have my mother's eyes," Monk said.

"Indeed you do, but now and then you get an expression, the way you set your jaw when you're concentrating, and before me stands Tooth DeCay."

Percy returned to flop down on the bench. "I'm too tired to dance anymore, Monk. Let's go home."

"You both excelled today," Quinton said. "It was a pleasure to watch you perform."

When they got beyond the crowds, Monk mounted the handlebars, his pockets heavy with money they'd collected.

"How much you think we made?" Percy asked.

"I don't know. A lot."

Percy took a different winding route to avoid gang boys. The pavement was rough, and there were no sidewalks. Monk's bottom ached and his legs cramped. "Percy, stop and let me off."

Monk stretched his limbs and rotated his feet to ease the spasms. He could hardly walk. Percy pushed his bicycle across the canal bridge, and Monk stumbled along, groaning.

When they reached the house, Grandmama was sweeping the porch. "Miss James," Percy hollered, "Monk is having muscle knots."

"Go inside and take off your pants, Monk."

"I'll be all right, Grandmama." But even as he said it, a charley horse seized him and he yelped.

She held his arm and led him to the bedroom. "Sit your cute little money-earning ass on the bed," she said.

"Can't you think of a better word than that?" Monk asked.

Grandmama spoke as she massaged his bare legs. "Ass is a part of the body," she said. "Ass is not swearing."

"Suppose you're looking for ass?"

"Thelonious Monk," she said, "I'm surprised at you! However, if you're looking for ass, it means you've lost a long-eared, slow, patient, domestic animal often used as a beast of burden."

She slapped his bottom and said, "Put on your pants. Let's go to the kitchen and give Percy his share of the money."

Monk was dressed in his Sunday best and Grandmama wore her slimming blue outfit with gloves, purse, and hat. They climbed into Willy Bouchard's pickup truck for the trip to church.

"You going to have seedless grapes this next week, Mr. Willy?"

"From South America, Miss James. Sweet, plump, and juicy."

"Save me a pound or two."

Monk sat beside Cherita, next to Percy's younger brother, Benny. "My mama say we bout to get us some weather," Cherita said.

Monk had heard the report. "Just another storm way out there," he commented.

"My mama said, sooner or later, one's going to come right down our throat, grab us by the tail, and snatch us inside out."

"My coon ass uncle says don't worry about it," Benny remarked. "He been through a lot of weather."

Monk looked around. "Benny, where's Percy this morning?"

"Riding on new rubber in Uncle Earl's Cadillac."

On the other bench, Grandmama asked her friend, "Is your husband out of jail, Lucille?"

"No, Miss James, he's still there. They got him working on a levee with a whole lot of other men. They ought be done by next Sunday. Some say the Levee Board is going to pay for work this time."

"They are?"

"Ten dollars a day after deductions for room and board at the jail."

The truck lurched, the passengers jolted, and they rode the rest of the way in silence.

When the congregation at Baby Jesus Spiritual Church settled into their pews, Aunt Bishop Beulah gave a sermon about how sinning made us lie, and one lie led to another. Grandmama played piano. She sat on a sturdy bench that Mr. Willy had built special for her and sang "Amazing Grace." The music made chill bumps run up Monk's back and spill over his shoulders.

Bishop Beulah called for a witness and three people stood up to testify. Lucille told how she'd been tempted by the flesh of a shrimper from Slidell while her husband was in jail. Nothing happened, she said, but she was sorely tried. Lucille promised God and everybody in church, she would not be looking for more shrimp while her husband was locked away.

Willy Bouchard testified, too. Monk had the feeling Aunt Bishop Beulah put him up to it because she didn't have any witnesses last week. His testimonial seemed insincere, about short-changing a customer in Faubourg Marigny.

The most interesting witness was five-year-old Cherita. The Spirit came upon her, and she fell to the floor writhing. Her mother was overcome with emotion, and began to speak in tongues. Finally, there were three adults and two children in rapture, and Bishop Beulah shouted, "Praise God Almighty. Thank you, Jesus!"

Percy arrived too late to see Sister Julianne in rapture with Cherita twisting and kicking on the floor. He came to sit beside Monk. He bent over and pretended to tie a shoelace, looking up the skirt of a young woman who convulsed on the floor before them.

"Praise the Lord!" Bishop Beulah yelled. "Bless us, Jesus!"

The service was much better than last week.

After church, Monk and Percy hurried home, changed into tatters and went to Jackson Square. Quinton wasn't there, and they had to settle for a different spot to perform. Without Quinton, and in a new location, they had trouble building an audience. Spectators paused briefly and then walked on. Monk's legs cramped and he stopped to rest.

He sat on the curb rubbing out knots in his muscles and while he did so, a mime stole their place.

"I'm sorry, Percy."

"It's okay, Monk. I don't feel like dancing anyway."

"We didn't make three dollars," Monk said.

"That's enough for red beans and rice. Let's go to Central Grocery."

One bowl, two spoons, a handful of paper napkins, and Tabasco sauce—Percy got most of it because it was too spicy for Monk.

They sat in a small park outside of Jimmy Buffet's Restaurant in the French Market.

"What do you want to do now?" Percy asked.

"I think I'll stop by Quinton's place," Monk said.

To his surprise, Percy said, "Okay. Let's go."

Quinton's address was a three-story house, exactly what Monk expected of a man who loved history and antiques. The roof was red terra-cotta tile, the downspouts copper, and the shutters a dark green. Many of the windows were trimmed with stained glass. A high wrought iron fence fronted the property. From the street Monk saw a brick courtyard wall in the rear, covered by flowering vines.

"Are you sure this is the address?" Percy chained his bicycle to a cast iron coachman at the curb. Upon reflection, he said, "The old queen must be rich."

An historical shield mounted beside the front door said, "Spanish Colonial style circa 1820."

Monk rang the doorbell and heard a musical peal inside.

Nothing happened.

He rang again.

The door opened abruptly and Quinton stood there in a silk robe. "Monk, this is not Monday."

"We weren't dancing too good, Quinton," Monk said. "We decided to come visit now."

"Wait here." Quinton shut the door.

"First time I ever saw him without feathers," Percy commented.

Minutes passed. Finally, the door opened again and a young man stepped out. He wore leather sandals on tanned feet, a tropical print shirt unbuttoned down to his navel, and khaki shorts. He brushed past Monk and descended the steps.

"All right, boys," Quinton said, irritably, "come in."

Monk had never smelled a house like this one. Lemon oil and roses. The walls were dark paneling to a height of his shoulder and from there up plaster. A clock in the hallway chimed eleven.

"Quinton, if you want us to come back tomorrow, we will."

"You're here now."

Everything was heavy: the drapes, furniture, and a naked marble man on a pedestal. Paintings were framed with ornately carved woods. A staircase rose to the second floor. A man's underwear hung on the newel post.

"What do you want?" Quinton asked.

Monk felt uncomfortable. "You said come by, Quinton."

"You told me Monday. This is Sunday. But, I'm asking what do you want to eat or drink?"

"Oh," Monk said. "What do you have?"

"Juices, tea, and water."

"Tea would be good," Monk said.

Percy paused to look at a chessboard. He picked up an ivory piece and Quinton took it from his hand. "Don't touch things, Percy."

They followed him to a kitchen where Quinton selected glasses, coasters, and napkins. He took a pitcher of iced tea from an avocado green side-by-side refrigerator. He placed the items on a tray and led the way back up front.

"We'll sit in my office," he said.

Bookshelves covered a long wall to the ceiling, and a ladder attached to the top shelf could be rolled the length of the room.

"Did somebody make you read all these books?" Percy pulled one off a shelf.

"Percy," Quinton said, "please do not touch things without permission."

Photographs filled every inch on the walls. Monk saw vaguely familiar images. "Who are these people, Quinton?"

"That one is William Faulkner, a famous author. He lived in the Quarter while he wrote his first book, *Soldier's Pay*. The picture next to it is Tennessee Williams, another writer, and the one to the left is Truman Capote. They've all been guests in my home at one time or another."

Quinton untied the sash of his robe, tightened the wrap and secured it again. His ankles were bloodless, covered with a web of blue veins. Caught looking, Monk turned away and stared at the picture of a beautiful African-American woman.

"That's your mother," Quinton said.

In this picture her mouth was closed and her eyes were open. Monk studied the face, but still didn't see himself. He shifted his gaze to another image. His father, Tooth DeCay.

Percy lifted the lid on a grand piano exposing the keys.

"Have my parents been guests here too?" Monk asked.

Quinton gave him a glass of iced tea. "Elaine and Tooth were here at a party to celebrate the release of a recording. Which is what you came to see about, isn't it?"

He pulled open the door of a wooden cabinet. It was filled with records, eight-tracks, and CDs. "You know, Monk, getting music is only the beginning of it," Quinton said. "You need equipment upon which to play it. Do you have a CD player?"

"No."

"Well then," Quinton shut the cabinet. "You'll have to come over someday and I'll play the music for you."

Percy pressed a piano key and the sound resonated richly.

"Percy," Quinton said, sternly, "don't touch the Steinway unless you intend to play. Do you play?"

Percy moved to shut the cover and Monk said, "Give us some boogie woogie, Percy."

Percy felt the foot pedals with his bare toes and ran his fingers lightly over the keyboard without making a sound. Then he began playing the repeated bass notes that are the backbone of boogie.

Rich tones filled the room. The beat was infectious. Percy hit the high notes with his right hand, dink, dink. His left hand went down an octave and then shifted up again.

"Come help me, Monk." Percy slid to one end of the bench. But Monk couldn't play like that. He said, "You're doing good, Percy."

Quinton took the seat instead. He had long slender fingers that spanned the keyboard from C to C. On the upper keys he established a riff and worked his way down. "Contrapuntal har-mon-i!" he cried, and together he and Percy boogied. Monk couldn't stand still. He clapped his chest and slapped his hands, wheeled and kicked. Quinton grinned and Percy took off on a side bar. Boogie-boogie-boogie-boogie, boogie-boogie-boogie-boogie, dink, dink ...

"Don't stop," Quinton urged. "Take it on down."

The music gave Monk gooseflesh. He whirled, snapped his fingers, and clapped hands.

"One more time," Quinton yelled, and they ran the keys in opposite directions until their arms crossed and Percy played tenor, Quinton on bass. Boogie-boogie-boogie-boogie, boogie-boogie-boogie-boogie, dink, dink ...

Monk watched them build to a crescendo, and suddenly, as if they'd practiced it a hundred times, they stopped abruptly.

"My God," Quinton threw an arm around Percy and hugged him. "That was fabulous. Where did you learn to play like that?"

"My coon ass uncle Earl. Miss James taught me keyboard."

Still in Quinton's embrace, Percy grinned sheepishly.

"You're astonishing, my boy." Quinton stood up. "Can you do jazz?"

"Fast or slow?"

"Whatever pleases you," Quinton said.

Percy did both; from a bluesy opening to tangent asides running scales in unfettered freehand, the music dipped, rose on melodic wings only to plummet again.

Quinton sat beside him with an arm around Percy's shoulder, eyes closed, buoyed by the notes, rocking his body in syncopation to the refrains.

Monk knew Percy had never played a fine instrument like this. The keys responded to his fingers with more power than Monk could've imagined. Hammers on the strings darted, raced, leapt, and bound. Sitting there under the arm of a man Percy had always called "the old queen," Quinton's touch did not repel him this time.

He liked it.
Monk had never felt such resentment.

{CHAPTER FIVE}

Monday morning was so hot the handlebars of Percy's bike burned Monk through his trousers. The bicycle's front tire threw up tiny flecks of melted asphalt, stinging his bare feet.

He was surprised when Percy had shown up, but glad to be going and eager to make more money before school started. He grabbed his taps and hat, and they were on the way to Jackson Square.

Percy detoured onto Esplanade and stopped in front of Quinton's house. "What're we doing here?" Monk questioned.

"You know Monday is a lousy day for tourists," Percy said. "It's too hot to dance for nothing." He chained his wheel to the iron coachman at the curb. "Quinton's place is air conditioned. We'll stay here until it cools a little, and in the meantime, Quinton said I could play piano today."

"When did he tell you that?"

"Yesterday."

"I didn't hear him say anything about us coming back."

"I'm not surprised," Percy said. "You stayed in the other room pouting."

While Quinton and Percy had played piano yesterday, Monk spent his time looking through brittle yellowed clippings in scrapbooks that spanned most of Quinton's life.

In one book Monk found a postcard from Club My-O-My on Lake Pontchartrain. It pictured Quinton posed with men pretending to be women. They wore fancy low-cut dresses and big hats to match.

The nightclub Le Chat Noir advertised in a newspaper, "The Most Interesting Women in the World Are Not Women at All." Quinton had directed a revue there.

In another scrapbook Monk was surprised to find his father's photograph on the front cover of an album. A youthful Tooth DeCay stood with his foot on a piano stool, elbow on his knee. "Best of the Best," the text said. Monk put the picture in front of Quinton at the piano.

"Do you have this recording by my father?"

"I'd have to look for it, Monk."

"Would you mind doing that?"

"I need to concentrate to keep up with this young virtuoso, Monk. Why don't you turn on the television?"

Stung by the dismissal, Monk returned to Quinton's den and switched on the TV. A newsman at WWL said, "a chance of showers today, tomorrow, and Wednesday."

Here he was, earning no money while the sun shined.

He flipped to another channel.

"The eleventh named tropical storm of the season is approaching the Bahamas," a weatherman reported. "We expect it to reach hurricane strength tomorrow."

Monk muted the sound.

On a shelf behind sliding glass doors he saw history books written by Quinton Toussaint. He reached to pull one out and Quinton spoke from the piano bench, "Monk, don't handle those. They're special leather-bound editions."

Quinton turned back to Percy. "You sight-read quite well." He positioned a sheet of music. "Try this piece," he said.

Monk's stomach ached as if he'd eaten too many grapes. He had never suffered such an awful feeling, and he didn't know a name to call it.

He watched Percy as Quinton demonstrated "a cascade." Quinton ran his fingers over the keys from high notes to low, one hand chasing the other like pale spiders racing across the keyboard. The tumbling sound was a musical waterfall. Percy seemed hypnotized.

During a break, Quinton reminisced about his younger days. "My favorite restaurant was Galatoire's, and the best dinner was heart of lettuce, shrimp rémoulade, and trout amandine with new potatoes." He pressed the tips of his fingers to his lips and made a kissing sound. "Délicieux."

Percy listened as if he understood every word.

"In those days a dinner jacket and necktie were de rigueur at a fancy restaurant," Quinton said. "God-forbid going someplace in shower shoes." He laughed and Percy laughed with him.

"We'll go to Galatoire's sometime," Quinton offered.

Monk realized Quinton talked to Percy as he would an adult, and in that instant, he knew he'd always been treated as a child. "May I help with your shoes, Monk?"

Percy went to the bathroom and Monk followed. "I'm going home, Percy."

Percy responded as if Monk had not spoken. "That piano is sweet," he said. "I wish I could put it in my pocket and take it to Jackson Square."

"Okay, so I'm leaving," Monk said.

They returned to the living room. Quinton sat on the piano bench, hunched forward, shoulders rounded, idly picking a melody with one hand.

"That'd be better if you jazzed it up," Percy suggested.

"Perhaps you could show me," Quinton said.

Percy sat down, took up the melody, and embellished it with such ease Monk groaned. Would he ever be that good?

"I'm going home, Percy," Monk announced.

Percy quit playing. "You want to play the piano? Is that what's wrong?"

"There's nothing wrong. I'm ready to go." He headed for the door.

"You're leaving?" Quinton said. "I was about to ask you to run an errand."

"What is it?"

"I made gumbo last night and baked cheese sticks in anticipation of your visit. I always take something special to Jon Latour on Monday. Would you deliver it to him? It will only take a minute to heat in the microwave."

"Who is Jon Latour?" Percy asked.

"He's a friend of ours," Quinton winked at Monk. "The ghost of Vieux Carré."

Thinking he had a momentary advantage, Monk said, "May I borrow your wheel, Percy?"

"Sure. You know the combination on the lock, don't you?"

Quinton gave Monk a wide-neck thermos filled with hot gumbo. He put cheese sticks in a Ziploc bag.

Riding toward Toulouse on Bourbon, Monk tried to understand what he felt. He was furious. Percy had taken his place with Quinton, and Monk was angry with Quinton for allowing it.

Monk pedaled the bicycle between moving traffic and parked cars. The odor of automobile exhaust filled the humid air. Residents sat outside on their balconies hoping for a breeze. Somebody was cooking on a grill and the odor of barbecued meat made him hungry. He passed a tattoo parlor and the Old Opera House.

The more he thought about Percy, the angrier he became. Everything was easy for him. Monk had practiced playing boogie until his fingers throbbed. No matter how hard he tried, he couldn't make the sounds Percy did with little effort.

It was the same with harmonica. Percy's cupped hands and double-tongue harmony made a ten-hole mouth harp sound like two harmonicas playing as one. When the instrument lacked a sharp or flat, Percy combined two notes to fake his way through a song.

By the time Monk reached Jon Latour's drop site, he was on the verge of tears. He leaned the bike against the ivy-covered wall and peeked through the hole. The shadowed and littered corridor seemed empty. Then he caught the scent of sour laundry.

"Jon?" Monk called through the opening. "It's Monk. Quinton sent gumbo and cheese sticks."

He turned the thermos on its side and pushed it through the hole as far as he could. The receptacle was pulled out of his hand.

Monk parted vines and peered through the opening. A figure moved away down the narrow passage.

"Don't forget the cheese sticks, Jon."

For the first time he saw the man's face. Dark shadows circled his eyes and a scraggly beard fell over a faded unbuttoned shirt.

"Come get it," Monk called.

Latour stood there, gazing toward him.

"Come on," Monk urged, "you don't want to miss Quinton's cheese sticks."

Jon's head wobbled and he came back.

The plastic bag was so full some of the cheese sticks were crushed when Monk shoved it through the hole.

He felt Jon take the bag.

Monk peered through and jumped back. Jon was inches from his face.

"Thank you," Jon whispered.

"You're welcome."

The man departed with a curious sidewise gait, as if his left shoulder led the rest of his body. Monk watched him climb a trellis using one hand, gumbo and cheese sticks clamped to his chest by the other arm. He walked along the balcony, scaled another lattice, and disappeared over a rooftop.

It was like viewing a wild creature in its natural habitat. For a second, Monk had been near enough to see that Jon's eyes were so dark they appeared black.

When he returned to Quinton's house, Monk chained Percy's bike to the stanchion and went inside.

They were at the piano.

"I saw Jon Latour, Quinton."

Quinton didn't turn, but raised a hand for silence.

"Right there, Percy," Quinton coached. "Don't hit the key. Caress it."

"I had my foot on the soft pedal."

"It isn't the same. Let your finger slide over the key. The way you stroke a note gives it a particular inflection."

Monk felt tears well in his eyes and that made him angry again. "Percy, I'm going home."

"Okay, Monk. Take the wheel."

But he didn't.

Monk ran down the street to get away. He hated Percy for making him feel this way. He hated Quinton, too. He fantasized about breaking Percy's fingers. He wanted to punish him for being better at everything.

"Hey, whoa!" Percy came up behind him on the bicycle. "Get on. I'll take you home."

"I don't want to stop you from playing the piano," Monk said.

"I was ready to quit anyway."

He got onto the handlebars. They rode in silence for a few blocks. Monk said, "I thought you didn't like Quinton."

"I thought I didn't."

"You seemed mighty friendly," Monk said.

"Yeah. Well. He's not so bad."

Tuesday morning a ship's horn roused Monk and he woke still angry with Quinton and Percy. Grandmama was in the kitchen listening to weather reports on the radio. He didn't have to hear somebody say bad weather was coming, he felt it. The air was heavy and humid. Sunlight came through the bedroom window filtered by haze.

"Monk?"

"Yes ma'am, Grandmama?"

"I need you to go buy batteries and candles."

"Are we going to have a storm?"

"Sooner or later," she said.

Monk dressed and went into the kitchen. "Where is it blowing now?"

"Over the Bahamas east of Florida." She gave him twenty dollars and a list of battery sizes for her portable radio and flashlight. "Go to the Dollar General Store and get the biggest candles they've got," she said.

"May I buy a sno-ball?"

She dumped her purse onto the porcelain kitchen table. She pushed aside an aluminum doubloon from a long ago Mardi Gras parade. She picked up one of Fiona's gris-gris she carried for luck, and a St. Joseph lucky bean, which added to her chance for good fortune. She selected coins and gave them to Monk. Then she checked her shopping list.

"While you making groceries," Grandmama said, "pick up ready to eat meat in a can, peanut butter, and saltines."

"Is the storm coming here?" Monk asked.

"The weatherman doesn't say so," Grandmama said. "But if folks begin to believe it might, there won't be a battery or candle left to be bought."

Several years ago, Aunt Bishop Beulah gave Grandmama a two-wheel luggage cart she'd bought at a garage sale. Willy Bouchard attached a wire basket for hauling home groceries. Monk pulled it across the canal bridge and trudged to the nearest time saver store. The owner, Mr. Benoit, was Cherita's father, a man as handsome as Sister Julianne was beautiful.

His hair was coal-black, his teeth perfectly shaped and absolutely white.

The owner greeted him, "Where yat, Monk!"

"Everything good, Mr. Benoit. I need a grape sno-ball."

To Monk, Mr. Benoit was the luckiest man in the world, married to a woman so beautiful. There was no chance his wife would ever be lured away. He was movie star good looking, tall and slim with a dimple in his chin. When he smiled women wiggled and looked weak. He was just the kind of man anyone would expect such a breathtaking beauty to marry.

"How's the world treating you, Monk?"

"The world treats me good," Monk said.

"Accept nothing less." Mr. Benoit gave Monk the shaved ice treat doused with an extra squirt of grape flavoring. Monk ate it on the way to Dollar General. Up ahead he saw Percy and his uncle Earl Thibodeaux entering the discount store. Percy's aunt Fiona sat in the Cadillac waiting for them. Monk hurried to get there.

By graffiti scrawled on walls he knew this was gang boy territory. He saw two of them loitering across the street.

"Hello, Miss Fiona."

"Hey yourself, Monk. How's your grandmama?"

"She's all right. I came for batteries and candles."

"Getting ready mighty early," Fiona said, meaning a possible storm. "That's smart, though. If it weren't for me, Earl wouldn't lay up a bucket of water or a gallon of coal oil. Go on inside, babe. Hurry along and we'll give you a ride home."

It was an offer he wouldn't turn down. Across the street the gang boys were now four in number and looking this way. Monk pulled his cart through aisles of the store. He found Percy and his uncle buying discounted canned foods.

"Where yat, Monk?"

"Doing good, Mr. Earl. Miss Fiona said you'd give me a ride home."

"If she say do, I will. Getting ready for the storm?"

"Yes sir."

Percy pulled him aside. "Want to go to Quinton's house?"

"No."

"You still sulking over that?" Percy chided.

"I'm not sulking. I just don't want to go."

Monk selected cans of sardines, tuna, potted meat, and Vienna sausage. He bought Christmas candles that had been on the shelf so long the sale price had been further reduced. Batteries, peanut butter, two boxes of saltine crackers, and he was ready to go. He kept a count of cost in his head and went back for more sardines. Grandmama liked sardines.

"I'll be outside, Mr. Earl."

"We be long shortly, Monk."

Monk paid for his purchases and wheeled his cart outdoors. He stood in shade next to the wall.

"Come get in the car if you want to, Monk," Fiona offered.

It was too hot to sit in the sun. "I'll wait here for Uncle Earl, Miss Fiona."

Uh-oh. Here came the gang boys.

The oldest one among them lived beyond the Quarter on Tchoupitoulas Street in New Orleans. Randy Bernard had a car. He came to Bywater to expand his influence with younger boys. He was old enough to grow a kinky beard, and he had a space between his front teeth, which he used regularly to spit at anything that made a sound, like a metal downspout or an empty garbage can.

"Felonious Monk," Randy deliberately mispronounced his name. His complexion was yellow with dark freckles. He claimed to be Cajun. Percy's coon ass uncle Earl said Randy's people were not from any of the twenty-two parishes that made up the Cajun homeland in South Louisiana. They came from Georgia. Randy's father was a policeman in the Quarter, known to defend his son in time of trouble.

"Felonious Monk," Randy said again, and his companions laughed as if they knew what felonious meant.

Randy lit a cigarette and inhaled. "We need two dollars for sno-balls, Monk."

"I don't have two dollars."

"That mean if we turned you upside down and shook good, we wouldn't get some change?"

"A few pennies, maybe."

Monk saw Fiona get out of the car and hurry inside.

"Soc au lait, boy." Randy liked to throw out French now and then to strengthen his claim to Cajun ancestry. "You come in our territory and don't bring a fee to pass? Let's see what you got in the basket, dawlin'."

He reached into the foodstuff and as he did so, Mr. Thibodeaux came out, grabbed him by the collar, and snatched him upright.

"Hey, little shit," Earl lifted him so high only Randy's toes touched the ground. The other boys scattered to a safe distance. "Were you about to contribute to my friend's cane money, Randy?"

"I was just looking, Mr. Thibodeaux."

"Your worthless père still stealing from street people, Randy? How you reckon that worthless piece of meat stay out of jail so long? Ain't you sorry to pick on Monk?"

"I am sorry."

"Give him back his money."

"I didn't take money, Mr. Thibodeaux."

"Give him what you stole from anybody else, then."

Randy pulled several dollars from his pocket and Earl took it. He shoved the boy away. "Stay off my friends, Randy. Next time I break you neck."

"Keep looking over your shoulder, boogalee," Randy said from afar. "Someday it'll be just you and me."

"I like that, yeah," Earl replied. "Might maybe you be wise to do the same, petit con. Keep looking over you shoulder."

Getting into the Cadillac, Fiona asked Earl, "Did you get chicory coffee?"

"I look stupid?" Earl said. "Ain't no other kind but chicory, baby."

They had to wait for the bridge to open and close before crossing the canal. They sat in silence, watching a ship pass.

"Thank you, Mr. Earl," Monk said.

"Neb mind, boy. Some day you got to whip his ass, though."

"Yes sir."

"When you do," Earl said, "whip it good and be done with him."

Monk could not imagine a day when he would stand up to someone the size of Randy, especially a boy whose father was a cop.

"Aren't you afraid of Randy's father?" Monk asked.

"I had me a little vacation time with Randy's père up to Angola," Earl said. "I robbed a all-night time saver and got caught walking out wit the money. Eustis Bernard ain't smart, but no, he ain't stupid. He don't mess with me."

Monk got out of the car at home, and he said again, "Thank you, Mr. Earl."

The long blast of a ship's horn put a tremor in the marrow of Monk's bones. Another ship answered with a low drone. The drawbridge whistle blew. Incoming ships were looking for safe harbor.

The next morning, Monk pulled on his trousers and joined Grandmama in the kitchen. Bacon sizzled in a skillet. The radio was set to WWL.

"Her name is Katrina," a radio voice announced. "Upgraded to tropical storm this morning, Katrina continues to move toward Florida."

"That's a long way from here," Grandmama remarked.

The radioman confirmed it. "At present, Katrina is no threat to the New Orleans area."

After breakfast, Grandmama took to bed, fans wagging back and forth, blowing warm air across her body.

"Anything you want me to do?" Monk asked.

"Stake the tomato plants to keep fruit off the ground, Monk. I'm not going to move unless the house catches fire, and then only because it'll be hotter in here than it is now."

Ten minutes after he started, the tomato plants were staked. There weren't many tomatoes left. When Monk finished, there was nothing else to do. He went in to tell Grandmama he was going over to the levee, but she was asleep, sprawled on her back, arms outstretched. Monk left a note anticipating her warnings:

> Dear Grandmama:
> I'm going to the levee not to fall in or wade.
> Love Thelonious.

He sat on the bank watching caramel-colored water flow south toward the Gulf of Mexico. Thunderheads piled high in the sky. Watercraft came and went. The drawbridge whistle blew. Monk waved at crewmen walking the deck of a barge being pushed toward New Orleans. They didn't see him, or didn't care. Nobody waved back.

Home again, Monk sat in the porch swing and wished for tomorrow when he could earn money in Jackson Square. Every tick of the clock paused before it passed. The day crawled by. Grandmama stayed in bed. When he heard her stir, Monk called from the porch, "Are you all right, Grandmama?"

"Marinating in my own juices, Monk."

"May I bring you something?"

"No. Thank you."

After a minute, Grandmama asked, "You need anything, Monk?

"No, ma'am. I'm fine."

He just wished this day would get on by and be done with. This last week of August would be his final chance to make money.

Thursday, Monk was dressed and ready when Percy arrived. Grandmama listened to the radio while they ate omelets cooked with tomatoes, onions, and banana peppers.

The weatherman said, "Katrina became a hurricane this morning only two hours before landfall near the Miami-Dade county line."

"You think it's coming this way, Grandmama?"

"Puny storm if it do," she said. "Going over Florida makes it weaker."

"I hope we don't have a hurricane," Percy said. "My mama runs every time she smells the Devil's breath. Last year in Hurricane Ivan we were out on a highway with half of New Orleans looking for a place to buy food and gas. I was jammed in our car with kinfolk. The women got to use a toilet. Only there ain't no toilet."

"Not ain't," Grandmama corrected. "Isn't."

"Isn't no food or gas either," Percy said. "After a while, they sold out of everything. There was a tornado. That scared me worse than any hurricane. Next time I'm going to stay home."

That was how Grandmama felt, too.

"People gritting at one another like they want to fight," Percy said. "You don't know who's got a gun. Next time I'm staying with Uncle Earl."

"Will he let you?" Monk asked.
"He still owes me money. He better let me."

{CHAPTER SIX}

Everything irritated Monk this morning.

While he adjusted his taps, at the far end of Jackson Square a steel drum band tested their instruments with rubber-tipped hammers.

Quinton spoke as if someone had asked a question. "The rhythms originated with the bottle-and-spoon bands of Trinidad and Tobago," he said. "In the late 1800s, steel bands were formed by freed African slaves trying to re-create the traditional percussion sounds of their homeland."

Monk thought they were distractingly noisy, and their clamor pulled tourists away from his side of the Square. His harmonica and body slaps felt piddling by comparison.

On top of it all, he and Percy weren't working well together. In the middle of their routine, Percy skipped a step and Monk broke rhythm.

Percy stopped dancing. "What're you doing, Monk?"

"Doing what we always do. You changed step."

"No, I didn't."

"Yes you did," Monk said, "and that's twice. A few minutes ago instead of holding a beat you went to melody and threw me off."

Watching the dispute, spectators shifted uneasily. A woman and her daughter walked over to the horse-drawn carriages. Percy stood very close to Monk crowding him backward. He smelled like sweat. "What's the matter with you?" he accused. "Can't you count anymore?"

"Boys, boys," Quinton soothed.

"Quinton, which one of us messed up?"

"I didn't notice."

That was a lie; of course he noticed. Trying to adjust to Percy's variation, Monk had shifted from tap to slide and stumbled. It was so awkward some of the spectators groaned.

"How often do we have to practice before you get it straight?" Percy seethed.

"It wasn't me, Percy, and you know it."

"I've been doing this routine longer than you have," Percy leaned into Monk's face. "I taught it to you, remember?"

"Now, boys," Quinton pushed between them. "Let's take a little break. Go to Maspero's for lunch. I'm buying."

"I'm not hungry," Monk said. The remaining audience drifted away.

"You know what's wrong," Percy taunted. "Monk is jealous."

"I am not."

"He's pissed off because we made piano music. He sat in the next room sucking his thumb and sulking."

"That's a lie, Percy."

"Come now, fellows," Quinton smiled at each of them. "Let's be friends and have lunch."

Monk removed his taps and tied the laces together. He dangled them around his neck. He turned his back to hide trembling hands. Along the line of wagons, a horse snorted and shook his head, rattling the harness.

"If you're not going with us," Percy said, "the least you can do is watch the wheel."

It was chained to a Dumpster where he always left it.

"We'll feel better after we've eaten," Quinton said, "you boys need a little protein," and that comment irritated Monk, too.

"I'm not going, Quinton. I think I'll take something to Jon."

"That's a nice idea," Quinton gave Monk five dollars. It was the money he used to sweeten the pot. "Buy Jon a Lucky Dog and a root beer."

"Who is this Jon you two keep talking about?" Percy asked.

"The ghost of Vieux Carré," Quinton said. "I'll tell you about him over lunch at Maspero's."

Monk watched the pair move off through the tourists. A photographer stopped them and asked if he could take a picture of barefoot and ragged Percy standing beside Quinton, who was dressed in purple and yellow. They posed, and walked on. A week ago, Quinton wouldn't have left Monk. Today he strolled away with an arm around Percy's shoulder, and neither of them glanced back. And Percy, damn him! He accepted the invitation quick enough. Free meal? Yes sir, he wanted to go!

Acadian dancers in red-checkered blouses and short skirts began to perform. Two men played accordions. They whooped and hollered as the women whirled and shouted. They looked like it was fun, and that's what it took. Grandmama always said, "If you're having fun, people will have fun watching." One of the women coaxed a man in the audience to dance with her, and they all clapped hands to a vigorous zydeco beat.

Monk hadn't made as much money as he should have this morning. He and Percy performed as if it were hard work. Obviously they weren't enjoying themselves and neither did their audience.

When Monk reached Bourbon Street he bought two Lucky Dogs from a pushcart vendor, and then went into the Old Opera House Bar to buy a cold drink. While he waited for service, he sat on a stool at the counter and watched a TV mounted near the ceiling. At nearby tables, tourists drank beer and stared at the screen.

"Passing over South Florida this morning," a newsman reported, "Hurricane Katrina weakened to a tropical storm."

A woman behind the bar said, "What's up, babe?"

"I want an ice-cold root beer with little pieces of ice running down the side of the can. Don't open it."

"No cans."

"Could I take a bottle opener with me if I bring it back?"

"You don't need an opener, dawlin'. It's a bottle with a twist-off cap. You're too young to sit at the bar. You want the drink or not?"

He bought the soda and went outside into searing afternoon sunshine. The sidewalk was hot to his bare feet. He took the shady side of Toulouse to Jon Latour's place. When he got there he stood next to the wall and waited for pedestrians to pass on by.

"Jon," he said. "It's Monk."

He didn't smell anything but the hot dogs.

"Jon, are you there?"

He looked through the hole and called louder, "Jon!"

A heavy wooden gate was the only opening to the entrance and it was locked. Monk looked both ways up and down the street. In the distance, young lovers held hands and strolled toward him. They weren't paying attention to him. He pushed the food, drink, and his shoes under the gate. Then, quickly, he climbed up and dropped to the other side.

In the corridor it was shaded and cool. The cobblestones were rounded by years of wear. Moss grew on brick walls. From in here he saw where Jon must have stood, hidden by ivy. Out on the street the lovers spoke softly as they passed, and he heard every word.

Stepping around broken glass, Monk went the way he'd seen Jon go, down the passage to a balcony at the end. He looked up, and called, "Jon, it's Monk!"

He clutched the sack of hot dogs and clamped the bottled drink to his chest with one arm. Climbing the trellis wasn't easy with only one hand completely free. As he advanced upward he secured his position with his feet and the hand holding food, then reached for a new grip with his free hand, just as he'd seen Jon do it.

On the balcony, Monk passed shuttered doors and shattered windows. He climbed another grillwork to a flat roof covered with tar and strewn with pebbles.

From up here he could see all the way to Bourbon. People appeared and disappeared as they walked beneath balconies. He could hear them talking and laughing. A dray filled with sightseers clip-clopped by, and the voice of a tour guide was clear, "The Old Opera House Bar is home to many famous New Orleans performing artists. It is not unusual to see a celebrity jamming with local musicians."

Monk heard a clatter and moved across the roof toward the sound. He rounded a rusty turbine and discovered an access door hanging by one hinge. Somewhere deep inside, an exhaust fan rumbled, and in the airflow he smelled sour laundry.

"Jon? It's Monk. I brought you—"

The man loomed out of the interior, taller and larger than Monk expected. Dark eyes peered from beneath thick tangled brows, and he stood there wearing nothing but trousers torn short at the knees. His chest and shoulders were covered with a mat of curly hair. Perspiration glistened on his face and arms. Drops of sweat hung from his earlobes and from the tip of his nose.

Monk felt as if he'd been caught invading a home. "I brought two Lucky Dogs," he said, flustered. "I also got you a root beer."

He wasn't certain Jon understood. "Quinton Toussaint gave me money to buy something for you," Monk explained. "It cost more than he expected, so I added fifty cents from what I earned this morning."

The sound of electric guitars pierced the air from the Old Opera House Bar.

Monk extended the hot dogs and soda. "Here, Jon."

The man moved like a slow motion film. One hand rose to take the frankfurters; the other hand accepted the cold drink. Then he stood there in the blazing sun staring at Monk.

"I hope you don't mind my coming up," Monk babbled. "I called and you weren't there. I thought if I left the food, roaches or ants would get into it. The drink would be warm. The cap on the root beer is a twist-off the lady told me."

Jon turned his head in slow motion and looked at it.

"Well," Monk said, "it's awful hot out here, Jon. I guess I'll go."

He started to leave and Jon said, "Thank you."

"You're welcome."

Monk stepped gingerly across the painfully hot pebbles and peered down the trellis. It seemed a lot higher from up here than it had from down below. He sat on the roof, turned onto his stomach, and felt for a foothold.

When he looked back, Jon was still there, watching.

"Did you know we might have a hurricane, Jon?"

No reaction.

Monk lowered himself over the eave.

In the space between buildings he walked carefully to avoid stepping on glass. Out on the sidewalk he reached back under the gate, retrieved his taps, and then hurried toward Jackson Square.

Quinton and Percy were waiting.

"You left my wheel," Percy accused. "Can't I depend on you for anything?"

Anger and tears erupted at the same time. Monk shoved Percy in the chest and the unexpected assault sent Percy stumbling backward.

He recovered his balance, jaw set, and came back infuriated. Quinton stepped between them. "Now, now," he said. "What's the matter with you two? Stop the nonsense."

Quinton pulled them to a bench in the shade. Monk could hear Percy breathing hard. Quinton held each of them by a wrist. The Acadians playing accordions started up again. The steel drum band down the street beat a competing rhythm.

Quinton's skin felt slippery on Monk's arm. "I cannot rest easy while there is a dispute between my dearest friends," Quinton said. "I want you boys to shake hands."

Begrudgingly, Monk took Percy's hand, shook it hard one time and let go. The afternoon sun cast dark shadows across the square. Shopkeepers turned on their lights and stood in doorways trying to tempt buyers inside.

The steel drum band began to pack their gear. The zydeco dancers claimed what remained of the tourists. Most people were going back to their hotels to get ready for dinner. The best of day was done.

A black man came to the bench and spoke to Quinton, "Been a long time, Quinton. Are you out of the business?"

"Too old to trot and can't hold what I got," Quinton replied. "Mr. Neville, I'd like you to meet my two friends. This is Percy Brown."

Percy shook the man's hand and walked off to get his bicycle.

"And this is Thelonious Monk," Quinton said. "Monk, you've heard of the Neville Brothers."

Mr. Neville pulled in his chin and stared at Monk. He accepted the hand to shake and held it. "This wouldn't be Tooth DeCay's son, would it?"

Astonished that someone so famous as a Neville Brother knew his father, Monk said, "Yes, he's my dad."

"You got some big boots to fill, boy. Tooth has always been my hero."

"Thank you."

Percy returned with his bicycle, jaw clamped, expression grim. "I'm ready to go home," he said.

Percy didn't speak until they reached the Bywater. "Are you going to want to dance tomorrow, Monk?"

"If you do," Monk said.

"How much did we make today?"

"A few pennies over eight dollars each."

They hit a bump and it went straight through Monk's skinny rump and up his spine. Percy said, "Sorry. I didn't see the hole."

When they reached the canal bridge it was open. A tugboat maneuvered barges in the waterway. Monk stood at a rail, watching.

"I'm not believing what Quinton said about the ghost of Vieux Carré," Percy commented. "He said there are people in the Quarter who have never seen the man and he's been living there all his life. He goes out in the daytime only when it's very foggy. I don't think he's real."

"He's real," Monk said.

"Quinton said he hasn't had a job in years. He doesn't get unemployment or disability. How does he eat?"

Out of garbage cans, Quinton had told Monk. Handouts. Now and then a cook left food outside a restaurant backdoor. If dogs didn't get it, Jon did. There were people who claimed a ghost had stolen leftovers off of an unattended dinner table. Quinton suspected it was Jon Latour.

The tugboat tooted thanks to the bridge tender. The drawbridge cranked and groaned and closed. The smell of the river rose into Monk's nostrils.

"I think the whole story is made up," Percy said. "Like gold and diamonds supposed to be hidden around the Quarter by Jean Lafitte and his brother. That's all a tall tale, there is no pirate's fortune."

Traffic began to move again. Percy pushed his wheel across the bridge and Monk followed.

"Quinton told me that I remind him of Tooth DeCay," Percy said.

The remark took Monk's breath like a fist to his chest.

"Quinton said the way I take a tune and jazz it up is the same way your daddy did it. Smooth and easy."

Monk brushed past Percy and ran toward home.

"Hey, tomorrow, right?" Percy yelled. "See you in the morning!"

Monk burst into the house so choked he couldn't speak.

"Hello, Thelonious. How did the day go?"

He ran past Grandmama, down the hall, into his bedroom. He shut the door and fell across the mattress, muffling cries with a pillow.

Beyond the door he heard Grandmama say, "Thelonious, are you all right?"

Monk lifted the pillow long enough to holler, "Yes!"

He felt as if he were bleeding inside. His belly was empty and heavy at the same time. He'd been stupid to trust Quinton. He fell for everything the old man had said—charisma—stage presence. "Thelonious, babe," Grandmama opened the bedroom door. "What's wrong, honey?"

"Nothing."

"This makes me think of the time you ate all the Halloween candy at one sitting and broke out in a rash. Nothing wrong, you said. But you looked like a walking pox."

She sat on the edge of his mattress. "So tell me. What's wrong?"

His eyes filled with tears and Grandmama pulled him into her arms. "What it is, baby? Tell me."

"Quinton Toussaint told Percy he's like my daddy."

"Percy isn't white. Your father didn't play harmonica or dance the taps. So what did Quinton mean?"

"He means Percy can jam like my daddy did."

"Well, he can't, Thelonious, and that's all there is to it. Nobody jammed better than Dean DeCay. I told you not to pay attention to Quinton. He's a prissy old fool. Born rich and raised by his mama and a fussy aunt, he never had to work a day in his life if he didn't want to. He used to come to Jazz Fest with a little fold-up canvas chair and he'd sit there with his hands clasped, ankles together, the biggest sissy ever was. By the end of day he'd be so sunburned you could feel him walk by in the dark."

Grandmama stroked Monk's back. "I see an ugly green monster on your shoulder, Thelonious."

"What do you mean?"

"Jealousy. Mean little green bugger casting doubts about you on yourself. Jealousy means you think somebody is better than you," she said. "Surely you don't think Percy is better than you."

"He is better than me."

"Why do you think a thirteen-year-old boy drags around a nine-year-old to go dance for the tourists?"

"They give more money because I'm younger."

"You have a mysterious and wonderful quality," Grandmama said.

"You have stage presence."

"Charisma?"

"Where'd you learn that word?"

"Quinton told me."

"I have to admit," Grandmama said, "he's right about charisma. You look at a chorus line and all the dancers are smiling. In the whole group one girl stands out. When she's onstage, nobody sees anybody but her. It's star quality, Thelonious. That's what you have."

"Percy plays piano better than I do."

"Then practice! That's how you get to be as good as somebody else, practice. How much money did you make today?"

"About eight dollars."

She pushed down on her knees to get up on her feet. "Maybe tomorrow will be better. In any case, that storm down in the Gulf has gotten strong again. If it turns our way you won't have an audience. Tourists will fly away home."

Grandmama paused in the doorway. "I made a huge vegetable and beef soup for dinner. I want the freezer empty if the power fails. Are you hungry?"

"I can always eat."

Grandmama smiled sadly. "That's what your granddaddy used to say."

It was one of the few things Monk knew about his grandfather.

"Night or day, just ate or not," Grandmama recalled. "I axe Lincoln was he hungry, and he'd say, 'I can always eat, Diane.'"

Late that night, Monk recalled the memory of this afternoon and ran it by his mind's eye. One of the famous Neville Brothers was impressed to meet Tooth DeCay's son. Monk remembered the expression on his face, the tone of his voice, the way he held Monk's hand after shaking it. *You got some big boots to fill, boy. Tooth has always been my hero.*

Filled with pride, Monk turned on his side and looked out the open window at bright stars winking through boughs of the willow tree. Someday he hoped he could repeat those words to his father. "You were always Mr. Neville's hero," he'd say. "He was impressed to meet me."

The willow murmured and a mockingbird sang night songs. A refreshing breeze came though Monk's window and swept heat from the room. In her bedroom, he heard Grandmama say, "That air feels good."

"Yes ma'am," he said, "it does."

A moment later, Grandmama said, "Can I get something for you, Thelonious?"

"I'm all right, but thank you."

He heard her sigh, and as if speaking to herself, Grandmama said, softly, "Nobody's better than you, baby."

It was in his genes ...

{CHAPTER SEVEN}

If tourists knew there was a storm brewing, Monk couldn't tell by attendance in the French Quarter. Friday morning it seemed there were more people in the streets than had been any day this summer. Pedestrians walked along the banquettes with paper cups of beer in hand. Didn't they know a hurricane was on the way?

He mentioned it to Quinton.

"That's Nawlins for you," the historian replied. "Hurricanes are a good reason to party. Not that anybody in this town needs cause to celebrate. If a meteor were coming to destroy the world, Nawlins would rush to Bourbon Street and wait for the final blast."

From Monk's corner on Jackson Square the nearest musical act was a guitar, violin, and bull fiddle. They stood a hundred feet away so there was no competition from noise this morning. Nearby, the mimes struck mechanical poses, and in the shade along the square artists stood by their easels adding paint to pictures.

Percy's harmonica rang loud and clear. Monk danced until his legs buckled, and the hat filled with money. They had worked so steadily and energetically, Quinton's morning whoops became afternoon peeps. His voice croaked from shouting.

Exhausted, they climbed the levee overlooking the Mississippi River and watched muddy waters churn the channel flowing south. The paddle wheeler Natchez pulled away from the wharf filled with passengers going for a river cruise. The air was clear and clean. It was hot, but not insufferable.

Quinton slouched on the bench, both hands on his chest. Monk heard him wheeze.

"Are you all right, Quinton?"

"Indigestion. Chopped celery, onions, and bell peppers are the holy trinity of Cajun and Creole cooking. Last night I should've stopped with a salad and skipped the crawfish jambalaya and crème brûlée."

When he stood up, Quinton teetered and sank back on the bench. "I need a minute to catch my breath," he said.

Ships approached one another in the main stream and one signaled with two toots, "bearing starboard." The other ship answered in kind. Down on the street the music of performers blended into a pleasant racket.

Percy stood up and started back toward Jackson Square. "Let's go, Monk."

Monk went over to him. "Quinton doesn't look too good."

"He said he's all right."

"He doesn't look all right, though."

"He's old, Monk. That's the way old people look."

Monk watched Quinton take a deep breath and straighten his feathered hat. He sucked in air.

Sitting on the handlebars, Monk felt Percy's breath on his neck, talking as he peddled toward Faubourg Marigny. "Old people don't do like young people," Percy said. "My Aunt Delia by marriage, Uncle Earl's cousin, got bit by a mosquito that gave her some kind of lepsy. She'd be pushing a cart making groceries at Schwegmann's, and she'd fall asleep standing up in the produce department. She'd stand there dead to the world, ice cream dripping on the floor, until somebody bumped her awake. That's the kind of thing old people do."

"Watch the hole, Percy!"

Percy managed to avoid it. "Whatever Aunt Delia had, it must've been catching. Her husband, Uncle Howard, he'd sit in a settee on the front porch and snore so loud it set dogs to barking half a block away. Sounded like a Harley with a bad muffler. He was old."

The canal bridge whistle warned traffic to stop. Monk heard the tender cranking up the draw. The tall mast of a yacht passed through going toward Lake Ponchartrain. In an incredibly blue sky, geese flew inland. Caught by a storm, where did they go for shelter?

Monk thought about Jon Latour. He hadn't taken him anything to eat today.

"Uncle Earl had another cousin," Percy continued, "I forget her name. Lived in the bayou; got around in a pirogue. Didn't wear underpants. She got so old she couldn't hold her water and wouldn't wear diapers. Uncle Earl said he gave her a ride in his pickup one time and ever after that on cold days when he turned on the heater, the truck smelled like he'd been hauling goats. She was old."

They crossed the bridge, finally, and rode the bike into Holy Cross Community. Grandmama was waiting at home with pork chops, potato salad, and deviled eggs.

"How many eggs can I have?" Percy asked.

"All you want. I got to empty the refrigerator."

"This is the best part about a hurricane," Percy grinned. "We eat all the good stuff before the power goes off."

"Where is the storm, Grandmama?"

"Last I heard, west of Florida north of the Keys."

"Uncle Earl says he goes sailing in a storm less than category three, Miss James. How many categories is it?"

"Radio said it's a two."

Percy mimicked his Uncle Earl, mouth turned down, sneering. "Good weather for flying kites, Miss James."

That night, lying in bed, Monk heard Grandmama fill plastic milk bottles with water. Through the opened window of his bedroom a breeze stirred and the willow whispered. Frogs burped, insects shrilled. If a storm came, Monk hoped it would bring cooler evenings, but he knew it wouldn't. After a hurricane it would turn breathlessly hot.

As he did almost every night, he wondered if his father was thinking of him. He imagined Tooth looking up at the same moon Monk could see. Did the whine of cicadas ring in his ears? Was he lulled by the peeps and burps of amphibians as he recalled a son in far away New Orleans?

Monk's thoughts shifted to Jon Latour. He hoped the man managed to find dinner somewhere. Poor Jon, how miserable he must be, crawling in and out of trash bins in search of food.

Even though Monk attended the Baby Jesus Spiritual Church every weekend, he rarely prayed. But tonight he asked for God's blessings upon those less fortunate than himself, especially Jon Latour. Here he was in a dry bed, clean and well fed, with a grandmother who cooked and took care of him. Bless them all, he thought.

"Oh, and one other thing," Monk whispered. "If my daddy is thinking about me, tell him I said hello."

Saturday morning Percy came for breakfast and they finished off Grandmama's deviled eggs and leftover pork chops.

"Last night on TV," Percy reported, "Governor Blanco said we have a weather emergency. Are y'all going to leave out this house if a storm comes, Miss James?"

Grandmama concentrated on the radio. Percy came back to Monk. "My mama and the women kin plan to leave town tomorrow. Mama said they're going where water flows and electricity goes. I ain't for that leaving myself. I'm staying with my coon ass uncle Earl."

Monk got his taps and hat from the bedroom. Grandmama sat with her ear close to the portable radio. He touched her elbow to get attention. He wouldn't have been surprised if she said don't go, but instead she said, "Pay attention to traffic riding on that bicycle, Monk. People drive crazy when there's a storm in the making. If it starts to cloud up, you and Percy come on home."

There were as many tourists out and about as usual on a summer Saturday. The clickety-clack of their taps brought them over to watch, but after a few minutes most of the audience became bored and wandered off.

"They're like birds," Quinton said of the tourists, "restless and don't know why. Birds can't sit still when the air pressure drops because they have hollow bones. When the barometer falls, their bones swell and the birds get uncomfortable. They land on a roost, fidget a while, and then fly some more before settling down again. That kind of bird behavior was one of the signs primitive man used to predict the coming of bad weather."

Grandmama must have bird bones, Monk thought. Her knees and feet started to ache when a squall was building.

Hollow bones or not, and despite clear skies, the weather affected them all. Monk felt listless, but when he sat down he couldn't get comfortable. Percy wanted to take more breaks than usual. Quinton was less enthusiastic; he'd forgotten to take his vitamins, he said. By midafternoon they were ready to quit.

Quinton offered to buy lunch, and they headed for the Clover Grill. The old man halted several times to watch apartment dwellers cover their upstairs windows with plywood. At each stop he sat down to rest a few minutes. "The lingering effect of Cajun cuisine," he said. "I feel the magma of Mount Vesuvius building from within."

Inside the Clover Grill, the music was deafening.

The waiter brought hamburgers and French fried potatoes to the table. He studied Quinton critically. "You don't look too good, Sweetie-Cue."

"Indigestion," Quinton said.

"Looks more like thrombosis. Better see a doctor."

Percy met Monk's eyes and he mouthed one word: "Old."

When they left, Monk and Percy walked the bicycle to keep Quinton company on his way home.

"Would you boys like to come in?" Quinton offered. "You could play the piano. I'll see if I can find Tooth DeCay's music."

"I best go home," Monk said. "If there's going to be a storm, Grandmama might need me to help get ready."

"It doesn't look like bad weather to me," Percy reasoned.

The afternoon sun was bright. Clouds rose in the south, but with none of the gray base that meant torrential rains. "Seems like storms always come at night when you can't see anything," Percy grumped. "I wouldn't mind a hurricane if we could see things."

"Hold your tongue between your teeth when you think thoughts like that," Quinton said. "Nawlins is a city below sea level. We don't need a hurricane."

After they separated from Quinton, Monk climbed onto the bike and Percy peddled toward the Lower Ninth Ward.

"This was our last day to make money before school starts," Monk said.

"Speaking of school," Percy commented, "I might not come to class this year. Cherita's daddy said I could work at his time saver store. As part of my pay, he said I could have all the sno-balls I want."

"I wonder if he'd give me a job?" Monk asked.

"You're too young, Monk. I have to lie about my own age to work there."

Once more, the drawbridge was up. Monk watched the passing of pleasure craft, commercial fishing boats, and cutters bringing workers home from oil platforms in the Gulf.

Impatient drivers blocked by the uplifted bridge began to turn around, going to look for other crossings. Somebody's car radio boomed so loud Monk could feel it. He gazed up, and as he watched, the sky changed colors, from blue to crimson and then to gold.

Willy Bouchard's pickup truck arrived with several neighbors in the rear. "The Baby Jesus Spiritual Church is having a hurricane party," he said. "Everybody's invited to bring what they got for a cookout."

Grandmama took frozen catfish, a bowl of baked beans, and day-old bread. Monk stripped the garden of the last vegetables. He pulled up tomato stakes and stored them under the house.

Riding to the church, the women showed varying degrees of anxiety.

"I'm steady dialing on the cell phone trying to round up my family before night," a passenger related. "I'm getting me prayed up; I'm getting my husband prayed up. My mom, which is eighty-five, she's crying like a baby because the last hurricane was peeling our shit apart and that was not as bad as they say Katrina's going to be."

Her mother was still crying, sitting close to the cab of the pickup, unnoticed by everybody but Monk.

Another neighbor reported, "My son called me this morning. He said the bars are rocking on Bourbon. There's cookouts on every corner. In the middle of it all, street bands are playing some hot jazz."

Monk slipped his hand into Grandmama's and she pressed gently.

Cars and trucks filled the vacant lot next door to Baby Jesus Spiritual Church. Plastic barrels held ice and beer, soft drinks, fruit, and milk. Uncle Earl and Mr. Benoit stood at homemade grills turning slabs of meat over fiery coals. Every drip of fat sizzled and smoked. Ice cream sandwiches, cones, and containers in smoky dry ice were free for the taking. Monk had never seen so much food, and whether they brought an offering or not, everyone was welcome.

"Better eat it now," somebody said. "Mayor Ray Nagin says get out of town cause this is going to be a bad one."

"He say we got to go, or ought to go?" another man questioned.

"He said anybody didn't go, take a axe to the attic to chop his way out."

"Did he say how we suppose to go? Last hurricane when they cut off electricity, the trolleys couldn't move and buses quit running. I got no car and no money to pay anyway."

A band formed, as bands do when people get together in the Lower Ninth Ward. Monk counted eleven musicians playing string, brass, and percussion, using anything that could be drummed upon.

Cherita and her beautiful mother came to sit with Monk and Grandmama. Sister Julianne spoke softly so others wouldn't hear. "Alan doesn't want to leave the store because of possible looting. I guess Cherita and I will stay home. What about you and Thelonious, Miss Diane?"

"We're not leaving," Grandmama said.

"You want to come to our house?" Julianne asked.

"No, thank you, Julianne. We'll be fine. I was here during Hurricane Betsy back in '65," Grandmama said. "That storm came to town eight o'clock in the evening and blew steady until four the next morning. Levees overflowed on both sides of the Industrial Canal. We lived through that, we'll get through this one."

The Big Chief and his Mardi Gras Indians played bamboula drums. People danced, and day gave way to evening. Long lines formed a twisting, kicking congo. Quinton had taught Monk the name of one star, Venus. It now appeared in the western sky. A breeze blew fitfully, quit, and blew again.

The smell of burning oak and seared meat brought saliva to his mouth. The crowd spilled into the street and down the block. There was laughter, backslapping, and hugs.

With each new influx of people came more food to be cooked and eaten. Children ran in and out of shadows playing hide-and-seek. Travelers passed on the North Claiborne Avenue Bridge. Headlights formed a glowing line of cars as they slowly advanced toward main highways out of town.

"I've been through a lot of storms in my lifetime," Grandmama said to Sister Julianne. "The news people come on the air trying to scare you half to death. But most storms are like Hurricane Ivan last year. We were told to evacuate, and the storm missed us. Folks spent a lot of money running from nothing. When they came home, everything was just as it had always been. No, I'm not running. We'll stay here."

Somebody set up a television set on the front porch of Baby Jesus Spiritual Church and turned the screen to face the crowd. There was nothing on but the weather.

"Hurricane Katrina is now a category three storm with winds of 115 miles per hour," an announcer said. "The National Hurricane Center predicts landfall will be at Buras, Louisiana, sixty miles southeast of New Orleans."

It was eleven o'clock and Mr. Willy was helping several other men board up windows of the church. Grandmama didn't want to interrupt him by asking for a ride home in his pickup truck, so they sat there and watched the activity.

Burning tires helped drive away mosquitoes. Oil drums held smoldering wood. Uncle Earl went from one barrel to the next sprinkling water on embers to create more smoke. A new musical group took over the entertainment. They played zydeco and sang Cajun songs. After a little while they were hooted into silence and the music returned to jazz.

Monk lay with his head in Grandmama's lap. It was one o'clock in the morning. The TV weatherman said, "Katrina is a destructive category four, and may become category five when she comes ashore in the next thirty hours."

People stopped dancing to listen.

Monk heard a woman say, "Hurricane Camille was a five, and look what happened in Mississippi."

People walked away into the night. Others got into their cars, or onto bicycles, and Uncle Earl began to put out fires and store the oil drums.

They rode home in the back of Willy Bouchard's truck, dropping off people here and there through the community until Grandmama and Monk were the last passengers.

"Thank you for the lift, Mr. Willy."

"Yes ma'am, Miss James. If you need anything, I'm afraid you can't send Monk to get me. Beulah and I may have to leave the church. You know it floods around there every time we get heavy dew. I wanted to stay, but Beulah says we're too old to be riding out storms, and maybe she's right. It makes me tired just to think about all the work that comes with a big blow. Anyway, you folks take care of yourselves."

"Y'all do the same," Grandmama said.

She went up on the back porch one step at a time. In the kitchen she turned on a light and put on her eyeglasses to see the thermometer.

"Ninety-six degrees," she said. "Drink plenty of water, Thelonious."

He went to bed so tired he fell asleep half dressed.

His last thought was of his father, "Are you thinking of me?"

{CHAPTER EIGHT}

Donna Marie DeCay had read studies about the psychological connection between twins. Identical, that is, not fraternal. And yet, all her life, whatever trauma her twin brother experienced she felt also. When Dean first went to prison, any confinement made her claustrophobic. Even a blanket on the bed at night left her choked for air, thrashing for more space. She entered therapy. The psychiatrist said her anguish was a response to the distress of a loved one.

"Empathetic reaction to the troubles of others is not unusual," the physician had said. "A wife's pregnancy might cause a husband to suffer morning sickness. In extreme instances he may develop a bloated abdomen and crave odd combinations of food. He may even believe he has felt the baby move. You have imagined your brother's suffering and it has caused a sensitive response in your own mind."

During the terrible months after Dean's conviction, besieged by anger and disappointment, she lost weight and couldn't sleep. Finally, as he must have accepted his situation, so did she. She threw away tranquilizers and concentrated on teaching eighth grade students at Central City Junior High School in Atlanta, Georgia.

Then last night she started thinking about their childhood. Not bad memories, those she could handle. It was the happy times that hurt her: Dean helping her learn to roller skate, building an ant colony between panes of glass for a science class. He taught her how to embrace a boy when dancing, a clever hold that pulled him close and held him off at the same time. The memories brought a smile and tears of remorse.

Plagued by these thoughts, she fixed hot tea spiked with rum, lemon, and sugar, soaked in a tub of warm water, and suffered reminiscences even more painful: the evening Dean announced his engagement to marry Donna's best friend, a girl loved by the entire family; then when he broke up with her to marry an African-American girl in Louisiana.

Donna returned to bed and lay awake staring at the green glow of her luminescent bedside clock. With the approach of daylight she got up for good, bone weary, and went into the kitchen where she brewed a pot of strong coffee and waited for a call she was sure would come.

Later that morning the telephone rang. Collect call from Angola Prison. "Hey, Donna."

"Hello, Dean."

From his end of the line, she heard the hollow sounds of men confined. Their voices echoed, and metallic things rattled. It must be a jarring environment, awful for a man who treasured silent contemplation and time to compose.

Their conversation began with tight amenities:

"How's Mom?"

"Fine."

"Dad?"

"He's all right."

"You, too, Donna?"

"Yes."

Without further preamble, Dean said, "I need your help, Donna."

"If I can, Dean."

"There's a hurricane bearing down on New Orleans."

She'd seen it briefly on the news, but normally Louisiana weather was of little concern here in Atlanta.

"At seven o'clock this morning," Dean said, "the eye was 250 miles out in the Gulf of Mexico. They predict it'll come ashore in twenty-four hours as a category five, which is a killer storm, Donna."

She could tell he expected to be rebuffed. He acknowledged objections before she mentioned them. "I know this is a busy time of year for you," he said. "School starts in a few days."

"Actually, classes began last week."

"The thing is," he persisted, "my son's grandmother has no transportation. I'm not sure she'd leave New Orleans if she could. Mrs. James is a large woman. Moving around is a problem for her."

Donna heard raucous shouts and wondered how Dean could hear over the turmoil around him.

"If the grandmother won't leave, what can anybody do?" Donna asked.

"She'd have to be convinced," he said. "Have you been keeping up with what's happening down there?"

"Not really."

"I was listening to our radio station."

"Your radio station?"

"We have our own radio station here at Angola," Dean said. "KLSP, 91.7 on the FM dial. We call it the 'incarceration station.'" He laughed, a sound so precious Donna almost sobbed. "It reaches about five thousand inmates, staff, and visitors. We play gospel, blues, rock 'n' roll, jazz, and country; anything but rap. I have a sixty-minute program once a week. Four fellows and I put together a jazz ensemble. We were six, but our sax player got paroled. We lay down some mean sounds."

For an instant this was the brother she'd always loved, upbeat, happy, productive.

Then his voice fell. "There are probably a hundred thousand people in New Orleans who will not evacuate for one reason or another. They don't have the money or the means, and they won't go. CNN says the Superdome will be opened as a shelter of last resort. They say it's built to withstand winds of 200 miles per hour."

He spoke aside to someone, "Back off, pal!" He cleared his throat. Prison racket had filled the void. He returned to ask, "Are you still there, Donna?"

"I'm here."

"My son, Thelonious, is nine-years-old, Donna. His grandmother doesn't have a telephone."

"I'm a long way from New Orleans, Dean."

"I know you are, and I wouldn't ask you, except there's nobody else I can turn to. I tried to call an old friend, but he's out of pocket."

"What do you expect me to do?"

"I don't know. Just—just—I don't know. Go there and get them if you can."

"Dean, I've never met those people. I can't show up and tell them what they should or shouldn't do. Maybe they've gone to the Superdome."

"I hope they have," he said. "Do you know someone in New Orleans who could check on them?"

"Not a soul."

"If I could reach Quinton Toussaint, I know he'd take care of this for me. You remember Quinton?"

"No."

"Years ago, he produced my first records. Didn't you meet him when we came through Atlanta one time?"

"I don't think so."

"He's a sweetheart of a guy," Dean said. "Gentle, wonderful friend. He keeps me posted on Thelonious. He says the boy is smart and talented."

"How could he be otherwise?"

"Let me give you Quinton's phone number and address."

Looking for paper, she added his message to a scant grocery list of items she intended to buy this week: yogurt, brie, croissants, and Toussaint. Sunlight cast the windows in shades of gray. Donna wrote down the information Dean dictated. In turn, she gave him her cell phone number.

"It's difficult to make calls out of this place right now," he said. "You have to constantly dial a number to get past busy signals at the other end. Every man is lined up to call his family about the storm. We're on a timer to keep conversations short. Donna, I know this is an imposition."

"I'll see what I can do, Dean."

"Thanks," he said, and then she lost the connection.

It occurred to her she hadn't told Dean she loved him, or that she missed him and thought of him every day. She forgot to ask if he needed any personal items. How was his health? Was he still composing music? It had been five years since she last heard his voice when he called to tell her he'd been convicted and wouldn't be eligible for parole until 2017. Given the opportunity this morning, she failed to say anything heartfelt. He must wonder if anybody cared for him anymore.

She studied her notes. Quinton Toussaint: an address on Esplanade. Diane James and her grandson lived at the corner of Andry and Royal in the Lower Ninth Ward, but there was no house number.

She dressed in loose slacks and a cotton shirt, called her principal, and then drove to his home on Decatur-Flat Shoals Road in Dekalb County. She and Bob Miller had gone to the University of Georgia together. They dated one another until the news broke about Dean's arrest. She wasn't sure which of them had withdrawn, but the relationship stalled.

Perhaps it was just as well. Poor literal Bob Miller was not blessed with southern wit. She once told him a joke about a girl in Hahira, Georgia, born with breasts on her back—a tragic story—but she made a great dancing partner.

"Breasts on her back?" Bob was horrified. "There's no surgical procedure to correct that, is there?"

Donna telephoned Bob to say she was coming, and when she arrived at his house he met her with an awkward hug. She came straight to the point. "I have a family emergency. I need a few days off."

"Your father?"

"No."

"Your mother?"

"No. It's—"

"Dean," he guessed.

"He has a nine-year-old son in New Orleans," she said. "I can probably go down and be back in a few days."

"Right here at the beginning of our school year," Bob worried. "Well. It can't be helped. Trouble rarely makes an appointment. Have you called the Louisiana state police? I heard on the news that all major highways in New Orleans are now one way going out to facilitate evacuation."

That was only one thing she hadn't thought of. It was Sunday; she couldn't go to the bank, so she had to withdraw cash from an ATM. She packed a pair of jeans, shorts, underwear, and polo shirts, gathered a few toiletries and stuffed them into an overnight bag.

By the time she was ready to leave, it was almost noon and she hadn't eaten, which made her think, with thousands of people fleeing south Louisiana, would restaurants have food? Could she get fuel for the car? She decided to carry twenty-five gallons of gasoline in plastic containers she bought at Wal-Mart. Throughout the preparations, every fifteen minutes she redialed her call to Quinton Toussaint in hopes she wouldn't have to go at all. There was no answer.

At last, she was on her way, driving west into the sun and south toward the storm. Had she forgotten anything? As she drove, she tried Quinton Toussaint again. The circuits were busy.

Even though all the windows were opened, the smell of gasoline fumes from containers in the trunk filled the car.

She stopped in Montgomery, Alabama, for dinner, and from there, telephoned her parents back in Atlanta.

She kept it light. "Mom, I'm on my way to the windy city."

"Chicago?"

"New Orleans."

She could imagine her mother stiffening. "What for, Donna?"

"Dean called. He wants me to check on his child and—"

"Donna, really now. Don't get caught up in that mess."

"He's worried about his son and the boy's grandmother."

"I saw on the news there's a six p.m. curfew down there. The storm is due to reach land early tomorrow morning. You should wait until it's over, and then call somebody. Shame on Dean for putting you in harm's way."

"I'll be all right," Donna said.

Her mother dropped the receiver and yelled, "Alfred! Pick up the phone. It's Donna. She's going to New Orleans!"

Donna heard him answer on the kitchen extension. "Bad time of year for a vacation in Sin City."

"I figured the room rates would be reduced."

"That storm has winds of 155 miles per hour," her father said. "It's nothing to fool around with. Wind of that velocity will bring a huge storm surge. Do you know New Orleans?"

"It's somewhere in south Louisiana, right?"

"Wait until the thing blows over," her father counseled. "Then you should take along ice and drinking water. They'll need it. Come over to the house and we'll discuss it."

"I'm in Alabama, Dad. On my way there."

She heard her mother, "Dear God, Alfred, talk some sense into that girl."

But Dad said, "Be careful, sweetheart. If there's anything we can do, let us know."

"Thanks, Dad."

"So we won't fret needlessly," he added, "let us know where to hunt for your body. Do you have your camera?"

That's what she forgot. "I never go to a disaster with proper equipment, Dad."

"Stay safe."

Paying the bill for dinner, Donna heard someone say, "Every motel is booked in Louisiana and Mississippi. Now they're coming over here."

She dialed around on the car radio for news.

"Katrina is 226 miles southeast of New Orleans," a reporter said. "She's a category five with winds gusting at 202 miles per hour. There's lots of pre-storm excitement in the Crescent City."

Looking through the windshield, a few clouds blocked the stars. Traffic increased in Mississippi as refugees from coastal areas inched north in search of safe haven. Every motel displayed a "No Vacancy" sign. She pulled into a service station to top off the fuel, but on each pump a paper sack covered the nozzle with a note that advised, "No Gas."

At a roadside picnic area she took two five-gallon containers from the trunk and poured petrol into the gas tank. A sudden breeze swept her hair and cooled her skin. But then it was gone, and a deathly still remained. She watched the last peek of stars disappear behind clouds. She put the gas cans in the trunk again.

Back roads were her best routes to avoid slow-moving traffic. In small towns the stores were closed, streets empty. A light drizzle dampened the pavement, raising oil, which made the surface slippery. She had to slow down.

South of Hattiesburg police cars blocked the road. Flashing lights made a mask of the trooper's face.

"I need to get to New Orleans," Donna explained.

"No ma'am. They're about to have a hurricane."

"I have to check on a child and his grandmother."

"No one is allowed in, ma'am. Turn around, or park across the street at the mall."

Using her cell phone she tried again to call Quinton Toussaint.

No answer.

All she could do was pull off the highway into a strip mall parking lot crowded with other cars. A family with several children had set up a charcoal grill. As the father cooked supper, the youngsters ran between cars yelling and laughing. In a car next to hers, Donna heard an apocalyptic weather advisory that locked her heart.

"Devastating damage is expected," the radio newsman said in a monotone. "Large areas will be uninhabitable for weeks. Half of well-built homes will have roof and wall failure. All windows will blow out. Persons, pets, and livestock exposed to winds will face certain death if struck by airborne debris; damage will be widespread."

A bank clock sign said the temperature was 90 degrees, humidity 90 percent. Her lips were chapped from gas vapors seeping out of the trunk.

"At this hour," the radio continued, "nearly ten thousand people have taken shelter in the Superdome. The French Quarter is empty. It is quiet and warm here in New Orleans. The most recent advisory on Katrina reports winds have diminished to 160 miles per hour. We have been warned that most parts of the city will lose electricity around five o'clock this morning. This is a safety precaution to prevent electrocution from fallen power lines."

Donna dialed Quinton Toussaint.

The circuits were busy.

Mosquitoes pestered her, and Donna endured them because it was too hot to sit in the car with windows closed. She tried to get some sleep to compensate for last night, but it was not to be. Her clothes were soaked from perspiration, and she itched for want of a bath. Somewhere in the parking lot a baby cried. From the roadblock, revolving lights of police cars threw red and blue reflections onto dark windows of the strip mall shops.

I wouldn't be sitting here if Dean had married Gail.

The thought brought renewed regrets.

If he had married Gail, he'd be living the good life in fashionable Buckhead, north of Atlanta. His son would be—white, and out of danger.

Donna slapped an insect biting her ankle.

The memory of an argument she had with Dean was as painful now as if it happened yesterday. He had taken her to the Varsity Drive-in

Restaurant near the campus of Georgia Tech in Atlanta. It was Saturday night, following a football game. Cars circled the lot trolling for parking space. Students blew their horns and shouted at one another. Dean said, "I've decided not to marry Gail."

"What?" Confounded, Donna said, "But, Dean, you've always loved Gail."

"I did. I do. I still have tender feelings for Gail, but I love another woman more."

The other woman was Elaine James. He met her while playing a gig in New Orleans. He'd known her for one year.

"A year? Dean, you and Gail have been going together since high school. Gail is my best friend. We always planned to be bridesmaids at each other's wedding."

"Yeah, I know, Donna. I'm sorry."

"I can't believe it," she said, hotly. "When will we meet this woman?"

"That brings me to the second part of this confession." He tried to grin but the expression came off anguished. "Elaine is not Caucasian."

"She's—"

"African-American," Dean said. "She's a beautiful woman, Donna. Talented, intelligent, a great singer."

"Is she pregnant?"

"No, no. Thank God. No."

"Have you told Gail about this woman?"

"No."

"Gail will be devastated, Dean. Her parents and our parents—they'll all be devastated."

"I know that. I need you to help break the news gently to Mom and Dad."

Then Donna said something totally out of character for her. She said, as though making an announcement to people in the circling cars, "Folks, my twin brother is going to marry a Negro!"

She wasn't a racist. At least she'd never been before. "What kind of people are her parents, Dean? I mean, other than the obvious."

"Her mother is a well-known singer. Her father is deceased."

"Did he die of natural causes, or was it during the commission of a crime?"

"Okay, you're angry." Dean stiffened. "Because I won't live my life by your conventions, you're upset. Well, here's the way it is, Donna. I'm going to marry the woman I love. Take it or leave it, I don't give a damn."

He got out of the car and slammed the door so hard the carhop's tray fell off the window. His last words to her were, "Take the car. I'll catch a bus."

That had been ten years ago.

Donna slapped another mosquito and then pressed redial on her cell phone. It rang, and rang, and rang. "Come on, Quinton Toussaint," she snarled softly. "Answer."

A man and two boys came by with boxes of Krispy Kreme doughnuts offered at a dollar apiece. Despite the outrageous price, they were selling briskly. Donna wished she had a cup of hot coffee. Another slap sent a bloodsucker to insect heaven.

She asked a man in the next car, "Do you have a Louisiana map?"

"I do."

She spread it on the hood of her car and studied the roads by flashlight. "I've got to get to New Orleans," she said. "I'm worried about a nephew living in the Lower Ninth Ward. Do you know that area?"

"Yes, I do," he said. "You know about the storm?"

"Of course."

"Then you don't want to go tonight," he said. "You're liable to get stranded somewhere. Are you by yourself?"

She hesitated. "I am for the moment."

He extended a hand. "I'm Barry Hampton, reporter."

She laughed. "Donna DeCay, educator."

She turned off the flashlight. In the dark, he said, "Who do you educate?"

"Junior high students at Central City School in Atlanta. Whom do you report for?"

"The *Probe*, a maligned and underappreciated periodical that keeps tabs on extraterrestrials, birth anomalies, celebrities, and oddities of human nature."

"Is that the *Probe* I see displayed on grocery counters when I go shopping?"

"One and the same," he said. "Our entire staff has vacated the premises in New Orleans, gone to Houston from whence they will put together future issues until they can return to the French Quarter."

"You didn't go with them," Donna noted.

"No. I was left to guard our offices. However, the storm predictions became so dire, I borrowed this automobile from a used-car dealer who was anxious to sell before the storm arrived. I told him I wanted to take a test drive, and here I am. The car did not pass the test, incidentally. I got this far when it quit."

He refolded the map and gave it to her. "Keep it. Obviously I won't be going anywhere for awhile."

"You know this area?" Donna asked.

"Like my own navel. That might not mean much to you, but as a student of Eastern religions, I practice omphaloskepsis, which is contemplation of one's navel as the center of the universe. I know my navel. Are you looking for a guide?"

She had no reason to trust this man, but Donna said, "Could you find a way into New Orleans tomorrow?"

"As a matter of fact, I should be there in the morning to protect the assets of my employers. While we wait out the storm, would you like to share a twelve-dollar box of day-old doughnuts? I also have a thermos of coffee, sans chicory. I live in New Orleans, but I'm not a native. Chicory is for Cajuns."

She sat in her car and he sat in his, doors open, talking in shadows. The police lights shot red and blue daggers of light across their windshields.

He was fifty years old, Barry said, a would-be novelist who had lost his way. He'd been writing quirky stories for the *Probe* most of his adult life. He described himself as a dropped ball before the bounce. "Since my wife died, I have fallen from a lofty height," he said, "but the peak of the rebound will define me as a man. Toulouse-Lautrec was a slave to absinthe; Arthur Conan Doyle was hooked on opium. My addiction was my wife, and I had been on a twenty-year high when I lost her."

He talked constantly and made her laugh; Donna needed to laugh.

"Most people think what we publish in the *Probe* is a pack of lies," he said. "Actually, we do not knowingly publish anything untrue. We merely look at truth from a different perspective. For example, the cover photo might be a strange creature with pointy ears and fangs, and the headline says, 'Bat Boy Brings Luck.' You read the article and it's about a winning streak a ball club has had since they hired a new bat boy. Or a story may be ludicrous, only meant to be funny. One of my favorites was the picture of a woman holding a very large child. 'Two Hundred Pound Newborn and Ninety Pound Mother,' the headline said. Read the article: the baby was an orphaned elephant being bottle fed by a lady at the zoo."

They ate doughnuts and sipped coffee. His wife had died in surgery five years ago. "It was a routine procedure," Barry recalled. "Appendicitis. Go in today and be home day after tomorrow; nothing to it, they said. For some reason, my wife's heart stopped beating and they couldn't get it started again."

To ease the moment, Donna asked, "What's the best story you ever wrote?"

"My favorite would have to be, 'Baby Born with Bungee Cord Umbilical.' The kid kept going back where he came from."

Donna turned on her car radio and Barry Hampton came over to sit in the front seat beside her.

A news report said Katrina had weakened to a category three and was about to hit southeast of New Orleans. "That's good for us," Barry remarked, "and bad for the Mississippi Gulf Coast. The west side of a hurricane is the weakest. Maybe New Orleans will dodge the bullet."

Donna tried Quinton Toussaint's number and listened to the burr of an unanswered phone.

"I've been calling this man for the past twenty hours," she complained.

"If he has any sense," Barry said, "he left town long before now."

The breeze picked up and with it came a patter of rain. It was too hot to raise the car windows. Mosquitoes buzzed around her ears. Donna put her head back and closed her eyes.

Here she was trying to get to a hurricane and about to share her car with a man she'd just met. Had she lost her mind?

An actress once said she'd never met a dumb comedian. Donna had always been a sucker for wit, and she admired intelligence. With humor, Barry Hampton had lifted her spirits, and he wasn't stupid. Conversation ranged from politics to haute cuisine. "With me it has been less haute and more cuisine," he patted his middle. "I've gained thirty pounds in the past few years." Sitting beside her, he'd fallen asleep. She heard a crude rhoncus. Okay, he snored. Nobody is perfect.

From the radio came another report, "Katrina has reached the south Louisiana coastline pushing a storm surge of fourteen to seventeen feet. If you ain't out, baby, it's too late to go."

In a car sharing the parking lot there were now two infants crying. Donna heard a woman cursing. "I need help with the babies, damn you!"

"What do you want me to do?" a man replied.

"Change a diaper," she replied. "Feed the baby."

"Hell, woman, the baby is breast fed."

"The other baby, you ass!"

Donna slapped another mosquito and stared into worsening weather. What was she doing here?

{CHAPTER NINE}

Sound from the radio in Grandmama's bedroom was too low to understand and too loud to ignore. Monk lay beside his opened window and the willow swished under gusts of wind. Rain lashed the roof and swept the walls. Lightning streaked across black clouds and in each flash he could see debris blowing in the street.

He got up to go to the bathroom and Grandmama called, "You all right, baby?"

"Yes ma'am, I am."

"You can come in here if you want to."

But it was too hot to share a bed, and besides, watching the weather through his bedroom window was interesting.

Lightning flashed.

Thunder clapped.

He hurried back to bed and lay with his face at the windowsill. Sometimes during summer rains the air filled with chemical smells, as fertilizers washed down from the sky or got stirred up from the earth. Right now the rain smelled like freshly cleaned vegetables.

A jagged tongue of flame flashed brightly and the concussion was so strong it slapped him in the face.

The electricity went off. Fans whined down and quit. In the kitchen the refrigerator stopped. Absolute darkness engulfed the house and the street.

He heard Grandmama switch to the portable battery-operated radio.

The announcer's voice came alive again.

"We have unconfirmed reports of minor flooding in St. Bernard Parish along the MRGO."

MRGO—the Mississippi River Gulf Outlet. Monk heard of, but had never seen, the waterway. It was five miles east of here.

A limb cracked and for an instant he thought it was a gunshot. The next glimpse by lightning revealed the willow tree had split down the middle. He loved that tree. He liked to climb into the branches and sit in a crotch hidden from everybody, surrounded by green leaves and lost in his own world. One of the broken limbs lay up against the house. It blocked the wind that had been coming through his window. Wet leaves were plastered against the screen.

He heard a bumping, rattling noise and in a lightning flash he saw a garbage can bounce across the street. Monk felt his way down the hall to Grandmama's bedroom door. "I'm going to sit on the back porch, Grandmama."

"Stay out the wind, Thelonious. Don't get hit by flying trash."

"I'll be careful."

He took his pillow and stretched out in the porch swing. The roaring wind buffeted his back. This was the most boring exciting night he'd ever endured.

Down the street he saw flashlights waggling as people gazed out of their windows to see if there was damage. Despite the wind, he heard voices, and then laughter. The flashlights extinguished. Rain came harder, striking the roof with such force it sounded like hail. Water poured from the eaves and blew on him in the swing. He didn't care. It was better than being too hot.

"Thelonious?"

"Yes ma'am?"

"You all right?"

"Yes I am, Grandmama."

"All right then."

A bird flew onto the porch and hit the screened kitchen door. Monk sat up, waiting for the next bolt of lightning. The creature clung to the screen and even when he walked over to it, the bird did not fly.

"Did you lose your nest?" Monk asked.

He was tempted to stroke it, but decided it might scare the bird into flying. For the time being, right here was the safest place to be. He eased open the door and let himself in.

He passed Grandmama's room. "I'm going to bed," he said.

"I love you, Thelonious."

"I love you, Grandmama."

Even with the cooling wind it was still hot. He threw back the covers and fell onto the mattress. He pretended the pillow was beautiful Sister Julianne. She wrapped his arms around her body and hugged her to him. He imagined he could smell her perfume, like crushed orange peels mixed with tea olive.

Then he thought of Cherita and wondered if she was all right in the howling wind and lashing rain. Was she frightened? Not with Jesus holding my hand, she'd said.

Monk dozed off and on, snoozing during the cool steady flow of wind pushing through the house. He awoke once to find Grandmama standing over his bed, her flashlight directed aside so the light wouldn't disturb him.

Things slammed into the outside walls, rain hit the roof like a handful of pebbles; now and then the eaves moaned and the house creaked. But half-asleep in his bed, Monk was not afraid. He had imagined monstrous waves coming over the levee, a hiss of foam flung from whitecaps. None of that happened.

It was time for dawn but daylight had not come. A gray veil had been draped over the world, half-light without shadows. He went to check on the bird and the terrorized creature still clung to the screened door. Beyond the porch, Monk saw the garden was underwater and ruined. The split tree covered part of the back steps; willow branches thrust onto the floor and touched the swing. He was glad he'd been inside when that happened.

He paused in the hall at Grandmama's door. The man on the radio said, "At seven o'clock; the eye of Katrina is still south of New Orleans. The storm surge has topped levees in St. Bernard and Plaquemines Parishes. We have reports of minor flooding in the Lower Ninth Ward due to overtopping along the Industrial Canal. Power and telephone lines are down. Hold on a minute …"

"Are you awake, Grandmama?"

"More or less, babe. Do you need something?"

The announcer came back on the air, "In the past fifteen minutes," he said, "there has been rapid flooding in the Lower Ninth Ward."

"Grandmama, there's water in the house."

"Where about, Thelonious?"

"Right here on the floor."

He heard the bed creak as she swung her legs over the side of the mattress. She turned on the flashlight. "Lord," she said.

She was a dark hulk moving ahead of him toward the kitchen. She said again, "Lord!"

Through the opened back door he saw limbs of the broken tree floating in water. The bird held fast.

"It's up to my knees, Grandmama!"

"Put on a sweater, Thelonious."

"I'm not cold."

"You may get cold. Hurry, put on a sweater and get your shoes."

He hadn't worn anything but the taps all summer. Monk sloshed back to his bedroom, pulled open the bottom drawer and it was filled with water. "Grandmama, the sweaters are wet!"

"Monk, come here!"

The tone of her voice carried the shrill cry of alarm. Monk waded back into the dark hallway.

"Help me pull the bureau under the attic door, Monk."

He wrestled his end of the furniture, and Grandmama pulled her side. The water buoyed the chest of drawers slightly and it toppled against the wall.

"I'll hold it," Grandmama said. "Climb up there and see if you can open that trapdoor, Thelonious."

She steadied him, her grip on his ankle so tight it hurt. Monk stood on the chiffonier and reached up. He pushed. "It won't move, Grandmama."

"Let's go to the kitchen then," she said. "We'll sit on the table until the water lowers. Climb down, baby."

When he got off the furniture, it bobbed slightly. The water was up to his thighs. Grandmama held his arm, splashing water down the corridor. In the kitchen she lifted him bodily and put him on the tabletop. She went to the back door with the flashlight and pushed open the screened door. The bird stayed put.

The wind howled and moaned and growled in the eaves. Lightning flashed and Monk smelled an odor like one piece of flint struck against another.

"Are you going to get on the table, Grandmama?"

"I will when I have to, Thelonious."

Something in her voice scared him. "You know how to swim, don't you, Grandmama?"

"Big as I am," she said, "I float."

When he didn't respond, Grandmama added, "It was a joke, Thelonious."

He said to her what she sometimes said to him, "I got it. It wasn't funny."

"Stay on the table, Thelonious. I'm going to see what we can use for a ladder."

"I'll go with you."

"No!" she said, sharply. "No telling what's in this water. I'll be right back."

His rear end felt wet. Monk reached over the edge of the table. "Grandmama, it's getting deeper!"

He heard her moving in the hallway, stirring water here and there. She came back with the flashlight and radio.

"Katrina is moving ashore at the Louisiana-Mississippi border," the announcer said. "Here in New Orleans, we have reports of six to nine feet of standing water at the Seventeenth Street Canal area."

"It's coming up fast, Grandmama."

She went to the backdoor again. Wind hurled objects at the shed; the willow cracked and broke again.

By the vague light of day he saw the bird had flown. Water came in the kitchen windows. Grandmama was right; he'd gotten cold.

Monk knew they were in trouble. He crouched on the table and Grandmama bobbed in water up to her breasts. "What are we going to do, Grandmama?"

"Don't be scared, Thelonious."

And yet, he detected fear in her voice.

Objects kept striking the roof. He heard a heavy thud like broken limbs, and the clang of something metal that ricocheted away. Water in the kitchen covered the stove and countertops.

"If it gets much deeper, Grandmama, we won't be able to breathe."

"We can't go outside," she said. "Let's us see if we can get that attic door open, Thelonious."

Something hit the house on the porch side, and to Monk's horror, he heard a grinding wrench of metal and saw the front end of an automobile pushed through the kitchen door.

"Grandmama, what're we going to do?"

"Can you swim to the hall again, Thelonious. That attic trap used to open years ago.

A cabinet door swung free and spices floated out. A box of sodden cereal emerged and Grandmama's thrashing arms made it move away on ripples. Outside, the din of wind and rain had become a scream. Or, maybe it actually was a scream he heard.

"I'll go first and reach back to hold you by the arm, Thelonious. Don't swallow any of this mess. Are you ready?"

"Yes ma'am."

She disappeared and a second later her hand grabbed him by the shirt and snatched him through.

It was completely dark.

Grandmama had left her flashlight in the kitchen. "I have to go back for it," she said. "Can you keep your head above water, Thelonious?"

She left him and Monk panicked. He took a deep breath to follow, but she reappeared, gasping for breath. "Are you here, baby?"

"Here I am, Grandmama."

He felt the bureau and stood on it. Grandmama wedged her body between the furniture and a wall, holding it more or less steady. Monk blew water out of his nose and Grandmama said, "Don't swallow this stuff, Thelonious."

"Not if I can help it," he said.

Grandmama's flashlight was a Boy Scout, waterproof, with an adjustable head that swiveled. She shined light on the attic door. Monk stood on the dresser and banged the door with his fist. "It doesn't move," he said.

“Seems to me like it used to open coming down, not going up,” Grandmama said. “See, do you find a latch, maybe.”

“Here it is.”

“Can you open it?”

He was so cold his fingers were numb and trembling. Monk fumbled with the sliding bolt. It had been painted over and stuck shut.

Grandmama gave him the flashlight. “Hit it with the lantern, baby.”

He did, and the latch broke free. He bashed it again and the door fell down. Dust poured onto his face.

“It’s dry up here,” he said.

“Climb through, Thelonious.”

He did so, flashing light over rafters and wiring. If possible, this area was even darker than the hallway below. He turned around to help Grandmama and she stuck her head through the trap door. He heard her cough and sputter. “Might be I swallowed some of this mess myself,” she said.

“Come on in, Grandmama.”

She slipped back down. “The chiffonier got away from under me,” she said. She ducked under water, trying to pull it back. When she emerged again, Monk said, “Can I come down and help?”

“No, baby. Stay where you are. I may end up floating through this hole. Better stand back. I’m liable to shoot through like confetti out of a party popper.”

Something smashed the roof so hard the attic shuddered.

“Did you hear something, Thelonious?”

“On the roof?”

“Not that,” Grandmama said. “Something else. Like a boom. A bomb.”

“No ma’am, I didn’t hear it.”

“I wonder did white folks dynamite those levees again.”

“I didn’t hear it, Grandmama.”

“I wouldn’t put it past somebody to do that,” she said. “Take the flashlight and see if you can find a place at the end of the attic where we might crawl outside, Thelonious.”

There wasn’t much headroom between ceiling rafters below and the slant of roof above. Barefoot, Monk felt his way from one rough timber to the next.

"See if there's a place where we can break through the roof, Thelonious."

The roof was decked with sheets of plywood. Roofing nails jabbed through from one end to the other.

He flashed the light down at his feet to gauge the next step and he saw water seep through from below. He turned the light back to Grandmama and water surged up around her, into the attic. He hurried back. "Come on, Grandmama, climb through."

"I'm trying."

She wedged one arm through, and then the next. Her blouse ripped as she pulled up one breast, and the other. "I guess I stopped up this hole," she joked. "Big titties and a whopping belly don't make for good squeezing."

"It isn't funny, Grandmama! Try harder."

"I'm far as I can come, Baby."

"Can you go back down, through the kitchen, outside?"

"I don't think so."

Water lapped between her breasts.

"Save your battery, Thelonious. Turn off the light."

"No. I want to see you."

"I'll be right here. Turn off the light and hold my hand."

He'd always been intrigued by her slender, tapered fingers, piano hands, just right for playing the keyboard.

"We should've dragged the piano under the trapdoor," he said.

"Too heavy," Grandmama gasped. "We did all we could."

The wind was a shriek, the rain torrential. Water rose more slowly, but it was rising.

Standing on a rafter, he felt liquid around his insteps.

"Your Granddaddy built this house," Grandmama said in the dark. "He wanted it to last as long as we did, he said. He used tongue-in-groove flooring and tongue-in-groove beaded board ceilings, too. I disremember how much more it cost than using plasterboard, but it was more than we could afford at the time. I wish you'd known your granddaddy, Thelonious. He was a good man. He would've been crazy about you."

She choked, coughed, sputtered.

"Grandmama, don't die."

"We all die sometime, Thelonious. If I die, I get to see your granddaddy, Lincoln, again. He never once asked me to lose weight. Not once. He said he liked to have something to grab hold of. Somebody told him these were love handles and Lincoln said I had banisters and balustrades. He knew words like that because he worked in the building trade. He was a good man."

"Please don't die, Grandmama."

"Do you remember being born, Thelonious?"

"No ma'am."

"Dying is like being born all over again. It's nothing to be scared of. You tell a baby in the belly you going to push him out into bright light and most likely he'd scream and holler. He'd want to stay where he is, warm and safe. Dying is natural as childbirth. No reason to be fearful. It's getting there that takes some courage."

The house groaned, a sound Monk once heard while on a seagoing clipper ship that came to the Port of New Orleans as a tourist attraction. Quinton took him to see it. The rigging stretched and yawned. The deck creaked.

That's the way the house sounded. Monk hoped they were afloat.

Grandmama choked and coughed. She strangled and heaved to expel liquid. Monk turned on the flashlight. Her head was tilted back to hold up her chin.

"Save the batteries." She pronounced it batt-trees. Under stress she stopped worrying about diction and pronunciation. "I left the extra cells in my bedside table drawer."

Water lapped on her face and she spit it out. "Lincoln knew how to build a house solid," she said. "How many storms we been through and never lost a shutter? He knew how to double-nail roofing shingles to hold them down."

Crouched on a rafter, Monk felt water around his ankles.

"Grandmama, can you come any higher?"

"No, baby. This is good as it gets."

She looked up at him, and incredibly, she smiled. "When I knew you were coming to live with me, I thought, Lord God, at my age, what would I do with a three-year-old boy? It turned out to be the best thing ever happened to me, Thelonious."

She twisted her head, strained her neck, and raised her chin. "You've been the joy of my life, Thelonious."

He sobbed. "I love you, Grandmama."

"And I love you with every ounce of my soul and body," she said. She gasped, coughed.

Monk straddled her and pulled up on her head.

"That's not helping," she said. "Best let me do it, babe."

But when he let go, her chin dropped into the water and she snorted, spit.

She gripped his hand so hard it hurt.

"Grandmama?"

She trembled, sucked water into her mouth and spewed it out. Monk grabbed her head and lifted. "Grandmama!"

Her head was so large he couldn't hold it. The flashlight floated away and he grabbed it back. Monk stood over her body, hands under her chin, lifting. She gurgled, rasped, choking.

"Grandmama!"

He pinched her nose to keep out the water and she pushed away his arm. He shoved water away from her face and tried to block it with cupped hands. The flashlight bobbed away on ripples. He pulled up on her arm. She didn't budge.

"Grandmama," he screamed, "please!"

And then, out of the dark, he thought he heard Cherita call his name. Monk stumbled after the flashlight. He banged his head on a beam. The water was up to his hips. A roach tried to climb onto him and he pushed it away. Attic dust rode the surface of water like a thin gray blanket.

By the dying light of spent batteries, he saw Grandmama's hands float up higher than her head and he screamed.

Cherita called again.

It must've been the wind. Cherita wasn't here.

He was alone.

{CHAPTER TEN}

Trapped in close quarters and rising water, Monk was terrified. There was barely enough room between the flood and peak of the roof to keep his nose above water. He couldn't stand up straight because the roof was too low. Despite Grandmama's warning not to swallow water, he accidentally gulped some down, coughed, and spit.

He slammed the roof with his fist and stabbed his hands on protruding roofing nails. Roaches crawled over floating attic dust. He reminded himself of something Grandmama once said, "Roaches don't have fangs, Thelonious. They won't hurt you."

Uncle Earl had said something about roaches, too. "When the bomb drops there won't be nothing living bigger than a man's finger—but there will always be roaches." Uncle Earl read that in a magazine at a dentist's office. "Roaches are hard to kill," he'd said. "Step on one, squash out his guts, and a minute later he sucks 'em back in and crawls off."

One day Percy and Monk were racing roaches across the living room floor. Sister Julianne came in and recoiled. "Roaches are disgusting," she said. "They crawl through dirty things. They lay egg pods in garbage. They live in filth."

"My mama says you can't get rid of them," Percy remarked.

"In the Deep South where we live," Sister Julianne admitted, "there are going to be roaches. But you don't have to play with them."

"I saw one in Mr. Benoit's meat locker," Percy said. "He calls them palmetto bugs."

"No matter what my husband calls them, they're still roaches, Percy. Both of you go wash your hands. Use lots of soap and hot water."

Every move Monk made in the attic was slow and deliberate to keep from sloshing water or stirring up the palmetto bugs. Stooped over, mouth shut tight, he went from one end of the attic to the other feeling for a way to escape. Outside, the wind still roared. Now and then something struck the roof.

He had to go to the bathroom, so he did.

The glow of the flashlight turned a sickly yellow as the batteries died.

He had cried his eyes dry and screamed until his voice gave out. When he touched his face in the dark, the wrinkled fingers didn't feel like his own. His feet slipped off the joist and dropped several inches, dipping his chin in dirty water. Panic seized him.

To calm himself, he thought about when he first met Percy and his brother, Benny. They played hide-and-seek at Percy's house. Monk was there to study arithmetic, but Mrs. Brown had to leave and deliver "the tolls" to a bookmaker. Monk climbed into a kitchen cabinet, hiding, knees drawn up against his chest. He pulled the door closed behind him and it locked.

He had never forgotten that first experience of sudden, blinding fear. It was so intense it drove out common sense. He bucked his body, thrashed at pots and pans, kicked the locked door and screamed.

Percy opened the cabinet and said, "What kind of way to hide is that? Neighbors could've heard you next door."

Monk remembered how cool the kitchen air felt after the confinement, and how his heart hammered for several minutes afterward.

On the spot that day, he decided panic was dangerous. That decision was wasted here in the attic with water up to his neck and Grandmama stuck in the trapdoor. He'd first tried to run and where could he go? He threw himself against the roof, bashed his head, and beat the ceiling. What good did it do?

At last, the panic eased, replaced by exhaustion. He forced himself to think.

He'd been on the roof of this house. One day he'd climbed the willow tree and crawled across a limb to get there. He remembered the asphalt shingles had a prickly feel to them, covered with glittering grit to reflect away heat. Jutting up through the roof were vent pipes from the kitchen sink and bathroom. He remembered putting his ear to a vent and hearing Grandmama flush the commode and run water in a lavatory down below.

The slant of the roof was not steep. Outside and on top, he had walked the length of the building looking down on lawns around him. The neighbor's dog was in the yard. Monk called his name. Befuddled, the pup barked and ran around. He couldn't find Monk high overhead.

Below the eave was a louvered wooden vent. He went to where he remembered it being. A current of water flowed against his legs and over his bare feet. He felt the louvered boards with a foot, braced himself against the roof and kicked.

He stubbed his toe, but it didn't yield.

Monk waded back past Grandmama to the other end of the attic. Through murky water he saw a faint glow of light from outside.

Holding against the roof, he pushed the louvered boards. He groped with his hands, pulling, instead of shoving. Then he kicked, and slowly it moved.

To get through he'd have to hold his breath and dive down. What if his clothes snagged and he couldn't get loose? What if he got through and the other side was worse than here?

He recalled the time Quinton Toussaint took him to the battlefield at Chalmette where Stonewall Jackson defeated the British in the Battle of New Orleans. Monk remembered gazing at the open field. Advancing Redcoats had marched toward their enemy under deadly rifle and cannon fire. Imagining himself there in 1814, he was struck by the bravery it would take to run toward gunfire. He said so to Quinton. "Why did they do it?" Monk asked. "Were they all heroes?"

"They were well-trained soldiers who followed orders," Quinton said. "A hero is often a man who does something brave without thinking. Later, when he looks back on what he did, he is astonished that he committed such a perilous act. In retrospect, what he did may seem foolhardy to him. Another day, another time, the same man might be a coward. Heroism is usually something that happens without aforethought."

The trouble was, here in the attic, Monk had already had time to think. He was so afraid his chest hurt. He kept thinking about the way

Grandmama coughed and spit, sputtering water out her nose as she died.

If the water rose a few more inches he'd have no air, and then he would drown, too. Outside had to be better.

He inhaled and exhaled, filling his lungs with oxygen. He read in a book that a man about to be hanged did that so he'd live a few seconds longer after a noose broke his neck.

Then Monk closed his eyes and dived down.

The storm was quieter underwater than it had been above. He pulled himself through the hole and clawed his way free. He came up in a roaring blast of wind that shoved him back under the eave. He scrambled to climb on the little bit of roof still above water. On top, he lay on his back. The sky was gray, clouds dark, and yet everything looked bright after being in the attic. He was on a slant of roof sheltered a little from the wind. Objects flew by overhead and skipped across the floodwaters. He heard the crack of a tree limb. In the distance, somebody cried for help. He thought it was the people with the rabbits.

After a few minutes, the shouts stopped.

His teeth chattered and he couldn't stop trembling. His fingers and feet were swollen and puffy. Monk stuck his hands between his legs to warm them. He turned on his side and gazed across the tops of broken trees and peaks of sunken houses. He saw a dog on a roof, and while he watched, the animal skittered sideways and blew off. He was incredibly thirsty. His lips were parched and cracked. He couldn't stop thinking about Grandmama wedged inside. He heaved to throw up, but there was nothing for his body to expel. He sobbed, coughed, retched.

He thought about Grandmama and her photographs and piano in the water. Everything was lost.

Monk's hands were punctured and swollen from beating against roofing nails. He couldn't stop the spasms in his legs.

At the house next door, the dog reappeared, paddling frantically to reach the roof again. Monk called to him, but his voice was a whisper lost in the wind. He watched the animal paw the eave trying to pull himself up.

Thoughts of Grandmama kept coming to mind as she choked and strangled. When Monk closed his eyes, he remembered the way she looked at him as he struggled to hold up her chin and brush away water from her mouth.

"That's not helping," she'd said. "Best let me do it, babe."

When the flood splashed her face, he pinched her nose trying to keep her from inhaling liquid. Nothing he did helped. Everything he did made it worse.

He shook and shivered. Through thin clouds the sun shone weakly.

He watched the dog go under again. He came up paddling hard only to sink from sight once more. Finally, the pooch got both front feet on the roof, trying to pull free of the flood. He slipped back and drifted away. Then he went under and didn't come up again.

Monk was so thirsty he was tempted to drink water at the edge of the roof. "No telling what's in this mess," Grandmama had warned. So he didn't do it.

He'd never been so tired. He sucked the purple punctures in his hands and shook convulsively. Grit on the roofing material dimpled his skin. The sun appeared briefly and then disappeared behind fast moving clouds.

Without Grandmama, who would look after him? Where would he live? He'd heard stories of orphaned children sent to stay with strangers. Baby daddies and crack mamas who didn't want responsibility gave up their children to government agencies. Would that happen to him? If it did, would he ever dance at Jackson Square again?

He thought about his money, in a jar hidden behind boxes in a closet. Did he have enough cash to find his father?

Nobody wanted him but Grandmama. She was the only parent Monk had ever known. Looking at photographs of his mother and father, he could never imagine them as real living beings. In all these years, not one letter had he received from Tooth DeCay. Grandmama said, Of course his father loved him. But saying so didn't make it be.

Monk's leg jerked and cramped. He rolled onto his back and rubbed his thighs. He went to sleep wondering if his daddy ever thought of him.

Monk awoke confused. He heard Grandmama calling, "Thelonious! Come here, Thelonious!"

Startled, he sat up. Where was he? What happened?

He was on the roof.

Grandmama was in the attic.

The wind blew in quick sharp gusts. Monk crawled to the crest of the roof and on all fours crept to the end of the house. In every direction there was floodwater.

He tried to yell for help, but his throat was dry and raw, and the wind swallowed his voice.

Percy's uncle Earl had a boat. Surely Fiona would send him to check on Grandmama and Monk. With voodoo powers, wouldn't she sense the fix he was in? Monk cupped his ears with both hands and turned full circle trying to catch a sound. No dog barked. No voice shouted. Over at the drawbridge there was no traffic.

Monk waded to the eave and looked down on the backyard. He remembered the car that crashed through the kitchen door and wondered if there was anybody in it. A day ago such a thought would have horrified him, but right now it was an idle question.

Nothing seemed real: the sting of rain, or objects plucked from the current by wind to be thrown like skipping stones across the water. Even colors were strange, submerged leaves of the broken willow were more green than he'd ever seen, the water a curious shade of yellowish tan. He was here, and not here, alive but dead, hot but shivering cold.

When he touched his lips with the tip of his tongue the taste was bittersweet, like burnt molasses. He was in a silence so complete he believed himself the last living being. But then he saw a rat swim to a shattered wooden door and climb aboard. A water moccasin slithered through the water and joined the rat. The snake coiled into a fat black heap. The rat licked his wet feet. A bedraggled orange and brown housecat came aboard, three odd survivors sharing a raft.

As if his eyes suddenly focused, Monk saw a domestic rabbit hop across a distant roof. Chickens roosted on a fallen light pole. He spied another cat, and then a dog! It wasn't the same dog he saw earlier. This was a mother with swollen breasts. Monk did not see her puppies.

The wind rose once more, pushing ripples across the street. Rain returned, every drop raising pimples on the water. He held his mouth open to catch the moisture. His stomach ached, though from hunger or bad water he couldn't be sure.

He lay down on the roof again. His hands throbbed, legs cramped, and his mouth tasted terrible. He wished he had a sweater.

The thought made him cry for Grandmama. He wished he could climb onto her lap and put his head against her breasts. She would never sing to him again. He sobbed until it set up a shudder in his chest.

More snakes arrived, slithering up onto the roof with Monk. Another cat and a traumatized dog joined him in the scant shelter his house provided. He was too tired to worry about reptiles, too spent to comfort the animals.

He closed his eyes and dreamed they were having a birthday party for Cherita. From the convenience store, Mr. Benoit had brought a big cake and strawberry sodas. Sister Julianne was especially beautiful in a blouse with puffed sleeves and a lace collar.

In his dream, Cherita opened a box and inside was a strange little dog with wet hair plastered to a frail body. The puppy was so ugly everybody laughed. But Cherita clutched the wretched animal proudly, and Sister Julianne said, "In your hands he is a champion, Cherita."

Still dreaming, Monk asked, "Did you die in the storm, Cherita?"

"Yes."

"Were you afraid?"

"No."

"Did you see Jesus?"

"Yes."

"What did he look like?"

"He's a black Jesus, not a white one," Cherita said. "But he do glow around his head like it show in Bible pictures."

"Did you see my grandmama?"

Cherita clung to her puppy and gazed away.

"Cherita, did you see Grandmama?"

"I heard her."

"What did she say?"

"She sang to me. Amazing Grace, how sweet the sound, that's what she sang. Amazing Grace, how sweet the sound. She said tell you it was like being born again and didn't hurt but a little while."

"Was that heaven?" Monk asked.

"Had to be," Cherita said. "Jesus held my hand. Too bad you didn't get baptized, Monk. You could be here with us. We having a good time.

Percy plays piano and my mama cut the cake. We blew up balloons."

"Are they all dead, Cherita?"

"Everybody's dead," Cherita said. "Dead and come to heaven. Too bad you don't be baptized, Monk."

"I'll do it!" he promised.

He writhed and sat up, bewildered. Bits of roofing gravel had stuck in his arm and on the calves of his legs. His hands shook and his fingers were so thick he couldn't pick out the particles.

He was thirsty.

Monk went to the eave and cupped water in both hands. He put his tongue in it, and then spit. He splashed his face.

He'd swallowed water in the attic. A little more wouldn't hurt.

Don't do it, Grandmama's voice murmured in his ear.

"I'm so thirsty," Monk wept.

"Go get you some good water," she said.

"Where?"

"Quinton," she said. "Go to Quinton."

Monk had no idea how far the flood had spread. From here it looked like everywhere. The nearest high ground was the levee, more than two blocks away. He never swam that far before. Last summer in the pool at Louis Armstrong Park he swam two laps, but it took all his strength to do it.

Monk lowered himself off the eave. The water was shockingly cold. His arms were stiff, his back and shoulders ached. He swam away a short distance, then wheeled and thrashed wildly to return. His heart hammered. He was ashamed of himself because he wasn't brave.

Bravery is something that happens without thinking about it, Quinton had said.

Monk forced himself to let go of the eave. He struck out for another house across the street. He pretended this was a swimming pool. All he had to do was get to the other side and he'd be safe.

He paused and felt below with his feet. It was bottomless. Frantic, he kicked, paddled, forcing himself to swim as Quinton had taught him in the municipal pool.

"You have the lean body of a champion swimmer," the historian praised him. "All you need is a little training. Lie on your side and swim, let your legs do the work."

But that was in the shallow end of a pool. Quinton was there beside him, his belly bleached and slowly burning in the summer sun. He was ready if Monk needed help.

"Measure your strokes, Monk. Count to yourself. One-kick-kick, two-kick-kick. Relax, my boy! Turn your head to take a breath. Breathing is important. That's the way, like that! You're doing very well. Keep it up. Breathe, Monk. Your muscles need oxygen. Breathe."

He told himself, Quinton was at his side. Quinton would help, if need be. It wasn't much farther. He could do this. He could do this.

His ribs burned as if he'd run as far as he could and now must run some more. He gulped water, and this time he didn't spit. It was gritty and oily.

Amazing Grace, how sweet the sound … he could do this …

One-kick-kick, two-kick-kick. He told himself, Quinton was beside him.

"That's my boy, like that, Monk! You're doing well …"

{CHAPTER ELEVEN}

Donna DeCay was a hundred miles northeast of New Orleans and more scared than she would admit. She had never seen this much rain. It fell not as drops, but in solid sheets that pounded her car so hard she worried the windshield might break. Electrical lines whipped and sagged; transformers exploded. Lightning pierced the gloom and a clap of thunder left her eardrums humming.

Barry Hampton slept in the front seat of her parked car beside her.

She dialed around on the car radio until she found news. The eye of the storm had blown into Mississippi just sixty miles south of where she seemed stranded, and it was headed this way. The newsman relayed messages from shortwave radio operators and military forces near the scene, reporting extensive damage to coastal areas.

"Water is up to my knees," one ham reported. "I'm on the second floor of my home half a mile north of Waveland, west of Bay St. Louis. My transmitter won't last much longer."

Twenty minutes later he was gone.

"The bridges are down to the east and west," a military officer announced. "Bay St. Louis is now isolated. Nothing can withstand the pounding of this storm surge. Beach property has been washed away."

Wind rocked her car and Donna watched the roof of a nearby business peel off and crash onto automobiles parked a short distance away. There was nothing anybody could do to help. Anything torn loose from its anchor became deadly shrapnel hurled by winds of tornadic strength.

The car swayed and shook. Barry snored blissfully.

Out at the roadblock, rain had swamped police cars. The officers were as helpless as everyone else.

Donna lowered her window a couple of inches, causing a shrill whistle of wind that forced her to close it again. Barry smacked his lips and turned slightly, the snoring temporarily abated. But only temporarily. It was infuriating that anyone could sleep through this. She wondered if he had come to her car drunk or drugged.

In the half-light of dawning, she could see he looked younger than he claimed to be—forty maybe, but not fifty. He had a full head of unruly dark brown hair with a broad stroke of silver at the temples. Good complexion, even under the stubble of a day-old beard. A square chin and strong jaw gave him an appearance of strength. His eyes were gray. She could tell the color because he slept with eyes half open, the visage of a corpse.

Across the street, a telephone pole splintered and fell. A lawn chair flew by. She shoved Barry's shoulder and he said, "Yo!"

"Do you think we should try to move the car elsewhere?" she asked.

"This is as good a place as any." Then he returned to the wheezing, rasping, asthmatic rhythms of deepest sleep. Objects flew toward the windshield and spun out of sight.

The only radio station Donna continued to receive was WWL in New Orleans. "Operating with emergency power from our own generators," the announcer proclaimed. "Hold on a minute ..."

The radioman came back a few seconds later. "In the past fifteen minutes," he said, "there has been rapid flooding in the Lower Ninth Ward."

Oh, God! Dean's son was in the Lower Ninth Ward.

In the lull of the passing eye Donna got out of her car and hurried to check on people covered by a damaged roof. Amazingly, nobody was injured. In fact, the roof seemed to give them some protection from the elements. She ran back to her own car, got in, and slammed the door. To hell with the whistle. She rolled down the windows.

Barry Hampton snored.

She helped herself to the last of his thermos of coffee and ate the only remaining doughnut from last night. Hey, she was going to be giving him a ride. This was her price for the fare.

Once the eye of the storm passed, wind returned, albeit with less rain. By midafternoon, the temperature became uncomfortably warm. The opened car windows gave some relief from rising body odors—her own and Barry's.

Reports from the New Orleans radio station sounded ominous. "Twenty thousand people at the Superdome … Mayor Nagin is running city government from the twenty-seventh floor of the downtown Hyatt Hotel … flood waters are pouring into the city."

Barry Hampton awoke at last. He checked the dry thermos and grunted. He looked in the empty box of doughnuts and grunted again. Then he closed his eyes and went back to sleep.

"The French Quarter is wet, but not under water," a newsman reported. "However, there is extensive flooding elsewhere in the Greater New Orleans area. The Superdome has become an island in a lake of water."

A wrecker arrived and pulled submerged police cars to higher ground. Other policemen set up sawhorses to block traffic. Donna braved the rain and ran to a patrol car.

"I must get to New Orleans," she explained.

"Nobody is allowed to enter," the cop said. "They're telling us that three-fourths of the city is underwater."

It was a horrifying thought. "Is there any way I can have somebody look in on an elderly woman and a nine-year-old boy?"

The policeman peered at her from under a wide-brim hat rimmed with rainwater. "I don't know who it would be."

"Can you tell me another way to get down there?"

"Lady," he said, emphatically, "all highways are blocked."

Drenched, she returned to her car. Barry Hampton was awake. He scratched his abdomen and yawned. "Oh, man," he said, "I needed that sleep."

"The police say nobody is allowed into New Orleans, Barry."

"First things first," he said. "We need breakfast."

Donna followed his directions and drove into Hattiesburg. She maneuvered around fallen trees in the streets. Trash cans floated in gutters. Roof damage was evident everywhere. Commercial signs were shattered. Traffic lights dangled from torn lines. The rain seemed to be falling harder.

"Turn right at the next corner," Barry said.

A block later they arrived at a National Guard Armory. He got out in the deluge and waded toward the building. Donna sat watching between windshield wipers that flung water left and right. Men in yellow slickers climbed into army vehicles. Other soldiers got into the back of trucks, rifles slung over their shoulders.

Thoroughly soaked, Barry returned with two large Styrofoam cups of steaming coffee. "I have ham and egg sandwiches, biscuits with sausage, and several packages of food the army calls 'Meals ready to eat.'"

"How did you know to come here?" Donna asked.

"Always go where the army is," Barry said. "The American government feeds the military."

"How much did it cost?"

"It's free. You're right; they said nobody is being allowed into New Orleans. Do you want a ham and egg sandwich, or sausage biscuit?"

"Either one."

"I'll take one of each," he said. "Boy, what a storm!"

Sarcastically, she asked, "Do you remember any of it?"

"Oh," he acknowledged, "the sleep. See, the thing is, in stressful situations my body shuts down. I got caught in a bank robbery once. We were hostages for ten hours. I fell asleep and didn't wake up until after a SWAT team stormed the place. You dropped a piece of ham. Are you going to eat it?"

The coffee was strong, the sandwiches good.

"Did you learn anything about conditions in New Orleans, Barry?"

"Yeah. You said the kid you're looking for is in the Lower Ninth Ward. It flooded."

Stricken, Donna wondered how to tell that to Dean.

She was astonished to hear her cell phone ring. Collect call from Angola.

"Donna," Dean spoke loudly to overcome his surroundings, "where are you?"

"Hattiesburg. The police have stopped all traffic going into the city."

"You can't let them stop you," he shouted.

"I'm with a reporter who has offered to help me get there," she said.

Beyond Dean the clamor of prison reached a crescendo. He yelled away from the telephone, "Knock it off! People are trying to use the phones."

"Donna," he said, "the worst of the storm hit Mississippi. Drive west and approach New Orleans from Baton Rouge. Who is the reporter you're with?"

"Barry Hampton. With the *Probe*." She looked at her companion and said to him, "This is my brother, Dean."

Barry lifted a hand in a mock wave, "Hi, Dean."

"The *Probe*?" Dean said. "That's not a newspaper. It's a scandal sheet."

"Which in this case is unimportant, Dean. He's from New Orleans and knows the area. When I find your son, I'll call immediately."

"They won't accept incoming calls here," Dean said. "I'll telephone you every time I get a chance. Have you been able to reach Quinton Toussaint?"

"He doesn't answer his telephone."

"Maybe he took Mrs. James and Thelonious out of town after all," Dean said. "God, I hope so."

Abruptly, the call terminated. Donna plugged her cell phone into the cigarette lighter to recharge.

Barry Hampton wiped his mouth, crumpled the wrapping his sandwiches came in, and then heaved a sigh. "That was not eggs Benedict," he said, "but it filled the void. Let's go back to my car and then we'll leave."

From the trunk of his automobile, Barry brought out magnetic signs that he stuck to the doors of Donna's car. They read:

"REPORTER

STORM NEWS"

He gave her a heavy old Graflex camera with a pan-style flash unit. "I hereby designate you official photographer for Probe International."

"I didn't know they made these cameras anymore," she said.

"They don't. But a Graflex looks more authentic than those sissy little digital cameras. My father gave this to me thirty years ago. He was a reporter for the *Atlanta Journal-Constitution*. Also the *Memphis Commercial-Appeal* and the *Birmingham News*, and half a dozen other rags around the country. The Graflex is the sum total of my inheritance. Dad was something of an authority on wines of the Mogen David and Thunderbird variety. Okay, my dear, go south on State Road 11 to Poplarville."

At every roadblock, a guard read their signs: "REPORTER STORM NEWS" and turned them back. "Usually that gets me anywhere," Barry said. But not this time.

Cypress and pine trees lay on the roadway. Water flowed out of borrow pits on either side of the pavement. A splintered trailer home was on its side, its furniture strewn across a field. Donna had to stop repeatedly while Barry got out and dragged aside broken boughs. Snakes were draped over barbed wire fences. A small bear watched the car pass. Deer swam out of cypress thickets and peered from a jumble of fallen pine trees.

The cell phone jingled again.

"Where are you?" Dean demanded.

"Near Bogalusa."

"I told you to go in from the west."

"Dean," Donna responded angrily, "everything is a mess. The National Guard and police have blocked the major highways. We're trying to get there on back roads."

"Every minute is life-threatening to Thelonious, Donna. CNN just showed pictures of water up to the rooftops in the Lower Ninth Ward. Mrs. James lives in a one-story house. They could be trapped there."

When they were children Dean had directed games with the same strident voice. Teaching her tactics in Monopoly, he'd say, "What are the odds that somebody will land on your property? You have to analyze your opponent's position to win a game. Think, Donna. Think!"

After his conviction for murder, she was incensed because he did not think before he killed a man. He had not calculated the odds of escape or consequences of his decision.

"Listen, Dean, damn you, I'm sure everything looks easier from where you are. Out here, we've been through a storm and everything is torn up!"

His tone of voice changed instantly. "I know, babe. I know. I'm sorry. Do the best you can. I'm frantic with worry about my boy and his grandmother. There's nothing I can do from here, and it's maddening."

After the call disconnected, Barry Hampton said, "If he's so keenly interested, why isn't he here himself?"

"He's in Angola," Donna said.

"Oh." Barry gazed out the car window.

Most low bridges were submerged in the flood. Barry got out of the car and waded ahead in water up to his knees. He tested the depth with a stick to be certain a span was still there. Donna followed cautiously, worried that the motor would drown out. Water seeped through the floorboard and soaked her tennis shoes.

"What are those huge rats I see, Barry?"

"Nutria. It's a large aquatic South American rodent brought to Louisiana by the government to provide trapping for fur traders. They have pelts kind of like muskrat. Some people eat them."

Donna and Barry had to double back several times searching for a clear road south. Finally, they emerged at Covington.

"Can't cross Lake Ponchartrain," a local resident advised. "One bridge is out completely, the other may not be safe."

"Any recommendations?" Barry inquired.

"If you haven't got a boat, go back."

In the community of Mandeville, the lakefront was swamped and water lapped at foundations of houses built close to the ground. Structures had been barricaded against the weather, but despite that, siding was ripped loose and shingles torn off. What the wind had not destroyed, surging water finished.

A message in spray paint covered the side of a building:

"BATTEN HATCHES
HOLD YOUR BREATH
THE BITCH IS COMING"

"You have gasoline in the trunk?" Barry questioned.

"About fifteen gallons."

"There's a bait and tackle store up ahead. Pull off and we'll walk over to it."

An elderly man sat in a lawn chair buoyed by two large inner tubes. He had moored himself to a corner of his building. He puffed a pipe and dangled his bare feet in dark waters.

"You own that fishing boat and outboard I see at the dock?" Barry asked.

"I do."

"What'll you take for it?"

"Yesterday, two hundred. Today make it four."

"Will you accept a credit card?" Donna asked.

"Well, golly, no, ma'am."

"Suppose we leave my car as collateral," Donna pointed at her vehicle. "When we come back, I'll pay cash."

"If you don't come back, I keep the car?"

"The registration slip is in the glove compartment," Donna said. "The key is in the ignition. Do you have anything to eat in your store?"

"Go in and help yourself," he said. "Everything's going to ruin anyway. You plan to cross this lake in my boat?"

"We're going to try," Barry said.

"I like my new car," the old gent grinned. Meaning they'd never make it.

Dean always joked that Donna took showers to avoid drowning in a bathtub. Her fear of water began when they were children. For a vacation, their parents took them to Pahokee, Florida, to fish in Lake Okeechobee. Until that time, Donna had never feared swimming.

On the shell beach at Lake Okeechobee an old motor launch was partially submerged in the seashell shore. Donna climbed on deck and peered down into the dark interior. She could hear water lapping against the wooden hull.

"Don't go in there, Donna," Dean cautioned. "It may be full of water."

Being braver than her brother had always been a challenge. "Come on, Dean," Donna teased. "I dare you."

"I don't think we should."

She was in a bathing suit and barefoot. She went down three steps and cool water closed around her ankles. "There is water," she taunted, and her voice echoed around her. "Don't be a sissy."

Donna inched forward toward the sunken bow. She extended her hands feeling for obstacles and there were none.

"Come on in, Dean!"

She turned to look back, and by a rectangle of light from the companionway she was shocked to see the boat was full of snakes. She stood absolutely still, suddenly aware of things slipping around her ankles.

"Dean?" She didn't want to scare him. Donna held her voice to an even tone. "Dean? Go get Daddy. I've hurt myself."

"I'll come in," her brother said.

"No," Donna said. "Go get Daddy. I'm hurt, Dean. Please hurry."

She heard him climb off the deck. She was afraid to move, riveted to one spot, her eyes adjusting to the dark and the sight of slithering reptiles all around her. It seemed an eternity passed before her father arrived.

"Hey in there, baby," her father called. "Is something wrong?"

"Daddy, the boat is full of snakes. I'm afraid to move."

"Stand still, sweetheart. I'll get help."

Men came with axes and chopped a hole in the deck over Donna's head. With every blow, snakes rained down around her. At last, her father reached in and lifted her up and out. Then the men set fire to the boat and waited to kill hundreds of poisonous water moccasins as they crawled out.

She'd been afraid of water and snakes ever since.

Barry unloaded the gas containers. He bailed out the boat and dried the spark plug.

The old fellow bobbed in his chair, watching. "Not that I don't treasure the prospects of keeping the car," he said, "but there's two Mae West life jackets hanging inside the porch. You may need those."

"How far to New Orleans from here?" Donna asked.

"Depending on where you plan to land, twenty-five or thirty miles."

"We're going to Esplanade," Donna said. "It's somewhere near the French Quarter."

"Yes ma'am, I know Esplanade. If you get to New Orleans, you can get to Esplanade."

Donna went into the store and gathered cheese crackers, bottled water, bread, pimento loaf, and salami sandwich meats. "How much?" she asked the proprietor.

"In light of our trade for my boat, the food is free for nothing. I ain't greedy."

She waded to the car, got her overnight bag of clothes and went back to put them in the runabout. The boat smelled fishy. She strapped on the life jacket. Barry yanked the starter cord several times and the motor caught. "Get in, sit down, and don't stand up," he said.

The cell phone rang. Collect call.

"Where are you, Donna?"

"Going across Lake Ponchartrain in a fourteen-foot wooden boat with low gunnels and an insane captain."

"Good," Dean said. "That's the way to do it."

No acknowledgment of her phobia. No recognition of the courage she had to muster just to sit in the damned boat! "Go first to Quinton's house," Dean ordered. The signal broke and Dean faded. She caught a word, he faded, and finally, she lost the call altogether.

From here to the southern horizon she could see nothing but choppy open water. The wind shifted and blew against her arm and neck. The tiny craft pounded across peaks of small, sharp waves.

"There's water in the bottom, Barry."

"Bail," he said, and bail she did, using a rusty Maxwell House coffee can. Behind them, the north shore of the lake diminished and disappeared.

Precipitation fell in a fine mist that gathered like beads on her clothes and in her hair. They ran alongside the twin bridges traversing the lake from north to south. Torn loose from the bridge, slabs of concrete slanted down to the lake below.

Clouds cleared and she was stunned to see the sun setting. "Are we going to be out here after dark, Barry?"

"Unless the earth shifts on its axis and the sun begins to rise in the west, we will be here after dark."

He was such a smart ass. They were going to be caught out here on open water at night! Sitting at the stern, Barry steered the craft. He yelled, "I quit smoking."

It was relevant to nothing, but Donna nodded.

"Wish I hadn't," he said.

The motor coughed and stopped. Donna gripped the gunwales, her heart slamming her chest. Waves slapped at the boat. She looked about for the oars. Had they left them behind? Had there ever been any? Without a motor or oars they could be adrift for days.

Barry hefted another gas container and the boat rocked under his weight. Donna held onto the gunwales, arms rigid. He inserted the fuel line, and after two yanks the motor cranked again. In the twilight, the lake had smoothed. The skiff slipped along steadily.

After several minutes, she carefully turned around on the seat to face him, and damned if the man didn't seem to be asleep.

"Barry!" she screamed.

He jumped. "Yo!"

"Don't sleep," she commanded harshly. "If you do, I'll throw you overboard."

"Resting my eyes," he said. "Your brother is in Angola?"

"Yes."

Barry pointed at the food, and Donna prepared a sandwich. She wished she'd gotten mayonnaise and mustard. Barry held the tiller with one hand and ate with the other.

"The reporter in me demands to know," he said over a mouthful, "What did he do?"

"He killed a man."

"Ah, yes, Tooth DeCay," Barry mused. "I know about him. This is interesting. Here I am in the middle of a lake with the sister of a murderer, going to search for her nephew somewhere in the flooded Ninth Ward. This has the makings of a story. Do you mind sharing details of the crime?"

He had gall. "Some other time," she said.

"Premeditated," Barry guessed. "Actually, I know about the case. Everybody in New Orleans knew about Tooth DeCay. Who would've thought I'd end up with the drenched sister of a famous jazz musician, navigating Lake Ponchartrain, headed to an adventure?"

Donna turned and faced forward again.

"You and your brother are close?"

Used to be. "Like twins," she said over her shoulder.

The sunset was every hue that could be derived from crimson. Pink and rose, blood red and blush, coral and vermilion spread across a rain-scrubbed sky. Out here on a lake in a rickety boat with the sun going down, she was frightened, but she wouldn't show it to this blasé somnambulist at the rear. She bailed water with one hand and held fast to the gunwale with the other, staring ahead into the unknown.

There were no city lights to guide them, nothing to define the shoreline of New Orleans.

The motor quit. In the dark, jostling the boat with every movement, Barry set up the last can of fuel, pulled the cord, and the craft moved forward again.

She ached for a tub of hot water. Perspiration had evaporated leaving salt rings under her arms. The crystals chafed flesh and her raw skin burned.

"Did you say something, Barry?"

"I said, 'Bail!'"

She felt around for the coffee can and scooped water overboard. "Who goes there?" a voice hollered from the dark. Barry cut off the motor. Water gulped against the boat.

"Who's there?" a man shouted.

"Who's asking?" Barry yelled.

"We need help."

Barry hesitated. "We'll send somebody."

"Food, water. People are trapped here. Bring an axe, a chainsaw."

"What's the address?" Barry called.

No reply.

"Hello! What's the address?"

In the silence that followed, Barry said, "I have no idea where we are." He yelled again. "Where are we?"

From farther out, a woman screamed, "Gentilly!"

"Gentilly," Barry marveled softly. "How the hell did we get to Gentilly? We're in the city south of the lake."

Donna saw the beam of a flashlight, then farther away, another one. Voices rose around them, "Help! Help!"

Near and far, their voices were like the croaks and peeps of frogs. "Help! Here! Help!"

Alarmed, Donna said, "What can we do?"

"Nothing," Barry said. "And we do not want to get caught by a mob. Let me get my bearings here. He reached over the gunwale and paddled with his hand. On the other side of the boat, Donna did the same. Someone fired a flare and a garish red light swept over the scene.

"Hey!" a man called. "We need help. We have women and children here."

By the cherry-red luminance of the descending flare Barry read a street sign that was barely above water. "Mirabeau, for Christ's sake. We're surrounded by a flood."

In the last light of the flare, Donna saw people on roofs, water up to the eaves. There were homes with the roof missing.

"Hey!" a man yelled again. "We need help."

Cries came from every direction. "Help! Over here. Help! Please, God. Help us!"

Barry yanked the starter cord and throttled the motor down to a soft putter. They struck something and it moved aside sluggishly. Another soft bump and it too passed. Bodies. People begged for assistance and when they realized it wasn't forthcoming, they cursed and threatened. Donna heard a gunshot and ducked, then another one.

"I don't think they're shooting at us," Barry said. "Probably trying to get our attention."

Dogs barked. Women wept. Children screamed.

"Help ... please ... help ..."

Incongruously, Barry said, "Watch for a street sign, Donna. We're looking for Elysian Fields Avenue."

"I can't read the signs, Barry. It's too dark."

Anguished cries fell away behind them in a diminishing wake. Help ... please help ... somebody, please ...

Shaking, Donna held fast to the gunwale, her abdomen ached from tension and distress. Behind her, Barry must've felt her trembling. He reached over and patted her shoulder. "We're going to be all right," he said.

Perhaps they were, but what of Dean's son and the grandmother? By the light of coming day, the devastation was shocking. She saw dead dogs, cats, even birds floating in black water.

"Unbelievable," Barry said. "The levees must've given way. We had to pass right over them to end up here. This is unbelievable."

And it truly was, unbelievable.

In the garish light of dawn a dead man lay on the front porch of a clapboard house, and after Barry cut off the boat motor, the only sound was the tinkle of a mobile made with bits of old bottles hanging above the body of the deceased. On another porch, three rocking chairs seemed undisturbed. Potted plants graced the residence, while next door the dead man lay exposed, and the bottle-built mobile tolled mournfully.

The gasoline lasted until they reached shallow water, and then Barry got out to wade, pulling the boat behind him.

It was barely daylight and a shirtless man stood outside a flooded bar, shouting, "I spent enough money in this dump to put your children through college. I want beer!"

From an upstairs window another man hollered down, "We're closed, goddamnit! In case you don't know, the distributors ain't delivering!"

The odd thing was, the front window was broken out. The buyer could have stepped through and helped himself. However, Donna saw a man wearing a pistol a few doors away. He'd used spray paint to post a warning on the wall of his house: "LOOTERS WILL BE SHOT."

The boat bumped aground and Barry pulled it up on a curb and came back to sit with Donna. They took off the life jackets and finished the last sandwich meat and bottled water.

"I hope Governor Blanco and President Bush are sending help," Barry said. "We're going to need it."

{CHAPTER TWELVE}

Monk swam to the levee and crawled out of the floodwater. His lungs burned for want of oxygen. His throat was seared from swallowing foul water. His arms and legs felt leaden. He was covered with mud, barefoot and battered. His punctured hands throbbed and were swelling. He dragged himself to the crest and collapsed.

Chickens, ducks, egrets, and wind-blown anhingas shared high ground with snakes, rodents, dogs, and cats. Feathers and fur were ruffled and soaked. Their eyes looked glazed from shock. Most of the animals lay quietly. No creature threatened another. Family pets lay side by side with wild rabbits and squirrels. The water was higher up the riverside of the levee than Monk had ever seen. Now and then in the rushing current he saw an animal float by, swimming furiously, but helpless to escape.

He was exhausted and in too much pain to move. The morning sunshine was comforting. A cool breeze stirred the air around him.

He was too tired to grieve. Too spent to think. He was, he thought, as nearly dead as a living person could be. His stomach cramped with such intensity he wondered if swallowed water had poisoned him. His throat felt sore and burned as if he had a fever. Mosquitoes drew blood, and he didn't have the energy to slap them. Ants crawled over his arms and legs. It took less strength to ignore them than to fight.

The whump-whump-whump of a helicopter passed overhead. He saw a man holding a big camera pointed down at exposed roofs in Holy

Cross. Monk didn't stand up or wave, and he didn't see anyone who did. The morning sun reflected off water the color of coffee with cream. East and south, the sharp angles of peaked roofs looked like children's blocks dropped into syrup.

After the helicopter passed, he tried to stand. He forced his legs straight and cramps brought him back to his knees. He knelt there until he summoned strength to get up again. He had scratched his arms and legs until they bled. His mouth tasted terrible. When he tried to spit through swollen lips he drooled.

Up the levee between him and the drawbridge were rusty metal buildings. He crawled, stumbled, walked. The gate was down. He went in and circled a shed looking for a water faucet and found none.

"Hey, boy!" a man yelled. "Get away from here."

Monk staggered along a chain-link fence and went north. If the guard caught him, what would he do? Beat him, shoot him, call police?

He'd always heard terrible stories about police. They robbed the helpless and stole from the poor. Innocent people were thrown in jail and put to work doing hard labor. Nobody he knew spoke well of cops. They nickel and dime you to death, people said.

He didn't want to be caught and arrested. When a young person of color disappeared from New Orleans, the law insisted he'd run away. Police never believed he'd been kidnapped. Cops said the child must've fallen into the river, and perhaps now and then that was true.

From time to time lawmen swept through the French Quarter rounding up the homeless. "Best be you got a home address if they get you," Uncle Earl warned. "Don't be do no begging in the Quarter, or you disappear." Miss Fiona said that was ridiculous, but Uncle Earl said cops shipped beggars to other cities, or put them in jail.

Percy suggested a fate much worse. He spoke of dead bodies that floated downriver to the swamps. "That's how the mob gets rid of a corpse," Percy said. "In the swamps, alligators, rats, and maggots eat every ounce of skin and clean the bones. What's left settles into the mud never to be seen again."

When Monk repeated those stories to Grandmama, she said, "I doubt that's true, but I wouldn't put it past some I've known."

Moving north along the levee, Monk came to depots and warehouses that did business with the shipping trade. "A hundred years ago," Quinton once said, "this end of the river was busy moving contraband." Nowadays, the businesses offered fuel to ships, and temporary docking if needed. Buildings were constructed on piers bordering deep water. The gates were locked, high fences topped with barbed wire. NO TRESPASSING signs warned everyone to stay out.

The smell of diesel fuel and chemicals hung in the air. When the wind blew out of the northwest, caustic fumes drifted over the Ninth Ward driving people indoors. The steel-sided buildings were scary places patrolled by unfriendly watchmen.

Normally, Monk wouldn't go near there. But thirst drove him to take a chance. He crossed a concrete span to a warehouse. He looked through oily windows.

"What do you want, Son?"

A tall heavy white man in a uniform stood between Monk and freedom. He wore a shoulder patch that read "Industrial Security."

"Thirsty," Monk said. "Please."

The watchman carried a ring of keys attached to his belt. He unlocked a steel door, stepped aside, and said, "Come in."

Monk hesitated so long the man said again, "Come in. It's all right."

The door closed behind them and the guard led the way down an aisle between barrels stacked three high. He walked with a limp, one leg stiff. The scuff of his good boot echoed with every step. The only light came from high windows and skylights in the roof. "Upstairs," the guard said. He climbed steel steps to a glassed-in office on the second floor. It was a dusty dimly lit room filled with desks and filing cabinets.

"Where are your parents, Son?"

To say he had none would be sure trouble, so Monk said nothing.

"Did they come through the storm all right?"

Monk trembled so hard he grabbed one hand with the other and held it tightly.

"Are your folks all right?"

There was a five-gallon jar upside down in a dispenser. The watchman pulled a paper cup from a bracket on the wall and filled it with water. In the jar a bubble gurgled up. Monk took the cup with both hands and fought the tremor in his arms. He gulped liquid and looked up at the man.

"Drink all you want," he offered.

Monk fumbled the button and filled his cup. He did it again and again, until his belly ached, and still he was thirsty. "I've been here since before the storm," the watchman said. "They're paying me overtime. I don't think I'll ever do it again though. It was like being inside a drum in this building. There were times when I thought the place would come apart. Go ahead, Son, have more water if you want it."

The man sat down on a swivel chair, his bad leg stuck out straight. He looked Monk over. "You're about what? Eight, nine, maybe ten years old? You look like you've been chewed up pretty bad."

Monk stared at him.

The watchman opened an ice chest and took out sandwiches in plastic Ziploc bags. He gave Monk two of them. "My wife put together enough food to last a month. Eat all you want."

Monk would've done so, but suddenly he threw up all the water he'd drunk. Shocked and embarrassed, he staggered backward.

"It's all right," the man soothed. "Don't worry about it. I'll clean it up later. Get another cup of water and eat a sandwich. Sip it. Don't hurry."

Monk drank more water. He ate ham and cheese sandwiches made with mayonnaise dressing. He'd never had a sandwich that tasted better.

"Did your folks get through the storm all right?" the man asked.

Monk choked down a bite.

"Do you live near here?" the guard persisted.

Monk swallowed without chewing and the man said, "Chew each bite thoroughly, or you'll be sick again. Take your time. There's no hurry. Everything is flooded around here. How did you get to the levee? Did you come in a boat? Swim?"

His uniform was dark green and he carried a gun but probably he wasn't a real policeman because he was old and lame. Monk bolted down the other sandwich.

"There's no electricity here," the guard said. "The telephones are out. I don't have a way to call anybody. All I can do is wait for the company to come check on me. It may be a few days before someone shows up. You can stay here long as you like."

Filled with food and refreshed by water, Monk dashed for the stairs and nearly tumbled going down. He ran to the exit and grabbed the handle. It was locked!

"Hold on," the man called. "I'll open it for you."

Monk shied away from his reach. When the door opened he dashed through. The sun felt good. He hobbled back to the levee, stopped, and turned around. "Thank you!" he called.

The man waved.

The way Monk had just acted made him think of Jon Latour.

Monk had to swim again to reach the drawbridge. He climbed up a slope to steel girders and looked down at the swollen canal below. On the walkway, a Mexican man and his wife huddled under blankets with two small children.

"*Tengo hambre, Mamá*," the little boy said. "*Tengo sed.*"

The woman cried and her husband took the boy in his lap.

On the Bywater side of the drawbridge, the streets were wet, but not flooded. Monk trudged toward Mr. Benoit's store. He stopped when he saw a crowd of people out front. Gang boys pushed past other looters, their arms loaded with food and drinks. Cherita's father stood there unable to stop them. "Does anybody have a boat?" Mr. Benoit yelled to the crowd. "My family lives across the canal. They need help. Can someone tell me where to get a boat?"

People shoved and cursed. Gang boys grabbed an elderly woman and snatched food from her hands. She stood there a second, and then turned and went back inside again.

"I'll pay for a boat!" Mr. Benoit hollered. "Anybody! My family is flooded. Help me."

Monk returned to the drawbridge and went down railroad tracks that followed the river to New Orleans. Close by the levee the land had not flooded. People sat on the cinder-strewn incline too busy with their own problems to pay attention to him.

His muscles cramped and he fell. He massaged his legs, then trudged on toward the city. From houses nearby men shouted to one another. Babies wailed. In the street two cur dogs snarled and ripped a third pup. A girl kept hitting them with a broom, shouting, "Stop it! Stop it!"

It began to rain a steady downpour. New Orleans had always flooded when it rained. Now, added to the storms of Sunday and yesterday, fresh rivers of water filled the system and gushed up through sewer grates.

A large woman stepped out of her house, raised her fist to the sky, and screamed, "God, that's enough!"

Monk trod as if in a trance. One mindless step followed the other, past Louisa Street and Clouet. He and Percy never came this way because on a bicycle it would be a rough ride over graveled bed and creosote ties. Besides, there was no place to run if gang boys saw them. Today the gang boys were busy looting stores on St. Claude Avenue.

Drenched and chilled, Monk's teeth chattered. His chest heaved from crying and every breath was a rib-shaking shudder.

He got off the tracks at the edge of Vieux Carré and followed Esplanade through broken trees and fallen limbs. The ground was a carpet of green leaves glued to the street by rainfall.

When at last he saw Quinton's house, Monk sobbed with relief. He crawled under debris past the wrought iron fence and up the steps to Quinton's porch.

There was no doorbell since the electricity was off. His hands were too sore for knocking. He bumped the door with his elbows. Weeping, he held his breath and put an ear to the glass. Somewhere in the distance a siren wailed. From inside, he heard nothing.

Monk used his knee and bumped the door harder. He tried to call, but his voice was gone. He went along the porch peering through windows. It was dark in there and the curtains were closed. Nothing moved.

He followed a driveway around the house. Quinton's courtyard was covered by torn foliage. Limbs draped a fountain from which no water flowed. Through a mat of leaves, Monk saw goldfish. He went up the back steps to a narrow porch. The door was locked. More steps took him to a second level. Everything was bolted. A third flight of stairs ended at a single door. It too was secured.

Monk bumped the door with elbows and knees. Then he put his head to the wood and listened. Nothing.

At every window descending, he banged on beveled glass. Quinton did not answer.

Monk walked out front again. Where to go from here? What if

Quinton left town and wouldn't be back for a week or two?

A car came toward him from down the street. Monk hid behind a fallen tree and watched it go by. It had begun to rain again and windshield wipers flung water from the glass. NOPD it said on the side, New Orleans Police Department. The car turned toward the Quarter.

He went up on Quinton's porch to get out of the rain. Where could he stay until Quinton came home? He remembered a shed in the back. Monk stepped into cold rain and picked his way through debris to the rear courtyard again. From a locked room on the back porch he heard a motor start, run a moment, and then stop. A generator.

The shed was an old carriage house. Monk entered through unlocked double doors. A horse-drawn buggy sat there, the convertible top cracked from age. On the walls hung bridles and harness. Two saddles rested on short sawhorses.

Beyond the buggy he saw stalls for animals. Straw covered the floors. Monk recognized items he'd seen on horse-drawn carriages at Jackson Square. Blinkers and bits, trace chains, reins, hames, and collars hung on tackle trees.

He climbed into the buggy. The seat smelled of old leather. He found a dusty lap blanket and covered up.

Rain on the roof lulled him as he finally warmed under the quilt.

Maybe Quinton went to stay with friends. But it seemed more likely they would come here to Quinton's house. He closed his eyes, hands throbbing, legs aching.

Images of Grandmama's face flashed through his mind, her features drawn as she gasped for breath.

"Sometimes people hurt when all the reason for hurting is gone," Grandmama once commented. "Those are echo hurts. A man's leg gets cut off and he still thinks his foot itches. The foot is gone. What the man feels is an echo of a leg that is no more."

Horrible memories of Grandmama dying were echoes of what he'd been through. His ribs were sore from sobbing. He pretended his head was in her lap and she stroked his brow, singing as he always imagined his mother sang, Amazing Grace, how sweet the sound ...

Pain woke Monk, pain and voices. He heard a man say, "We shouldn't be poking around back here. Somebody is liable to shoot us as looters."

Double doors of the shed creaked open. Monk lay motionless in the buggy.

"Look at this antique carriage," the woman said. "My great-grandmother owned one of these. She kept it long after they bought a 1922 Model-T Ford. She said you never knew when you might need a buggy again."

The speaker was scarcely three feet away from Monk, behind the carriage.

"Really, Donna," the man urged, "come out of there. People get pretty testy after a disaster. We're trespassing."

Monk heard the doors close. The voices faded as the couple walked away. He slipped out of the buggy and went to the door. He peeked through a crack and watched the woman climb the stairs to the back porch. She knocked on a door and called, "Yoo-hoo! Anybody home?"

She went up to the second floor and did the same thing again. "Knock-knock," she said. "Anybody here?"

She was tall and slender, dressed in slacks and tennis shoes. Her hair was pulled into a knot at the back of her head.

Descending again, she rapped on doors and looked through windows.

Both man and woman were soaking wet. The woman's blouse stuck to her back. She wiped moisture from her face and looked down at the man two floors below. "I could use a bath," she said.

"Not much chance of that here," he replied. "Let's go to my place. At least we can get dry clothes."

His deep voice was like a growl, but pleasant to hear.

Monk watched her come down the stairs. "Well," she remarked, "obviously he isn't here."

"Let's go to my house," the man said again. "Get clean dry clothes."

"What about the boat?" she asked.

"By now," her companion replied, "somebody has stolen it. We owe the bait man four hundred dollars. For God's sake, let's go, girl."

An NOPD car pulled up out front and an officer challenged them, "Do you have business here?"

"Reporters," the man said. "Looking in on a friend."

"We're under mandatory evacuation," the policeman responded. "May I see identification?"

Monk crawled back into the buggy and pulled the lap blanket around his body. He could feel every pulse of his heart in the injured hands. He flexed stiff fingers and rotated his wrists. If Grandmama were here, she'd say, "Better put something on those cuts, Thelonious. Infection is always looking for a way to get inside our bodies."

Quinton would have something to put on Monk's swollen hands. Applying medication was the kind of thing the old historian enjoyed doing. He would cluck sympathetically and dab on salve. "You need an aspirin," he'd say. Quinton was a great believer in aspirin. "I took one aspirin a day long before it came into vogue," he said. "Acetylsalicylic acid is Bayer's gift from God to anyone in discomfort."

He liked to tell Monk the same stories he'd told before, about how the American Indians discovered that tea made from the bark of a birch tree eased headaches, cuts, and bruises. "Then a doctor named Bayer figured out how to make the ingredients synthetically, and voila! Aspirin."

Monk dozed. The rain was a soothing patter on the roof. Lying here would be pleasant if he weren't hungry, if Grandmama weren't dead, if he didn't ache from head to toe ...

It was getting dark when he woke again. The lap blanket had absorbed water from his body and the buggy seat was wet. It was still raining. He went into the courtyard and dipped throbbing hands into the goldfish pond. His clothes smelled sour. His scalp itched. If he had a bar of soap, and the fish didn't mind, he would've bathed in the fountain.

He didn't, of course. Quinton might not approve, and the soap wouldn't be good for tender gills.

Monk went through the process of climbing stairs, bumping doors, and peeking through dark windows. He heard the generator again, a soft putter off the back porch. Quinton was not home.

He trudged into the Quarter. All the clocks were stopped at 6:45, as if time stood still when the storm hit and power failed. In a newspaper rack he saw sodden copies of the *Times-Picayune* dated Sunday, August 28, the time of last delivery. The appearance of a police car made him duck into an alcove until they passed. Rain and dusk were his friends now, a screen, which hid him as he went from door to door.

Bourbon Street was empty. Curtains dangled out of shattered windows. Garbage and broken glass littered the street. He saw rats climb in and out of a dumpster. Even they looked soaked and miserable.

He went by Fiona's voodoo store. Nobody there. Nobody anywhere as far as he could see. Shops were boarded up, doors padlocked. Clover Grill and the Old Opera House were closed. Trash floated in gutters moving toward Jackson Square.

He arrived at Jon Latour's place not by plan, but because he didn't know where else to go. He did not expect a welcome. Monk stood close to the ivy wall.

"Jon?"

He tried to raise his voice, but his throat was sore. "Jon! It's Monk."

He climbed the gate and dropped inside. Rain gurgled in downspouts and trickled down mossy walls.

"Jon?"

He scaled the wrought iron grill and walked a balcony past shuttered windows. At the far end he pulled himself onto the roof. Rain beat on the metal turbine. In the distance, a siren screamed and klaxons blared. Monk went to the broken access door and called again, "Jon?"

The bearded man stepped out of shadows. He wore shorts and no shirt.

Monk could barely speak, his words a hoarse rasp. "I went to Quinton's place and he's not there, Jon. Mr. Benoit may have lost his family. He was looking for a boat. Miss Fiona isn't at the voodoo shop."

He sucked a shuddering sob. His arms fell limp at his sides, rain dripped off his brows. He was quivering, lips so swollen they hardly moved when he spoke.

"I hope Quinton brought you something to eat," Monk said. "I don't have anything."

Jon stared at him.

"My grandmother is dead," Monk's voice quavered. "The house flooded and I couldn't pull her through into the attic. She got stuck halfway and drowned."

Jon came forward three steps and snatched Monk into a hug.

He was crying.

{CHAPTER THIRTEEN}

Donna carried the overnight bag on her shoulder in an attempt to keep it dry, but the effort was wasted. Everything she'd brought was soaked. She was so tired each step took concentrated determination. Walking across the Quarter, Barry led the way several paces out front. Broken shutters and pieces of roofing littered the street. Garbage turned the gutters to sewers. Now and then, Barry said, "How're we doing back there?"

"A lot better if a gentleman provided portage."

He didn't even glance back. "It is one of the fallacies of modern society that men should suffer the brunt of a disaster so women will survive," he said. "When the *Titanic* went down in the icy waters of the North Atlantic, men were denied seats in lifeboats to provide women a dry space. Women have a layer of fat that insulates them from frigid temperatures. They are thicker of thigh and more hale and hearty than the skinny bastards who went into the freezing sea under a misguided sense of chivalry. Drop the bag. Nothing in it is worth the energy needed to get it where we're going."

"Where are we going?"

"My house."

Donna read a sign, Canal Street. "How much farther?"

"Couple of miles."

A police car drove up and blocked their way. The officer hit the siren for a second, turned on flashing lights, and got out. He was a rectangle of a man, with a low center of gravity. "Where do you think you're headed?" he asked, sternly.

"My house, in Uptown," Barry reached for his wallet.

"Keep your hands where I can see them," the cop said.

"Hey!" Barry turned on Donna. "What did you do with the Graflex?"

"I left it behind."

"What kind of photographer are you?" he cried. "How can you shoot pictures without a camera? What do you think our editors will say about that?"

"You guys are reporters?" the cop asked.

"Yes, we are." Back to Donna again. "All right, we'll get another camera at my place." Then to the cop he said, "I'm looking forward to a hot bath, a good steak, and beer so cold it'll set my teeth on edge."

"When you find it, I'll come join you. Where did you say you're going?"

"Uptown near Tulane."

"Tulane is flooded," the cop scolded. "Where have you been?"

"We rode out the storm on Esplanade. You say Tulane is flooded?"

"Eighty percent of the city is under water," he said. "Get in the car and I'll give you a ride as far as I can go."

The officer's car parted a crowd standing in the street despite a steady rainfall. "The Convention Center wasn't a designated shelter, but look at them," the cop said. "No food or water there. The mayor didn't know people had taken cover there until an hour ago."

He dodged downed trees. On side streets to the north Donna caught a glimpse of immersed automobiles. She could see the Superdome off to her right. Every high point of ground was teeming with people trapped by the flood.

"What's the fatality rate so far?" Barry asked.

"Nothing official," the cop said. "But it'll be high. Levees collapsed at the 17th Street Canal near the lake, two places on London Avenue, and three sections of the Industrial Canal. It flooded so fast people didn't have time to get out. My family lives east of 17th in Lakeview." He stopped talking as if he couldn't bear to speak the obvious.

"I'll remember them in my prayers," Barry said grimly.

The policeman pumped his brakes. "This is as far as I go. The water gets deeper north of here."

Donna stepped out into cold rain that fell straight down. The huge drops plopped like nuggets of mud. Water squeezed from her tennis shoes with every step. Her clothes felt weighted. Across the street the body of a dead dog was tethered to a fence where he'd drowned. Donna swallowed hard.

"How much farther, Barry?"

He stopped and looked around. "Farther than we can go," he said.

Ahead of them stretched a flooded street. Donna saw a man's body on top of an automobile, his arms and legs spread as if to hold down the car.

"He's dead," Barry said, as though she doubted it.

She closed her eyes and a wave of exhaustion nearly toppled her. "What do we do now?"

"I can see from here, my house is flooded."

"I'm sorry, Barry."

"Yeah. For years after it's cleaned up I'll still smell the mud. Do you swim?"

"No, but if I could, I wouldn't swim through that mess."

"Okay, come on. Let's go back to the Quarter. We can stay at the newspaper office."

"I'm not sure I can make it," Donna warned.

"Of course you will," Barry said. "Don't get near the fire ants."

The stinging insects clung to one another and floated in clumps the size of basketballs, the ants on bottom giving their lives to save those on top.

They neared the Convention Center again. Donna could smell sweat, urine, and feces. She remembered stories her grandfather told about battles in the South Pacific during World War II. "The Japanese could smell us coming, because of our diet," he had said. "I later met a Japanese man who attended college at Harvard. He said Americans stink of garlic, fried food, and red meat."

Near the Convention Center the stench of many unwashed bodies trapped in the heat and humidity was overpowering. Elderly men and women slumped in wheelchairs or leaned on walkers. Donna saw no medical personnel.

"Who will rescue all those people?" she asked.

"Where will they take them when they do?" Barry compounded the question.

Canal Street had become a canal. Commercial signboards lay on the ground or floated in floodwater. She thought she saw a body adrift in the distance. Rain cast the city in somber shades of gray. Donna spotted a park bench and collapsed on it. "I have to rest," she said.

Barry dropped beside her. Raindrops dangled from his eyebrows. He looked at his watch and joked, "I think the trolley runs every twenty minutes. But we have to have correct change to ride it."

She shivered. He pulled her into a hug, and inexplicably, Donna began to weep. He patted her wet shoulder and held her.

"If the Lower Ninth is flooded worse than this," she said, "Thelonious and his grandmother probably drowned."

"What's the kid's name?"

"Thelonious Monk DeCay."

"Thelonious Monk?" Barry said. "What kind of name is that to hang on a child?"

"His father admired a man named Thelonious—"

"Pianist. Yeah, I know who he was. But to name a kid Thelonious—hey, but of course, I have to remind myself this is Tooth DeCay's son. One pianist paying homage to another, right?"

He seemed re-energized. "I'll be damned," Barry said, softly. "Fantastic musician. Okay, Donna, stand up and let's go. It's only a few more blocks to the office."

He talked as they trudged into the French Quarter. "During Tooth's trial, I sat in the courtroom from start to finish. I was a stringer for several out-of-state papers, including the *New York Post*. Did a short piece for *Time* magazine. People would've lynched the drug pusher if Tooth hadn't shot him."

Donna stopped and removed her sopping wet tennis shoes. She thought they weighed at least three pounds each. Barry took her overnight bag, and they waded down Bourbon Street.

"Your nephew, Thelonious Monk, he's a mixed-blood boy," Barry mused. "Yeah, I'm connecting the dots now. Even though I should have known better, all this time I was thinking you were looking for a white kid."

It seemed they'd never get to their destination, but finally, Barry announced, "This is it." He unlocked a heavy wooden door that was swollen and he had to kick it open. "Shut it behind you," he said and started up a dark stairwell.

The exertion of climbing steps left her breathless. At the top she emerged into a small sitting area furnished with a worn couch and several chairs. Beyond that lay a large open room with computers, copy machines, and at the far end a glassed-in space identified by a sign that read, "Editor Damn It." She sat down in the first chair she came to, put her head back against the wall, and closed her eyes. The roof was sheet metal and the beating rain sounded like a hundred tympanis.

She heard the squish of Barry's shoes moving toward her. He presented a bottle of water and three tablets. "Take these."

"Quinine?"

"No."

"Arsenic?"

"Buffered aspirin."

She swallowed them and drank the entire bottle of water. When she looked up, Barry seemed stricken. "Oh, I'm sorry, Barry. Did you want some of that water?"

"Oh, no," he whined. "Don't worry about me. I'll be all right. I'm sure there'll be another oasis just over the dunes. I always let my camel drink first."

As inexplicably as she had wept, she now laughed.

Donna wanted to call her parents in Atlanta to tell them she was all right. Her cell phone battery was nearly dead and the signal was nonexistent. The call failed. She could imagine Dean frantically dialing without any response, but there was nothing she could do about that. Even if he reached her, she still didn't know anything to tell him about his son.

She pulled chairs together in a makeshift bed, and fell asleep. When she woke, her joints ached. Rain drummed softly on the metal roof. She was wet, although now from perspiration as much as precipitation. Confused, she lay with her eyes open trying to remember where she was and why. New Orleans. Hurricane. Dean's son.

Across the room, Barry mopped up a leak. He wore nothing but boxer shorts. His clothes were hanging over the backs of desk chairs.

"I'm hungry," she said.

"Pretend you're on a diet."

"Do I smell alcohol?" Donna asked.

"Isopropyl," he replied, "not ethyl or grain, unfortunately. To be used as a topical antiseptic and sanitizer it says on the container. If you want to take an alcohol bath, we have several gallons. I found it back in the art department. I have no idea what they use it for."

He grinned. "This is no time for modesty. Take off your clothes and let them dry."

Donna walked to the front of the building and gazed out a window overlooking Bourbon. Across the street she read a sign, Cajun Cutie Lingerie and Gag Gift Shop. In the window display was a T-shirt emblazoned with a leaping fish and a sign that said, It's not how deep you fish, but how you wiggle the bait.

A recent cover of the *Probe* had been tacked to a wall. "Girl Impregnated by Alien Sperm," she read aloud.

"That story came from Eddy Ellerby, our office tout and odds-maker," Barry explained. "The girl swore the sperm found her in a public swimming pool. Eddy had ultrasound pictures to prove the thing had a tail."

Looking at the photo, Donna said, "That's an umbilical cord."

Barry wrung out his mop by hand. "Nothing shocks people anymore. There was a time when an affair between a sitting president and some floozy would have been a world-class scandal. Not these days. The evening news has more sex and violence than a Hollywood film. Tabloid television rakes muck for daily consumption. The world is numbed."

Barry put away the mop and bucket. He stood over a desk and spread an array of melted candy bars. "Baby Ruth, Hersheys with almonds, Butterfingers, Reese's Peanut Butter Cups. These belong to Tiny, our receptionist and would-be lady wrestler. I found them in her desk. What's your choice?"

Donna's stomach twisted. She wanted real food. "Baby Ruth," she said.

He sat behind a desk and peeled the wrapper from a candy bar. He propped his feet up on the desk and crossed his ankles. She saw freckles on his legs. He never stopped talking. "In the past fourteen months we've run nine stories that claim 'Elvis Lives,'" Barry said. "That doesn't include 'Elvis Turned Over in the Grave' when his daughter, Lisa, married Michael Jackson."

"Barry, I have to go to the Lower Ninth Ward to find out about Dean's son."

"Lower Ninth Ward is flooded, babe."

"They may be sitting on a rooftop waiting for help. I have to try and get there."

"Okay," he reasoned, "we don't have a boat. The cabs aren't running. So before we don't do anything because we can't, let me finish my breakfast. Would you like Hershey's with almonds, we have two of those, or you may prefer the Butterfinger?"

And he talked ...

"There's a formula to our publication," he said. "Every issue has a freak feature, movie star exposé, and a health piece on how to lose weight while constantly eating."

Donna took tiny bites of the candy to make it last. Hunger twisted her insides.

"Then we have regular columns on astrology, which include numerology and advice for lovers of every persuasion. At the back of the publication are personal ads in which hopefuls correspond with like hopefuls in cryptic shorthand: PWF40 SEEKS BWPM20'S. If the 'Professional white female age forty' meets a 'black or white professional man in his twenties', Will they be happy? It's one of our most lucrative features."

He didn't sound proud of his work. "Do you like your job?" Donna asked.

"The pay is good. I respect my colleagues. I'm not ready to write a novel. This pays the rent, and it's interesting. Are you going to undress or not?"

Donna went into the bathroom and removed her wet clothing. In the dark, she scrubbed her teeth with water from the cooler and raked her hair with a brush. She used alcohol to bathe, a suffocating procedure, but it left her feeling cleaner and more refreshed. When she came out wearing clean but damp clothing, Barry was dressed again.

"The only way to get to the Lower Ninth is by walking," he said. "It's several miles. Are you up to that?"

"I have to do it," she said.

He pulled a revolver from a desk drawer, stuck it in his belt, draped a camera around his neck, and gestured toward the stairwell. "Let us go," he said.

The rain had eased to a steady drizzle. When the sun finally appeared, it turned wet streets into sweltering canyons. They waded, at times up to their knees. Donna recognized Esplanade as they crossed it. All the while, Barry amused himself shooting pictures and talking about the *Probe.*

"A third of every issue is advertising," he said. "But we don't accept just any ad. We rejected one for a Jeffery Dahmer cookbook, because the serial killer had cannibalized his victims, and we thought promoting it would be in poor taste. However, we ran one for 'designer' condoms on the grounds that it's a public service."

As they walked along, Donna heard gunshots. Barry looked around, and then detoured to a back street nearer the river, "To avoid unsavory sorts," he advised.

Traffic lights dangled askew from wires overhead, twisted street signs looked like crippled statuary, and trash littered the walkways and streets. Fallen trees covered houses and cars.

She already had an idea of the havoc wreaked on New Orleans because they'd come into town by boat. And yet, where they'd been seemed to have fared better than where they were now, standing on a drawbridge at the Industrial Canal looking across absolute devastation. Only the peaks of roofs were above water in a lake that was the Lower Ninth Ward. The flood extended as far as she could see. Coast Guard helicopters flew back and forth searching for survivors. Now and then they dipped low to pluck somebody off a rooftop. Here and there small boats moved from building to building looking for stranded residents. Barry's camera whirred and clicked.

"Who could survive this?" she said. "What will I tell Dean?"

Walking back toward the French Quarter, a gang of tough-looking young men took notice and moved to block their way. Barry drew the pistol and walked with it held loosely by his side. The boys saw his weapon and turned aside.

At a small shopping center, men and women crawled through broken plateglass windows to steal items inside the shops. A police car drove up. Two officers walked past looters into one of the vandalized stores. A few minutes later they came out with CD players and a couple of cameras.

"So much for law and order," Barry observed.

Apparently when he was awake, Barry talked compulsively.

"So why didn't Tooth's family attend the trial?" he asked without warning.

The question made her uncomfortable.

"I figured there must be a schism between Tooth and folks back home," Barry said. "Was it his marriage to a woman of color?"

Donna told him about Gail Winthrop, her best friend, jilted by Dean to marry a girl from New Orleans.

"So the estrangement is a racial thing," Barry said.

"It wasn't racial."

But that was a part of it she conceded to herself. On the way down from Atlanta, she found she was worrying how to explain a visiting African-American nephew to her friends. Barry was staring at her. She thought he saw through her. "It was not altogether racial," she said.

"Tooth adored his wife, anybody could see that," Barry said. "What was her name?"

"Elaine."

"Right. Elaine James DeCay. Light-skinned lovely woman. She had a voice tuned by God. I bought a couple of her albums. She was beautiful."

Donna had only seen pictures in newspapers and magazines.

To stop unpleasant questions, she tried to change the subject. "Barry, when we first met, you mentioned that you aren't a native of New Orleans. Where was your home?"

"This is home as much as any place. Growing up, I lived where my father worked, of course. I thought of cities by the banner of their newspapers. Memphis Commercial Appeal, Jacksonville Times-Union."

"You moved a lot?"

"Every time my father lost a job, which was about once a year. He was a good writer, so he always found work. Fruit of the juniper got him. So tell me, what kind of kid is Tooth's boy? Have you spent much time with him?"

God, he was an irritating snoop. "I'm too tired to discuss it, Barry."

"Meaning no," he said. "Watch where you step. If you get sucked into one of these storm drains you're done for. Did you ever communicate with the kid and his grandmother?"

"Barry, I don't want to talk about it."

"The answer is no."

"Please stop coming to a conclusion based on something I haven't said."

"Ah, guilty conscience. Okay. Sorry."

Back upstairs at the Probe offices, Donna gingerly lay down on the chairs she'd pushed together to make a bed. A headache pounded her temples. Her insides cramped from lack of food.

"Here we go!" Barry announced from across the room. "I've found Tiny's hiding place!"

He delivered a package of cheese crackers. "They were hidden behind the toilet tissue and towels in the bathroom," he said. "Tiny is an eater. She and her husband wrestle professionally as the Masked Marauders. She's one of the few women in the world trying to keep up her weight."

Donna ate the crackers, but they weren't enough to quell the ache in her abdomen.

"For months," Barry said, "Tiny trained to wrestle tag-team with her husband. After their first match she came to work with a puffy purple eye. She was proud of that shiner. I've seen Picasso paintings that looked better. Anyway, she's always on a diet, not to lose weight, but to gain. There may be more food around here somewhere."

"We can't live on junk food," Donna complained.

"Beats nothing to eat at all," Barry said. "I might be able to break into the Coca-Cola machine. How about a warm soft drink to wash down the crackers?"

Night came, utterly without light and oppressively humid. In the dark, Donna listened to Barry speak of his editor, a man "nervous as a banker under audit," with a smile "like an exhibitionist at a child's birthday party."

Maybe it was the nature of the business, but his co-workers all sounded strange to Donna. And what did that say about Barry, she wondered?

"Eddy Ellerby, our odds-maker, found a horse at the race track that could fart the 'Marseillaise'," Barry droned in the dark. "The horse wasn't always on key, Eddy said, but it was close enough to bring a Frenchman to his feet."

When Donna didn't react, Barry said, "Well, good night."

A few minutes later, he snored. The sound reverberated under the metal roof and filled the office.

Then, with a snort, he coughed and cleared his throat. "Know what we could do?" he said.

"What?"

"We could go to the various agencies who are bound to be handling survivors. Red Cross, Salvation Army, relief workers. There's sure to be a record of people who have contacted them. Maybe Tooth's boy and the grandmother will be on a list."

Almost immediately he snored again.

"Good idea," Donna said.

{CHAPTER FOURTEEN}

To reach Jon Latour's apartment, Monk followed him down a ladder into a ventilator shaft. At the bottom, Jon squeezed through a jagged hole in a plaster and lath wall, reached back, tugged Monk's arm, and pulled him inside. He lit a candle with a wooden stove match.

The floodwater Monk had swallowed upset his stomach. He was nauseated and the smell of this place made it worse. "I have to go to the bathroom, Jon."

Jon showed him where. The commode was dry and broken. A lavatory had been pulled from the wall and lay on the floor. Jon used a plastic grocery bag to make a liner for a bucket, which he gave to Monk with a roll of coarse paper towels.

The place reeked of mildew, a stench all the more distressing because of heat and humidity. Monk used the bucket as best he could. The rough paper towels left his flesh inflamed.

When he returned to the other room, Jon offered Monk a spoon. From a sack of canned goods, none of which had labels, he selected a container and opened it. He emptied half its contents into another can and gave the rest to Monk. First tuna, then anchovies, which Monk respectfully rejected. He identified each course by taste: green beans, tomatoes, sliced pineapple.

They ate without talking. Thunder grumbled and rain fell hard.

"That's all I want, Jon. Thank you."

He watched his host gather trash and put it in the toilet bucket. Jon tied shut the plastic liner and pulled it out. He left Monk and climbed up the ventilator shaft.

Alone, Monk could examine the room without being rude. There was a convertible couch opened into a bed. They'd eaten off the top of a scarred coffee table. A floor lamp with a tasseled shade stood in the corner. Rainwater dripped from a bare ceiling fixture and hit the dusty wood floor with soft sputs.

He heard Jon coming down the ventilator shaft again.

Jon took Monk by the wrist and led him across a short hall. He kicked a door at the bottom and hit it with his shoulder until he bumped it open. Air from the closed room smelled of mold and dust.

A bed was covered with a chenille spread. Plump pillows in embroidered cases leaned against an iron headboard. Framed full-length oval mirrors on stands reflected one another from opposite sides of the room.

Without a word, Jon pulled the door closed and left. As he departed, the swollen door swung back open and Jon's shadowy figure moved across the hall.

Monk didn't remember lying down to sleep, but he awoke in the midst of a terrible nightmare. In his dream Grandmama was up to her chin in thick mud. "Thelonious! Help me. Thelonious, please ..."

He tried to swim toward her, but no matter how hard he struggled, he couldn't get to her and she slowly sank into the mire. He sat up, breathless and confused. A crash in the next room woke him.

In the dim glow of a wavering candle flame he saw Jon fencing with a broom handle. Jon slashed the air, jabbed into a closet, fell on his knees, and stabbed beneath his bed.

"Jon?"

Jon didn't hear, or was too occupied to answer. He swiped and stabbed and sliced, until finally, he threw himself onto the daybed couch. Monk heard him groan.

A steady rain roared on the balcony roof. Monk watched Jon cover his ears with pillows and strap them in place with a belt. He then slapped the pillows with the flat of both hands and fell back on the bed.

Monk dozed until Jon shrieked again, his head still sandwiched between pillows. He whirled and jabbed at unseen enemies and collapsed once more.

Monk was too tired to stay awake. He slipped away to slumber until the next battle, when once again Jon fought off demons. If Bishop Beulah of the Baby Jesus Spiritual Church had seen this, she would've said Jon was possessed.

Dawn brought dim light and Monk had a view of where he was. He'd slept in a woman's room. Crocheted doilies covered nightstands just like at Grandmama's. Beside the bed was an old-fashioned rotary dial phone. Monk lifted the receiver. It was dead. On a vanity table were dried-out perfume bottles, and in an open closet hung fancy dresses, lacy blouses, and silken skirts.

He was startled to see a large brassiere hanging across a ladder-back chair. It was stuffed with tissue to round out the cups and clasped in the back, as it would be on a woman's body. On the seat of the chair was a pair of panties filled with rags to give them shape. Nylon stockings had been crammed with paper and dangled down to the floor. The toes of the hose ended in a pair of bright red high heel shoes. For an instant in the dim light it looked like a woman sitting there.

Monk felt as if he was seeing a private scene.

In the living room, Jon stretched and muttered, yawned and scratched, his ears still muffled by pillows. Living with Grandmama, Monk had learned it was not wise to talk until after she'd had coffee in the morning. He stood in the doorway and waited for attention.

By the gray light of day, he could see that the apartment overlooked the narrow courtyard where Jon had waited for delivery of food from Quinton Toussaint. They could have climbed onto the balcony and come in French doors, except the doors were nailed shut by heavy boards.

Somewhere in the distance a siren wailed and klaxon blared, an eerie sound in the otherwise silent Quarter.

He watched Jon take the pillows off his head. Jon felt around in his food sack. Empty.

Monk didn't want to be caught spying, so he said, "Good morning, Jon."

Jon seized his broom handle and threw himself backward against a wall.

"It's Monk, Jon."

Jon glared with a savage expression; then his features softened and he put the broomstick aside.

"Is there anything to eat?" Monk asked.

Jon put on tennis shoes without socks or laces, reached for his food sack and a bag of trash. He motioned, "follow me," and went up the shaft out into misty rain. The air duct smelled like sheet metal wiped with oil. A gentle updraft rose around Monk as he climbed the ladder. He remembered hearing the fan the day he'd delivered gumbo and wondered where the electricity came from. Looking down below through the stilled blades of the fan, he saw a large unoccupied kitchen. Apparently Jon enjoyed somebody else's breeze when the power was on.

Monk followed Jon into the rain, across the wet roof, around chimneys with loose bricks, along a gutter to a fire escape, and down below to a courtyard littered by storm debris. They scaled a wrought iron trellis to another roof, this one covered in slate tile and sharply slanted. Jon reached back and held Monk's arm as they stepped along a slippery gutter. When they descended to the ground again, Monk was astonished to find himself on a block far from Toulouse Street.

Jon crouched, hidden by garden foliage, while a police car slowly drove by. The cruiser turned a corner. Jon held Monk's arm and hurried across the street with a strange sidewise lope. He pulled Monk into an alcove.

More of the same: climbing balconies, onto roofs, along gutters, down to patios, watching for cops, and then dashing across another street. Monk followed Jon up a flight of stairs, through an open loft, out a window, over adjoining peaks, down a trellis, across a courtyard, and up again. Three-stories up, the height made his heart pound as Jon pulled him along. Finally, Jon stopped. Across an alley, windows revealed the interior of an apartment building.

Jon put the flat of his hand against Monk's chest. "Stay," he said. He dropped the bag of trash to the ground below and walked away on a ledge so narrow he had to place each foot squarely in front of the other. At the corner, he slid down a drain spout to the next level, walked another ledge, and disappeared. Monk shivered in the drizzle. He heard a clang and bent forward to look down.

Jon threw his trash into a garbage bin. He lifted the top of another dumpster, peered inside, and closed it. From where he waited, Monk saw a police car approaching from down the street. He called softly, "Jon," and pointed. Jon melted into shadows until the cruiser disappeared.

A minute later, Jon climbed a fire escape, paused at each apartment, and tried to open a window. When one yielded, he slipped inside. Through the windows Monk saw him enter a kitchen. Jon opened cupboards and put food in his sack. In other dwellings he did the same, each time adding to his fattening bundle. He poked around in a closet, selected something for his sack, and then like Santa Claus with a bag of goodies, he retraced his steps to Monk and they went back to Jon's place.

So this was how he survived, Monk thought. Stealing food.

Back home, Jon removed labels from every can. Out of the food sack he withdrew a red high heel shoe, took it to his kitchen and placed it in the oven where there were dozens of other red shoes. Now that Monk noticed, there were red shoes everywhere, under the bed, on top of Jon's refrigerator, in his closet.

Grandmama would not approve of stealing food, but hunger outweighed conscience. Monk feasted on cookies, applesauce, canned peaches, and salted nuts. He ate until he had that comfortable uncomfortable feeling that comes from eating too much.

Jon opened a bottle of wine, poured a cupful, and extended it. Monk had tasted wine only once before, offered by Percy's coon ass uncle Earl. He sipped a bit and grimaced. He hadn't liked it before and he didn't like it now.

Jon laughed, a pleasant surprise.

A little while later, Jon went to his oven and rearranged the red shoes. He took out some and put others in. Monk started to say something, maybe make a wisecrack, but Jon handled the shoes so seriously, he decided to keep quiet.

A cool breeze came through a broken window sweeping odors to the ventilator shaft. Soft rain on the balcony was a lulling sound.

Monk worried about Grandmama wedged in the attic door. What would happen when somebody found her? The thought brought an ache to his chest, and he couldn't breathe. He went to the bedroom, curled onto the bedspread, and cried himself to sleep.

The next day, Monk walked to Fiona's voodoo shop. He saw soldiers with rifles slung over their shoulders. Down the street they caught gang boys plundering a place and chased them away. Some policemen took things from stores for themselves. The voodoo shop was locked up.

He went to Quinton's house where he picked his way through a tangle of trash and knocked on the door. Still no answer.

At the foot of Esplanade he came to railroad tracks that followed the levee. Monk walked the tracks to the drawbridge at Industrial Canal. Spread out before him, the flooded Ninth Ward was a giant mirror reflecting blue skies and mounds of white clouds. In the distance, so far away Monk couldn't hear the motor, a boat moved from rooftop to rooftop.

Going back to Jon's, he passed Mr. Benoit's time saver store in Bywater. Windows were smashed, the door held open by a concrete block. He knew the school on St. Claude Avenue had been used as a storm shelter and that's where many residents had stayed. Now they walked the littered streets in a daze, and nobody paid attention to him.

The sun was hot. Water on the pavement evaporated and rose to join clouds in a sky so bright it hurt Monk's eyes. A pit bull in a yard growled at him and Monk threw a rock. The animal flinched, but didn't yield. Monk picked up another stone. "Don't mess with me, dog. I'll hurt you."

Back at the apartment, Jon slept. It was so hot Monk could hardly breathe. He climbed back up the ventilator shaft and went down to the balcony outside. He sat in the shade, wet with perspiration, his damp clothes itchy. The sheet metal roof crackled as it expanded in the midday sun. Minutes ticked slowly by.

He had never felt so alone.

He daydreamed about his father coming out of nowhere to save him. They would go to live in a house with musical instruments in every room. Monk would dance for him, and his father would be proud.

He heard Jon move around inside. Monk retraced his path up the trellis, across the roof, and down the ventilator shaft.

"Jon, I need clean clothes." As a second thought, he added, "We both need clothes."

Jon gazed away for a time, and then nodded. From his food sack he brought out two bottles of water. He handed one to Monk and they drank all of the lukewarm liquid.

"We could use a bath, too," Monk noted. "Do you know where we could steal a tub full of water?"

Jon laughed.

It pleased Monk so much he almost cried.

When they left the apartment, stars in the sky seemed near enough to touch. Monk followed Jon along the eaves of adjoining structures. Pools of rainwater on flat roofs pictured heaven beneath Monk's feet as well as overhead.

At the end of the block he was close behind Jon as they slipped through an alley, watched for the right time, then scampered across the street past overturned garbage cans, and back up to rooftops again. Monk moved with care on bare feet—there was broken glass everywhere. Even on top of buildings, twisted limbs and pieces of commercial signs lay among shingles with roofing nails intact. Damp lichen made for slippery passage and Monk stepped warily around old TV antennas and microwave dishes.

Jon snatched an antenna from a stanchion and threw it off the roof. "Dries blood," he said.

That struck Monk funny. Grinning, Jon uprooted another antenna and discarded it. Monk seized one and wrenched it free. He heard it hit a courtyard far below.

Somebody yelled, "Hey! What's going on up there?"

Jon grabbed Monk's wrist and they retreated off this roof onto another. Following a route Jon must've known well, they moved by the light of a rising half moon. Across an alley was a fire escape that zigzagged up the side of a block-long group of condominiums. None had electricity, but lanterns lighted two inside.

This time, Monk went with him.

They tiptoed up the fire escape, bypassing apartments that were occupied, trying windows where dwellings were dark. At last, they found one broken window and Jon pulled off the screen. He stepped inside, reached out, and drew Monk through.

First they went to the kitchen and Monk opened the refrigerator. The stench drove him back with a yelp. He slammed the door and leaned against it. On the counters and in the cabinets he found apples, sardines, oatmeal cookies, and snacks in unopened packages.

In the bedroom, Monk watched as Jon pawed through dresser drawers for shirts, shorts, underwear, and socks. Passing a chest of drawers, Jon saw his own image in a mirror and stood glaring at the bearded man with hollow cheeks. He and his reflection studied one another and then each turned away.

Back at the refrigerator, Jon opened the door. The stink sent Monk to the dining room. Jon took out packages of cheese sealed in plastic. He selected a piece of watermelon from a crisper. At last, he shut the door and they left.

Out of the building, across the alley, and up on a ledge, Jon stopped and leaned back against a chimney. He motioned for Monk to sit beside him. In the distance the Central Business District was a silhouette of dark buildings, except for a rare light here or there. They ate cheese and crackers, drank warm soda from pop-top cans, and devoured apples. Stars winked and thin clouds moved slowly across the moon. A breeze swept up from below and against Monk's moist body it felt cool and refreshing.

They raided several other places on the way home. Jon found a tub full of water apparently drawn by residents to use in flushing the toilet. A plastic bucket sat nearby.

"You first," he said.

Monk immersed himself and soaked. The water felt good. He got out, filled the bucket and using that water only, soaped up and rinsed off without getting the tub water dirty. He used the commode and poured in the bucket of water to flush it.

"Your turn, Jon!"

Jon came in naked, an unlit cigar clamped between his teeth. "Bad boy, bad boy," he said, and sat down in the tub. Monk heard him moan with pleasure.

As in the last apartments, the refrigerator smelled awful. Monk left that for Jon. When his bath was concluded, Jon came out wrapped in a towel, sucking on the unlighted cigar. He offered to share his fake smoke and grinned when Monk declined.

It took both of them to carry away the food and clothes they'd gathered. Monk had the smaller of two sacks and he moved as Jon did, clambering up ornamental ironworks with the booty clamped beneath one arm. When they reached Jon's place, down the shaft and into the living room, Jon lit a candle and plopped down on his bed.

"Did good," he said. Then, methodically, he removed the labels from every stolen can and jar.

Monk nibbled dry Cheerios from the box and tried on clothes. The trousers swallowed him, but a belt solved the problem. Jon adjusted the length with a large pair of scissors, lopping off fabric until Monk could see his feet. When he walked, the fabric rubbed against itself and Jon said, "Whisky britches." Monk didn't care, the clothes were clean.

They went onto the balcony and leaned against a wall. Jon lit the cigar. The aroma made Monk think of Percy's Uncle Earl, flicking ashes with his little finger as he imitated an actor named Groucho Marx, "Say d'secret woid and win fifty dollars." A long way off, sirens and klaxons broke the silence. "Fire trucks," Jon said.

When they went back up on the roof a glow of flames lit the horizon.

There were animals on top of the building. That was a surprise to Monk. Mice drank from pools of trapped water. An owl swooped in on silent wings and helped himself to a rodent. Against the moonlit sky, Monk saw bats dart in and out of chimneys. The owl returned for a second helping and the mice scattered, but too late for one of them.

Watching the drama, Monk realized an owl was not the only predator. A rat snake seized a mouse and wrapped it in suffocating coils.

Inside the apartment, ants appeared from somewhere and ran along a baseboard going elsewhere. Roaches skittered out of cabinets. Through broken windows moths were drawn to the flame of the candle. An occasional mosquito found its way inside. None of this seemed to bother Jon.

Because it was difficult for Grandmama to move about, Monk had often helped clean house. It made him feel good to have done the job well. Poking around in Jon's apartment, in a dresser drawer, he found folded sheets. He changed his bed and Jon's. He picked up old candy wrappers, crumpled aluminum foil, and the labels Jon discarded from canned goods. In the kitchen was a broom so old it molted straw. Monk used it to bring down cobwebs.

"Poor spiders," Jon said. Then he stepped on one.

"May I take boards off the balcony doors, Jon? We'd get more air with the doors open."

Jon showed Monk a paper that said the building was condemned and occupancy forbidden. It was dated ten years ago. "If they see me," he said, "I go to jail."

Monk nodded to show he understood, but then he said, "They won't know, Jon. We'll only open the doors at night."

Jon's beard wiggled as he chewed his lip. "All right," he yielded. He helped pull down the barriers, the boards squealing against the nails. Cool air flowed through to the ventilator shaft. Fresh air carried away the stink of things.

When it began to rain, Monk placed pans on the balcony and collected water for washing.

"We are friends," Jon said. Monk wasn't sure whether it was a statement or a question.

"We are friends," Monk replied.

There were two things in the apartment that Monk handled carefully: high heel red shoes and the broomstick. He lifted the shoes to clean, and put them back precisely as he found them. Jon watched closely.

"Who slept in my bedroom, Jon?"

"Mommy."

Monk dusted around the mannequin figure, but dared not touch it.

Apparently, Jon approved.

{CHAPTER FIFTEEN}

Monk sat on the roof at sunrise watching a lizard chase crickets. He'd discovered this hiding place while looking for a spot from which to watch Fiona's voodoo shop without being noticed by policemen or soldiers. He leaned back against a louvered shed on the roof that housed an air conditioner. Without electricity there was no cooling, so except for chirping birds, it was quiet.

In the distance on Toulouse he saw three gang boys going from one shop to the next looking for a way to get inside. Now and then he heard the tinkle of smashed glass, or the wrench of pried wood, as they broke in somewhere.

On Bourbon toward the Central Business District two soldiers were on patrol, rifles slung on their shoulders. He thought about calling to them, but what right did he have to blame those gang boys for doing what he'd done with Jon? Theft was theft.

It bothered Monk that he and Jon had been stealing, because he knew Grandmama would be shocked if she knew. But what else could they do?

Going out for food, Monk became Jon's spy boy in a game that could be dangerous. From high above the street, Monk watched for cops. He was more than a lookout; he was Jon's partner. He felt honored, but at the same time it disturbed him to be equal in the crime at hand. It bothered him most that he enjoyed it. Racing from building to building, weaving in and out of lofts and attics, scampering along peaked roofs, around old chimneys, the sense of freedom was exciting. It would be great fun if he could stop thinking about Grandmama.

Actually, because of the terrible circumstances, even Grandmama might have forgiven the kind of stealing he'd done. They snuck into homes for food that would spoil anyway. If she had smelled those refrigerators, Grandmama would agree how fragile food could be. Even the people Jon stole from might excuse him if they knew the desperate life he'd lived. Besides, he only took what he needed to survive.

The moment Grandmama entered his mind, Monk suffered dreadful images: bubbles from her nose, hands grasping for support and then quivering to motionless blobs floating above her head.

Monk's fantasies of heroic rescue by his father were growing dim. Before the storm he'd always told himself that Tooth was probably in another country unaware of what was happening here. Or, he was deathly ill and barely conscious in a jungle hammock nursed by nearly naked natives who had never heard of New Orleans.

The gang boys were still a couple of blocks away. Now and then in the stillness Monk heard their voices, laughing as they wrecked and burglarized.

When shopkeepers returned and buildings were occupied, theft would stop. Already Monk had seen a few owners in the Quarter sweeping up trash, cleaning leafy debris from their doorsteps. Yesterday evening, dodging them, he and Jon went north toward Congo Square at Louis Armstrong Park. They had to walk in plain sight. They couldn't travel over roofs because there were too many one-story buildings that did not connect to structures next door.

At Rampart Street, Jon balked. "Too far," he said, and turned back into the Quarter.

It was an upsetting trip. Monk saw two dead people. One in the middle of a street, face down, blown up like a balloon. The other was an old woman slumped in a rocking chair with a piece of cloth draped over her face. A pack of hungry-looking dogs pulled at her thin ankles. Horrified, he found a stick and threw it at them.

Two of the dogs snarled, but did not yield. Monk hurled a piece of brick, and still they did not run away. Finally, Jon helped him and they drove the mongrels off, but Monk was sure they would return.

Two helicopters flew over with huge packages hanging below. A few minutes later they returned without the bundles.

"Sandbags," Jon said.

Monk's thoughts returned to the present with a clatter of metal and smash of glass. The gang boys were working their way toward Fiona's voodoo shop. He looked for the soldiers on Bourbon. They had stopped walking and stood at a corner smoking cigarettes. Sound played tricks in these city valleys between buildings. Obviously the soldiers did not hear the vandalism in progress.

If Monk yelled at them, they'd know he was here and might discover Jon's apartment. The vandals would certainly know he was here and that meant future trouble. So Monk did nothing, watching the destruction in progress.

The morning sky showed no sign of rain, and that was good, Monk thought. He was sick of rain. In its place sunshine beat on metal surfaces making them too hot to touch. Water evaporated so fast he could see it happening as damp spots dried.

He had to change positions to stay in the shade. He saw a gang boy scrawl graffiti on a wall. A second boy bashed a window with a steel bar. They were no longer stealing, but working off their energy by causing damage.

A patrol car turned onto Toulouse and the young men ran. The soldiers saw them and shouted, but didn't give up their cigarettes to join the chase. Obviously there were too many vandals in the city to capture, and if caught, where would they put them?

Trash still littered the street at Quinton's house. Downed trees and shattered limbs lay alongside the fence and in the courtyard. For lack of anything else to do, Monk dragged branches out to the curb. He stood garbage cans upright and filled them with litter. It didn't seem likely the city would come by to pick up waste, so he left Quinton's containers in the backyard.

He found a leaf rake in the carriage house and swept the front porch, driveway, and courtyard. He removed rubbish from the fountain and discovered goldfish the size of mullet. The pond smelled like a swamp with rotting vegetation.

A neighbor caught Monk by surprise. He wore a canvas hat and an unbuttoned shirt that exposed a hairy chest and protruding brown nipples. He hadn't shaved in a while. "What're you doing here, boy?"

"Cleaning up."

The neighbor looked at the house. "Is Mr. Toussaint home?"

"No sir."

"Haven't I seen you with him a time or two?"

"Yes sir."

"Have you heard from him?"

"No sir."

"People who evacuated are not being allowed to come back," the man said. "All right then. If you need something, I'm next door."

"Do you have anything to feed the fish?" Monk asked.

"The fish?"

"There are fish in the fountain."

"I didn't know that. No, I don't have anything to feed the fish. Where do you live?"

"In the Quarter."

"Came through the storm all right?"

"Yes sir."

"Good preparation is the key," he said. "You're doing a fine job with the grounds. Mr. Toussaint should be pleased."

"Do you have water to drink?" Monk asked.

"Not much. Don't you have water at home?"

"Some."

"Better bring it with you when you come to work next time. The radio says we may be in this mess for several weeks. Water can be more precious than gold."

As soon as the neighbor disappeared, Monk ran back into the Quarter. That was close! Thank goodness the man wasn't a policeman.

He returned to Jon's. Monk took a warm ginger ale to the roof and sat by the air conditioner shed.

Two National Guard soldiers walked by below.

"Do you think New Orleans will ever recover?" one asked.

"If they do, the city will be a caricature of what it was."

Their voices faded as they strolled on toward Bourbon.

Monk wished he knew the meaning of caricature. It sounded like something dead.

Bad teeth were a torture for Jon. Monk had seen him take aspirin by the handful and chew the tablets dry. The pain drove Jon to break his own rules about going out in the daytime.

The next morning, despite bright sunshine, Jon staggered up the ventilator shaft and went out in search of relief. Sneaking about in daylight took more stealth than at night, and Jon didn't want Monk to go with him.

Something had died in the café downstairs and the odor of it drew houseflies into the apartment. Hot, sticky, and bored, Monk stalked the insects with an old-fashioned swatter made from screen door mesh hemmed in plastic.

Jon could be gone for hours. When he returned he would most likely read or sleep the day away. Restless, Monk poked through a dusty cedar chest.

He found a scrapbook filled with pictures and newspaper articles about Jon's mother. She was a beauty contestant an article said. There were photographs of her in an evening gown with a ribbon across her chest that said, "DELTA QUEEN."

In a faded color photograph she was pictured in a bathing suit wearing bright red high heel shoes. Her blond hair was piled on top of her head and she stood in a way that showed off her legs.

Monk read a yellowed newspaper article from the *Times-Picayune*. The headline said, "Beauty Queen Selects Wardrobe with the Point of a Gun." The Delta Queen and her boyfriend went to Memphis where they robbed a store for the bathing suit. In Shreveport they "shopped" for shorts. They also "shopped" in Natchez for luggage and sportswear. Jon's mother was fitted for an evening gown in Jackson where she held a gun on a seamstress who adjusted and readjusted the garment. She went back to the same shoe store twice because the first pair of shoes didn't match her gown exactly.

At every crime scene she cheerfully admitted the clothes were to be used in her bid for the title of Miss Louisiana. That was only one step away from Miss America, and she promised to mention where she got the clothes. A newspaper picture showed her posing with one hand behind her head, the other on her hip as she stood in the door of a jail cell.

Another article said that strangers offered money and sympathy, and the stores dropped all charges against Jon's mother. But it ended her career as a beauty contestant. Her boyfriend went to prison, and Jon's mother returned to New Orleans.

Monk was so caught up in reading he didn't hear Jon come home.

"No!" Jon charged into the room. "No. No!" It was the way you spoke to a dog.

Jon snatched pictures from Monk's hand, took the photo album and carefully replaced it in the cedar chest. "No!" he shouted. "Bad boy, bad boy."

Jon glowered down at him, dark eyes flashing angrily. Monk shrank back. Jon shut the cedar chest and hit the lid with a fist. "No."

"I'm sorry, Jon."

He watched the man go to the closet. Jon looked around as though he expected something to be missing. "No," he said, again.

He stepped over to a vanity table and examined a mirrored tray filled with empty perfume bottles, the contents long ago lost to evaporation. Eyebrow pencils and tubes of lipstick lay between tins of caked make-up.

Monk followed him to the kitchen. Jon sank to his knees and opened the oven door. He stared at the red shoes and whispered, "Mommy." He looked as if he were still in anguish.

"I'm sorry, Jon. I won't do it again."

Sniffling, Jon rearranged the shoes.

Upset because he'd upset Jon, Monk went to the roof. He was unhappy with himself for meddling in somebody else's belongings, he knew better than that. He kept telling Jon he was sorry, but the apology was not accepted, and Monk felt awful.

He thought about going over to the drawbridge to check the water level in the Ninth Ward. How much lower could the water be anyway?

He'd been checking every day. And what was he going to do when it did go down?

The thought of entering the house with Grandmama stuck in the attic made him queasy. Suppose he did go there, what would he do about her? He'd have to hang on her legs to pull her loose.

Nausea swept over him. He wasn't sure he could bear to look up at her from down in the hallway. The idea of dropping her to the floor was more than he could stand.

He needed someone who would help him do it with loving gentleness. He didn't want a stranger to reach up and yank her down.

Because of Grandmama, and because he'd distressed Jon, because he was lonely and frightened, he burst into tears.

When he got inside at Grandmama's, he'd get his money. It was in a tightly capped jar, so it should be all right. He would ask Quinton to help him find Tooth DeCay. Maybe he could use his savings to buy advertisements in music magazines. "Help Son Find Father," he'd say. "Looking for Tooth DeCay."

If Jon threw him out, and at this moment Monk worried that he might, maybe he could stay with Quinton. Or Percy, or Fiona.

Where was Percy? And everybody else?

He needed a bath with lots of soap and warm water. Sores festered on his arms and legs. He'd been bitten by insects and waded in dirty water. Scrapes and cuts oozed corruption. Grandmama always insisted that he bathe every day. Every day. In the week since the storm, he'd had one bath and that was out of a bucket.

"Feeling sorry for yourself don't never accomplish nothing," Uncle Earl often said. "Take the bit in you teeth and be strong about it."

From somewhere down the street he heard the voice of a man and woman. He went to the edge of the roof and looked west on Bourbon. The couple entered a door beneath a sign that said, "PROBE INTERNATIONAL." Maybe it was a clinic.

North on Toulouse, he saw furtive movements and realized the destructive gang boys had returned. Two more soldiers walked together on Bourbon Street, going out of the Quarter. Monk heard glass break. The vandals were at it again.

Monk heard a familiar voice and crept near the eave to listen.

"Break it down," the boy said, and he stepped back into the street to pick up something to throw. He threw it at Fiona's shop window. Glass shattered.

Randy Bernard, Monk realized. Randy and his gang boys. They went inside the voodoo shop. Monk glanced toward the soldiers. While he debated whether to shout for them, he saw that wonderful coon ass, Uncle Earl.

"Uncle Earl!" Monk called. His voice echoed up Toulouse. The soldiers on patrol turned to see who yelled.

"Uncle Earl!" Monk hollered again.

He heard Uncle Earl shout, but it wasn't at Monk. Earl reached through the door of Fiona's shop and grabbed somebody. The intruder wore long baggy pants that were so large he had to hold them up with one hand. Uncle Earl threw him on the pavement and stolen goods scattered across the street.

"You going to pay for all this shit," Uncle Earl promised. He had another boy by the seat of his britches and collar of his shirt. "I know you mama, boy. I be speaking to her about you."

Monk ran to the far eave, down the trellis to Jon's balcony, over another wrought iron fixture to the narrow brick passage below. He ran past broken glass and sodden papers, climbed the gate, and dropped to the far side.

He heard Uncle Earl say, "I ought kick yo' ass, boy!"

The first two thieves ran away as Uncle Earl went back inside. A moment later he dragged out Randy Bernard.

"Taking after you old man?" Earl scolded. "Going to be as big a thief as you policeman daddy?"

Randy rolled away from a kick aimed at his backside. To Monk's horror, he came up holding a pistol.

"Hey, hey," Earl backed away, "even you daddy don't approve of that, Randy boy."

The sound of the shot was surprisingly loud. Uncle Earl's knees buckled. He staggered and fell.

"What you think of that, you coon ass bastard?" Randy screamed. He advanced with the gun at arm's length.

Horrified, Monk screamed, "Stop!"

Randy wheeled. "Well look who's here," he said. "Felonious Monk."

Uncle Earl tried to sit up. "Run, Monk!"

Randy stood over Uncle Earl and pointed the gun at his chest. He pulled the trigger. For an instant, Monk was in shock. But as Randy turned the gun toward him, Monk jumped back and ran. He heard a gunshot and dodged instinctively. His feet felt weighted, his strides in slow motion. He rounded a corner and dashed away east.

"I'll get you!" Randy hollered. "You're dead meat, Felonious."

Monk darted down an alley, through a courtyard, over a fence. Another gunshot. He heard Randy jump for the fence and stumble with a curse. Monk went over a second wall and scampered up a trellis. Looking down, he saw Randy come over the fence in pursuit. On the roof Monk raced through an empty loft stirring dust as he ran to the other side. He doubled back to keep from crossing a street. His sides burned from exertion.

He heard Randy in the distance, "I'll get you Felonious! I'll get you."

Monk worked his way to a ledge where he could see Randy's retreat. The chase was over for now. But Randy Bernard was far more dangerous than he'd been before. He had committed murder, and Monk was his witness.

{CHAPTER SIXTEEN}

Upstairs at the Probe offices it was even hotter than the ninety-two degrees outside. Donna DeCay mopped her face with a coarse paper towel and loosened the top button of her blouse. Sweating profusely, Barry worked to open windows swollen shut by moisture and heat. A sudden popping sound made Donna stand still, listening.

"Barry that sounded like a gunshot."

He held up a hand signaling caution. "Stay away from the windows," he said.

Years of training as a schoolteacher had conditioned her to react immediately if she sensed trouble. Donna ran down the stairs and out the door. She heard a young man shout, "I'll get you!" She caught a glimpse of the youth as he raced across Bourbon and down Toulouse.

To the left toward the business district, two soldiers looked her way. Barry yelled at the National Guardsmen. "Hey, guys! Over here!"

Around the corner on Toulouse, Donna found a man on his back. Blood soaked his shirt and he gasped for breath. She knelt at his side and took his hand.

"We're getting help," she said. "Hang on."

He gurgled a bloody froth and coughed. "Monk," he whispered.

Horrified, Donna said, "Monk? Did you say Monk? Thelonious Monk?"

He coughed again.

"Did Thelonious do this?"

Barry was at the corner shouting to the National Guardsmen, "Hurry! Come here!"

She watched life fade from the fallen man's eyes. His last breath was a liquid rale. The coppery smell of blood sickened her.

The two soldiers arrived at a run. One of them ripped open the victim's shirt. "Gunshot," he acknowledged. He felt the neck. "No pulse."

He pumped the chest and blood oozed from a hole beneath the soldier's fingers. "Do you know this man?" the other soldier questioned Donna.

"No."

"Did he say anything?"

She hesitated. "He tried to."

A burly policeman in a short-sleeve shirt ran up and gazed down at the dead man. "Oh, yeah," he said. "I know dat coon ass. Did some time up to Angola five years or four ago. His wife owns the voodoo store. Is he dead?"

"He's dead," the soldier replied.

"Angola, yeah; I know him. Earl Thibodeaux. Mean as a moccasin that one. Leave him lay until we get a dray to haul him off."

The policeman walked over to the voodoo shop and looked inside. "The wife ain't here," he said. "Must be Thibodeaux caught somebody coming out and got himself shot. He's the kind of Cajun that begged for a hurt."

He pulled a notebook from his shirt pocket. He moistened the lead of a pencil with the tip of his tongue and poised to write. "Okay who saw what?" he asked.

"I heard gunshots," Donna said. "I ran out here—"

"Out here from where youse ran?"

"Probe International," Barry provided. "Around the corner and across the street on Bourbon."

"From around the corner youse came running?" the policeman said. "It ain't wise to run toward gunfire. You being brave or stupid?"

Donna persisted. "I saw a man run away."

"White man, black man, young man, old man?"

"White. He was young. He yelled; it sounded like, 'I'll get you.'"

"The shot man was dead when you came on the scene?"

"He died a few seconds later."

"Did he talk to youse?"

"He tried to," Donna said.

"This is my third gunshot dead man since Katrina," the policeman said. "Okay, youse two need to see Detective Gus Warner at Broad Street police station. Know where zat?"

"I do," Barry acknowledged.

The officer made note of both their names, and then he said, "Gus Warner, that's who to ask for." He produced a business card embossed with the New Orleans Police Department city shield. Donna took the card and read the policeman's name: Eustis Bernard.

"Tell Detective Warner I'll send a report when I know something," Bernard turned to the National Guardsmen. "Either youse got a bag?"

"No."

On the back of the card Bernard had written, Gunshot fatal. Earl Thibodeaux, Fiona Voodoo Shop, Toulouse N of Bourbon.

Eustis Bernard went into the voodoo shop and came out with a fringed tablecloth, which he used to cover the dead man's chest and head.

Donna felt her knees give way. "Barry," she said softly, and he grabbed her arm.

"Hold on, babe. You don't want to lie down here."

He helped her stumble back to the Probe, and Donna stretched out on her two-chair bed. Barry brought a bottle of water. The stink of garbage on the street below wafted through open windows. She drank in tiny sips to quell queasiness.

"When you feel better," he said, "we'll go see the detective."

"What a nightmare," Donna swallowed an urge to throw up. "What an incredible, horrible nightmare."

For the past two days she and Barry had gone from one relief agency to another, hoping to find Thelonious Monk DeCay on a list of survivors. The Salvation Army, FEMA, and the Red Cross all admitted that their records were incomplete. They were swamped; there was no cross-indexing. Now, miraculously, his name was presented to her on the lips of a dying man. Monk, he'd said.

It should've been inconceivable that a nine-year-old child would shoot somebody. But she'd seen violence in ghetto-bound city youths before.

She couldn't tell Dean that his son might be involved in murder. Donna closed her eyes and willed herself not to vomit.

Barry opened a ready-to-eat army meal and offered one to her.

"I'm not hungry," she said. "How can you eat after what we've just seen?"

"Food eases stress. That's why they feed you after a funeral."

"Do you ever take anything seriously?"

"When I have to," he said. "I'm sorry the man's dead, babe, but I didn't know him."

There was a fragile line between wit and witless. Barry spent less time dwelling on a murder than he would lamenting the loss of Dixie beer and Abita in the bottle. She'd seen him reduced to tears while recollecting Jazz Fest and Mardis Gras, and yet, fresh from the violent death of a man, he ate with gusto.

"Madame Marie Laveau, the famous voodoo queen was supposedly married in St. Louis Cathedral and buried in St. Louis cemetery," he said.

"What does that have to do with anything, Barry?"

"I just thought it would take your mind off the tragedy, thinking about something else."

"Thank you, but I'd like to mourn quietly for a few minutes before I dismiss what I've experienced today."

That evening, upstairs and down a hall at the back of the Broad Street Police Department, Barry held open an office door for Donna to enter. Detective Gus Warner sat hunched over a cluttered desk in a small cramped office. He looked like a man old enough to retire. Shoulders rounded, his belly so large the buttons were strained, bushy gray hair stuck out of his ears.

Men his age didn't work in tiny cubicles at the rear of an office after hours unless they were incompetent, she thought. He was a short man with a thick neck and barrel chest. His countenance made her think of an English bulldog. Detective Warner's jaw thrust forward and exposed his lower teeth behind heavy jowls and a slack lip.

Down the hall somebody cursed lustily. Detective Warner ignored the disturbance. He pointed at Barry. "You were here a couple years ago. Brought in a finger."

"Yes."

"Practical joke, I thought."

"It was delivered to me," Barry said. "I thought I should turn it in."

"You remember, I suggested it could've come from a joker at the morgue," Warner said. "Medical examiners have a dark sense of humor. Did you talk to any of them?"

"No."

"Believe me, they've got a warped sense of humor. Or it could've come from a medical student at Tulane. They buy cadavers over there. A student might have taken it home to study and dropped the finger out of his specimen bag."

"I don't think it was an accidental loss," Barry said. "It was delivered to me in a jewelry case while I was eating dinner with my editor."

"Um, well, yes, I recall. You're right. Do you want it back?"

"No, thanks."

"I've kept it in the refrigerator. I didn't send it to the morgue. Giving them the finger might appear inappropriate. I don't expect they can autopsy one finger anyway."

"You might have gotten a print from the finger and sent it to the FBI," Barry said.

"They'd get a kick out of that, wouldn't they? What would they do with one finger? Do you imagine it was a male finger or female?"

This was insanity. Donna felt as if she'd fallen into a Salvador Dali painting of melting clocks and distorted landscapes. They'd come here to report a homicide and these two men were discussing a prank played on Barry two years ago.

She gave Eustis Bernard's business card to Detective Warner. "A man was shot and killed," she said. "We were told to come to you."

"So this is not about a finger?"

"Not this time," Barry said.

"You remember the finger was manicured and lacquered," Warner mused. "Made me think it was female."

"And it may have been," Barry responded.

"Used-to-be-clues," the detective said. "These days you can't tell. We get sailors with ponytails, motorcycle gangs wearing earrings. And those are the straight guys. There's no telling where that finger had been. Would you call it a forefinger or middle finger?"

"Detective, please," Donna implored. "Could we do whatever it is you want us to do so we can leave?"

He stared at her. "You can leave now," he said. "Unless you have something you want to say. Did you shoot somebody?"

"No."

"Do you know who shot somebody?"

"No."

"Then you may go."

She started to stand up and the detective said, "Forgive me, Miss, that was testy. I apologize. Day before yesterday, a thirty-one-year veteran officer, a friend of mine, put a gun to his head and killed himself. He was pushed over the edge by a deep sense of disappointment and betrayal caused by desertions within the department and reports of police looting. Our police force here in New Orleans is 1,600 men. About three hundred officers abandoned their posts and left the rest of us here, understaffed and under pressure. The next day, our information officer drove out of town and killed himself."

"I'm sorry," Donna said.

"Police officers in the third district over at Gentilly got flooded out," Warner recounted. "Their motor pool was high and dry in a downtown garage, but they appropriated two hundred Cadillacs and Chevrolets for personal use and took off to Baton Rouge and the far west. Our police and fire departments are going through a meltdown. So I'm not altogether rational, you understand?"

"I do understand," she said.

He read the note on the cop's card. "Oh, damn," he said softly. "Earl Thibodeaux. That's too bad."

"Do you know him?" Donna asked.

"Oh yeah, long time. Everybody in the Quarter knows Earl and his wife, Fiona. She owns the voodoo shop on Toulouse."

He brightened. "Maybe you should take that finger to the Voodoo Shop, Mr. Hampton."

Barry smiled.

Down the hall, a prisoner rattled the bars of his holding cell and a policeman cursed him. The building had that odor peculiar to these places. Donna had been in police stations several times trying to help delinquent students. There was a residue of sweat, dirty ashtrays, and a coffee pot boiled dry. Wastebaskets overflowed with remnants of fast food wrappers that were weeks old.

"You have electricity," Donna noted.

"From a generator," the detective said.

"Is there any chance I could charge my cell phone?"

"If you have the transformer and proper connections."

But those items were in her car north of Lake Ponchartrain. "I don't have them with me," she said.

"Who you trying to call?" he asked.

"My parents in Atlanta."

He shoved a telephone toward her. "That may be the last phone working in New Orleans, Louisiana," he said. "Help yourself." Then he went back to Barry Hampton. "You going to write about all this?"

"I might."

"Be sure you mention my name," Gus Warner said. "I'd want my mama to read my name in the *Probe*."

"If I write it and they publish it, your name will be there," Barry promised.

In Atlanta the phone rang twice and Donna's mother answered breathlessly.

"It's me, Mom."

"Dear God, Donna, we've been worried sick. Where are you?"

"I'm in New Orleans."

"Are you all right?"

"I haven't been able to call because everything is a mess down here."

"I've seen it on television," her mother said. "It looks dreadful. Your brother has telephoned repeatedly. You know Dean wouldn't call here unless he was frantic to reach you."

"My cell phone is dead, Mom. Nothing is working in New Orleans. When Dean calls again, explain why I haven't been available. But Mom, tell him there may be one piece of good news."

"What is it?"

"I think his son, Thelonious, is alive."

"Thelonious?" the detective interjected. "Thelonious Monk DeCay?"

"Yes," Donna cupped the receiver and held it aside. "Do you know him?"

"I knew his daddy. What about Thelonious?"

"We're here looking for him," Donna said. "He's my nephew."

"I be damned," the detective muttered. "The dead man, Earl Thibodeaux, knew Monk. Black boy, right?"

"That's right."

"The kid hung around with a man named Quinton Toussaint."

"We've tried to locate Mr. Toussaint," Donna said.

"He lives in the French Quarter."

Donna's heart was hammering. "On Esplanade. We've been there, but he isn't home."

"Probably had the good sense to get out of town before the storm hit. That old boy loves talented people, and he's responsible for making some of them famous. He knew Tooth DeCay as well as anybody. In the old days, Quinton was a force to be reckoned with in the music business. I've seen him with Monk at Jackson Square. The kid puts bottle cap taps on his shoes and dances for tips. He plays a pretty good harmonica."

The detective gave Barry a lopsided bulldog grin. "You manage to get right in the thick of things, don't you, Hampton?"

Barry shrugged with mock helplessness. "It seems that way."

When Donna had heard the dying man speak her nephew's name, she'd tried to shake off the first thought that came to mind. Thelonious killed somebody? What did she expect? An orphaned mulatto child, son of a convicted murderer, living in a slum dwelling with his grandmother—what would anyone expect of a boy under such conditions?

New Orleans was like a war zone. Bodies floated in slime, crumpled cars were piled on top of other flooded vehicles. It had been a week since the storm struck and the abandoned citizens were furious with every level of government from local to national. People were hungry and dehydrated. Medical care was nonexistent, and the authorities had done little to help.

Wading from the Convention Center to the Superdome looking for Thelonious, Donna was repulsed by the sight of bodies adrift in an oily lake of floodwater. She met a heart patient desperate for digitalis. Diabetics were going into shock for want of insulin. Even analgesics were not to be had, and people were suffering. While she stood waiting for a Red Cross volunteer to check through a long list of refugees, a jaundiced man in a wheelchair passed away because he needed kidney dialysis.

There were rumors of rape and murder but when Barry pressed the issue he could find nobody who said it had happened to them, or to someone they knew personally.

At the Superdome there was no way to flush toilets. The smell of human waste, dirty diapers, and unbathed bodies was horrendous even out into the street. The stench was so terrible people inside had moved outdoors into blazing sunshine. National Guardsmen marked the periphery standing with weapons at the ready, maintaining control only with the constant threat of armed response. Dead people were being warehoused away from a milling throng of desperate survivors. Donna learned there was no way to view bodies and many remained unidentified.

Finally, refugees were being shipped out across America. Some were flown to San Antonio, Texas. In a convoy of fifty-six buses, hundreds of people endured a thirty-hour ride to Muskogee, Oklahoma. The diaspora extended to Utah, Colorado, Washington, New York, and Florida. Unregistered and unaccounted for, many children were separated from parents. Husbands were occasionally sent to one city, wives to another. The elderly in need of immediate medical care were parted from their families. Donna had no idea where they might have sent Monk if indeed he had come through at all.

The exodus was uncoordinated and impossible to catalogue. She was told that four-fifths of New Orleans was under water. Six days after the levees broke, the evacuation was still taking place.

She imagined months of searching nationwide. First response teams could not communicate with one another. There was no central clearinghouse for information. Confusion and chaos were compounded by frustration and fury.

"One tiny spark here could ignite civil disorder like nothing ever seen in this country," Barry observed. "We're on the verge of anarchy."

But so far it had not happened. People were in peril, and most of them were poor and helpless. But overall they were law-abiding.

In the meantime, out of the bayous of southern Louisiana came pirogues, flatboats, propeller-driven swamp buggies, and canoes, as local citizens stepped in to help with rescue efforts. Barry asked one of the boatmen to check the grandmother's home on Andry Street in the Lower Ninth Ward. The report was not encouraging.

"Houses in that neighborhood are flooded to the apex of roofs," the boatman said. "If there were people inside during the storm, they're dead."

Donna had been thwarted, exhausted, and ready to quit, convinced that she'd never find Thelonious.

But now she had hope.

From the lips of a dying man had come her nephew's name. "Monk," he'd whispered.

The boy she saw running away was white, older than nine years. "I'll get you," he shouted, perhaps chasing Thelonious. She didn't believe Dean's son shot that man, and now she had reason to believe Monk was alive. She wouldn't give up the search.

But, oh, how she ached for a decent meal, a steaming bath, clean clothes, and shampoo for God's sake! Her scalp itched ferociously.

"You got me into the city," she bargained with Barry. "Do you think you might get me back to my car?"

"Oh, sure, babe!" Barry quipped. "I'll go to a car rental place and get us one of those y'all-haul trailers. I'll tell them we need a ride, plus gas to get there."

Miraculously, somehow, he did arrange transportation. She and Barry rode out of New Orleans in a military truck with a tobacco-chewing National Guard corporal on his way north for supplies. Even on the interstate the army vehicle rode like a farm tractor over a washboard road.

The heart-rending sights of destruction held them to silence as they lumbered past submerged shopping malls, apartment houses, and private homes.

"It'll take years to recover from this," Barry said.

"I heard it'll take a decade," the corporal replied.

Donna spotted a baby carriage and shuddered to think what might have happened to the parents and infant.

"I got to let you out here where the interstates cross," the driver said. "My orders are to go on to Hattiesburg."

"How often do you get lost these days?" Barry asked.

"What do you mean?"

"If you accidentally got onto Interstate 12 going west," Barry suggested, "that's a mistake, but it isn't AWOL, is it?"

"Well, my orders are to go on up—"

"We might stand out here a week trying to get a ride," Barry said. "It wouldn't take you but half an hour to deliver us to Mandeville."

"Oh, please do," Donna begged.

"What the hell," the driver turned west. Donna kissed him on the cheek and he grinned.

Her car was where they'd left it, dirty, but no worse for wear. The storeowner decided he'd take a credit card after all. Donna paid four hundred dollars for his boat and motor. Barry talked a military convoy out of a tankful of fuel.

"Now that I have my car," Donna said, "Where can I drop you off, Barry?"

"Where're you going?" he asked.

She plugged her cell phone into the cigarette lighter, "After I've recharged my phone and my body, I'm going back to New Orleans to look for Thelonious."

"Suits me," he said. "Why don't we run upstate a ways and see if we can find some real food and hot water. Searching for Thelonious Monk will be easier if both of us are refreshed."

Pine trees along the road had been snapped and laid flat by the storm. Miles from any sign of habitation, household items were scattered in fields. The world had been taken apart and left in tangled heaps. When she got beyond the area most affected by the storm, Donna marveled with appreciation for the shine of electric lights, traffic signals that worked, and people following normal routines.

For supper they ate barbecued pork, baked beans, and potato salad. They drank endless glasses of sweetened iced tea. The motel where they stopped had only one room available with two double beds. Donna had been half-clad in the same clothes for a week, so modesty was no longer a concern. She soaked in a molded fiberglass tub with the bathroom door ajar. In the other room, Barry was smoking again, idly watching her reflection in a mirror. She didn't care. She'd seen him naked and he'd grown accustomed to her nudity as they shared accommodations at the Probe.

"Don't go to sleep," he warned. "I might crawl in that tub with you."

Donna laughed. "Come ahead," she said.

And he did.

{CHAPTER SEVENTEEN}

Monk saw Officer Eustis Bernard search Uncle Earl's pockets. The policeman removed a wallet, coins, and Earl's wristwatch as the soldiers stood by watching.

Monk wanted to shout at the guardsmen, "Randy shot him. Mr. Bernard's son killed Uncle Earl!"

Gang boys all knew the officer protected his son. Monk had heard how Randy bragged after he was sent to juvenile court for theft. He said the judge let him go because his father was a cop.

"Randy can do anything he wants," gang boys boasted. There were rumors that Eustis Bernard arrested his son's enemies for the slightest wrongdoing.

Randy Bernard boasted to his friends that his father had worked as a guard in Angola Prison, and they feared him. Gang boys said the police officer knew criminals who would cripple a person for a few dollars cash.

After searching Uncle Earl's body, the policeman walked off one way, the National Guardsmen the other. They left Uncle Earl where he was.

To escape Randy Bernard, Monk had run so hard he was giddy from lack of oxygen. He beat his chest to force a breath and then sank down in the shade of the louvered air-conditioner housing.

For a long time when he became breathless like this, Grandmama thought he had asthma. She once took Monk to a doctor at Charity Hospital and he said, no, it wasn't asthma. It was hyperventilation.

"When it happens," the doctor advised Monk, "sit down, relax, and breathe easy until it passes. It's a little scary, but don't worry. You won't die from hyperventilation."

In the street below, Uncle Earl lay in the blistering afternoon sun. A couple of times Monk thought he saw movement, but he decided heat rising off the pavement caused an illusion. He ached to go down and be certain Uncle Earl was really dead, but the soldiers kept coming by, and they would've caught him had Monk been on the street.

He thought things about Uncle Earl that he didn't know he remembered.

At Jazz Fest last year, Uncle Earl climbed onstage and astonished Monk, declaring, "I don't sing too good, but I love the songs I do sing. I'm gone sing a song writ by my friend, Tooth DeCay. 'I'm Sick and Tired of Sitting Home All Alone in the Same Room with You.'"

In Monk's mind, memories flared for a few seconds and then faded away: Uncle Earl trying to play harmonica, sucking and blowing, but he couldn't control his tongue. ... When Fiona teased him about it, he pulled her onto his lap and made a blubbery sound against her neck. She squealed with pleasure. He had a tattoo in the crook of his arm, so when he doubled the arm the tattoo looked like a little naked butt. "You boys ain't ever touched a girl," he said, "poke your finger right there." Fiona shrieked. She drove him out of the house, but laughed the whole time.

Monk's throat was raw and his ribs ached from running. Adding to his misery, sores on his arms and legs itched terribly. He sat on his hands to keep from scratching.

The sun slipped behind skyscrapers in the business district and long purple shadows crept over Vieux Carré. A ship's horn blew and in the emptiness of the Quarter the blast bounded and rebounded, and then echoed away to silence.

"Monk?" Jon Latour called in a raspy voice.

Monk stood up, and when Jon saw him, Monk pointed at the body on the street. "That's Earl Thibodeaux. Randy Bernard shot him. Randy's a gang boy, and his daddy is a cop."

Monk smelled Jon's musky scent and it made him think of the time Uncle Earl took him and Percy fishing on the Pearl River.

"Phew, Uncle Earl," Percy complained, "you smell awful!"

"Drives off mosquitoes and lures fish," Earl explained.

"And asphyxiates your friends," Percy said.

"What's that about my ass—fixes what?"

The sun had set and Uncle Earl's body still lay where he'd fallen. Mosquitoes buzzed Monk's face. Chimney swifts darted and dipped in the afterglow of sundown. Bats left their lofts and took up the hunt for supper. The Quarter hunkered under a darkening sky.

"I don't know where to find my daddy," Monk said to Jon. "Where did Quinton go? And Fiona? Who's going to tell her about Uncle Earl? Did Percy die? There's nobody left to look after me, Jon."

Awkwardly, Jon patted Monk's shoulder.

"I don't want to live in an orphanage," Monk sobbed.

Pat-pat-pat—

Monk cried himself dry. His upper lip stuck to his teeth. He had cried so long he had hiccups. Each convulsive spasm was another stab in the ribs. Jon tugged at him to go downstairs. He opened their last bottle of water and offered it to Monk. Monk held his breath and drank in long slow swallows. When he relaxed, the hiccups continued, even after he went to bed.

Several times during the night Monk woke and watched Jon thrash the air with his broomstick. Monk went up onto the roof where it was quiet and cooler. The moon was a sliver in a star-speckled sky. In the business district flashlights waggled, and from the river came a low chug of tugboats.

He itched miserably. He thought about times Grandmama told him to take a bath and he hadn't; he yearned for those baths now. He wished he'd been a better boy. If Grandmama were here, he'd beg her to forgive him. He'd tell her how much he loved her and how sorry he was that he let her drown.

He fell asleep sitting on the rooftop and dreamed of her death over and over again. In sleep he reconstructed the tragedy, altering it so he managed to save her. He dreamed she was wet and slippery but somehow he pulled her through the trap door into the attic. The vent to the outside was smaller than the trapdoor, but in his dream he kicked the wall and enlarged it. He held his breath and led the way underwater. His body screamed for oxygen. He pulled her onto the roof, his lungs screamed for air—

He awoke with a sudden and massive inhalation. He'd been holding his breath in the dream.

Grandmama wasn't here.

She was at home, caught in the attic door.

Uncle Earl remained in the street until a forklift came to scoop him up. The workmen wore rubber gloves and facemasks. Where Earl had been lying, there was a dark stain on the pavement. They sprayed the street with a foamy brown liquid and drove away.

Monk's itches were so uncomfortable Jon produced wintergreen alcohol and bathed his sores. Wintergreen smelled better than regular alcohol, but burned no less. Monk hopped around and sucked air between clenched teeth. When the discomfort let up, he asked for more, because burning was better than itching.

Jon doused Monk's head with Listerine mouthwash and massaged it into the scalp. The treatments stung, but when it was over, Monk felt better.

He returned the favor. He poured alcohol over Jon's chest and down his back, and chased Jon around the room trying to fan him and hasten evaporation. The apartment smelled like a hospital, but itching eased, and alcohol repelled mosquitoes.

The next morning, Jon reached up into a closet and brought down a cardboard piano keyboard. He placed it on a table in the kitchen. Monk watched him sit down, straighten his back, and place his feet as if to press pedals on the floor. He touched a key here, another there, as though testing notes to be certain the instrument was properly tuned. He used one finger on each hand to strike two keys—Chop Sticks.

He quit and flexed his fingers. He had large hands and a good span. And then, Jon began to play.

He closed his eyes, fingers moving over the paper keyboard. It was a fascinating performance; he had no sheet music, he played from memory. By the tempo of movements and power of crescendos, Monk knew the piece was not improvisation. He was a better mime, Monk thought, than those who practiced at Jackson Square.

"Play boogie, Jon."

But Jon was lost in the exercise. He bent forward in concentration, and then threw back his head, eyes closed, and performed an intricate run of imagined notes. Monk saw his foot move on invisible pedals as he dampened or extended tones.

Like the demons that only Jon saw, this was music only he could hear. Perspiration gathered on his face. He threw himself into the performance. The end came with a slam of the keys. Bam. Bam! The piece was finished. Jon slumped, arms at his sides.

"That was beautiful, Jon."

He gazed away.

"Will you play boogie-woogie for me?" Monk asked.

Jon fell to the keyboard again. From hours of practice, watching Percy and Grandmama play, Monk recognized the notes and tempo; by gestures and timing, he imagined the beat.

Jon raked the keyboard from high notes to low, and then up again. Boogie-boogie-boogie, Monk could almost hear it.

He whirled and jumped as Jon pounded the keys. Monk twisted his body, stamped his feet, and whooped with the joy of infectious rhythm.

When it ended, he fell to his knees, laughing.

"That was good, Jon."

Jon folded his paper piano and put it back in the closet. Monk saw him stare at his own hands.

"Quinton Toussaint has a piano," Monk said.

He wasn't sure Jon understood, so Monk spoke louder, "Quinton has a grand piano."

"I know."

"My daddy is a musician," Monk said. "Quinton talked to you about him when we first met. Did you know Tooth DeCay?"

"Quinton likes him," Jon said.

"Do you know if my daddy is still alive?" Monk asked.

Jon rubbed a fingernail with his thumb.

"Do you know where my daddy is, Jon?"

As always, when pushed too far, Jon ignored further questions. The conversation was ended.

The food sack was empty and they were out of bottled water. More people had returned to the city, which made raids hazardous. A dark apartment was not always empty. They had to take extra care before entering. Squatting on eaves three floors high, Jon stared at windows of condominiums to be sure they were unoccupied. Then he studied other apartments nearby to judge whether neighbors might see him. The yap of a dog or voices in the dark sent them on their way.

Monk followed over a rooftop route, doubling back, retracing their steps. They ended up where they started, near Jackson Square. The crescent moon was growing, but still too slight for light. They moved as much by feel as sight along eaves Monk had not traveled before.

Good food was scarce. Bread products were moldy, dry cereals crawled with weevils. The stench of refrigerators was so overpowering, Jon no longer opened the doors. Canned goods were their safest choices, but because of the weight they had to go out more often for supplies.

Jon was inside an apartment rummaging through the kitchen when a flashlight beam caught him holding a sack full of food.

Monk heard a woman yell, "I've got a gun!"

Slowly, Jon backed toward an open window.

"I'll shoot you," she screamed. "Put down the bag."

Monk's heart hammered so hard his ears throbbed. "You're not taking anything out of here," the woman shrieked. She kept the light on Jon's face. He reached the window and stepped out. He still held the bag.

"Don't ever come back," she shouted. "Next time I'll shoot you."

Monk watched as Jon scampered down a fire escape and across a dark courtyard. A few minutes later he appeared on the roof beside Monk.

"Whew," Jon said.

It made Monk consider, suppose Jon had been caught? What if he got arrested? Or was shot?

"What should I do?" Monk asked.

"Don't steal," Jon advised.

It was strange advice from a man who lived by theft.

"Have you ever been in jail?" Monk questioned.

"Yes."

"More than once?"

"Yes."

Monk remembered stories Uncle Earl told about hard labor, bad food, and knife fights in prison. "It ain't no place to go on vacation," Earl had said.

"Was it bad, Jon?"

"Yes."

"Did you ever get hurt?"

"Yes."

"Jon, do you think you could talk to me with more than one word at a time?"

"No."

That ended that.

Monk discovered the *Probe* was a newspaper when he and Jon entered through a back window in search of toilet paper and aspirin. Front windows of the office looked down on Bourbon Street. The rear windows opened onto a flat roof that extended to the next building. Jon dismantled a jalousie and stepped inside. It was like entering an oven. The heat took Monk's breath.

The Probe office was filled with desks and computers. On large tables there were photographs that had been cut apart and spliced together again. Monk walked around the room, curious about odd pictures he saw: a pig with wings, a goose with four legs, a small parakeet sitting on a very large egg.

On a desk he found a stack of newspapers. The headlines intrigued him. "Royal Blood Truly Blue," a story claimed. It was about a prince's depression when his princess died in a car wreck.

"One-Pound Parakeet Lays Two-Pound Egg" … that should be interesting. He studied the photograph of a parakeet perched on an egg and tried to imagine what that must have felt like.

"Hitler Was a Woman" … Monk had learned about Hitler in home school. He was surprised to discover a woman could have a moustache.

"Man Swallows His Own Glass Eye and Sees Cancer" … early warning saved his life …

Jon would not steal things they didn't need, but he let Monk select several issues of the paper to take home. Back at the apartment, while

Jon sat on the bucket, Monk read to him from a copy of *Probe*. The story was about a zookeeper cleaning an elephant's compound. The zookeeper started to light a cigar and the elephant passed gas.

"'The methane ignited, and the zookeeper received third-degree burns to his face and ears.'"

Jon laughed so hard he nearly fell off the bucket.

In the back of the newspaper—it was really more of a magazine—there were advertisements that anybody could buy. The *Probe* was printed in Spanish, German, French, Italian, and English. It was possible to advertise in all those languages at one time. This would be a good place to ask for help finding Tooth DeCay.

By himself, Monk returned to the Probe to get paper and pencils. While Jon napped, Monk wrote advertisements.

"Son Looking for Jazz Muscian Tooth DeCay. Contact Monk DeCay."

Contact him where? Monk had no idea where he'd be.

Suppose somebody answered the ad? No matter where he ended up, Monk could write to the newspaper to collect his mail. It was a good idea.

In the classified ads section it said he could advertise in "all languages" for $22.30 a word. "Son Looking for Jazz Musician Tooth DeCay. Contact Monk DeCay, at the *Probe*."

If he used their address that was an additional six words, P.O. Box whatever, plus New Orleans, LA, and zip code—nineteen words = $423.70.

On the front page of the *Probe* it said every issue was read weekly by three million people. Surely out of three million people somebody would know where to find his father.

All Monk needed now was his money ...

Randy Bernard was searching for him. Monk saw the gang boy and several of his friends climb over fences and prowl through courtyards in Vieux Carré. They came onto balconies and crossed roofs. They nearly caught Monk coming out of a loft. He had to duck back inside and hide in shadows. They were near enough he could hear their voices.

"He ain't up here, Randy."

"He's here somewhere. I saw him go up a trellis like a monkey."

"What do we say if somebody catches us?"

"Tell them we're looking for food."

Monk was pretty sure if Randy Bernard caught him, he was good as dead.

Like Jon, Monk was safest going out at dusk. On his way to the Ninth Ward he went by Quinton's house. So far, the old historian had not come home.

He didn't dare go back to Bywater in daylight. So he walked the railroad tracks at sundown, working his way around to the drawbridge. From there, he dared to approach Mr. Benoit's time saver store. He was close enough to see that the door was still propped open. Broken windows hadn't been repaired. Trash was piled in the parking lot. There were still no lights in the area.

Every minute in gang boy territory was dangerous. Monk returned to the railroad tracks, and in the dark he walked toward the city. He saw a woman standing over a campfire. The smell of cooking beans made his stomach ache. He went to the fence and called to her.

"Please ma'am, could I have some beans?"

She stood motionless, staring into the dark, and then she said, "Whose child you is, boy?"

"I live in the Ninth Ward."

"Y'all get through the storm all right?"

"No ma'am."

"I got no way to give them to you except in an old cup."

"That'd be good." He was shaking.

"Come on over the fence, babe. I got some cornbread, too. I make it with jalapeño peppers. You like it that way?"

"Yes ma'am. That's how my Grandmama cooked it."

She handed him a cup of field peas and a piece of cornbread, with a thick slice of onion on a paper towel. Monk's hands trembled as he ate, and she watched him swallow fast and hard.

"Chew the food, baby," she said.

He couldn't see her face. She was big like Grandmama, her head tied in a bandana, dress so thin he saw her legs backlighted by the campfire.

"You lose somebody in the storm dawlin'?"

"My grandmama. Maybe some other folks, too, I don't know for sure."

"Who's keeping you?" she asked.

"A friend."

She filled his cup again, cut another slice of onion. "That's all the cornbread I can spare," she said. "I got my own to feed, too."

"Yes ma'am. Thank you."

The onion poured tears down his cheeks; the hot beans raised a sweat.

Out of the dark a boy appeared and the woman said, "This is my son, Nathaniel."

"Hey," the boy said, "ain't you Felonious?"

Monk dropped the cup and scampered over the fence.

"Nathaniel," the woman rebuked, "what you doing?"

"He killed somebody, Mama. We saw him do it."

"I did not!" Monk shouted from the tracks.

"Shot him twice," the gang boy said. "They going to get you, Felonious. The cops know you did it."

Monk ran over creosoted ties and the graveled bed of tracks. He looked back and there was nobody behind him. Randy had a car. They might try to get ahead and intercept him. He jumped off the tracks and stumbled along Esplanade. A dog barked and that set off other dogs as one animal after another picked up the cry.

Quinton's house was dark.

Where was he?

Monk saw a car coming and darted into Vieux Carré. Past the French Market he ran, up an alley, onto the roof of a building; he stopped and looked down. A patrol car drove by slowly, flashing a spotlight on doorways and into alcoves.

When he dared move again, he made his way to Jon's apartment.

"Jon, gang boys told police I shot Earl Thibodeaux."

Jon peered at him out of dark eyes shadowed by the candles.

"Do you think the cops will shoot me?" Monk asked. "A gang boy named Nathaniel told his mama they saw me shoot Uncle Earl."

"He lied," Jon said.

"I know he lied, Jon. But the police won't know it. Do you think they'll shoot me?"

Jon seemed less positive.

"Randy's daddy is a cop," Monk worried.

Jon opened an unlabeled can of food and extended it.

"No, thank you," Monk said. "I had supper."

Jon looked at him so long, Monk explained, "A lady gave me a bowl of beans and a slice of cornbread."

Jon was like a statue, staring.

Monk had to start at the beginning and tell the whole story. Jon completed his meal, listening without comment.

Monk was in bed when Jon came to the door. "Be careful," he said, and that was all he said.

{CHAPTER EIGHTEEN}

Donna drove south toward New Orleans while Barry Hampton snoozed. In the trunk were three five-gallon plastic containers of gasoline, and on the back seat, two large thermal chests, one of which was filled with ice in plastic bags and bottled water. At roadblocks set up to keep out looters, guards noted the "STORM NEWS" sign on her vehicle and waved her through.

She listened to WWL talk radio. Most calls were from somewhere else because New Orleans had few working telephones. Callers praised the Coast Guard for their rescue efforts, but vilified every other branch of the federal government up to and including President George Bush.

Her cell phone rang. Donna turned down the radio.

"Well, Godalmighty, at last!" Dean shouted. From his end of the line, she heard the usual racket of humanity confined in a hard-surface environment, voices reverberating. Every sound was harsh and unpleasant. "Where are you, Donna?"

"In my car, driving back to New Orleans."

"I've been trying to reach you for two weeks."

She reminded herself of the frustration he must feel, imprisoned and immobile.

"Okay," Dean began, "Mom said you believe Thelonious is alive."

"But I haven't found him, Dean." Donna explained about the chaos at disaster relief services, incomplete lists of survivors, and a lack of communication between agencies. "Barry Hampton sent a boat to check on the grandmother's house," she said.

"The tabloid guy? What does he expect out of this?"

"Actually," Donna said peevishly, "outside prison walls there are people who help one another merely because help is needed."

Long pause. "I apologize," Dean said. "What did you start to say?"

"The house is flooded to the roofline. The boatman said anybody who stayed there is dead."

"But you think Thelonious survived?"

Donna told him about the dying man who spoke the name, Monk.

"You don't think Thelonious had anything to do with the shooting?"

She described the white youth running away. "It wasn't Thelonious," she concluded.

"Have you talked to Quinton Toussaint?"

"His house is still shut. He must've left town."

The cell phone signal weakened as she neared the city. Dean issued directives, "Talk to neighbors. Leave a note. Go to … café … ask …"

The signal was gone.

Barry roused up, sleepily. "There are women who are attracted to men in prison. That's not you, is it?"

"Dean is my brother, you idiot."

"A woman gives the prisoner money and he receives conjugal visits. I don't know what she gets out of the relationship. It's like owning a large pet in a cage. She knows where her sugar is at night, and he tells her she's beautiful. That must be enough, since he's not available to carry out garbage or mow the lawn."

Barry yawned. "You never know what will appeal to a person. W. C. Fields said he met the perfect woman: she owned a liquor store and hated sex. That wouldn't do for me, but for a misogynous old souse it might work."

An automobile accident ahead brought traffic to a standstill. Donna rolled down the windows and turned off the motor to conserve fuel. Hot humid air smelled of rotting humus. People in other cars looked tired and grim. In the distance, city buildings appeared as gray and lifeless steles. Haze had filtered the brilliance of sunlight, and foliage beside the highway was whipped and wilted. Good times did not roll in New Orleans these days.

Nobody blew their car horns. The long line of traffic sat unmoving in mounting heat, silent and resigned to the frustration of waiting helplessly. Entering the city, Donna passed through streets lined with discarded refrigerators, the doors held shut by duct tape. A brown muck covered household items piled upon mounds of wet Sheetrock and insulation. A few businesses were open for trade despite the lack of electricity and other services.

She turned up the radio again. A woman on a talk show said, "New Orleans is my home. I was born there, my people have lived there all the way back to my great-great grandparents. I always said no matter what happened I'd never leave; I'd stick with it. I wouldn't be happy anywhere else in the world. I stayed there through the storm. It was like, you don't leave a longtime friend when he's in trouble, and so I didn't leave New Orleans to run from the hurricane. But a good friend of mine was murdered. It was a senseless, stupid murder. The killers took two dollars from his pocket, and a cheap watch off his wrist. A few days later, I was walking home and two men attacked me. I got to tell you, it scared me. That did it. I'm in Chicago. I yearn for New Orleans. But I'm not coming back."

Sewage, decomposing animals, and occasionally the smell of dead people filled the air with a putrid stench that had not diminished while Donna and Barry were out of town.

"Where should I park, Barry?"

"Stop at the Probe and we'll unload everything," he said. "Then we'll find a parking garage in the Central Business District where the car is less likely to be stolen or vandalized."

The garage they selected was attached to a luxury hotel. Barry lifted a crossbar blocking entry to a ramp that ascended to upper levels. Nobody challenged him. On the sixth floor, Donna picked a space away from other vehicles. She placed a note on the windshield listing their names and address of the Probe.

Standing outside the car she could see across the city from a height of six stories. Blue tarps on damaged roofs formed a crazy quilt pattern in residential areas. Armed National Guardsmen patrolled streets. Stray dogs scavenged in dangerous packs. There was no place to put abandoned animals and no one to catch them. Soldiers had little choice; they shot the dogs and left them where they fell. Donna could see tons of garbage surrounding the Superdome.

They left the garage and walked toward the Quarter. Civilians on foot were considered suspicious.

A sentry confronted them.

"Your names?"

"We're reporters," Barry explained. He gave his home address and then said, "I was flooded out. We're staying at offices of the Probe on Bourbon Street."

The guardsman studied Barry's identification. "The Probe?" he said. His accent was Louisiana. "You write for the paper that carries stories about people sexually abused during alien abductions?"

"We may have reported on matters like that," Barry confessed.

Donna stepped aside as if she weren't really with him.

"Did you write the story about a woman who got pregnant from swimming in a pool with alien sperm?"

"That particular piece was not mine," Barry said cautiously. "It was written by an associate."

"Where does somebody come up wit shit like dat? My wife won't let our daughters swim in a public pool because of dat story."

"Ah," Barry said. "Tell your wife there'll be no problem if the youngsters swim with cotton balls in their ears."

"In their ears?"

"Conception on other planets is achieved by an entirely different canal. A rubber swim cap with earflaps will also provide excellent protection."

The patrolman nodded and pumped Barry's hand. "It's an honor to meet you, sir."

Barry made note of the soldier's name and confirmed the spelling as though he intended to include it in a future article. "You fellows are doing a great job," Barry said. "We couldn't make it without you, and I'll tell you, man, you look good in that uniform."

Walking to the Probe, Barry said, "Ego is the one trait all men share in common. If a beautiful woman tells an ugly man he's appealing, the damn fool believes it when every mirror testifies otherwise. That's why women spies are successful. Wax a man's ego and he'll give you anything."

He looked at her slyly. "Consider that a hint," he said.

She still had not decided how enamored of him she was. Her experience with sex was limited, but she knew enough to know Barry Hampton was a cut above the norm. He was gentle, patient, attentive, and surprisingly athletic.

Their tryst in the motel bathtub consisted of bathing, and it was nice. There'd been none of that frantic teenage got-to-have-it-now stuff. Barry was mature enough to contain himself. From the tub they moved to one of the double beds to dry off and he massaged her with lotion. Because he progressed so methodically, she assumed age had tempered ardor. That turned out to be a false assumption. The third time they made love was even better than the first two. She used muscles she'd forgotten were available for such activities.

Afterward, Barry ran another tub of warm water and knelt on the bathroom floor to bathe her like a baby, with tender strokes and loving care.

He didn't discuss it later. No stupid questions, "Was it good for you?" He lay there beside her and groaned himself to sleep.

The next morning they had a Grand Slam breakfast at Denny's Restaurant, with a double rasher of thick-sliced bacon and eggs scrambled softly. Then they returned to the motel and slept until evening. Before leaving this morning, they went shopping. Barry bought bottles of wine, a small hibachi, a bag of charcoal briquettes, and a dozen steaks, which he packed in ice at the bottom of a cooler loaded with beer. He also purchased candles. It looked like a romantic evening in the making.

Donna wasn't anticipating physical activity without air conditioning and a bathtub. "You aren't thinking about more of what we've done, are you?"

"Lord, no," Barry said. "It's too hot for that."

A heavy-handed pounding on the door at the Probe brought Donna downstairs. Detective Gus Warner didn't say hello. He said, "There are no movie houses open; horses aren't racing at the Fairgrounds. Nobody's standing in line outside Galatoire's, and the Saints aren't here. No Swamp Fest or Voodoo Fest or Film Fest. The Hornets are gone. The National Guard is using helicopters to look for dead people, laying them out at

Zephyr Field. I've just come from St. Gabriel Morgue where I identified several dead cops. I'm feeling pretty low."

"Come in," Donna said. "Close the door behind you. It sticks."

They climbed the stairs to the office and Barry emerged from the bathroom pulling on a clean shirt. "What say, Gus?"

"The mayor announced he's laying off three thousand city workers," Gus said. "Do you think anybody will notice?"

Barry took two ice-cold beers from his cache and gave one to Warner. They each popped the tops, took a big swig, and sighed.

"There's a shop down on St. Charles near Lee Circle," Warner said. "Right after the storm, the owner spray-painted a message on plywood sheets covering the windows. It said, 'Don't try. I am sleeping inside with a big dog, an ugly woman, two shotguns, and a claw hammer.'"

Barry laughed.

"About a week later," Gus reported, "the sign was updated. 'Still here. Woman left. Cooking a pot of dog gumbo.'"

Donna sipped bottled water and watched them chuckle, slug beer, and chuckle some more.

"This morning," the detective said, "the newest message is 'Welcome back, y'all. Grin and bear it.'"

"That's New Orleans," Barry mused. He opened another beer and offered it to Warner.

The two men drank and said nothing for a long time. Then Barry broke the silence. "I miss the good smells of New Orleans. Ligustrum, sweet olive, confederate jasmine."

And then to Donna's amazement, both men cried. Unashamedly, tears poured down their cheeks.

With onset of evening, Barry climbed out on the roof behind the office to set up the new hibachi. He lit the charcoal. If he'd invited Gus to dinner, Donna didn't hear it. But Gus Warner would stay, that was obvious. She cleared a photo table for dining and brought over three roll-around chairs.

Despite heat radiating up from the flat roof, the men stood by the hibachi drinking and talking. Now and then they directed a comment at her, mostly about food. Red beans and rice, cochon de lait, shrimp Creole, oysters on the half shell, and crawfish étouffée. They debated the better place to get fried chicken, Dunbar's or Willie Mae's, a little corner store restaurant run by a black woman in her eighties.

"All those places were damaged by Katrina," Gus said hoarsely. They lifted their beers in a silent toast to what used to be.

As the steaks seared over glowing embers, Gus related one horror story after another. "Nobody knows what all is in the floodwater," he said. "Human waste, human remains, oil, lead, battery acid, chemical spills, and asbestos. I heard about a pregnant woman who left her seven-year-old son to fend for himself. She swam through that mess having contractions the whole way, looking for a safe place to give birth to her baby."

He sipped his drink and licked his lips. "A woman was gang raped on the street." Thugs had raided hospitals for drugs, snipers took shots at would-be rescuers.

"Have you actually spoken to the victims of these crimes?" Barry asked.

"It's common knowledge among police officers," Gus replied.

"So far," Barry said, "I haven't met anyone who actually claims to have been robbed, raped, or shot at."

"Well, gee whiz, Mr. Reporter," Gus Warner said coldly, "you'll have to come down to the police station and interview a few victims for yourself."

"I'm not disputing your word, Gus, but I wonder if a lot of those claims aren't unsubstantiated rumors."

"According to the coroners," Gus said, "they've picked up a few hundred bodies."

"Killed by the flood, or murdered?" Barry asked.

"That's what the coroner is trying to establish, Hampton."

"When you know for certain," Barry said, "I'd like to hear the final figures."

Barry lit a lantern, shared more beer, and Donna watched mellow go to mush. Finally, after dinner, the detective lifted his shoulders to ease muscles, tilted his massive head to one side and then the other. "This has been nice," he said. "I almost forgot what I came for."

Donna stopped breathing. "News about Thelonious?"

"If what I hear is true," Warner said, "he's alive, and that much is good. There've been reports of private home invasions by a scruffy, bearded white man, possibly a vagrant. Apparently he goes into apartments in search of food and clothing. We've been lenient with looters who steal to survive. For one thing, we're too short-handed to investigate petty crime. Anyway, according to reports, the bearded guy is accompanied by a young light-skinned Negro boy."

"What makes you think it's Thelonious?" Donna challenged.

"We have a report from three young men who know Thelonious," Warner said. "They say he was burglarizing Fiona's Voodoo Shop and Earl Thibodeaux caught him at it."

Her chest seized and Donna forced herself to sit still.

"They say," Gus continued, "they saw Earl haul the kid out of the store by the nape of his neck and kick him. Thelonious jumped up and shot him. While Earl was on the ground, wounded, Thelonious walked over, took careful aim, and shot him a second time."

"My God," Donna said.

"An eyewitness report becomes the most powerful evidence available under these conditions," Gus concluded. "Anyway, if the boy gets picked up, at his age he'll go to juvenile detention until the matter can be settled in court."

"I don't believe Thelonious shot that man," Donna said.

"Do you know him?"

"No." She could see Gus thinking: his father is a murderer. She repeated her story about an older white boy running, shouting, "I'll get you."

"The white boy is the son of a veteran police officer," Gus said. "He claims he chased Monk—that's what he calls Thelonious—Monk."

"He saw a man shot, and he chased after an armed assailant?" Donna said. "Does that sound reasonable?"

"No, it doesn't," Gus admitted.

"You said there were three boys. Where were the other two witnesses during all that?" Donna argued. "I only saw the one white boy running."

"Good point," Gus said.

"Another beer, Gus?" Barry offered.

"Don't mind if I do." The detective changed the subject. "You know, the press is saying Katrina was the worst natural disaster in American history. Thing is, it was an unnatural disaster, a man-made failure. If the levees hadn't collapsed, we'd have come through the storm in good shape."

Somewhere out in the city a siren warbled. Donna was sick of screaming sirens, blaring klaxons, and the whump of helicopter blades.

Chainsaws whined endlessly as workmen cleared streets. The noise was constant and wore on her nerves. Then late at night, when silence finally came upon the dark city, it was like living in a void.

"They've finally evacuated the poorest segment of this city," Gus continued. "The thing of it is, poor people are what gave New Orleans the exotic food and unique music we love. The day the Ninth Ward died, the soul of the city died with it. People think we can re-create the culture that made jazz and zydeco. But you can't fake the complexities of several hundred years of suffering and surviving. Even if those people come back, there are no jobs for them and no houses to live in. Schools have been destroyed or severely damaged. Hospitals and medical care are nonexistent."

"The schools weren't good anyway," Barry said.

"But who's going to make them better, Hampton?"

Donna's concern wasn't the local culture. She was worried about a nine-year-old boy accused of murder. Where was he? Was he scared, hungry? He could be hurt and to whom would he turn for comfort? Certainly not his father.

Dean had always said he didn't want Thelonious to know he was in prison. He wouldn't write to the child, nor would he accept letters Donna had written to him.

The last time she saw her brother, a few days before he went on trial, Dean said, "I am dead. Think of me that way. My life is over."

The first year after he was convicted, she wrote to him every week, but he never answered. Eventually, her letters were returned unopened, and she gave up trying to communicate.

"Businesses can't get money or materials to make repairs," Gus droned on. "There's nobody to haul away trash and clean the streets. Rumor is, of twenty-seven major corporations with headquarters here, only a few intend to return. Shell Oil says they will. Most of the others have pulled out for good. Hell, I don't blame them. We had problems with crime before and it's worse every day. Who wants to live in a city that looks like a Third World country? If the corporations leave, there goes our tax base. If they return, who's going to work for them? The labor force is gone. Assuming they work out those problems, there's no assurance the levees won't fail again with the next hurricane. This is a wretched mess, Hampton."

"People who grew up here will want to come back, Gus."

"Maybe. I don't see it."

"They'll try, Gus."

Donna's head pounded. Her stomach was upset. When flesh touched flesh, it stuck. She sat with legs spread so her inner thighs wouldn't adhere to one another. While she and Barry were out of town she'd bought a loose fitting summer dress in an attempt to be cool. Wearing it now, she was thankful for the drape of fabric to keep her knees away from one another.

"Gentlemen," Donna said, "I hate to break this up, but you're visiting in my bedroom."

The detective stood up and drained his beer can. "Now, it looks like we might have another one coming."

"Another what?" Donna asked.

"Hurricane. Her name is Rita. The weather bureau says it will become a category five and may be headed straight for us."

Donna felt a wave of exhaustion. "Go away, Gus. I can't stand anymore."

She urged him to the stairs and he descended with heavy footfalls. "Lock the door on your way out, Gus."

"Right-o."

She sat on the top step, pressure pounding her temples from within. Behind her, Barry called, "Want a brew?"

"No."

Whether it was reasonable or not, she blamed Dean for what she was going through. He'd jilted Gail Winthrop to marry a woman he hardly knew. When the family disapproved he withdrew, and the schism between them had deepened ever since. Dean had made a fateful choice, and everything now, including Donna's misery here in New Orleans, was a result of his early decisions.

It struck her that by now she'd probably lost her job in Atlanta. She hadn't telephoned the school to say she was still here looking for her nephew. Bob Miller must be worried about her.

He would worry.

Wouldn't he?

She heard a strange rhythmic sound and turned to look back into shadows of the office.

"Barry, what're you doing?"

"It's a surprise."

She stood up and felt her way through the darkened space.

Barry grinned at her, and his teeth caught the lantern light like luminous pearls on a string.

He pointed at the floor.

It was an inflatable mattress. He flapped a sheet in the air and spread it loosely.

She let him take her into his arms and he poked the mattress with a foot. "Not too firm, not too soft," he said.

"It's awfully warm, Barry."

He smelled of charcoal smoke, grilled steak, and beer. He eased her down on the inflated cushion and put a pillow beneath her head. "There," he said, "isn't that comfortable? It's cool down here on the floor."

"I didn't see the mattress or the pillow in the car," she said.

"No," he grinned. "Because it was a surprise."

When it came to surprises, nothing seemed to catch Barry off guard. The *Probe* was an epicenter for genetic oddity and abnormality. He'd been around the extraordinary for so long monstrosity was commonplace. He found joy in the most grotesque subjects. She couldn't imagine him being surprised by anything.

"What's the most surprising thing that ever happened to you as a child?" she asked.

He stopped moving. "This seems a strange time to ponder that question, Donna. Is it something I'm doing?"

"I wondered if you're ever surprised by anything," she said.

He paused in place. "Well, let me think. I was surprised just now when you asked that question. I was surprised when I met you in Hattiesburg trying to get into New Orleans during a hurricane. I knew right then, you were my kind of girl."

He resumed his activity, and Donna recalled a line from Lord Byron:

A little still she strove, and much repented,
And whispering "I will ne'er consent"—
consented.

{CHAPTER NINETEEN}

Monk stood on the drawbridge in afternoon sun looking across a shallow lake that was the Ninth Ward. His gaze followed men in rowboats as they searched for survivors, but the only living things they found were half-starved pets terrified of the strangers trying to grab them.

At a bend in the river a seagoing ship blew a horn to warn of their approach to the Industrial Canal. The giant vessel was surprisingly quiet in passing. Seamen on deck coiled lines and stowed gear preparing for a cruise outbound. Monk had always wished he could get on a ship like that and sail away to foreign ports. Uncle Earl said sometimes they hired cabin boys, if a parent gave permission. There was no chance that would happen to him without a parent to agree to his wish.

The flood level in the Ninth Ward was lower today and dead things had begun to surface. Flies swarmed around the bodies of cats and dogs. Dead birds were nothing but feathers and bones, completely stripped of meat by ants. A sickening stench clung to the nostrils and fouled his clothes. Monk covered his nose and breathed through his mouth.

He hoped to see someone he knew. He'd made a mental list of everyone in his life by order of those most likely to take him in. He was not encouraged. He couldn't get to Percy Brown's house, which was farther into the Ninth Ward than Grandmama's. Since Percy wasn't with his uncle when Randy Bernard shot Earl, Monk was afraid that Percy was dead too.

Aunt Bishop Beulah's Blessed Jesus Spiritual Church was often swamped by summertime rain. Surely it was underwater too. Aunt Bishop Beulah and her husband, Willy Bouchard, lived in back of the sanctuary because the building was their residence before she made it into a church. Mr. Willy told Grandmama they'd be leaving, but they might not have. Sister Julianne and Cherita lived only a few doors away. Monk thought they probably drowned, too. The last time he saw Cherita's daddy, Mr. Benoit was outside his time saver store begging for a boat to go find them.

Every day Monk had come to the drawbridge to gauge the depth of water, and every day he'd gone by Quinton Toussaint's. Quinton's house was still locked shut.

Walking back to Jon's apartment was like wandering through a junkyard. The City of New Orleans was a pile of rubbish since the storm. Kitchen appliances, upholstered chairs, couches, mattresses, and carpets lay in muddy heaps. In flooded sections of town, buildings with broken windows and open doors seemed to gape at passersby.

Utility workers from other states had come to help clear trees from the streets and repair electrical lines. The smells of split wood and pine sap made Monk think of Christmas trees. He pushed the thought away. He had all the grief he could stand without memories of Grandmama baking cookies while he decorated a tree for the holidays.

Most residents still had no electricity and people cooked on outdoor grills. The aroma of broiled meat brought saliva to the tongue and an ache to his abdomen. It was dusk and a few neighbors sat on their front steps and talked to one another in low voices.

Another storm coming, Monk overheard them say. Levees might break again.

Near Jackson Square some stores had opened, but without tourists for customers, the owners stood in their doorways looking sad. Grocers at the French Market sold what was left of canned and dry foods. A sign hung in the front window of a delicatessen: "CORRECT CHANGE ONLY."

On Rampart Street, and also at the Convention Center, army trucks brought in packaged ice, bottled water, and fuel for lanterns. Several times, Monk had warily approached an army truck to get ready-to-eat meals.

"Where're your parents, son?"

"Home."

"What's your address?"

The soldiers didn't know New Orleans. Monk said, "Esplanade."

A couple of times a National Guardsman called for someone else to come talk to Monk, and he ran off without the food he came for.

Clinics were set up to inoculate people against diseases. Signs read, Tetanus Shot Here. Monk wasn't about to go there.

Breaking into apartments had become more dangerous. Jon had been threatened with a gun. Monk told Jon he wanted to do the invading from now on.

"No," Jon said.

"They might shoot you, Jon; they won't shoot me."

"No."

"I run as fast as you." That was not true, but Monk said it anyway. "I can get away easier than you." That wasn't true, either.

"No," Jon insisted.

Before the storm, Jon had prowled through dumpsters behind restaurants. The trouble was, restaurants weren't cooking. Dumpsters were flooded and the contents rotten.

"From now on," Monk offered, "I'll slip into places. You be the spy boy and look out for me."

"No," Jon said.

It was the return of electric power that changed Jon's mind. Lights exposed him. He was tall, bearded, with glowering dark eyes, and his appearance frightened people. After a few nights searching unsuccessfully for empty apartments, Jon yielded.

Monk's first attempts were clumsy. He didn't have the strength to open stuck windows or doors. He was so frightened his legs trembled and hands shook. But across an alley up on a nearby rooftop, Jon was watching. He didn't want to look afraid.

Once inside a home, the first thing Monk did was peek in bedrooms to be sure nobody was there asleep. He figured if he woke someone in the dark they might shoot first and see he was a small boy later. But then one evening he didn't notice a man sleeping on a couch and walked right by. In the kitchen, Monk dropped a can of food in a stainless steel sink. It made a terrible racket. Lights came on.

Monk wheeled to face a very big man dressed only in underwear. He had hairy arms and an aluminum baseball bat. He swore softly and held up the bat with both hands. Monk grabbed the food sack, ducked under a table, and scampered for an open window. He heard the bat bash a cabinet.

Out the window and down a fire escape, he met Jon coming up. "Run," Jon said, and put himself between Monk and the man in pursuit.

"Let's both run, Jon!"

Later, catching his breath after they climbed to a rooftop, Monk said, "You shouldn't have come for me, Jon. Next time let me escape by myself."

"No more," Jon wheezed.

"I would've gotten away all right," Monk insisted.

Jon seized Monk by the shoulders and shook him. "No more," he said.

His ferocity was frightening. "Okay, Jon. No more."

The next day Monk went out alone and stole half a case of bottled water from an army vehicle. After midnight he went back to climb inside a huge military truck looking for food. A guard blinded him in the beam of a flashlight. Terrified, Monk dropped the rations.

"Everything is free, son," the guardsman said. "What do you need?"

"Food."

The soldier climbed into the truck, and Monk dashed past him and jumped out.

"I'm getting it for you," the guard called. "Hold on a minute."

Monk shrank into shadows as a second soldier came over. "Who're you yelling at, Martin?"

"A kid trying to steal food. I told him it's free, but he took off."

"Put it on the ground and leave it."

"Hey, boy," the first soldier called, "here it is. You can have it."

After they walked away Monk grabbed as much as he could carry and ran. Through parking lots, up the levee, past the old Jax Brewery, he rounded Jackson Square. A police car came toward him and Monk wiggled through a fence and raced down an alley. Behind him the cop turned a searchlight into the alcove. Monk crouched.

"Think I should go after him?" he heard a cop question his partner.

"Nah. Just a kid."

Monk waited until they drove off, and then hurried on to Jon's.

The apartment was empty. Monk lit a candle, opened an army meal and ate the wedge of chocolate it contained. He heard something scurry in the kitchen. He'd grown accustomed to sharing the apartment with critters. Jon ignored every creature except those that bit him, like mosquitoes. Monk once saw him scoop a mouse out of the bathtub and let it go. The fat little rodent paused as if grateful, then waddled away across the floor.

Monk washed down the army meal with lukewarm bottled water. He bathed himself in alcohol. He'd come to like the smell of wintergreen; it left him feeling cool and clean.

He placed the sack of MREs where Jon would see them, blew out the candle, and went to bed.

Two mornings later, Monk woke to a vague uneasiness, the same feeling he had before Katrina. He was hot and yet the air felt cool. He heard the low moan of an updraft in the ventilation shaft. Outside on the balcony he watched a fine mist drift down from steel-gray clouds. Wind gusts seized the rain and hurled it like grains of sand. Behind him in the apartment, Jon sat up on the side of his bed.

"Another hurricane is coming, Jon."

Jon mumbled and yawned. He scratched his beard, chest, and armpits.

They needed many things. The last candles were waxy puddles in lids of jars, the wicks so short Monk couldn't light them anymore. They were out of plastic grocery bags to line the toilet bucket. Food was running low. Jon refused to go out before night and most apartments were occupied except when residents were away for the day.

Owners of the café downstairs had been cleaning the kitchen. Out of the shaft came the metallic odor of a grill scoured with pumice. Now and then the vent fan started up with a jolt, the belt squealing for traction before turning the blades. When it stopped running, Monk's ears hummed. He climbed quietly through the vent shaft so they wouldn't know he was up here. Crossing the roof in a torrent of rain, he was quickly soaked.

Water poured from eaves and gurgled in downspouts. He reminded himself to be careful because so many people were home again. Passing through an attic he saw a sliver of light shine up from below and went over to peek down at a woman about to have breakfast. She sliced a banana on top of corn flakes and doused the cereal with condensed milk from a can. He was hungry, but not starving. He couldn't stand evaporated milk.

In every dwelling where he heard residents, TV news reported on the weather. Hurricane Rita is a category five storm … 175 mile per hour winds … expected to make landfall along the Texas-Louisiana Gulf Coast day after tomorrow.

At a dormer, he dared to peek inside. A couple still in bed watched television with the sound turned off.

"I can't take another storm," the woman said.

"We'll leave tomorrow morning," the man replied.

Monk made mental note: tomorrow there'd be food here for the taking.

He ran through the rain and didn't stop until he reached Quinton's house. He took cover on the porch, and then knocked. Where was Quinton?

Over on the railroad tracks Monk trudged with head down to avoid the stinging pelt of rain. His wet clothes stuck to his body and brisk winds chilled him. He worried that the Ninth Ward would flood again, and indeed, when he got to the drawbridge, the water had deepened from yesterday.

If he was ever going to Grandmama's, he decided, he had to do it now even if it meant wading in murky water. He followed the levee over ground he'd covered getting out of Holy Cross—how long ago? It seemed months had passed. At last, he was three blocks from Grandmama's house. Monk slid down the embankment, pushed through a tangle of weeds, and crossed a soggy yard. Water was ankle-deep in most places, up to his knees otherwise.

On the outside of Grandmama's house somebody had painted a giant "X" with orange spray paint. He read the date, 9/16, and a note: "One dead." The message paralyzed him. Grandmama was dead, and that's all it said? He had to force himself to breathe.

The sky was darkening. Lightning zigzagged across the horizon so far distant the thunder was a soft grumble. Near the levee were several houses built in three tiers, like layers of a wedding cake. The highest floor was the smallest with a view of the levee and river beyond. He didn't know the tiered-home owners by name. He knew they were rich and rode around in Mercedes and Cadillacs. White people came to mow their lawns and prune shrubs. They hired maids to clean house. Workmen repaired their fences and painted gingerbread trim.

"They're nice folks," Grandmama once said. "But we leave them alone, and they appreciate that."

Another bolt of lightning flashed, and this time Monk heard a clap of thunder. The raindrops were larger, downpour heavier.

He stood in the deluge looking at the painted message: one dead.

That would be Grandmama.

A car was still lodged in the back door, hanging over the porch and steps. Somebody had jimmied open the trunk. Monk eased around it and squeezed into the kitchen.

Sticky mud sucked at his bare feet. A horrible stink made him hold his breath. As his eyes adjusted to dim light, he saw pots and pans scattered across the floor. Grandmama's cookbook was a soggy pulp. Cabinet doors hung open. The refrigerator was tilted. Monk waded back to the porch door, exhaled, and took another deep breath of fresh air.

He thought how distressed Grandmama would be if she knew this terrible odor came from her. She bathed everyday, sometimes twice a day, and she always smelled good.

Standing in the kitchen, Monk threw himself at the porch door again and gasped for another breath.

Grandmama's kitchen was always spotless. How many times had he watched her take apart the stove to reach down deep and scour inside? His feet slipped on mud and he fell to one knee. His throat closed. He blinked away tears and swallowed a hard lump.

The hall was a black hole. Was she there? Oh, God—was she there?

He dashed back to the door for another breath, gagged and retched, but his stomach was empty, he had nothing to give. He had rubbed against the muddy car, table, and refrigerator. His hands were covered with an awful, smelly slime, but there was nowhere to wipe them.

He was here to get his money!

Set a goal and let nothing distract you, Quinton always said. He was talking about a career in music, but the lesson applied to anything. To get inside his bedroom, Monk would have to pass below the attic trapdoor. What if Grandmama was still stuck there? The chest of drawers blocked his way and he'd have to climb over that and under Grandmama if she was up there.

All of a sudden, in a panic, he wanted out of that hallway, out of the kitchen, and into the yard. There wasn't enough money in the world to make him go under Grandmama. He slipped and fell and clawed his way toward the door.

In a flash of lightning he saw the painted X: one dead.

He fell to his knees in the yard and scooped puddled water over his arms and chest. Streaks of electricity formed a spider's web of lightning and waves of thunder rolled above him. Might he be struck and killed? All right if he was! He'd be with Grandmama. He looked up at the sky and let rain splash onto his face.

The pain of this—the way he hurt—he'd never felt such a deep unrelenting ache. He screamed and the wind and rain and thunder carried away his voice.

Aunt Bishop Beulah preached, "Ask and you shall receive."

"God! Give back my grandmama. I'll never ask for anything again. Please! Don't take Grandmama."

It wasn't going to happen. He knew before he prayed it wasn't going to happen. Sister Julianne told stories in home school about the Holocaust, when Jewish people were put into rooms to be gassed to death. Some turned away from their own faith and prayed to Jesus, but they died anyway. Others appealed directly to God and they weren't saved either.

Grandmama wasn't coming back; he knew that.

He wished he could go with her.

He trudged straight through the Bywater. He didn't look for gang boys and didn't care if they saw him. Mr. Benoit's time saver was just as it had been days ago, the broken glass door propped open with a concrete block. Lightning streaked so near Monk smelled flint, and a crash of thunder shuddered his bones.

Drenched, cold, and sad, he walked down the middle of the street. The Dollar General Store was still boarded up, plywood covered broken windows and ruptured doors. He went through Faubourg Marigny to Esplanade. At Quinton's he shouted at the dark house, "Where are you?"

Another strike of lightning cleaved the heavens with a sound like the split of a ripe melon, followed by a deafening clap of thunder. The street flooded as it often did in heavy rain. Monk slogged into the Quarter through floating trash.

Upstairs, Jon played his cardboard piano again. When he saw Monk dripping wet and empty-handed, he grinned and turned to boogie-woogie. Monk could tell by his expression he expected a dance. Jon traced the keys with a finger and returned to the beat.

This time, Monk didn't hear the music.

After a few minutes, Jon realized Monk wasn't going to respond and he stopped. His head fell forward and with chin to chest, he played one of the classical pieces he enjoyed.

Monk went in and fell on the bed.

Gales ripped awnings and snatched tarpaulins from roofs already damaged by the first hurricane. Torrents of rain pummeled the city. Several levees were topped, and once again parts of the Lower Ninth Ward flooded.

Hurricane Katrina had frightened people. This time there were no hurricane parties. Nobody joked and drank and partied. This time, when they were told to evacuate, they went.

Bad weather for everybody else, it was perfect for Jon.

Barefoot and soaked, Monk followed him on a raid for supplies. Jon moved across roofs in his curious sidewise gait, looking for empty buildings.

They discovered a box of heavy-duty plastic leaf bags in someone's pantry and began to fill them. When the bags were too heavy to carry comfortably, they returned home to drop off the booty, and went right out again. Soon they had enough of everything to last for several days.

They rested under the wide eave of a two-story structure. A screen of water poured past them into a courtyard below. The noise of pounding rain and howling wind was deafening, but reassuring. They could not be overheard, and nobody was out and about to catch them. Monk shivered and Jon put an arm around him to provide warmth.

They began again, on the eastern end of Vieux Carré, near Quinton's house, entering homes they'd never plundered before. The cupboards of well-to-do residents were filled with canned fruits and meats. Monk helped himself to toilet tissue nine rolls in a package. Jon found red high heel shoes to take home for his collection.

Monk carried the lighter of their bags, and Jon led the way. He looked like a funny, skinny half-drowned Santa Claus under bulging sacks. Wind whipped street signs and loose objects skittered along the banquettes.

"Cop!" Monk shouted, and they ducked into an alley.

It was a dead end with no balconies. No trellis to climb. They were trapped, but the cops didn't see, or didn't care, and they drove on by.

Jon said what he always said after a close call, "Whew!"

They should've stopped. Jon's apartment was filled with stolen supplies. But the storm was perfect cover during daylight hours, and who knew when they'd have such an opportunity again?

Storm clouds lifted, and the wind eased. Monk followed Jon east toward Esplanade. Twice they spied patrol cars and had to hide.

Because the territory was new to Jon, he hadn't tested the strength of wrought iron banisters and the wood to which they were anchored. He climbed aloft as agilely here as he did on familiar grounds deep in the Quarter.

From his high perch he reached down to help Monk climb up beside him. Next door, a woman yelled, "Get the cat. The cat got out!"

Jon listened for a moment and then released Monk's wrist. "Enough," he said, and turned to climb down again. Suddenly, bolts yanked out of water-softened wood and Jon grappled for a hold. He hit the ground on his feet, but off-balance, collapsed on the brick courtyard, and rolled on his side. His left leg was twisted at an odd angle.

Monk scrambled down as far as he could, and then dropped the rest of the way. Jon lay in drizzling rain. He tried to turn over and cried out in agony. "My leg."

Below the knee his leg jutted at an unnatural angle. The sight of it turned Monk's stomach. "What should I do, Jon?"

Jon's eyes rolled back and he swore loudly.

"Should I go for a doctor, Jon?"

Jon dragged himself to a wall and propped against it. "Quinton," he said. "Go to Quinton."

{CHAPTER TWENTY}

Donna woke to a sound so alien it confused her. She rolled over on the inflated mattress, listening. Telephones were ringing. Barry roused up, walked to a desk, and answered, "Probe."

Then he said, "Yeah, hey, Art."

Two days ago the eye of Hurricane Rita had gone ashore west of New Orleans, sparing them the brunt of a second storm. In certain areas breached levees and heavy rain caused more flooding. Now, the sun rose brightly. Office lights came on. Through open windows a cool, fresh breeze stirred the air.

Donna rolled off the mattress and gathered her clothes.

Barry hung up the telephone. "That was Art Findley, our editor. The staff is coming back to reopen the office next week."

She put on denim trousers and a T-shirt.

"That means I have to go to work answering telephones at the very least, Donna. I won't be able to help look for your nephew."

Using small amounts of bottled water, she brushed her teeth.

"We'll have to move out of this place," Barry grumped. "I suggest we run by my house and see what shape it's in."

Several telephones rang at the same time. Barry answered one, "Probe." A second later he said, "The office is closed because of the storm. Can you call back next Monday?"

He repeated the message in one phone after another.

Donna felt exposed, as though the world could suddenly see her. She heard a knock at the door downstairs and went to answer. Across the street a shopkeeper washed his windows. Two women joggers in running shorts ran down Bourbon Street. Detective Gus Warner leaned on a lamppost, watching them.

"Come in, Gus."

Warner followed her upstairs and caught Barry in his underwear, still answering telephones.

"I came by to see if you'd found the kid," Gus explained.

"We haven't," Donna said.

"I've taken depositions from witnesses who claim they saw Thelonious shoot Earl Thibodeaux," Gus reported. "There's a warrant out for his apprehension. In a few days every cop in the city will be on the lookout. We'll catch him before long."

"They won't hurt him, will they, Gus?"

"If he threatens them with a gun, they will. They'd be stupid not to."

Barry dressed while the telephones continued to ring, incessantly. "Should I help answer those, Barry?" she asked.

"No. Hey! You look different in this light. Doesn't she, Gus?"

"Blue tint. It's the fluorescents, I think."

Barry shortened his message and went from one ringing phone to another: "The office is closed. Call back next week."

"I did background on the boys who've accused Thelonious," Gus said to Donna. "Two are from the Bywater; the policeman's son, Randy Bernard, is a New Orleans kid. They're all truants and run in a pack. They wanted to know if there was a reward for turning in Thelonious. Randy Bernard's father was a guard at Angola before he came to New Orleans and joined the police force. Soon as I get permission from him, I'll do a polygraph on his son."

"You think he's lying?" Donna asked.

"We'll know when we get a polygraph. Kids usually buckle when faced with a lie detector. Let's hope Thelonious isn't found until we get the truth sorted out."

After Gus left, Donna and Barry headed down Bourbon to get her car.

"You know what Gus is saying," Barry said. "He's telling you to find Thelonious quickly, and get out of town."

"He didn't say that."

"But that was his message, Donna. If cops get the kid before you do, he'll be in the juvenile court system until they decide his future. There's no telling where he'll end up. Baton Rouge, probably, but he could be sent anywhere in Louisiana, caught in a system that is inefficient at best. The process will take weeks, perhaps months."

Months. "What day is it, Barry?"

"Tuesday, September 27th."

"I've been here twenty-eight days," she said. "It feels like a year. I've probably lost my job."

They passed a woman walking a dog. Donna thought what a pleasure it was to see an ordinary pedestrian. Huge street sweepers cleaned gutters. The city was wet and in shock, but struggling to get going again.

"What will your parents say when you show up in Atlanta with your brother's son?" Barry asked.

"What kind of question is that?"

"By things you've said," he reasoned, "I assume they resented Tooth being married to an African-American woman. How will they react if a black child comes into their lives?"

Donna bristled. "My parents aren't racists, Barry."

"How will they feel taking a mulatto boy shopping at the mall? Or going to a sporting event at his school? What will be the reaction of their neighbors when Thelonious takes a white girl out on a date? Or a black girl, for that matter? Will they cringe when he calls them grandmama and granddaddy?"

Donna had come to New Orleans thinking Thelonious and his grandmother needed a temporary safe haven. She hadn't considered sheltering Thelonious for an extended period of time.

After a long silence she said, "I love my brother. I'll do whatever Dean expects of me."

"That's a good point. What does he expect? Is he going to take a more active role in the boy's life?"

"He's somewhat restricted, Barry."

"He could write letters. He can talk on the telephone. Thelonious can visit him. Tooth abandoned his son to the care of his wife's mother. Now he's shifted that responsibility to you."

Were these not some of the thoughts, albeit subconscious, she'd already had?

They climbed six floors up the elevated garage. The car was as she'd left it. A note on the windshield said move the vehicle or it would be impounded.

"No problem," Barry said. "From now on we'll park at my house."

The weekend visit of Hurricane Rita left the city rain-washed, but relatively intact. Driving to Barry's house, Donna maneuvered her car around street crews who, for the second time in four weeks, cleared debris from St. Charles Avenue. The morning calm was shattered by a shrill screech of chainsaws and heavy industrial shredders as they pruned and pulverized. The smell of hewn wood recalled memories of Dean's boyhood hobby, building musical instruments. She still had a zither he'd made for her, and a rather crude ukulele constructed from plywood.

"Turn here, Donna," Barry instructed. His home was a block from Tulane University. The street was puddled, muddy, and slippery. Lawns that had once been carefully tended were now dead or dying, covered with a greasy, odiferous blanket of flood residue. At his direction, she pulled into a driveway and drove around back to an empty garage.

His house was on a slight elevation, built up off the ground. When they reached the porch, Barry unlocked the door, looked inside, and grinned. "I am one lucky rascal," he said. The flood had reached the porch, but didn't get inside.

He flipped light switches. "Still no electricity," he noted.

Like a realtor conducting a tour, he named the rooms as Donna followed. "Kitchen, downstairs bath, my office-at-home."

The place had the musty smell of a basement, but it wasn't moldy. He was lucky. "Umm," Barry commented. "The refrigerator and freezer need to go out. I can smell them with the doors shut."

"When we came out this way the first day," Donna observed, "you said you could tell the place was flooded."

"The houses around us were under water. I assumed my house was, too."

Upstairs were four bedrooms with two baths. In one room a canopy-covered bed and sheer curtains lent a feminine touch. The closet door was open and Donna saw dresses. It looked as if his wife had just stepped out. Barry followed her gaze to a hairbrush and perfumes. He put the items into a drawer.

"You don't have to change anything, Barry."

"I never felt the need to until now. What do you think? Can we stay here?"

"It's nice."

For several days, he'd been posing questions with an eye to "do we have a future together?" He didn't say those words, but it was a subcurrent to everything spoken.

"What will you do with Thelonious when you find him?" he'd asked.

"I guess it depends on the kind of boy he is," Donna said. "I imagine he'll live with me for now."

"You've never even seen a photo of the kid. What if he's a hulking, sulking juvenile filled with antisocial angst, will you want to take him in anyway?"

It was her worst fear verbalized. "I'll have to wait and see, Barry."

She stood in the feminine bedroom looking at photographs on a dresser, pictures of Barry with people she didn't know. Everybody seemed so happy. Barry and a pretty woman shared a kayak on a river run. Riding a lift at a ski slope. Playing tennis. They were an active, healthy couple.

He caught her staring and Donna said, "Is this your wife?"

"Cathy," he answered. "I think I told you, we were married almost twenty years."

"You look happy together."

"We were," he said. "My life began when she came into it and ended the day she died. When I met you I felt renewed. I dared hope again."

There. It was out in the open, now. "Maybe you should know me longer than a few weeks before you make that judgment, Barry."

"Twenty-seven days, twelve hours," he consulted his watch, "thirty-two minutes and two hurricanes later, I have confirmed what I thought the moment I fed you a doughnut in Hattiesburg, Mississippi."

"Relationships forged under duress are subject to review when things calm down," she cautioned.

"I'm calm."

"Let me ask a hypothetical question," Donna said. "Suppose I find Thelonious and take him in. Would you be happy as a surrogate father to a nine-year-old boy you don't know?"

"Every child needs a father."

"A boy approaching his teens can be a handful. I've taught a lot of them in Atlanta schools."

He looked away, and by his expression, she saw reluctance.

"I'm not a Boy Scout leader," he said. "Mankind has advanced too far for me to give up air conditioning and color TV to go camp in the forest with wood ticks and tykes. Little League baseball is out of my realm of interest. I'm more of a billiards and backyard barbecue guy."

"You look athletic enough in these photographs."

"I did those things because Cathy wanted to."

"Then I guess the question is, would you want to do similar activities with a nine-year-old boy?"

"If you're asking whether I'd make a good father, I don't know. But I can tell you, I'll make a great husband."

"Are you proposing marriage, Barry?"

"Eventually."

"Would you move to Atlanta with me?" she asked.

He hesitated. "If that's what I have to do to be with you, I guess I would. Let me turn that around. Would you stay in New Orleans with me?"

"I don't know."

"Okay," he said. "When you know, we'll have this discussion again."

In the hours that followed, for the first time, they began to have serious conversations about themselves. While they wrestled his refrigerator out to the sidewalk, Barry said he'd gotten a degree in journalism at the University of Missouri. Driving back and forth from the Probe with personal items, she learned he came to New Orleans for the music, food, and ultimately Cathy, whom he met when she was a student at Tulane University. The house had been hers, Barry revealed, inherited from her father, a professor of English literature.

"I took a job at the *Probe* because I couldn't get work at the *Times-Picayune*," Barry said. "A year or two later when I had a chance to move over there, I had to admit to myself that I enjoyed working for a tabloid. I've been with the *Probe* ever since."

He turned questions back to Thelonious. "How long will you look for him?"

"I don't know."

"If you never find him, what then?"

"That's a horrible thought, Barry."

"But a realistic one. The boy may be dead. The kids who said they saw him shoot somebody could be mistaken. If he's alive, Thelonious might be in Seattle or New York City, already settled into a new family somewhere."

That night, she made the bed with clean sheets and lay next to Barry, wide-awake and tense.

"What's wrong?" he asked.

"I can't sleep knowing your wife is over there on the dresser watching us."

He got up, gathered photos and took them down the hall to another room. When he returned, he said, "I loved Cathy, but I'm not being unfaithful to her. She would be happy for me knowing that I'm here with you. Which reminds me, have you ever been married?"

"No."

"Who is Lionel?"

"Lionel? I don't know a Lionel."

"You speak about him in your sleep," Barry said.

"I never heard of anybody named Lionel. What did I say?"

"You said, please move, Barry, you're lionel my arm."

He said he loved her, which was ridiculous after only twenty-seven days twelve hours et cetera. But the funny thing was—funny strange, not ha-ha—the funny thing was, he immediately became more appealing to her.

The next morning Donna dropped him off at the Probe and drove around New Orleans alone, watching for young African-American boys. In the French Quarter there were no children to be seen. Meanwhile, driving aimlessly, she tried to analyze what had changed with Barry. He still made corny jokes. He continued to chatter constantly, but there seemed to be more substance to what he said. One of the most perplexing things he did was to talk while they made love.

"You are the sexiest woman I ever knew," he murmured at a most unpropitious moment. "I love the lobes of your ears. They feel like gumdrops on my tongue. You have that one dimple on the left cheek. Did you cultivate that or—"

"Will you shut up?" she said. "Concentrate."

"I am concentrating. Most people have two dimples or no dimples. You have one dimple. When you were a child, did you poke your cheek with a finger to make a dimple? Hmm-mm, you feel good, woman."

Because she had not attended Dean's trial, Donna had never known the whole truth about the charges against him. Being excluded from his life was the most hurtful thing in a series of hurtful things Dean had done: jilting Gail Winthrop, marrying out of his race, killing a man—

She knew her relationship with Barry had changed when she confided these unhappy thoughts to him.

"We'd always been so close," she said. "If Dean got a headache, I began to hurt too. If he was thirsty, I wanted something to drink. When he was happy, so was I. Then, suddenly, he shoved me out of his life."

"Maybe he was trying to protect you," Barry said.

"He would probably say that," Donna agreed. "But in fact, it compounded the pain I felt. The only news I had about the trial came from reading the *Times-Picayune* online. Dean wouldn't discuss the matter with me."

"I'll tell you what the prosecutor told the jury," Barry offered. "Tooth's wife, Elaine, had been singing since she was a child. She performed professionally and loved it. Then, for a reason she didn't understand, after appearing in public hundreds of times, she began to suffer stage fright."

He spoke as they strolled across St. Charles Avenue to Audubon Park, "to feed the mosquitoes," Barry said. It was dusk; the air was absolutely still and warm. His voice was soft and low-pitched in the gloaming.

"Because Elaine was having jitters about going onstage," Barry continued, "her manager gave her a pill to settle her nerves. The next time she had a show to do, even before she became nervous, she wanted one of those pills. Over a period of months, the pills changed to increasing strength. That's the story the prosecutor put before the jury. The manager was trying to help the girl through a difficult phase. The truth was something else."

Mosquitoes, love bugs, and biting flies turned them back toward home.

"Everyone who knew the murdered man knew what he was," Barry said. "Killing him should've been morally justifiable homicide. He was a worthless piece of humanity. He latched onto Elaine when she was a child prodigy, directing her career and feeding her drugs when she was in her teens. That was his control over her. Tooth knew nothing about that until the bastard had Elaine hooked on the tough stuff, cocaine and heroine."

Barry finished the discourse at his house. "Tooth tried to wean Elaine off the dope. Sent her to rehab, spent a fortune trying to break the bonds, and she'd do well for a while. For example, she stayed clean throughout her pregnancy with Thelonious, but after the kid was born she relapsed."

Barry fired up the hibachi and put on their last two steaks. Fumes from the burning charcoal drove away insects.

"Over the years," he said, "Elaine had snorted coke, smoked weed, dabbled in LSD, but never mainlined. She had a TV show coming up. A lot of folks thought it would catapult her to international prominence. She was nervous and under a lot of pressure. The manager loaded her up with Percodan, Dilaudid, and finally, a pure heroin off the street. It killed her."

The steaks sizzled over charcoal. Donna stared into glowing embers.

"Tooth loved that woman," Barry declared. "But he shouldn't have killed the sonofabitch. He deprived his motherless son of a father, and I find that hard to understand. The murder was premeditated—he had to hunt down the guy over several days. The prosecutor called it revenge. Public sentiment was on Tooth's side. Probably the jury was too, until they were told he'd orphaned his three-year-old son. If Tooth had waited for the law to take that man to court, Elaine's manager would be in prison today, and Tooth would be home raising Thelonious. Of course, then I wouldn't have met you."

"If you'd been in Dean's place," Donna asked, "what would you have done?"

"Oh, I would've wanted to kill the pusher."

"But you wouldn't have killed him?"

"Honestly, I don't know, Donna. But if I had done it, I would've tried to get away with it. Tooth shot the guy in front of witnesses, and then went home to wait for police to come arrest him. He didn't plead temporary insanity or mitigating circumstances. His attorney admitted he killed the creep, he just didn't make a case as to why, and Tooth showed no remorse whatsoever. You know, in the Deep South, lawyers used to say, 'He needed killing,' was a valid defense. Tooth's lawyer did a lousy job showing that the manager needed killing."

He turned the steaks and fat sputtered on hot charcoal. "The prosecutor made Tooth look like a manipulator rather than a despondent husband who had been deprived of the most precious thing in his life. The main reason Tooth lost sympathy was the kid. He apparently didn't give a thought to his son. The prosecution hammered that point repeatedly. Tooth was a selfish, single-minded control freak, that's the thought jurors took with them when they retired for deliberation."

"You think he should've gotten off?" Donna asked.

"No. He should've served time, but less of it."

While they were eating steaks, the electricity came on. The house flooded with light and outside street lamps brightened the neighborhood. It should've been a festive moment but it came in the midst of a disturbing conversation.

This had been a day of mixed emotions.

Donna drove to the grandmother's address on Andry Street in the Lower Ninth Ward. From her car she saw the orange "X" painted on an outside wall. "One dead." The message stopped her heart. One dead, a stingy epithet. A rusting vehicle was wedged into the back porch. Mud had covered everything and dried to an ugly gray-brown veneer. Across the street a neighbor worked on his house. Donna walked over and introduced herself.

He was an elderly man, stoop-shouldered and unshaven. His flesh was the deep ebony of anthracite. He wore a gauze mask to avoid noxious odors and poisonous dust. When Donna spoke to him, he pulled off the mask. Creases in his face testified to years of exposure out-of-doors.

"Did you know Diane James and her grandson?" she asked.

"Everybody knew Miss James and Monk."

"On the house it says 'one dead,'" Donna said. "Who died there?"

"National Guard folks found Miss James stuck in a hole trying to get in the attic out the water. They never found Monk."

"Do you think he might have survived?"

"I don't see how. We lost three people around the corner from me.

My best friend died in his place down the street. All told, seven of my neighbors drowned right here in Holy Cross, maybe more. They found another body day before yesterday. The water came up so fast there wasn't time to get away."

"How did you survive?"

"I wasn't here. I always knew those levees might give way. I left."

Donna looked back at the grandmother's house. What a horror it must've been for Mrs. James, gasping for air as floodwaters drove her to the ceiling where she foundered and drowned. Maybe Thelonious was dead after all.

Standing in the street looking at the small house that had been their home, she wondered what authorities did with so many bodies. Would there ever be a ceremony to bid them good-bye? The only memorial to mark the passing of its victims was this house with that oddly placed automobile sticking out of the back porch.

She returned to her car and sat watching the old man work on his place across the street. He picked up a small limb and shuffled out to the edge of his yard where he placed it on a pile of other limbs. He returned to the house, stooped for another piece of trash and trudged back to the street in short, sliding steps. Donna felt like she was observing Sisyphus, doomed to push a stone uphill only to have it topple down again.

The agony of it all, the loss these people had suffered, was unbearable. She wondered if Monk could still be alive. If he was, how was she going to find him?

{CHAPTER TWENTY-ONE}

Monk ran through the most recent debris to Quinton's house and confirmed what he already knew. Quinton was not home. In the meantime, Jon had crawled under an azalea bush to hide. He'd covered himself with black leaf bags. Monk returned to lie beside him. The rain cleared, and bright sunshine dried the ground around them. Monk heard the woman who'd lost her cat come out to call, "Here, kitty, kitty; come to mama."

His clothes had been wet and dried so often they were stiff and scratching his skin. Lying under the bush with Jon, he heard people talking, cars passing on the street out front. The woman came nearer, calling, "Come to mama, kitty, kitty, kitty, come to mama."

Suddenly, Monk's face was full of cat. The animal was a longhaired calico with yellow, black, and white fur. She arched her back and rubbed against his cheek, purring.

"Kitty, kitty, kitty," the cat's owner was just beyond the courtyard wall. For fear she'd come onto the patio searching for her pet, Monk pushed the animal away. It came back, tail high, purring. Jon pulled farther into the shrub and tried to adjust his position slightly. He trembled with the effort.

"Come to mama, kitty."

The cat droned, Jon groaned, and the lady peered over the wall, calling, "Kitty, kitty, kitty."

Monk pushed the cat again and it darted across the patio, bounding up the wall into the lady's arms. "There you are! Come on, sweet baby, let's go home."

Monk turned on his side and whispered, "Are you ready to go, Jon? There aren't many people." Jon didn't answer. There was no point pressuring him, he wasn't coming out in daylight.

Finally, at sundown, Jon struggled upright and used Monk for a crutch. His weight bore down on Monk's shoulder as they limped toward Esplanade.

To be sure Jon had understood, Monk said, "Remember I told you, Quinton isn't home."

It didn't matter; that's where they were going.

Monk was thirsty and hungry. His stomach growled. Under the pressure of Jon's weight, his shoulder ached as they hobbled one painful step at a time. Every few feet, Jon stopped and sank to the ground, making low mournful sounds. Diamond-bright stars winked down from the sky, and Monk thought of nights when he and Grandmama sat in the backyard studying constellations for Sister Julianne's science class.

When Jon regained his strength, he arose, limped, hopped, and then sat down to rest again. It took all night, but they finally reached the house at daybreak.

Jon and Monk both collapsed on Quinton's back porch. After a moment, Jon looked down at his oddly angled leg. "Pull my foot, Monk."

"No. It'll hurt you."

"Do it."

Monk lifted the swollen ankle and tugged gently.

"Pull hard!" Jon cried.

Monk held the foot and leaned back. Jon slapped at him. "Damn it, Monk. Yank it."

He did, and Jon cursed. "Pull," he ordered.

"I did pull, Jon."

"Straighten it," Jon said.

Monk held the foot, leaned back, and yanked. In agony, Jon slapped the porch floor, wailed, and fainted.

While he was unconscious, Monk snatched the leg so hard the lower part moved and it was straight again. Jon woke and groaned. His face was gray as ash. "God," he said.

Monk made a decision. He would never consider breaking into Quinton's house for selfish reasons. But he was sure the historian would understand if he broke in for Jon.

"I'm going to smash a window and get inside, Jon."

"Wait." Jon hauled himself up on the porch railing and limped over to a wrought iron trellis. He felt underneath and removed a magnetized box. He opened it, dumped a key into Monk's hand, and replaced the container.

"You knew about a key?" But of course he did, Monk realized; he and Quinton had been friends since Jon was a boy. Monk unlocked the door and an unpleasant odor drove him back. The memory of Grandmama's house made him queasy. "There's something dead in there," he said.

Jon leaned on Monk and pushed him inside. A generator kicked on and the refrigerator hummed. Monk helped Jon through the kitchen out into the hallway.

When they reached the hall, Jon sank into an overstuffed chair and motioned for a hassock. "Water," he said hoarsely. Monk helped him lift the broken leg onto a footstool.

In the kitchen under a table Monk found four cases of store-bought bottled water. While Jon sipped liquid, Monk gulped water from another bottle and explored a walk-in pantry. Shelves from floor to ceiling were filled with canned foods. Crockery canisters contained teabags, coffee beans, sugar, and flour. He flipped a switch and lights came on.

"Turn it off," Jon snarled. Then, more gently, he said, "Somebody might see."

"The kitchen is full of food, Jon. Do you want me to get you something to eat, and find aspirin? I can go upstairs." He made the offer even though he thought the awful smell was coming from up there.

"No. Stay down here."

Monk wandered onto the back porch. In a storage room he discovered the generator. A sign on the wall warned, "Carbon monoxide. Do not block the vent." While he stood there the motor started again, ran a minute, and stopped. The exhaust went through a hole to the exterior.

Back in the house again, Monk dared to open an avocado-colored refrigerator. The interior light revealed champagne, bottled beer, soft drinks in cans, and a drawer filled with cheeses and sealed packages of sandwich meats. A note on a rack said, "Do not touch without permission from Quinton."

"Jon!" he yelled. "Food in the refrigerator is still good."

Monk tore open a pack of bologna and crammed his mouth full. He unwrapped a wedge of cheese, ignored mold on the edge, and ate hungrily. Cold root beer washed it down.

He took another can of cola into the hall. "Jon?" He walked through the den, living room, and Quinton's office. "Where are you?"

Monk hollered up the staircase, "Are you up there?"

The foul odor grew stronger as he climbed stairs.

Quinton liked heavy furniture, picture frames, marble lamps. At one end of the wide upstairs hall two soft leather chairs and a coffee table made a sitting area. Off each side of the space were bedrooms with opened transoms above closed doors. Monk found Jon sitting on a king-size bed in a large room with high ceilings.

"I brought you a cold drink," Monk said. "Did you find aspirin?"

A light glowed beneath a bathroom door. Monk started toward it.

"Stop!" Jon demanded.

Frightened, Monk said, "What is it?" Jon was crying.

"Quinton," Monk realized. He stared at the sliver of light beneath the door.

"In the bathroom?" he said. "Is he dead, Jon?"

Jon sobbed. "Yes."

For a long time Jon wept while Monk sat beside him. He patted Jon's shoulder, moaning with pain and shock, but tears would not come. Jon pulled a blanket off the bed to block space under the bathroom door. Still sniffling, he closed the transom and shut off the bedroom.

Monk felt he should apologize for something, but wasn't sure what. He'd invaded Quinton's home, but he was certain the historian wouldn't mind. After all, he expected Monk to look after Jon someday, and someday was now. If Aunt Bishop Beulah was right about the way things worked, spirits watch over the living, and Quinton would certainly recognize their needs.

For their use, Jon chose a bedroom down the hall. In the adjacent tiled bathroom was a deep tub with a high back and feet shaped like a lion's paws. The faucet coughed, spit, and spewed yellow water. Monk filled the tub and sank up to his chin. He sat in the dark and soaked, listening to Jon weeping in the adjoining room.

Surely Quinton would understand the situation. Monk came here because of Jon's hurt leg. They hadn't come to steal, although the pantry full of food would not go to waste. Since Quinton's absence was permanent, Monk would look around the house for his father's recordings, and if he could figure out how, he would play them.

Monk scooped hot water over his face and dug in his ear with a finger. This bath and bedroom were obviously meant for guests. He had turned on the light long enough to see little bottles of shampoo and conditioner arranged on doilies beside the tub. Embroidered hand towels hung on the racks.

In a sermon, Aunt Bishop Beulah once preached that all wrongs are pardoned upon death. When spirits moved to another plane, she said, they looked back and understood the weaknesses of others. In which case, Quinton should forgive Monk if he poked around looking for Tooth DeCay's recordings. Nevertheless, it wouldn't hurt to soothe Quinton just a little.

Monk whispered, "I wish you were here to show me how to play the music if I find it, Quinton. I'm glad you let me be your friend, and I wish you hadn't died."

In the event spirits could read the selfish thoughts in his mind, Monk said, "It's all right that you let Percy play the piano like you did. I guess I was jealous." He still was, when he thought about it. "And listen, Quinton, if you see my grandmama, tell her I love her. She died, too. Earl Thibodeaux, did you know him? He was murdered."

What more could he say to a dead man?

Monk stood in front of the refrigerator with the door open, wondering what to make for Jon's breakfast. A knock at the back door jolted him. Exposed by light from the refrigerator, he shut the door and flattened himself against a wall. A man called, "Yoo-hoo, Sweetie-Cue! Are you home?"

He recognized the waiter from Clover Grill whose friend had taken Quinton's sterling silver sugar bowl and creamer. The waiter rapped again.

"Hello, Sweetie-Cue," the visitor called. He moved to a window, cupped his hands against the glass, and tried to peer in. He gave up and went around to the front porch. Monk hurried to the living room and watched from behind heavy drapes. The waiter wrote a note and stuck it in the mailbox on the porch, which was already stuffed with mail.

After he left, Monk peeked out, and then grabbed the note:

> Thinking of you, Sweetie-Cue. When you get home,
> come by the Clover Grill. We're open again.
> Love, Merlin

He took the message upstairs to Jon, and Jon said put it back in the mailbox.

"There's a lot of mail in the box, Jon."

"Leave it there."

Downstairs, Monk removed the light bulb in the refrigerator so he wouldn't get caught exposed like that again. In the freezer he found loaves of bread. He toasted half a dozen slices, brewed hot tea, set it all on a tray along with a stick of butter and a jar of orange marmalade. Carefully taking small steps so as not to spill the tea, he mounted the stairs and delivered the tray to Jon.

"I made toast for my grandmama sometimes," Monk explained. "At home I used the oven. Here, Quinton has a toaster, so it's easy."

Jon pulled up on the headboard, propped himself with pillows, and buttered toast while Monk watched. Then he said the longest sentence he'd ever spoken to Monk.

"If the police catch us here, we won't have Quinton to say it's all right."

It was one more thing to worry about, along with gang boys, how to retrieve his money jar, and finding Tooth DeCay.

Later, while Monk washed dishes, someone tapped on the front door. A woman tried to peek in windows. Monk had closed the drapes, so he saw her but she couldn't see him. She looked at Quinton's mail, read the waiter's note, and placed it back in the box.

She returned that afternoon. By then Monk remembered he'd seen her on Bourbon Street at the Probe. Why would she come here, he wondered.

It kept him on edge. He didn't dare use a light anywhere in the house, and he had to tiptoe from room to room. In the kitchen, he handled dishes and pans very carefully so any unexpected visitor would not hear him clattering about.

As was his habit, Jon got up at night, eating aspirin by the dozen. He said the pain killers made his ears ring, but the leg didn't hurt as much.

The two of them drank many bottles of water, but thirst could not be quenched. Monk bathed so many times his flesh puckered and his skin squeaked when he rubbed it with a finger.

When Jon ran low on aspirin, Monk volunteered to go into Quinton's bathroom to search for more. There was no need, Jon insisted. His leg felt better.

It wasn't true. In his sleep he tried to turn over and woke up yelling.

Monk searched for aspirin in the baths downstairs and the pantry, with no luck. Jon writhed in agony.

Grandmama always said, "A hot bath does more to mend a man than medicine can."

He ran a tub of water and helped Jon into it. Jon drank Quinton's beer to numb the hurting. His beard and scalp itched, so Monk gave him a shampoo. He had to wash and rinse three times to get lather, and throughout, Jon protested. Monk scrubbed Jon's back and head as Grandmama had once washed his, and after several beers Jon began to find it funny. He squirted Monk with a flexible hose on the spigot, which Monk had used to rinse him off.

Jon limped back to bed. Monk gently lifted the leg and covered the man with a sheet. A few minutes later, flat on his back, Jon snored so loud Monk could hear him down the hall. He shut the door to muffle the sound.

The only place Monk hadn't looked for aspirin was Quinton's bathroom. He didn't want to go in there, but Jon's leg was so tender even breathing made him hurt.

In Quinton's dark bedroom an electric clock blinked the same numbers over and over. Monk unplugged it. He took a deep breath and felt his way to the blanket blocking the bottom of the bathroom door. He wasn't sure whether the bad odor had diminished, or he'd gotten used to it. It was ridiculous to knock, but he couldn't bring himself to enter without announcing his presence. Hair bristled on the back of his neck as he called softly, "Quinton? I have to come in."

He pushed open the door and light blinded him. The bad smell was still here. Monk held his breath. He avoided looking at the tub. He heard water from the spigot trickle and overflow as it drained away. Despite his intention not to look, out of a corner of his eye he saw a black blob and one discolored arm hanging over the tub.

He quickly checked the medicine cabinet. Good. Two unopened bottles of aspirin. Leaving the bathroom, Monk said, "I'm sorry, Quinton."

He closed the door, blocked the base, and went to Quinton's closet. When he opened the heavy doors, a light came on automatically. The closet smelled like cedar. Monk selected trousers that were too short for Jon and too long for himself, but better than nothing. He gathered shirts and underwear from bureau drawers. Jon's snore rumbled down the corridor.

Standing in the hallway, Monk changed into fresh clothes, rolled up the trousers and shirtsleeves. He dropped his old clothes into a wastebasket and left the aspirin on Jon's bedside table. Walking quietly was becoming a habit. He tiptoed downstairs to the grand piano.

Oh, how he would love to pound those keys with boogie-woogie, but he dared not. He covered the strings with two lap blankets from a couch. He closed the lid and struck middle-C. It sounded a subdued note.

Grandmama would've been proud; he practiced before he played for pleasure. Sitting in the dark, he ran through chords and scales, and then simple melodies, repeating routines that bored him. As he tapped the keys, he thought of Grandmama listening as she always had, ready to correct him if he made a mistake. His fingers were stiff and he stretched for notes. Warmed up at last, he began to play the music he most enjoyed. He imagined Grandmama tapping a foot and nodding in time to the tune. He played for her.

Jon came in and listened. When Monk finished the piece, Jon sat beside him, his bad leg extended to the side. He smelled of beer. He touched a key, then another.

"Play, Jon."

Jon ran a short refrain and the muted strings delivered a quiet response. He began with something Monk did not recognize, heavy with chords, too slow for dancing.

"What is that?" he asked.

"Mozart."

"Mozart! You play that kind of music, Jon?"

The style changed, and Jon said, "Shostakovich."

"Ugh, Jon."

Jon smiled. Again the style changed, and Jon's fingers skipped across the keyboard like dragonflies flitting over flowers. "Beethoven," he said.

"How about boogie-woogie?" Monk insisted.

At last he played something upbeat, "William Tell Overture," Jon said. "The Lone Ranger." But Monk didn't know the music or the ranger.

Jon switched to another quick tempo piece and identified it as "Offenbach. Can-Can."

"That's better," Monk said, "but it isn't boogie."

But suddenly it was, the beat that grabbed Monk and held him, boogie-woogie! He jumped up to dance and Jon switched tempo and tune.

Disappointed, Monk sat down again and watched him play.

Long into the evening without a page of music, Jon played. The pain of his leg seemed forgotten. It was not for himself he performed, Monk was pretty sure of that. Jon played and he wept. It was for Quinton.

Monk had one memory of his father. Tooth playing the piano and crying. Every piece was a slow, aching melody. Monk remembered climbing onto his father's lap. He put his hands on top of his father's hands, riding the music from one sad note to the next. Watching Jon grieve for Quinton, the old, faint memory took shape again in Monk's mind.

He went to the couch, closed his eyes, and fell asleep.

The next morning, Jon came downstairs bleary-eyed and reeking of liquor. He swallowed aspirin with champagne; the beer was gone. Monk warmed cans of chicken noodle soup and opened a box of saltine crackers. He sliced cheese and put a jar of olives on the table. Jon mouthed food around bad teeth.

"Tastes good, Monk."

They spoke in murmurs, and good that they did. A knock at the back door made them freeze. The kitchen was dark, and outside sunlight bright, so the caller couldn't see in.

"It's that woman from the newspaper office on Bourbon Street," Monk whispered.

She was a pretty white woman with shiny eyes the same honey color as her hair. She tried to peek through the glass, and for a moment Monk thought she looked like a picture framed in the pane. He watched her step into the backyard and gaze up at the second and third floors. She walked down the driveway, and from the hall window he saw her go next door.

After a few minutes, she and the neighbor came out onto the sidewalk together and talked. As she spoke, she tilted her head to the side and smiled. Now and then she reached out with a gesture so warm and friendly, Monk wished it could be his arm she touched. He'd watched Uncle Earl in the company of pretty women as he waved his hands too much and ducked his chin as though bashful. The neighbor was enchanted. He gestured the same way as Uncle Earl. Monk saw him shrug his shoulders as though helpless to say where Quinton Toussaint might be.

They both turned in his direction, and startled, Monk stepped back from the window. They'd done nothing to make him think he'd been seen. Nevertheless, he had a sinking feeling. Did the curtain move? Had they spied his face in the shadows?

He peeked out again. The man rocked back and forth, heel to toe, evidently hypnotized by his guest. Again, she reached over and touched him. It was an endearing gesture, and this time her hand remained on his arm for several seconds. It was like watching a puppy get his tummy scratched.

Behind him, Jon had come into the room. "Did she see you?" he asked.

"I don't think so."

"Maybe we should leave," Jon said.

There was food in the pantry; the bed was comfortable, bathwater hot and plentiful. The thought of giving it up was so distressing, Monk said, "I think we're safer here than we were at your place, Jon."

It probably wasn't true, but Jon was willing to yield. He sat at the piano, a bottle of champagne on the bench beside him.

Monk looked out from behind the drapes. The man and woman were still talking …

{CHAPTER TWENTY-TWO}

Donna stood on the sidewalk in the cool shade of fractured oaks talking to Paul Ussery, Quinton Toussaint's next-door neighbor. Mr. Ussery didn't want to converse on the front porch, he said, because his wife was still sleeping, and she wasn't feeling well. He was unshaven, wearing a faded yellow golf shirt, his middle drifting over a belt. He wore blue shower shoes and his toes kept going up and down as he talked.

"I've lived next door to Quinton for fifty-five years," his bushy eyebrows lifted in syncopation with the toes. "We speak and wave, but he has never been a close friend. Still, you get to know somebody living next door for five-and-a-half decades, you know what I mean?"

The trees were filled with twittering, chirping, and whistling birds. "This is a migratory flyway," Ussery explained. He indicated the spattered sidewalk and said, "Fowl-weather time." He laughed at his own attempt at humor and then returned to her inquiry.

"I never thought Quinton would leave town for a hurricane," he said. "Maybe he's gotten old. Times past, he'd batten down the hatches and hunker in, or more likely, throw a party. We've been through a few storms in our day, and neither of us ever dodged a hard blow. That includes Hurricane Betsy in '65. At the height of every storm I'd look over at night and see Quinton's flashlight flicker from room to room as he checked for leaks and broken windows. A few years ago, he invested in an industrial generator and a thousand-gallon fuel tank." He pointed, and Donna saw the tank camouflaged by a low fence at the rear and off to one side of the house.

The breeze subsided and she smelled the mature-male-morning-musk of the man. "He told me once that he keeps plenty of food and fresh water on hand," Ussery said. "He called it his end-of-the-world syndrome. He was always ready for a storm. With Katrina bearing down on us, Mayor Nagin couldn't make up his mind about ordering an evacuation. The first advisories suggested people might want to leave. For the ten-thousandth time we were reminded that New Orleans is below sea level. There were the usual warnings of the potential for flooding and wind damage. The next thing we know, the mayor is hysterical. Evacuation is mandatory. Everybody must go. Get out! It's the worst storm ever! Maybe it scared Quinton. I haven't seen him since a day or two before the hurricane made landfall."

"You have no idea where he might've gone?" Donna questioned.

"None whatsoever. So far as I know, he has no family. There's an effete entourage that flows to his house for all festivities and holidays." He lifted a hand, wrist limp. "La-de-dah, know what I mean?"

"Genteel," Donna offered.

"Quinton chases talent like some men chase women," Ussery said. "He socialized with the (limp wrist again) boys, but it was talent that attracted him. He's associated with Tipitina's recording studios so he was always looking for performers who could do something better than everybody else. Have you talked to anyone at Tipitina's?"

"No."

Purple bird manure landed on Ussery's shoulder, but he failed to notice, and she didn't mention it, tried not to react, but it was like watching a dinner companion who is oblivious to spaghetti in his moustache.

"Somebody at Tipitina's might know Quinton's whereabouts," Ussery suggested. "He was also a regular customer at the Clover Grill. They may know something."

Birds flitted and flew. Droppings speckled the sidewalk, but so far she'd not been hit. Esplanade was almost completely cleared of debris. It was a beautiful street of solid old homes, some converted to bed and breakfast inns. A pleasant breeze blew her hair.

"Quinton's got money," Ussery chattered on. "He can afford to hop a plane and go anywhere in the world. In younger days he ran back and forth to Paris on vacation. Wherever he is, you can bet it's a five-star hotel with a superb chef. He makes perfection a fetish. Look at his house."

She followed his gesture.

"It's as perfect now as it was the day they sank the last nail in 1879. Even after a hurricane, there's not a shingle missing. Quinton hires somebody to power wash all three floors every spring. Painters come in to touch up. I wasn't the least surprised to find a little black boy cleaning the yard right after the storm. Only Quinton Toussaint would arrange to have someone spiffy up the grounds in his absence."

Donna's heartbeat quickened. "You said a boy? Do you know his name?"

"I didn't ask. It's a child Quinton spends a lot of time with. Mulatto kid, nine, ten, twelve, maybe younger."

Donna watched him gaze away for a moment. "It occurs to me," he said, "maybe you should contact our attorney, Ormand Delacroix. Quinton and I use the same legal firm. Ormand is mostly retired, but he still keeps an office in the business district. He's hard of hearing, so you have to raise your voice to communicate. If anybody knows about Quinton, it'll be Ormand."

"Thank you, Mr. Ussery."

She stepped carefully down the soiled sidewalk going to her car. The din of the birds had suddenly gone from melodious to raucous. When she glanced back, Ussery was still there, belly protruding, watching her depart. As Donna drove away, they waved at one another.

Ormand Delacroix answered his telephone in a gravelly baritone. When Donna said she was looking for Quinton Toussaint, the attorney rumbled, "Ah, yes, my dear friend, Quinton." He agreed to see her immediately.

His office was at 909 Poydras, a building graced with a colonnade of oak trees, a walkway of natural stone, and large bronze statues on either side of the entrance. Rising thirty-six floors into purest blue sky, the façade was mahogany-colored Dakota granite with alternating bronze-tinted glass. It was beautiful, and it reeked of money.

Ormand Delacroix was waiting when she stepped out of an elevator on the twenty-third floor. He looked to be about eighty years old, with a full head of snow-white hair, a thin moustache, and a crooked smile that gave him a mischievous charm. A flirtatious twinkle sparkled in cerulean eyes. He took her hand and held it, leading Donna down a carpeted hallway.

"Paul Ussery telephoned to say you'd be calling," he said, as though Quinton's neighbor was a mutual friend of hers. "He indicated you're worried about Quinton."

"Uh, yes," Donna stammered. "Mr. Ussery said Mr. Toussaint has never run from a storm, but he hasn't been seen for several weeks. Perhaps he's inside his house, ill or hurt." She remembered the attorney was hard of hearing and raised her voice, "I hoped that Mr. Toussaint could help locate my nephew."

Delacroix winced. "You need not shout. I have a state-of-the-art digital hearing aid that cost more than a first-class Mediterranean cruise. The Cajun otologist who sold it to me said that I would be able to hear a juror whisper at thirty feet. He was right; as the old joke goes, my heirs didn't know I could hear them, and I've changed my will three times. How do you happen to know Quinton Toussaint?"

"He's a friend of my brother, Dean DeCay."

Delacroix's smile vanished and she watched the twinkle wane from blue eyes. He studied her soberly as if looking for ulterior intent, and then said, "After Ussery called, I tried to reach Quinton by telephone and there was no answer. It's not unusual for him to unplug the phones. He hates talking on the wire. I assume you've never met Quinton?"

"No, I haven't. My brother asked me to contact Mr. Toussaint in hopes of finding Dean's son, Thelonious."

Delacroix settled into a leather executive chair behind a kidney-shaped desk. Through office windows still speckled by storm debris, she saw the Mississippi River and Central Business District far below. Here and there windows of nearby buildings remained boarded, and on the roofs she saw litter left by high winds.

"I haven't spoken to Dean since his conviction," Delacroix said, grimly. "How is he?"

"He's anxious about his son."

"I don't remember meeting you at his trial, Miss DeCay." The remark had the sting of an accusation.

"Dean didn't want me there."

"How unfortunate that you and your family couldn't attend. But you stayed away to comply with his wishes?"

It wasn't altogether true, but she said, "That's right."

"Tooth came across to the jury as an artistic oddball with strange friends," the attorney said. "Quinton sat right behind him, a toucan in turquoise, his appearance more distracting than supportive.

Delacroix laced together soft looking hands with manicured fingernails. He scrutinized her as he rocked gently in his chair. To deflect implied criticism, Donna said, "What is your relationship with Dean, Mr. Delacroix?"

"I defended him against the charge of murder."

"And lost, obviously."

"Yes, I lost, but I do not accept responsibility for it. The jury looked around the courtroom for somebody who cared about Dean DeCay and there was nobody. Not you, or his parents, or his wife's relatives. If you had sat there cradling Dean's son in your lap, it would've been good for a bit of sympathy, which we desperately needed. Your brother was not easy to defend. Early on, the prosecutor wanted to plea bargain to manslaughter and Dean refused despite the fact he was charged with premeditated murder. Had he accepted, he would've been incarcerated for seven years instead of twenty. After he was convicted, his friends blamed me because we didn't take the offer."

"What kind of criminal lawyer are you?"

"I'm not a criminal lawyer. I make my living in civil court, mostly investment management and corporate mergers."

"After Dean's conviction, did you appeal?"

"He wouldn't allow it. He wasn't going to spend his money on lawyers, he said. In the past, I had drawn up contracts for him. I composed his will. I handled probate of his wife's estate. Closed the sale on his house when he bought it, closed the sale when he sold it. I urged him to get an experienced defense team, and he insisted I was what he wanted."

Donna realized she had clenched her fists. She forced herself to straighten the fingers.

"Dean was depressed and thought his life was over," Delacroix recalled. "In fact the police had him on suicide watch for several weeks. He was surly, overtly rude to people, insulting to the court, and did nothing to endear himself to anybody. Your brother is an inflexible, single-minded fool."

"Yes," Donna admitted. "He can be."

"All right," the attorney's mood changed abruptly and the flirty smile returned. "We need a policeman and a locksmith. Let me telephone the Broad Street station and see if I can get a cop to join us at Quinton's house."

He did that, and then called the concierge in the lobby. "This is Delacroix," he said into the receiver. "I need my car and driver."

He was steady on his feet and once more he was back to being the affable old gent who greeted her half an hour ago. Descending twenty-three floors in the elevator, Delacroix said, "I haven't been to Quinton's home since your brother signed a recording contract years ago. What a shame, a terrible waste of intellect and talent. Dean had such a promising future."

Ormand Delacroix's car was a sixty-year-old Rolls Royce limousine with a glass partition between the chauffeur and passengers in the rear seat. The driver wore a uniform that was color-coordinated with the silver and gray vehicle. As they pulled out of the garage, the attorney never let conversation lapse.

"The real tragedy in this city is something you cannot see, Miss DeCay." He waved a hand toward buildings still unoccupied. "It is a tragedy that may foreshadow dissolution of the union someday. After the hurricane, the federal government sent in Blackwater Security," he said. "Do you know who they are?"

"I don't think so."

"They're the mercenary bodyguards who protect politicians and diplomats in dangerous countries like Afghanistan and Iraq. Blackwater is good at what they do; up to now they've never lost a client despite gunfight and bomb assaults. I don't know whether it's true or not, but they have a reputation for brutality. Their enemies call them professional assassins. They answer to nobody. They came into New Orleans in unmarked and unlicensed vehicles, heavily armed, and with a strictly business attitude.

We were told they were invited because of snipers shooting at rescue workers and citizens on the sidewalks. That turned out to be a false rumor perpetuated by careless news reporters."

The limo moved slowly, circling the French Quarter by way of North Rampart. Although a third of the residents had returned, the city still felt sluggish and empty.

"The Blackwater fellows seized an apartment to use for their headquarters," Delacroix continued. "They picked out a place, and without permission from anybody they moved in. There were things in the residence they didn't want, so they began to throw furniture and personal possessions into the street. The owner was understandably upset about that and wanted to sue. But Blackwater is not constrained by American law. They don't answer to anybody. It would've cost a fortune to bring suit against them."

He peered out his car window for a moment, eyes narrowed against the colorless light of the September afternoon. "We're in a hell of a legal mess these days, Miss DeCay. President Bush suspended habeas corpus to avoid bringing imprisoned terrorists to trial. This is how dictatorships get started. I fear the worst for America."

Over on the sidewalk, Donna saw an overweight man riding a rusted old-fashioned single-speed bicycle. He stopped to pick up an aluminum can, put it into the bicycle basket, and then pedaled into Armstrong Park.

"Not everybody has been hurt by the hurricane," Delacroix commented. "Blackwater got a lucrative federal contract. New Orleans has been good duty for them. It's safer here than it was in Baghdad, where some of them had been only a few weeks ago."

A police car passed and turned onto Esplanade. Delacroix's driver fell in behind him.

"I have a neighbor in the Garden District who came through the hurricane without losing electricity or her telephone," the attorney mused. "Yesterday she told me she didn't see what all the fuss was about. There was nothing wrong in her world, except now she can't get help to clean her yard."

The chauffeur parked behind the police car and came around to open Donna's door. A panel truck marked "LOCKSMITH" was in the driveway. Delacroix continued talking as they strolled toward the front porch.

"My pampered neighbor's husband is one of the so-called Drunken Santas who celebrate Christmas in July. They called her their Ho-Ho-Ho. I don't think she ever caught on to what that was about."

The police officer waited patiently for attention. Delacroix said, "We fear that the owner, Mr. Quinton Toussaint, might be incapacitated. Have the locksmith open the door and please go through the house to be sure there is nothing amiss."

"Yes sir, Mr. Delacroix."

The moment the door opened, Donna knew Toussaint was dead. The faint but unmistakable odor turned her aside. Delacroix pulled a handkerchief from his pocket and gave it to her. The policeman stepped into the hall and turned on lights as he advanced from room to room.

It was a home of exquisite taste. Velvet drapes and brocade tapestries, marble and brass statuary, crystal chandeliers, ornately framed original oil paintings. A concert-size grand piano dominated the den, but on the polished lid sat an empty champagne bottle. There were crumbs on the bench and crust of an uneaten sandwich in a plate on the floor. The policeman pressed the bread with a finger and said, "This is fresh. Somebody's here."

Dirty dishes were in the sink, a goblet had been abandoned on the table half-filled with cold orange juice, the contents so fresh the glass condensed moisture.

"I'm calling for backup," the cop said. He did so, and then loosened the pistol in his holster and headed cautiously upstairs. "This is the police," he yelled. "Step out where I can see you." He kept his hand on the weapon.

To Delacroix he said, "The smell is coming from up here."

Repelled and yet drawn to follow, Donna pressed Delacroix's handkerchief to her nose. In the hallway she saw dirty clothes in a heap. Outside, sirens yodeled as patrol cars approached.

"Don't touch anything," the policeman cautioned Delacroix. He stood at the top of the stairs and called down to new arrivals, "Check around for an intruder, then come up here."

There was evidence of habitation in a bedroom down the hall. A wastebasket overflowed with empty aspirin bottles, used facial tissues, beer cans, and champagne and wine bottles. There were towels on the bathroom floor, and the mirror was steamed as though someone had just finished a bath. Clothes hung over a cedar chest.

From downstairs rose a male voice, “Clear down below!”

The first policeman yelled, “Come on up!” He entered another bedroom. A moment later he came out and shut the door. “The deceased is in the bathtub,” he reported. “We need to be sure this is not a felony, so don’t go in there, Mr. Delacroix.”

“No, of course not.”

The policemen hollered up and down the stairs announcing, “Medical examiner … ambulance … detective …”

“I think someone else is here,” one officer said to another.

“No sign of breaking and entering,” the other advised. “But somebody has been cooking and eating.”

They searched the second floor, under beds, into closets, until there was no other place to go but a narrow paneled stairwell rising sharply to a third level.

The first officer advanced cautiously, pistol drawn. “Police!” he yelled. “Coming up. Police!” A second cop was close behind. Donna saw them flip a switch and lights ignited the top of the steps.

“Police!” they hollered.

She dared not go up, but stood at the bottom of the stairwell listening to their progress. She heard the scrape of heavy things being moved about.

“Hold it,” somebody shouted. “Don’t move!”

“Keep your hands where I can see them. Lie down.”

“Hit the floor, you sonofabitch! Lie down.”

A moment later she heard a scream and two of the cops dragged a handcuffed man down the steps. “My leg,” the bearded captive cried. “Broke leg!” But they yanked him roughly, the one leg bumping, the prisoner wailing.

Her heart hammered, breathing difficult. In the attic Donna heard a policeman curse and he hollered, “Here’s another one!” Suddenly, leaping down the stairs, a child hurdled into her arms and Donna reeled under his weight and momentum.

He tried to wrest free, but she clutched him firmly.

“Let go,” he yelled.

Upstairs, a male voice shouted, “Did you catch him?”

Donna said, “Thelonious?”

The boy stiffened.

"Are you Thelonious?"

He was a handsome child, with dark brown eyes, lightly tanned and with an even complexion, wavy black hair. He wore clothes ridiculously large, but within those folds she felt a wiry body, taut and strong.

Policemen stood ready to help her. By the way the child looked at them, Donna recognized an expression she'd seen on the faces of many inner-city youngsters. He was terrified.

"I won't let anyone hurt you," she promised. Her grasp was tight, but gentle. "I'm your friend," she said, and smiled. "My name is Donna. I am your father's sister."

He stared up at her, and then burst into tears.

{CHAPTER TWENTY-THREE}

Two white policemen put Monk in the rear seat of a patrol car and slammed the door. He scrambled to the far side only to realize he was in a cage with no way out. A grill separated him from the front seat. The cops got in, took off their hats, and faced forward. Monk stared at the backs of their pink closely shaved heads.

"What happened to Jon?" Monk demanded.

"Is that the man you were with?"

"His leg is broken," Monk yelled through the wire.

"Are you related to him?"

Monk remembered advice Uncle Earl offered long ago, "If cops catch you, watch what you say. They use it against you."

"Where do you live?" one cop asked.

Monk stared out the car window.

"You and that old fellow have been stealing in the Quarter. Is that where you got the gun?"

It was a trick. There was no gun.

"What did you do with the weapon?" the driver asked.

People on the street looked at Monk curiously as the police car passed.

One officer muttered, "Tough already."

The other said, "They learn early. What did you expect?"

Monk recalled stories about beatings and confessions forced from innocent men. "The only crimes cops can solve are the ones they commit themselves," Uncle Earl often said.

They delivered Monk to a small room with a tiled floor and flickering fluorescent lights installed behind a wire cage in the ceiling. There were two chairs facing one another on either side of a metal table that was welded to the wall. In a large mirror he saw his shaggy hair, baggy trousers rolled up to the knees, and Quinton's oversized shirt drooped around his shoulders. Beyond the mirror he sensed people watching. In a movie he'd seen on Percy's TV he learned about two-way mirrors. For the benefit of a possible audience he faked a yawn.

A black lady cop came in. She was thick through the chest with wide flat breasts and big feet set in sturdy shoes. She smelled like spice. Tightly braided cornrows held up her eyebrows so she looked surprised.

"I need the name of your closest kin," she said.

He had to think a minute. Was an aunt closer than a grandmother? He didn't know anything about the aunt, and Grandmama was dead. So he said nothing.

"What is their name, little bro?"

He stared at his reflection in the two-way mirror. He imagined cameras recording every move.

"You're already in trouble," she said. "Unless you want more of the same, you'd better cooperate."

He wouldn't have been surprised had she thrown him to the floor and kicked him, seized him by the throat and hurled him against a wall. He saw that happen on TV at Percy's, too. Monk could hear the thump of his heart. His nose burned as though he'd been breathing frigid winter air. Finally, the lady cop stood up and towered over him. "Suit yourself, little shit." The door lock clicked behind her.

He counted holes in the ceiling tile. There were a hundred forty-four holes in each square. He used the mirror to correct his posture, wiping an expression off his face that he thought betrayed fear.

The door opened and a gruff looking white man came in. He put a ring binder notebook on the table and sat down heavily.

"Thelonious, I'm Detective Gus Warner," the man said. He looked like an old bulldog. His cheeks jiggled when he talked, and he had watery eyes set in baggy folds of flesh. His jaw stuck out so far Monk could see his bottom teeth. "I'm not here to accuse you of anything," he said. "In fact, I'm here to see that you aren't accused of something unjustly. Do you understand?"

"I guess so."

"Do you know Earl Thibodeaux?"

"He's Percy Brown's uncle."

The detective stared hard at him. "Did you shoot Earl Thibodeaux?"

"Randy Bernard shot him."

"How do you know that?"

"I saw him do it."

"If you saw him, why didn't you report it to police?"

"His daddy is a cop. Randy can get away with anything. Mr. Bernard knows men at Angola who will hurt a person for a few dollars cash money."

The detective continued to stare as though watching for a lie from Monk's lips. "Randy and two other boys say they saw you shoot Earl Thibodeaux, Thelonious. That's three witnesses against you."

"They belong to the same gang. Randy shot Uncle Earl and they all know it. Randy was pushing me around one day and Uncle Earl jumped on him. They didn't like one another, that's why Randy shot him."

"Do you have a gun, Thelonious?"

"No."

"Have you ever fired a pistol?"

"No sir."

"Okay, lad. Sit tight. We're trying to round up a judge."

"What will happen to Jon Latour?" Monk worried.

"Does he talk to you?"

"If he has something to say, he does."

"Does Latour own a pistol?"

"I don't think so. I never saw one."

"You and Latour have been breaking into homes. What did you take?"

"Food."

He wrote it down, murmuring, "Food."

"And clothes. Some red shoes."

"Red shoes?"

"Jon puts the shoes in his oven because that's where his mama put her red shoes when they got wet. What will they do to him?"

"Set the broken bone, clean him up, and feed him. He'll be all right."

The detective's eyelids looked droopy. His cheeks quivered. "Did Latour ever hurt you, Thelonious?"

"No sir."

"All right." Warner stood up. "Someone will come and get you when the judge arrives. Are you hungry?"

He was, but Monk said, "No sir." As a second thought he added, "Jon might be. He hadn't finished eating when the police came."

After the detective left him, Monk slipped to the floor and crawled into a corner. The air conditioner in the ceiling blew cold currents. He rolled down his sleeves and trousers, pulled his legs up close, and shivered.

He must've dozed. The black lady cop woke him by poking his leg with her toe. "I have to put you in cuffs," she said. "Be my ass if you ran."

Where would he go? Not to Quinton's, certainly, and Jon was in jail. So he said, "I won't run."

She snapped on the handcuffs anyway and walked him out of the police station, around the corner, and down the block to another building. They rode the elevator to an upper floor. This building was warmer, the halls carpeted. The lighting was soft and more pleasant. She took him into an office. "Judge Seitz," she said, "this little bro is Thelonious DeCay."

Monk smelled food, as though someone had been cooking in the room.

The judge was tall and broad-shouldered. His head was shaved and red, as if he'd stood in the sun without a cap. He wore running shoes, blue jeans, and a yellow LSU sweatshirt. He stuck out a freckled hand for Monk to shake.

"Thelonious is tough to get my tongue around," the judge said. "What do your friends call you?"

"Monk."

"My friends call me Seymour," the judge smiled. "With a name like Seymour Seitz I should've been a travel agent, but my family wanted me to study law. I'm a rare beast in Louisiana, a Jewish jurist."

The judge said to the matron, "Let's get rid of the bracelets." She removed the handcuffs and left the room. Judge Seitz pointed at two upholstered chairs placed close to one another. "Sit here, Monk. Where's your home?"

"Andry Street in Holy Cross. Where do you live?"

"On the North Shore. Were you born in New Orleans?"

"I believe so. Where were you born?"

"Brooklyn, New York. Do you know where that is?"

"No, I don't."

"How old are you, Monk?"

"Nine. How old are you?"

"I'm forty-two. If you're going to turn back every question, I'd better be careful what I ask. How did you meet Quinton Toussaint?"

"I don't remember. In Jackson Square, maybe."

"I'm told that he was a friend of your father's. Would Mr. Toussaint mind that you went into his house?"

"I don't think so. He told me to look after Jon Latour and Jon broke his leg. I think Quinton would want us to eat his food because he was dead and didn't need it anymore."

"Speaking of food," Judge Seitz said, "Are you hungry?"

"A little."

"I brought in hamburgers and chocolate milkshakes. Does that suit you?"

"Yes sir."

Framed diplomas on the walls said that Judge Seymour Seitz had attended colleges in New York, New Jersey, and New Orleans. Monk decided he must like New places. On the judge's desk he saw a book by Albert Bandura called *Adolescent Aggression*.

"What is adolescent?" Monk asked.

The judge spoke as he pulled food from a sack. "Adolescence is that period in life when most of a person's characteristics change from childlike to adult."

"Am I adolescent?"

"That's part of what I have to decide. What sports do you play, Monk?"

"I don't play sports."

"Not baseball, football, or basketball?"

"I play piano. And dance."

"Really? Tell me about that."

Monk recalled home schooling, Grandmama's music lessons, and how he and Percy made money tap dancing for tourists in Jackson Square.

"Detective Warner tells me your grandmother died in the storm," the judge said.

The hamburger suddenly seemed too much to swallow. Monk took a sip of milkshake and washed it down.

"How about your friends, Monk? Did they come through the storm all right?"

Monk felt his throat tighten. "I couldn't find anybody." He had to quit chewing and swallow hard. "Sister Julianne and Cherita probably drowned. I saw Mr. Benoit trying to get a boat after the flood so he could go look for them."

The judge listened, brown eyes moist. He held his hamburger with both hands but didn't take a bite.

"Aunt Bishop Beulah and her husband, Willy, probably drowned, too. They live at the Baby Jesus Spiritual Church and it floods there with every little rain. If they stayed at home, I don't think they could've gotten out. The ceilings are low and it's close to the levee. It was hard enough to get out of our house."

"How did you manage to get out, Monk?"

He put aside his hamburger and pressed trembling hands between his knees. He described how Grandmama got stuck in the attic, and as he talked he remembered the way she looked at him when he pulled on her arm. Warm tears ran down his cheeks, but he refused to sob. He didn't describe the bubbles that came out of her nose, expression pinched as she sucked water down her throat. Instead, he told how he swam to the levee and walked to the Bywater.

"That's where I saw Mr. Benoit outside his time saver store," Monk said. "People were stealing everything and he was begging for a boat so he could go find Cherita and her mama."

The judge moved closer to him and Monk drew back. "I stopped at Quinton's house. I thought he was gone, but I guess he was dead. That's when I went looking for Jon Latour."

Judge Seitz reached for his hand, and again, Monk pulled away. "Jon let me sleep in his mother's bed."

"Where was his mother all that time?"

"She's dead." Monk peered away at the shelves full of books. "Everybody's dead."

The judge gathered up their trash. "Mr. Seitz," Monk asked, "what will they do to Jon?"

"He needs medical attention for that broken leg. A doctor will prescribe medicines that will help him think more clearly. He's emotionally disturbed, Monk. You knew that, didn't you?"

"He fights bad spirits with a broomstick. Quinton told me one time that Jon is a tortured man bedeviled by voices. I guess that's true. I've seen Jon strap pillows to his head so he won't hear the voices. At first I thought he was fighting his shadow, but shadows don't crawl into closets and under beds. I think he fights demons no one else can see. Quinton said Jon might be insane."

Monk started to take another bite of burger, but put it aside. "The first time I saw Jon wake up fighting the air, it scared me a little, because he did look crazy. But I've seen people twitch and twist at the Baby Jesus Spiritual Church when the Holy Ghost comes on them. Maybe Jon isn't crazy at all. Maybe he's just religious."

"Did he ever hurt you, Monk?"

It was the second time the question had been posed. Monk said, "Jon was good to me."

"Tell me what happened to Earl Thibodeaux."

"Is this my trial?" Monk asked.

"It's just you and me talking, Monk."

"Will you use what I say against me?"

"I'm trying to learn the truth about things so I'll know what should be done."

"Am I going to jail?" Monk asked.

"Do you think you belong in jail?"

"I stole food."

"I think we can forgive hungry people for taking food."

The judge stood up and walked around behind his desk. He threw the burger wrappers and empty milkshake cups into a trashcan.

Monk told Judge Seitz what happened to Uncle Earl, and how Randy chased him firing his pistol. All the while, Mr. Seitz arranged things on his desk and moved books around on the shelves, as though he wasn't really paying much attention. Finally, Monk had answered every question as honestly as he could. The judge sat down at his desk.

"We'll have a hearing in a couple of weeks, Monk. I want you there to repeat what you've told me. Mr. Latour needs someone to speak for him, and I think you're the person to do that. In the meantime, how would you like to stay with your Aunt Donna?"

"I don't know if she wants me."

"She says she does."

"Okay," Monk said.

When Monk came out of the judge's office, he was surprised to find the aunt reading a magazine in a side room. She stood up when they entered.

"We had a good meeting," Judge Seitz said. "I told Monk he'll be staying with you, Miss DeCay. I need time to check on a few things before we get together again."

"I was thinking about going back to Atlanta for awhile."

"If you leave this parish," Judge Seitz said, "everything will be in limbo and may never be decided. We won't chase you."

"In which case I'll stay."

"We're short of personnel and I have a full docket, but I'll try to rush things along and settle this matter as quickly as possible."

"Thank you, Judge Seitz."

The judge put his hand on Monk's shoulder and smiled down at him. "Monk is worried about his friend, Mr. Latour. I need to confer with the medical people who're evaluating Latour before that aspect of this situation can be adjudicated. In the meantime, Monk, be on your best behavior, and I'll see you in two weeks."

Going down in the elevator, the aunt said, "He called you Monk."

"That's all anybody calls me, except for Grandmama."

"You prefer Monk?"

"It's easier to get your tongue around," he said.

Her car was a four-door silver Toyota. It was streaked with dirt and spotted with pieces of leaves and pine straw. A cardboard fir tree hung on the rear view mirror making cedar smells.

"Is this your car? My grandmama didn't have a car. Mr. Willy had a truck."

She turned on Canal Street and passed a trolley running north. The car windows were rolled up tight, and sounds of the air conditioner covered all noise from outside.

"Who is Mr. Willy?" she asked.

"Aunt Bishop Beulah's husband. You live in Atlanta?" Monk asked.

"Yes."

"Is it as nice as New Orleans?"

"Like all large cities, some parts are nicer than others."

It was the kind of reply he expected from adults, an answer without an answer. He saw workmen replacing broken glass on storefronts and removing dangling signs. Parked on the banquettes were pickup trucks loaded with rolls of roofing. Men on the roof hauled up buckets of hot pitch. Everywhere he looked there was construction activity.

"If you go home to Atlanta, do I have to go with you?" he asked.

She looked at him so strangely, he said, "I don't need anyone to look after me. I can take care of myself. Don't worry about me."

"That's something we'll talk about and decide together, Monk."

"Why did you come to New Orleans?"

"Looking for you. I thought you might need help."

"Why didn't you come a long time ago then?" He felt tears again and blinked them back. "Do you know my daddy?"

"He's my brother, Monk. I'm your Aunt Donna."

"Is he alive?"

She pulled over to the curb and stopped the car. "I can't talk about your father, Monk."

"Grandmama said he's dead. Quinton said he wasn't. Do you know?"

She leaned on the steering wheel with both arms and stared straight ahead. "Doesn't he love me at all?" Monk said. "Why didn't he come help me? I nearly drowned! Grandmama drowned."

"I'm sorry, Monk."

He grabbed for the door handle and it was locked.

"Monk, don't get out of the car. If you give me a chance, I'll try to be the best friend you ever had. But I must talk to other people before I can discuss certain things. We have two weeks before we see the judge again. Until then, let's work on getting to know one another. All right?"

"All right," he said.

The aunt stayed in a house with a man she introduced as "Uncle Barry" Hampton. He was a reporter for the *Probe*, she said. He had a room in his house that was used for nothing but a library, with a heavy square desk and a wastebasket overflowing with crumpled papers. Upstairs were four bedrooms and two baths.

Having Monk as a guest seemed to make them tense. When the aunt brought food to the table and uncovered it, Uncle Barry said, "Pork chops." "With sauerkraut," the aunt replied. During dinner they sat at opposite ends with Monk in the middle.

Monk raked away kraut and took a bite of meat.

"You don't like sauerkraut?" his aunt asked.

"I never had it before."

"Perhaps you'd like to taste it."

He didn't want to and after he did, wished he hadn't.

"You don't have to eat it," she said. They watched him not eat it.

"The young man needs clothes," Uncle Barry noted.

"I'll see if I can find someplace to shop tomorrow."

After dinner, Aunt Donna said, "Monk, would you like to help wash dishes?"

"No, thank you."

Barry laughed and cleared the table. "I'll load the dishwasher."

The aunt and Barry watched news on television, which was boring.

After a while, Aunt Donna said, "Want some coffee?" and Barry said, "No, thanks."

They sat there watching people on TV talk about levees and water tables, but didn't speak to one another.

"Is there a program you'd like to watch, Monk?"

"I don't know."

"What did you watch at home?"

"We didn't have television."

On a fake fireplace mantel a clock ticked loudly. Finally, Barry said, "Just about bedtime, isn't it?" and Donna led Monk upstairs.

"This is your bedroom and the bath is here," she explained. "The big towels are for bathing and the small towels are for hands."

While the tub filled with steaming water, she directed Monk to the bed she'd made up when they first arrived. The covers were folded back. The bed was high off the floor with four tall posts and a tent top covering and curtains on the sides. He thought the curtains were to keep out mosquitoes, but the aunt said no, it was to keep out dust and that's the way they did it a hundred years ago.

"If you want anything that isn't here," she said, "let me know."

"Are you married to Uncle Barry?"

"No."

"But he's my uncle?"

She looked uncomfortable. "Not really. Calling him Uncle Barry seemed less formal than Mr. Hampton."

"He doesn't mind being called my uncle?"

"Not at all."

"But you're my father's sister, so you really are my aunt," Monk said.

"I am your aunt."

Then she did something that caught him completely by surprise. She removed his shirt, pulled off his pants, and sent him to the bathroom. It was too late to shut the door, so he left it open. But then she came and closed the door.

"You may want some privacy," she said.

White adults did things that were confusing. Monk sank into the hot water and trembled with the pleasure of it.

Through the door, the aunt called, "Good night, Monk."

"Good night—Aunt Donna."

Aunt Donna had taken his only clothes. Monk went to bed naked. The mattress was filled with soft feathers. As he lay there it sucked him under and folded around him. He didn't like it. He got up, pulled a blanket and sheets to the floor and made a pallet. Lying with his head next to a heater vent he heard Uncle Barry's voice.

"What are you doing, Donna?"

"I'll have to move to another room. I can't sleep in here with Monk in the house."

"Why not?"

"It sets an immoral example."

Barry laughed. "Are you suggesting we sneak around to sleep together?"

Monk put his ear closer to the vent.

"How far will you go to play the virgin queen?" Uncle Barry said in a low teasing voice.

"It's important that we don't send mixed signals to Monk until he feels more secure, Barry. He asked if we were married, and I told him we are not. There are already too many loose ends in his life."

"We shouldn't hide from that boy to be ourselves, Donna. I want you to stay in this room with me. Is anything else bothering you? "

"Have any of his friends survived, and if they have, where are they? What about his grandmother's body? Shouldn't there be some sort of funeral or memorial? His only anchor seems to be Jon Latour. Monk is obviously attached to the man. Detective Warner said Latour would be sent to an institution. He's probably schizophrenic. Also, there's a possibility the court will place Monk under state supervision, which means a foster home somewhere."

"Did you tell the judge you wanted custody?"

"He didn't ask, and I didn't volunteer. I have my own loose ends to tie up."

Monk smelled dust in the heater vent. He heard the creak of bedsprings.

After a long silence, Donna said, "Outside of emotional issues, there are practical considerations to worry about. Raising a child is not cheap. He'll need clothes, medical and dental care, education. I'm not asking you to take this on, Barry. He's my responsibility, not yours."

"He's not your responsibility until you accept it," Barry said. "But all right, let's talk about finances. Do you still have a job in Atlanta?"

"I don't know."

"Wouldn't it to be a good idea to call and find out?"

"I should do that."

Monk strained to hear more. "Did Monk's grandmother have a will?" Barry asked.

"I don't know, Barry. On the face of it, I'd say she didn't have much in the way of worldly goods."

"Was she Monk's legal guardian? Just because he lived with his grandmother doesn't make him a legitimate heir. Did Dean sign him over to her, or did she get a court decree?"

"I don't know."

"Those can be very sticky points in a court of probate," Barry said. "The irony is, the boy might not have a legal guardian. If you want to change his status, you will have to petition a court for the right to keep him."

"I'm not ready for that," she replied.

Monk realized again how completely and absolutely alone he was. Grandmama would never talk about him this way. In every bone and muscle of his body he felt emptiness. This wouldn't be happening to him if Grandmama were here.

The aunt said they were going to send Jon to an institution. Was that a place for crazy people? How long would they keep him?

Jon was the only person he trusted.

Through the heater grate, Monk heard Barry say, "Don't kid yourself, Donna. That boy needs a lot of work. I shook his hand and he never looked me in the eye. He's sullen and without social skills. I'm sure you realize that taking him on is a lifelong contract."

"I know," she said. "Hold me close, Barry."

It was obvious Uncle Barry didn't want him, and Monk wasn't too sure about his aunt.

He had to get his money and find Jon.

Judge Seitz said the doctors would give Jon medicine to help him think clearly. Good. They'd have to leave Vieux Carré, which Jon did not like to do, and travel by day. They'd go to New York where Quinton said Monk would be a hit dancing in Central Park and Union Square.

With his ear to the grate again, he heard Barry say softly, "Don't cry, Donna. We'll do this together. Just don't shut me out."

Monk covered his head with the blanket and stared into the dark. He and Jon had to run away. But he wasn't confident Jon would cooperate. New York City was a lot farther from the French Quarter than Rampart, and Rampart was the farthest he'd ever seen Jon go.

He imagined riding on a bus. Monk had never been out of the city before. What if Jon fell asleep and woke up thrashing at demons? The bus driver would put them off in some strange town and call the police, and maybe have them locked up in jail.

Monk had to convince Jon to behave and go along with his plans.

Did he have enough money for a bus ticket? Where would he go to buy the ticket? Whatever he did, Monk promised himself, he would not abandon Jon.

All they had was one another.

{CHAPTER TWENTY-FOUR}

The sun had not risen when Donna caught Monk at the front door. He wore his new clothes, but no shoes. "Where're you going so early in the morning?" she asked. He teetered on the top step of the porch as if about to take off.

"I left some money at Grandmama's house. I'm going to get it."

"It's a long way from here to your grandmother's, and it's awfully early to be going anywhere."

"I don't mind," he said, and took another step down.

"It's not a good idea to be wandering around the city at this hour, Monk."

He looked incredulous. "I've done it before," he said.

"I wouldn't want you to get hurt."

"I'll be careful."

"Monk, wait a minute. Let me take you in the car."

"I need to go by Jon's apartment, too."

"I'll be glad to drive you there."

"And maybe go by the jail to see Jon," he said, almost as if testing her.

"I don't think they'll let you in," Donna responded.

"I was going to tell them Jon's my daddy."

"That might get you sent away to a juvenile facility, Monk. It'd be better to say he's a friend."

"All right. Are you ready to go?"

She wished she'd had a cup of coffee. "You'll probably need shoes to get inside the jail."

Begrudgingly, he went upstairs, and she hurried to the kitchen to make a quick cup of coffee.

Back in the hallway, Donna waited with coffee cup and car keys in hand. She didn't want Monk to feel he was on a tether, but she intended to hover nevertheless.

Driving to the Broad Street Police Station, the streets glistened under the sheen of heavy dew. Most traffic lights weren't working, and neither were street lamps. Fog wafted between buildings in the business district. Morosely, Monk stared out the passenger window.

"Are you all right, Monk?"

"Fine."

"Is anything wrong?"

"No."

When they reached the police station, an officer directed them to the bus and train depot, which had been converted to a temporary holding facility for defendants. There, corralled like animals, men waited for legal disposition of their cases. Many detainees were still asleep on army cots and pallets. The smell of humanity was thick and unpleasant. Soldiers walked the perimeter of enclosures and a policewoman sat at a desk under a harsh light.

Monk hurried ahead and asked the female desk sergeant, "Is Jon Latour here?"

The policewoman looked exhausted. "We're so screwed up we don't know who we're holding half the time." She shuffled a loose pile of papers.

"May I look around for him?" Monk asked.

"No, I'm sorry. We don't have the equipment or manpower to search prisoners as we should. I can't allow you to see anyone."

"I won't touch him and he won't touch me," Monk bargained.

"We have no place for him to visit under supervision. I'm sorry."

Monk's expression soured. He returned to Donna and she took him to his grandmother's house on Andry Street in the Lower Ninth Ward. Despite a clear sky and the first rays of bright sunshine, it was still a dismal scene. Trees, lawns, and shrubs had been killed in the flood. The entire landscape was withered and brown. Most homes had been abandoned.

Donna saw the same old man shuffling back and forth to his pile of trash.

"If you want to come in," Monk advised, "you'll have to take off your shoes. The house is full of mud."

The thought of it was repugnant. "Unless you need me, Monk, I'll stay in the car."

He removed his shoes, rolled up the new trousers, and waded through weeds to the car still stuck in the back porch. Several minutes later he emerged clutching a dirty quart-size canning jar. His shirt was soiled, trousers smudged, feet caked with mud. He got in and put the jar between his feet.

"That's a nice sum of money," Donna said. For a child in the Ninth Ward she thought it a huge sum. "Is that your grandmother's money?

"It's mine."

"Saving money is always a good idea. What are you planning to buy?

"I was saving it to go find my daddy."

Donna drove up Bourbon Street to Toulouse, and Monk directed her to stop less than half a block from the Probe building. She parked on the sidewalk and watched Monk scale a fence to Jon's apartment. A moment later, with pounding heart, she caught a glimpse of him high up a trellis as he crawled onto a roof and disappeared.

She stared at Monk's muddy jar on the floor, jammed full of coins and paper currency. How was he planning to look for his father? She glanced up and saw him come back over the fence.

When he got into the car she said, "Did you find what you went for?"

"I wanted to see if Jon came home."

"Did he?"

"No."

An old woman wearing a long ragged dress came past the car. Her shoes had been cut to expose corns on gnarled toes. She carried a plastic garbage bag over her shoulder, and she wore a knit cap adorned with aluminum tabs from canned drinks.

Donna started the motor. "Are we ready to go home, Monk? We'll put your money away, and I'll treat those clothes to get out the stains."

"I can walk from here."

"No." She smiled to soften the command. "I'm in no hurry. Where else did you want to go?"

"If you're hungry," he offered, "I'll buy you something to eat."

She laughed. "All right. Where would you like to dine?"

"The Clover Grill."

It was around the corner several blocks away. The place pulsed with music so loud people shouted to be heard. The waiter saw Monk and smothered him in a hug. "Hey there, my man! Did you hear about our sweet Quinton? They found him in his bathtub. He's dead, honey!"

"I know."

With tears in his eyes, the waiter called to the cook, "This is Quinton's little dancing friend. Remember Quinton talking about Monk?"

The cook abandoned chores at the grill, wiped his hands on a towel and came from behind the counter to embrace Monk. "We'll all miss Quinton," he said. "What a darling he was. Are you coming to the funeral?"

"When is it?" Monk asked.

"Tomorrow morning. The parade will start at Jackson Square about eleven o'clock. There'll be two bands, one leading and another following, because there are so many friends gathering to celebrate Quinton's life. Oops, my onions are burning!" He hurried back to the grill.

The waiter gazed at Donna flirtatiously. "Who's your friend, Monk?"

"This is Donna."

He extended limp fingers for her to hold. "Hi there, Donna."

She could hardly hear over the din of music and loud voices.

"Have you seen my friend, Percy, who used to come in here with Quinton and me?" Monk asked the waiter.

"No, babe, I haven't. Didn't he live in the Lower Ninth near you?"

"Yes."

"Oh, tsk-tsk," the waiter lamented. "It's all such a tragedy. I cried for days and days." He bent over the table waiting to write down their order.

Donna noted lewd blurbs on the menu. She asked Monk, "What do you recommend?"

"The cheeseburgers are good. We could share one."

"Nobody threw a better party than Quinton Toussaint," the waiter spoke to Monk while writing on his pad. "I think half the Quarter is planning to join the parade. You want fries with that burger?"

"Yes," Monk said.

"Quinton's spirit will be so pleased to have you parade in his honor, Monk. What are you drinking, sweetheart?" he asked Donna.

The burger came cut in halves and served on two plates. The waiter bent and kissed Monk on the forehead. "I'll see you at the funeral, brave little man."

They ate saying nothing. Monk stared out the window at an odd assortment of characters on the street, the same raggedy woman Donna had seen earlier, two men swapping a cigarette back and forth and sharing a bottle between them. Donna had been gazing at Monk for several minutes before she realized he was crying.

Every evening in the privacy of their bedroom, Donna debated one thing or another with Barry, and after each dispute, somehow, incongruously, she felt closer to him. He sat in the middle of the bed now, naked and hugging one knee, trimming his toenails. He'd just had a shower and his hair looked slept in. "We're facing life-changing decisions," he said gloomily.

"Yes, we are, Barry."

He glanced at her. "We don't need to rush into decisions, do we?"

"I have to decide a few things before I see Judge Seitz next week."

He leaned over the edge of the bed to retrieve an errant toenail. When he came up again, he said, "Do you love me?"

Caught off guard, she faltered, "I think I do. I mean, sure. Do you love me?"

"I feel the same way."

He searched between his legs for another lost clipping. "There's no hurry," he said. "We can take our time. Are you going to call your parents?"

She'd deliberately waited until nine Eastern Time, allowing her parents to finish dinner and settle down for the evening. She used her cell phone.

"Donna!" her mother yelped. "Are you trying to give us heart failure? Why haven't you telephoned?"

"Like I said before, Mom, things are hectic down here."

"Bob Miller has called from the school every day for a week," Mom said. "He allocated sick leave and vacation time to your absence. You still have paychecks being deposited to your bank account. But Bob says he has to hear from you soon, or he'll be forced to replace you, Donna. He repeatedly asked if you're coming home. I said, of course she's coming home, Bob! She's been through two hurricanes and floods of biblical proportions. That's why we haven't heard from her."

"Mom," Donna interrupted, "I found Dean's son."

In the lull that followed, Donna thought she'd lost the connection.

"Alive?" Mom asked.

"Yes, he's alive."

After another hesitation, Mom said, "Well. All right. Good for you."

"I thought I'd bring him up to meet his grandparents," Donna suggested.

The pause this time conveyed her mother's feelings better than words.

"He has no other family," Donna said. "It's just us."

"That's unfortunate, isn't it, Donna? Some errors in judgment are lifelong and immutable. This is what Dean has done to all of us." She changed the subject abruptly, "I see on TV news that crime in New Orleans is rampant. They're calling it the murder capital of the nation. Stay out of badly lit neighborhoods, Donna. Be wary and alert."

"Okay, Mom." Damn it. "Let me speak to Dad."

"Call Bob Miller and tell him your plans," her mother urged.

"Right, Mom."

She heard her mother speak aside, deliberately unmuffled. "Donna is talking about bringing Dean's son here, Alfred. I don't recommend that."

"Hello, my love," Dad said. "Do you need anything?"

"I met a man down here, Dad. He's a wonderful person."

"A man? Umm, is this serious?"

She heard her mother demand, "Is what serious?"

"It might be, Dad. His name is Barry Hampton. He helped me find Dean's son, which was a colossal task. The boy is staying with us at the moment."

Staying with us was not lost on her father.

Her mother came back on the line. "Is what serious?"

"She's met a man, Maxine," Dad said.

"Dear God!" Mom cried. "What happens to you people when you go to New Orleans? Tell me what you just told your father, Donna."

"Dad can tell you, Mom. I have to go now."

When Donna disconnected, Barry was staring at her.

"She doesn't want Monk there," Donna said.

"Fine," Barry responded. "Stay here then. You don't have to go to Atlanta."

She turned off her lamp and rolled onto one side. Barry gathered his nail clippings, wrapped them in a facial tissue, and threw them into a wastebasket. He went to the bathroom without closing the door and made sounds akin to a leaking yak. He returned to bed and snuggled close. She felt his warm breath on her back.

Barry wiggled closer and exhaled on her spine. "Did you know, when I breathe warm air between your shoulder blades you get goosebumps on your arms?"

His hand slipped down her body and caressed her thigh. "More goosebumps," he murmured. "If you go to see your parents, when will that be?"

"After Monk goes to court."

He traced her abdomen with one finger. "I'll go to Atlanta with you."

"I don't think that's a good idea, Barry."

"You can present me as Casanova with short toenails."

Donna turned toward him. "I can guess how they'll respond to a love interest who writes for the *Probe*."

"I'll be a pleasant distraction from more weighty issues."

"For one thing," she tried to say it lightly, "you're older than I am."

"Were you looking for a younger beau? At your age I wouldn't be casting aspersions on maturity."

"They'll insist we stay at their house so we won't be seen around town by anybody who knows them. That means we won't be able to sleep in the same room."

"Yes, we can."

"No, we can't."

"When you feel a sexy hand creep up your inner thigh, it better be mine," Barry said.

A moment later he stroked her nipples. "Now those are goosebumps!"

Donna scrambled eggs and baked biscuits. She hadn't cooked breakfast in years, but with a nine-year-old in the house she thought she ought to. Besides, Barry was an appreciative diner, moaning with every bite. "Oh, so good," he groaned. "You're a terrific cook. The canned biscuits are perfect. Could I have a couple more?"

She was dreading the day because she knew Monk planned to participate in Quinton Toussaint's funeral procession and that meant a lot of walking. It had been drizzling rain all night.

Barry described the coming event: "A jazz funeral begins with a mournful dirge as grieving friends slowly follow a brass band to the place of burial. The body is transported in a wagon or hearse. After they leave the family at the cemetery, the mood shifts to an upbeat tempo. The bereaved become celebrants, dancing and rejoicing for the soul of the dead who is now released and going to heaven. Sidney Bechet, a famous New Orleans jazzman, said that 'music in New Orleans is as much a part of death as it is of life,' and he was right."

Barry buttered a third biscuit. "The tradition was brought to America by slaves. Four centuries ago, the Dahomean of Benin and the Yoruba of Nigeria, West Africa, laid the foundation for what we know as the jazz funeral today. They believed a man lived life to benefit his tribe. If he brought home an antelope, he shared it with the entire community. When he died, the tribe owed him a decent send-off. Quite often they supported his widow and children, sometimes for as long as they lived. They formed a parade all the way to the grave, and then, beating drums, singing, and dancing, they returned home. The jazz funeral procession is the celebration of a man's time on this planet, sorrowful at first and joyous at last."

"How did an erstwhile historian end up writing for a tabloid like the *Probe*?" she teased.

"It's just something I'm interested in," he said, and he munched his biscuit.

Donna went upstairs to wake Monk. He wasn't in his bedroom and the bath was empty. Every morning she had noticed a pallet on the floor made from his bedding, and she questioned Monk about it. He didn't like the feather bed, he said. The floor was more comfortable. This morning the bed was made and there was no pallet. The closet was empty, his jar of money gone.

Hurrying downstairs again, she said, "Monk has left the house, Barry."

"Probably went ahead to the funeral procession."

"No." She paced around the table. "The bed hasn't been slept in, and he took that heavy jar of money."

"More likely he hid it somewhere."

"I think he ran away."

"Where would he go?"

"Maybe to Jon Latour's apartment, or to his grandmother's house. I don't know where he went."

While Barry shaved and bathed, Donna ransacked Monk's bedroom. She studied the area. "Where would I hide money?" she asked herself.

She knelt on one knee to lift the heater vent and felt as far inside as she could reach. Across the hall and two rooms away, Barry coughed, cleared his throat, and spit. She paused, listening. A moment later, she heard him hum tunelessly.

In a conversational tone she said, "Barry?"

"Yeah, Babe?"

"Can you hear me?" she asked.

"Yes. Where are you?"

"Oh, God, Barry. I'm in Monk's bedroom. He's overheard every word we've said."

A moment later Barry appeared at the door with shaving lather on his cheek. "He's been eavesdropping?"

"He slept on the floor here beside the vent. I heard you clear your throat. He knows everything we said."

"What did we say that could be so wrong?" Barry questioned.

"It wasn't wrong, Barry, but we thought it was private."

Barry swore softly. "All right. Get dressed. We'll find him."

A steady mist fell onto a sea of brightly colored umbrellas around Jackson Square. In New Orleans, which Donna knew got sixty inches of rain annually, everybody owned an umbrella. From St. Louis Cathedral a horse-drawn carriage transported the remains of Quinton Toussaint. Over glistening cobblestone streets a phalanx of mourners and revelers waved handkerchiefs and parasols, keeping cadence with spirituals trumpeted by a brass band.

"Did you know this guy?" Barry asked a man in the crowd.

"Quinton Toussaint! New Orleans historian, patron of the arts, and a friend to the Crescent City's most talented jazz performers."

Donna ducked under an awning trying to spot Monk beneath colorful parasols and swirling handkerchiefs.

"Last year," the stranger said to Barry, "one of the founders of the Dirty Dozen Brass Band died. Anthony 'Tuba Fats' Lacen was his name. His fellow musicians held a celebration that lasted for hours. This reminds me of that turnout. You never heard of Quinton Toussaint?"

Of course he had, but Barry said, no.

"For half a century, Toussaint was a big man behind the scenes in the jazz community," the reveler said. "He kicked off the careers of people who became famous far beyond New Orleans."

"Like Tooth DeCay?" Barry suggested.

"Yeah! Like Tooth."

The crowd surged forward and behind her, Donna heard the second band take up "Just a Closer Walk With Thee," as strains of "Amazing Grace" faded in the distance up front.

"Where are we going?" Donna asked a woman in the crowd.

"St. Louis Number One Cemetery on Basin Street."

As the parade continued, more revelers came out of shops and off sidewalks to join the procession.

"Did you know the deceased?" somebody asked.

"Never had the pleasure."

"In New Orleans," Barry advised Donna, "citizens will drop everything for food or music. They don't have to know the dead man to celebrate his existence."

Donna stopped on the sidewalk—banquette Barry called it—and watched for a rain-soaked little brown boy. She didn't see him.

Barry took her arm and led her aside. "Maybe Monk doesn't want to be seen," he said, and that made her angry and fearful for his future.

They walked against the crowd back to a municipal parking lot near Jackson Square where she'd left the car. Sitting in a lot by the levee, Barry used her cell phone to call his office.

"Art, I won't be in today. No, I feel fine. Just a couple of personal things."

She quit listening as Barry discussed articles unwritten and pieces ready for print. She stared through the rain-dappled windshield at gray buildings without shadows, and low clouds moving overhead. This city had a hold on its citizens. A block away stood the old slave market where human flesh was once bought and sold. In Jackson Square, Indian men and women had been burned at the stake while white citizens turned out to watch. Out of the brutal past had developed a haunting charm that held sway to this day. Barry was caught in it. So was Monk. Maybe it was the idea of moving to Atlanta that upset Monk the most.

She realized she couldn't force her will on the child. She had not yet developed emotional ties with which to coerce him. She tried to remember what she and Barry had said to one another in the bedroom. Monk had heard them discuss whether or not to keep him. He learned that his grandparents didn't want him, and so far as Monk knew, his father was either dead, or unloving.

When Barry disconnected from his call, she said, "Monk thinks nobody wants him."

"Have you made a decision to give him up?" Barry asked.

"No, but he thinks I have. He believes nobody wants him."

The rain quickened, and in the distance she heard returning brass bands playing "John the Revelator" and "Jesus on the Mainline."

"What do you want to do now, babe?" Barry asked.

She started the motor. "Go home I guess."

"There's nowhere else you want to look?"

"I want to go home, put on dry clothes, and drink hot tea laced with Jamaican rum."

She drove around remnants of the funeral march, the last band playing a quickstep version of "Down by the Riverside."

When she got home, Donna telephoned Bob Miller at school in Atlanta and resigned from her teaching job. He asked, as he always asked, if there was anything he could do for her.

"No, Bob, I'll be all right."

"Are you sure you want to live down there?" he inquired.

"Actually, I'm not sure."

"That's a city with a hedonistic past, Donna. Iniquity tends to cling if you stand in it long enough. Before you know it, shocking behavior ceases to horrify."

He was right of course. A few days ago she'd caught herself reading a back copy of the *Probe* and actually laughed out loud at Barry's bizarre story about a baby born with a bungee cord umbilical. To someone who had never lived in New Orleans, how could she explain? Getting up in the morning was an adventure with people who were warm and generous, a blend of joys unlike any she'd ever known. The city was a carnival in a constant state of festivity. Yes, there was debauchery, but even that seemed harmless.

Why had she been resisting this place? It went against human nature to rebel against merriment. She remembered her feelings as a child the day school let out for summer vacation. Waking up in New Orleans with Barry at her side, she experienced the same childish surge of excitement.

How could she expect Monk and Barry to give up New Orleans to live somewhere else? No doubt, certain aspects of life in this city would lose appeal someday; it was a natural response to constant exposure. She knew people born and raised at the foot of Stone Mountain who had never climbed that granite mass. Barry had said natives of New Orleans rarely ate Lucky Dogs. Those born and raised here didn't stand on a curb for hours anticipating Mardi Gras parades. It was tourists who collected cheap beads and caught Moon Pies thrown from floats. Out-of-towners drank volatile Hurricanes, a local concoction designed to eliminate rational thought and sane behavior.

But even the most jaded habitué never gave up the desire for socializing by sharing the exotic foods of the Creole culture, and soaking up music as intoxicating to the soul as Hurricanes were to the body. It wasn't realistic to imagine Barry and Monk loving life in Atlanta. For them, anywhere else was as alien as rills of the moon.

She sat at the kitchen table sipping her hot rum tea, lost in worry.

Trying to lend comfort, Barry intruded on her thoughts. "Monk is a smart kid, Donna. He'll come back. Everything will work out."

"Not unless I handle this better than I have so far," she said.

{CHAPTER TWENTY-FIVE}

The exhaust fan was running and warm air flowed up through the ventilator shaft as Monk descended to Jon's apartment. He smelled cooking meat from the restaurant below. In the apartment he took off his soaked clothes and draped them over chairs to dry.

Naked and cold, he crawled into bed and wrapped himself in covers.

A few minutes ago he'd seen Aunt Donna and Uncle Barry watching for him at Quinton's funeral. She stood on the banquette looking over the crowd and peering under umbrellas while Barry moved around. Monk managed to avoid them and still attend services for Quinton.

He missed Quinton; Quinton, and everything else that had been swept away by the hurricane: meeting at Jackson Square, the whoop of musicians and acrobats, laughter and applause of tourists, the smells of candy kitchens and the clop of horses hooves; and Grandmama waiting at home to see how much money he'd made that day.

He missed Percy, too, and Holy Cross as it had once been with a neighbor who raised rabbits and egg-laying hens.

He shuddered beneath the bedding, seized by a chill.

He had his money and was ready to leave as soon as he found Jon.

Another deeper, longer shiver rattled his teeth. He put his head beneath the cover, warm breath his only heater. His cold feet felt like they belonged to somebody else. He wrapped frigid fingers in fabric to keep them away from his body.

Nothing would ever be the same again, he knew that. There was nobody to help him. He and Jon had to help themselves.

Monk closed his eyes in the dark of his undercover den, blowing warm breath between icy hands. He dozed, and in his sleep he thought he heard Jon sword-fighting spirits with a broomstick. When he roused up, he realized it was nothing. The apartment was empty and he was alone. Common sense told him it was not an intruder.

He didn't worry about Aunt Donna finding him here. When he got out of her car yesterday, he'd approached the apartment from down the block and come across adjoining roofs so she'd think he was going somewhere else.

He didn't have a plan, because he didn't know the circumstances of Jon's imprisonment. But he knew his friend was going to court in a few days, and Judge Seitz wanted Monk to speak on Jon's behalf. Whatever happened would happen then.

If he and Jon could get back to the Quarter, Monk felt sure nobody would overtake them. Over roofs and through attics, across courtyards and up wrought iron grillwork—who knew those routes better than Jon? There were dozens of places to take shelter in lofts and dormers, dusty stairwells, and empty shafts. But then he remembered, Jon had a broken leg.

So he didn't know what to expect. It would depend on Jon. Could he be convinced to venture out in daylight? Travel to New York City?

Monk wondered if he could teach the tall lanky man to dance with taps on his shoes. Maybe that was hoping for too much. If Jon would dance, what a team they'd make, hand clapping and thigh-slapping. Jon had rhythm; Monk knew that from watching him play piano. A long tall loose-jointed partner would make the act more interesting. They could do you-are-my-shadow, with Jon as the shadow.

Monk was daydreaming. He never talked about daydreams with Grandmama because she said it paid to be practical. If he began to weave fanciful ideas, she'd pull him into a hug and say, "Now, Thelonious, it's all right to dream. But dream dreams you can make come true."

That was one thing troubling him now. Could he make these dreams come true? Even if they made good money dancing at the parks and squares, Jon might want to come back to New Orleans.

Suppose he got Jon to New York City, and couldn't find a place to live? What if they had to steal food there? He'd seen pictures of buildings so tall the top floors were in clouds. The thought of running over roofs fifty or sixty floors above the street made Monk unsure of himself. Would he be scared? Jon might become confused and pull into himself, which he'd done a few times right here at home.

Monk assumed police in New York were like police in New Orleans. "Cops is cops," Uncle Earl used to say. "All alike and you can't trust one among them."

Worried, Monk shut off unhappy thoughts and tried to sleep in the blanket cocoon he'd made for himself.

He wished he had Grandmama to hold him close. He'd give anything to have her stroke his back and sing a lullaby, Hush-a-bye my baby, don't you cry. Hush-a-bye, lullaby. Close your eyes and sleep a while. Hush-a-bye, lullaby, close your eyes my sleepy child.

He dreamed that everything was all right. He dreamed the storm was a bad dream and bells of Holy Cross rang loud and true. In his sleep he smelled breakfast making and heard the pop of bacon in a frying pan.

He was so relieved. He wanted to jump out of bed and run to Grandmama. Tell her he'd had a terrible nightmare.

"Sleep on an empty stomach and it bends the sensibilities," she'd say. "Sit down and eat some potato pancakes, Thelonious. Everything is all right."

But when he woke, the stale smell of the apartment and cold wet air brought him to his senses. The dream was the dream—this was the real.

He went under the covers and tried to call up the fantasy again.

Here it was—the smell of bacon, fatback crackling in a pan, the floor creaking beneath Grandmama's weight as she moved around in the kitchen. He eased himself into half-sleep. There'd been no storm. No flood. He was home in bed, snoozing late and Grandmama let him, because he'd had a long, hard, good day at Jackson Square yesterday.

He wished he could sleep forever.

Because of their recent raids, Jon's apartment still held plenty of food. Monk carefully removed labels from cans to surprise himself with the contents: tomatoes, asparagus, hash, and apricots. None of these were his first choice for something to eat, but he ate everything except asparagus.

It was raining and a steady flow of water ran off the balcony roof and splattered on the brick passage below. The sound of it muffled music from the Old Opera House, and the steady drum of water eased his mind. He lit three candles, and from one of them a flowery aroma filled the room.

With nothing to occupy his time, he went back to bed.

That's how he spent the next three days. Eat, sleep, eat, sleep.

The rain finally stopped. By midday the temperature was rising and on the roof under a broiling sun, puddles began to evaporate. Monk gazed up at mounds of white clouds tumbling over one another, climbing ever higher into the blindingly blue sky. From the roof he watched people strolling on Bourbon Street, mostly military men with girlfriends they'd made since coming to New Orleans. Monk guessed that was the case because the girls clung to the arms of the soldiers and kept urging them to buy things.

He was so bored his leg jiggled. From where he sat he could see Fiona's voodoo shop and it was as it had been since Randy Bernard killed Uncle Earl. The door was still open. A few trinkets lay on the street. Obviously, she had not returned.

He had a problem to overcome and Monk was not sure how to do it. He didn't know exactly when Judge Seitz wanted him, and had no idea where they were supposed to meet. There was nothing else to do except go and ask.

He used bottled drinking water to wash his face and hands. He put on a clean shirt, pants, socks, and shoes. Careful to avoid an area near the Probe building for fear he'd run into Uncle Barry, he walked to the police station to get his bearings, and then to the judge's office.

A guard stopped him at the door. "What do you want?" he asked.

"I have to ask Judge Seitz a question."

"Hold on," the guard said. He placed a phone call, spoke softly into the receiver, and then turned to Monk again. "What's your name?"

"Thelonious Monk DeCay."

The man relayed that information, then disconnected. "You know how to get to the judge's office?"

"Yessir."

"Go straight there. Don't wander anywhere else in the building."
"Yessir."
Upstairs, a woman waited for him. "You're Thelonious?" she asked.
"Yes ma'am."
"Come with me."
She took him to the judge's office. Judge Seitz stuck out a freckled hand to shake. "How are you, Monk?"
"I'm all right."
"How are things going with your aunt?"
"Good."
"Where is she?"
"She couldn't find a parking place," Monk said.
"What can I do for you?" Judge Seitz asked.
"When do you need me to talk about Jon Latour?"
"Tomorrow morning at ten o'clock."
"Where?"
"Juvenile Court downstairs. We're using that room because there's a backlog in all the other courtrooms. I'll call security; when you go downstairs the guard will show you where it is. I'm sure your aunt will have you here on time."
"I may come alone."
"Oh?" the judge studied Monk's face. "Is everything all right between you and your aunt?"
Monk threw away a hand nonchalantly. "Oh, sure. I just don't need anybody with me."
Judge Seitz nodded. "Then I'll see you tomorrow morning at ten."
He walked with Monk to the elevator. "Is there anything you want to talk about, Monk?"
"No sir. Just Jon."
"Good then."
The judge stood with him until the elevator doors closed and Monk descended to street level.
The guard led him to the courtroom. It was small, with pews, like at the Baby Jesus Spiritual Church. "You'll go into this door," the guard showed him. "And wait in here until you're called to court. Understand."
"Yes."

The guard escorted him to the exit, and Monk tried to appear casual as he strolled away. He felt pretty good. It wasn't everyday you could fool a bunch of grownups, especially an armed guard.

Back at the apartment, he removed his clothes, carefully folded them, and buffed his shoes to bring back a shine. He wanted to look good tomorrow. He thought it would be the most important performance of his life, and everything depended on getting Jon free.

He was tired of eating odd combinations of food. That evening he read labels before he tore them off the cans. He began with Vienna sausage and applesauce, then canned boiled peanuts, pineapple slices, and baked beans. It was a fine meal, but it upset his stomach.

Later, he went out to empty the toilet bucket and carried trash to a dumpster a couple of blocks away. He came back and sat on the roof watching the wink of stars. Mice scurried here and there across the roof. They never seemed to learn. The owl was back in business, swooping down to pluck up a mouse before flying off to dine elsewhere. Bats rose from chimneys and lofts, chasing insects on the wing.

This was not a bad life, Monk thought. He was glad for his time here with Jon. He hoped that living in New York City would be as nice.

The next morning, Monk used a paring knife to clean his fingernails. He put on his new trousers and shirt and buffed his shoes again to make the leather glossy. If Grandmama were here, she'd tell him he needed a bath, but that was out of the question. He wished he had aftershave lotion to cover any natural smells, a trick he'd learned from various men in his life. Using more bottled water he took a spit bath using a washcloth wrapped around one finger to scour suspicious spots here and there on his body. The hardest part was his feet, but that's what shoes were for, to cover up dirty feet.

He descended the trellis carefully to avoid a smear of moss on his clothes, climbed over the gate, walked a block out of his way to avoid the Probe building, and went to court.

The guard said, "You're early."

"Yessir."

"Does your mama let you drink coffee?"

"Is it chicory coffee?" Monk asked.

"No."

"Thank you just the same," Monk said.

"How about a cold orange soda," the guard attempted, "and a couple of doughnuts?"

"That would be nice."

Actually, the guard gave him four doughnuts and some wet paper towels from a bathroom down the hall. "If you need anything," he offered, "come out and let me know."

He was real nice for a white man with a gun.

Twice Monk opened the door a crack and looked in at the courtroom. The first time nobody was there. The second time, a few people had come in and taken places in the pews. Monk returned to his seat and sat on his hands to stop his fingers from picking at things.

There was a huge clock on the wall, with a secondhand that ticked, and paused, and ticked again. The minute hand crept around the dial.

Finally, so bored he was sleepy, Monk went down the hall to the bathroom. He washed his hands and face in hot water, swished his mouth clean, scrubbed his teeth with a forefinger, and headed back to the waiting room. As he passed, the guard said, "It won't be long now."

Another hour ticked away.

Aunt Donna came into the waiting room. For an instant, Monk felt cornered and wanted to run, but he couldn't leave. He had to be here for Jon, so he sat still.

"Where have you been?" she asked.

He stared at his feet, hands beneath his bottom.

She pulled a chair around and sat facing him. "Did you ever run off from your grandmother?"

He stared at the new shoes, which he intended to take off the minute he got out of here. His toes felt like they were trying to hide under one another.

"Uncle Barry and I are trying to help you and you ran away. You didn't run from your grandmother."

"She loved me."

"I want to love you, Monk."

"But you don't," he said.

"It takes time to love someone. It doesn't happen instantly. People have to have a reason for loving one another. I like you, and that's a start. I'll learn to love if you let me."

"You don't want me," Monk said, "and that's all right. I'll go somewhere else to live."

"Where do you imagine that will be?"

"I haven't decided."

"I think you should give us a fair chance before you go off to live among strangers, Monk."

A deputy came to the door. "The judge is ready, young man."

Monk spoke angrily to Aunt Donna as he stood up. "I don't know why you're pretending to want me. I know it isn't true."

The courtroom was now full of people, some well dressed and others clad in baggy and soiled clothing that marked a person living on the street. Every pew was filled. Monk's heart pounded and there was a hum in his ears. The judge sat up higher than everybody else, his desk surrounded by dark wood paneling. He wore a black robe and looked serious.

The deputy led Monk to a chair beside the judge. "Sit here," he said.

To Monk's dismay, Uncle Barry and the bulldog policeman were in back of the courtroom. Aunt Donna came in and joined them. When Monk's eyes met hers, she smiled and nodded. He looked away. He was sure the wham of his heart was shaking his entire body.

"Good morning, son," the judge said.

"Yessir."

"Tell the court your name, please."

"Thelonious Monk DeCay."

"That's a very distinguished name," the judge said. "When you and I met a couple of weeks ago, you gave me permission to call you Monk. Is that still all right?"

"That's fine."

"How old are you, Monk?"

"I'll be ten in nine months."

"Where is your home?"

"Andry Street in Holy Cross."

"That's the Lower Ninth Ward, isn't it?"

"Yessir."

He asked Monk about Grandmama, and Monk talked about things they did together. He said Grandmama massaged his legs after he danced all day in Jackson Square, and when he wore a hole in his sock she'd put the sock over a light bulb to darn a hole in the heel. He said people loved her singing, and she played piano in church. He told the judge how she held him in her lap even though he was getting too big for that, and every night the way she tucked the covers along his body as though wrapping him up until morning. The courtroom was absolutely silent.

Judge Seitz asked Monk to tell about Grandmama getting stuck in the attic, and how he escaped and swam to the levee. Step-by-step, Monk repeated almost everything he'd said in the judge's office two weeks ago.

"When you couldn't find your friend, Mr. Toussaint," the judge prompted, "what did you do?"

"I went looking for Jon."

"Do you know Jon's full name?"

"Jon Latour."

"Do you see Mr. Latour in this room?"

Monk scanned the audience, looked at the table where lawyers sat. "He's not here," he said.

A tall, thin, clean-shaven man raised one hand. "Here I am, Monk."

He wore a dress shirt so big his skinny neck poked up in the middle of the collar like a plant stuck in a pot. He had on a suit and tie; his hair had been cut, which made his ears seem larger.

Monk blinked hard. "Jon?"

"They fixed my leg." Jon extended it and tapped the cast with his knuckles.

Monk went to the table. "I tried to find you, Jon."

"I saw you at the bus station," Jon said, "but I couldn't get to you."

"Monk," Judge Seitz called, "come back and sit down."

Monk whispered to Jon, "I got some money. If we can get out of here, we'll go away together. Maybe to New York City."

"I don't think they'll let me do that, Monk."

Monk realized people were listening. "You're talking good, Jon."

"They're giving me medicine."

"Monk," the judge called, "I need you to come and sit here by me."

Jon stroked Monk's head and Monk grabbed the hand and held it.

"Go on, Monk," Jon said. "Sit where the judge wants you."

The deputy took Monk by the arm.

When he was seated again, the judge said, "You love Jon Latour, don't you?"

He'd never thought about it, but now, with only a moment of reflection, Monk said, "Yes, I do."

"Tell us how you survived after the storm, Monk."

"I swam to the levee."

"I meant, where did you get food and water?"

Theft. There was no other word for what they did. Entering apartments, taking food. It was stealing. He described the rooftop routes they took and how they climbed fire escapes looking for unlocked windows. He told the judge about taking a bath in somebody's tub.

"I have to ask you, Monk," Judge Seitz said. "Did Jon Latour ever hurt you?"

"No. He looked after me."

"He never did anything that made you uncomfortable?"

"No. He's the best friend I ever had."

"When you were crawling around on rooftops, weren't you in danger of falling off?"

"No sir. Jon held on to me. He showed me the way to do things."

"All right," the judge said, "I guess that's it, Monk. Is there anything else you'd like to say about Jon?"

"I promised Quinton I'd look after Jon, but it turned out Jon looked after me. I want to live with him. I'll make money dancing for tourists. He won't have to work at all. We won't go into any more places for food, will we, Jon?"

Jon lifted his fingertips off the table and dropped them.

"I'll look after him and he'll look after me," Monk declared. "My grandmama would be proud of me, living with Jon. She'd see how nice he is, and my grandmama was not easy to fool. She said she could feel badness in people. She'd feel the goodness in Jon."

"All right, Monk," the judge said. "Thank you."

"Mr. Seitz, can I talk to Jon by myself for a few minutes?"

"Not today, Monk. Another time and I'll see what we can do."

"Do I have to leave the room again?"

"You may sit with Mr. Latour," Judge Seitz said. "But do not talk. Is that clear?"

Monk sat beside Jon and took his hand beneath the table.

"Doctor Wendell Johnson," the deputy called a short fat elderly man with wavy hair and bulging eyes. He went to the judge and promised to tell the truth.

"How long have you known Jon Latour, Doctor?"

"He's been under my professional care from time to time since he was in his teens. About twenty years."

"Give us your professional assessment of Mr. Latour's mental and physical condition."

"Physically, he's robust. Climbing around through the Quarter has kept him in good condition. Psychologically, he is schizophrenic with an inclination to paranoia. His fear of others is grounded in life experiences. His mother depended on the generosity of men for a living. Several years before Jon's mother died, she submitted him to electroconvulsive therapy because he was perpetually depressed and suicidal. The electric shock treatments were an attempt to break that cycle."

"Was the treatment successful?" the judge asked.

"It eliminated thoughts of self-destruction, so to that degree it was effective. However it wiped out Jon's memory. Some of that has returned, but he still has holes in his memory."

"Is he a threat to anyone else?"

"In my judgment he is not and never has been."

"Can he live outside custodial care, Doctor?"

"If he stays on medication he should be able to maintain a simple lifestyle. He's been administered Risperidone and that has ameliorated most of his hallucinations. For a long time he thought his mother's male friends were attacking him in the night. Jon felt he had to fight them off."

"Doctor, if I place this man in a private home with minimal duties to perform, will he function in a stable manner?"

"You are referring to the home of Miss DeCay?"

Surprised, Monk turned and looked back at her.

"I think Jon would do well under her care," the doctor said. "She's a school teacher with considerable experience working with troubled minors. This is not so far removed from what she has handled before. She has indicated she wants custody of Mr. Latour, and her brother's son, Thelonious. In my opinion, this could be a relationship that is beneficial for everyone. As his guardian, Miss DeCay can see that Mr. Latour takes his medications. I can treat him as an outpatient."

"Monk," Judge Seitz called, "will you agree to live with your aunt under these conditions?"

He turned to look back at Aunt Donna. She smiled and nodded.

"Sure."

"We'll give this a try," the judge said. "My docket is full. We can't schedule anything right now, but each of you will be notified when we can get together again. Does anyone disagree?"

Nobody responded.

"Then, so be it," Judge Seitz said. He hit his desk with a wooden hammer and said, "Next case."

Monk and Jon sat in the back of Aunt Donna's car on the ride home to Barry's house. Barry had his seat all the way forward to make room for Jon's broken leg in a cast.

"I was afraid the police would send me to Dr. Acee-Deecee," Jon said. "Some of his patients called him Dr. Ampere. He'd strap me down on my back and tell me to bite on something that shot electricity through my head."

"Did it hurt?" Monk asked.

"I didn't feel a thing. A nurse told me I flopped around like a fish out of water, but I didn't feel it."

Aunt Donna and Uncle Barry were very quiet in the front seat.

"Some people think being electrocuted for a crime is cruel, but I know it isn't," Jon said. "Dr. Ampere proved to me it's painless. The only bad thing was when I woke up. Each time it took longer and longer to remember things. I think if you electrocute a criminal he probably wouldn't remember his name."

Aunt Donna turned up the driveway and stopped outside the garage.

"Is this where we're going to live?" Jon asked.

"Yes, it is, Jon," Aunt Donna said.

He had a bedroom to himself, with a TV set. Jon shared Monk's bathroom. Monk helped him make up the bed, and he explained about the big towels for baths and small towels for hands.

It was like a dam that blocked his mind had burst, and words came pouring out of Jon. He cried when he talked about Quinton, telling Monk how Quinton wanted him to play jazz, and Jon didn't like that kind of music.

"He said I was born a musical high brow," Jon related. "I could read a sheet of music and remember every note, but I couldn't improvise."

"Who taught you?" Monk asked.

"Quinton did in the beginning," Jon said. "I read books and practiced when I was a little boy. I taught myself a lot. Quinton thought I'd give concerts and play with symphonies someday. He offered to send me to a music school in New York, but then Dr. Ampere put the juice to me and I couldn't remember my name anymore. That was the end of Quinton's plans for me."

For several nights Monk slept in the same room to reassure Jon when he woke, lost and frightened.

"Is this a hospital?" Jon cried in the dark.

"This is Aunt Donna's house, Jon. We're safe here."

Sometimes when Jon woke Monk, they were both confused. They yelled and jumped around together until they got their bearings. Aunt Donna plugged nightlights into receptacles and shadows loomed. Unlike shadows made from the flames of candles, these dark specters did not move, and that eased Jon's mind. After the doctor adjusted his medicine Jon slept more peacefully.

He did a few things that might have upset Aunt Donna, but she didn't show it. He removed labels from every can in the kitchen. Uncle Barry put a lock on the pantry door and Jon took the hint.

All things considered, life with Jon in the house wasn't bad. He didn't mind peeling potatoes or dicing onions. He took out the garbage and enjoyed working in the yard.

The broken leg had corrected Jon's strange sidewise lope. Because of the cast he still hobbled, but did it face on. Monk was proud of Jon. He wished Quinton could see him now.

{CHAPTER TWENTY-SIX}

Donna found herself thinking of Monk to the tune of the "Twelve Days of Christmas."

> On the first day of Monk he was sullen as could be.
> On the second day of Monk I thought he'd run from me.
> On the third day of Monk I finally took him shopping,
> Bought him pants and shoes and new cotton stockings.
> On the fourth day of Monk I began to see
> A bit of my brother and a tiny hint of me.
> The fifth day was golden; I dared to scold him,
> He completely folded, and came back tearfully.

She knew they were making progress when potential family crises were quickly defused and forgotten. She told Jon to stop dropping his clothes on the floor. He appeared resentful as he picked up after himself. She worried about reprimanding both Jon and Monk, but a household required discipline. Her concern was dispelled when Jon asked her to teach him how to work the washing machine and dryer.

Barry was a great equalizer. He managed to handle every situation with aplomb and humor.

For breakfast, she served pancakes, sausage, and orange juice. They were becoming a family, she thought. She had just congratulated herself that things were working out well when Monk astonished her with an embarrassing question. “You sleep in the same bed with Uncle Barry, don’t you?”

Trying not to overreact, she fumbled for a measured response.

Never one to be flustered, Barry said, “Yes, son, we do occupy the same bed. But in the interest of modesty, I sleep with my eyes closed.”

“Why would you ask such a thing?” Donna questioned.

“Grandmama used to let me get in bed with her when I was afraid. I don’t, I can’t –”

“Hey, hey,” Barry pulled Monk to him, “anytime you’re scared, come jump in bed with us. You’ll be welcome.”

He turned to Jon. “If you decide to come with him, bring your own pillow.”

It was the first time she’d heard Jon laugh.

The day before, Dean had called from Angola. It had been a month since Donna had heard from him.

“I’d been calling you over and over and getting no answer,” he explained. “A couple of other guys wanted me off the phone and we had a slight altercation. As punishment the guards took away my telephone privileges.”

“Dean,” she broke her news sorrowfully, “Mr. Toussaint is dead.”

“Yeah, I know,” he said. “I got a note from Quinton’s attorney, Ormand Delacroix. I’m named in Quinton’s will. I need you to handle it for me, Donna. Where can I mail the papers?”

“I’ll come get them.”

“No. Do not come here. I’ll send them to you.”

“Dean,” she said, firmly, “I’m coming up there.”

“I said, no.”

“I don’t give a damn what you said,” she snapped. “You and I have to talk, and I’ll be there. Make certain I’m on the visitor list.”

“I don’t want you to come to this place.”

“Put me on the list, Dean.”

Delacroix had told Donna about the will. “Toussaint left Dean his house and certificates of deposit. Shortly after Dean's conviction, when Quinton dictated the will, he said he was handling Dean's royalties as his own—at Dean's request—to prevent the funds being attached in a possible wrongful death suit by relatives of the man Dean shot."

"How much money are you talking about?"

"I haven't spoken to the accountant recently, but I would imagine close to three hundred thousand dollars in certificates."

Talking to Dean, Donna said, "I didn't realize you and Mr. Toussaint were such close friends."

"He produced my records, negotiated contracts, and he loved Elaine almost as much as I did. He was my best friend."

Raucous prison sounds forced them to silence for a moment. Donna heard Dean sigh heavily.

"Come up on Wednesday," he relented. "They require a picture ID to get in. A driver's license will do. Go first to the Front Gate Processing Center. They have metal detectors, an x-ray machine, drug interdiction devices, and a computerized system for processing visitors. Bring a roll of quarters so we can use vending machines in the visiting room."

This morning she'd left New Orleans before daybreak, stopped in Baton Rouge for breakfast, and now with the sun rising behind her, she followed State Highway 66 through vaporous bogs of West Feliciana Parish toward the prison. The fog and isolation made her feel she had slipped into another dimension.

On the bough of a cypress tree she saw an osprey perched beside a rough stick nest. Cardinals darted through roadside woodlands like flecks of red paint flung on a canvas. Twice she had to maneuver around alligators crawling across the pavement. The air was heavy with moisture and a musky smell of swampland. Now and then she smelled air sweetened by blooming plants.

Barry used a camera borrowed from the *Probe* to shoot digital images of Monk. He enlarged each photo to 8 x 10, and Donna had them with her. She also had a sheaf of papers Delacroix had prepared for Dean to sign, naming her the new executor of Quinton's will.

"When we drew up the instrument of disposition," Delacroix said, "I was executor. I would like to turn that over to you, if you'll accept. You will disburse funds and pay the bills, which will include my legal fee.

Dean must agree with this arrangement. Be sure to get his signature on the release."

The attorney turned pages, explaining legalese. "This document gives you the right to live free in Quinton's house so long as you pay property taxes and upkeep. If Dean elects to sell the place, and you decide to handle that for him, he should put his name on the addendum to the lease agreement giving you the right to dispose of the property at a price you consider fair. Have him call me in a day or two and I'll act as notary on all of this."

Hocus-pocus.

From the tiny town of Tunica, Donna followed markers pointing to the Louisiana State Penitentiary. Miasma spread across the land like a soft blanket. She had decided not to tell Dean about Monk's trouble with the law and the court appearance. Nor would she mention Jon Latour. Take this one step at a time, she thought.

Morning sun cast a shadow of the car before her as she reached the red and yellow prison entrance. A guard tower to her right overlooked a high chain-link fence topped with razor wire. She was filled with dread almost to the point of fear. Her palms and underarms were slick with sweat, and she couldn't stop trembling. She had visions of a strip search, somebody probing body cavities with a rubber-gloved hand.

As it turned out, visitor processing was surprisingly fast and simple. She was treated with solemn courtesy, passed through a metal detector, and then transported to Camp C along with other visitors. Waiting for Dean to arrive, she studied the visiting area. It was as she'd imagined, cold hard surfaces and resounding acoustics. Soft drink machines and snack food dispensers lined one wall. The place was in sad need of a decorator.

Dean met her with a tight smile but he lingered in a long hug.

She stepped back and looked him over. He was older, but then, so was she. Unruly graying hair swept back from an advancing brow. In his eyes she saw residual sadness. "You look good," she said, and actually he did, trim, tanned, and fit. They sat at a corner table across from one another, away from other visitors and inmates.

Donna presented the photographs. Anticipating his pleasure, she said, "We found Thelonious."

"Yeah," Dean said, flatly, "Delacroix mentioned it in his note about the will."

Well, damn him, that ruined the surprise. Donna sustained a smile. "Thelonious prefers to be called Monk," she said.

"His grandmother warned us that would happen." Dean shuffled through pictures with the long supple fingers of a born pianist. "The boy looks like his mother."

"There are moments when he is you," Donna said. "He gets a particular look in his eye, an expression of intensity when he's concentrating on something, the way he twists his lip."

Dean paused and touched one of the photos. "That's Elaine right there. God, she was beautiful."

"I want to bring him here to meet you, Dean."

"Absolutely not." He fixed her with a belligerent glare she'd known all their lives, obstinate and uncompromising.

"Well," she said mildly, "I'm bringing him anyway."

"Goddamn it," Dean rose to his feet. "I said no! Absolutely no!"

"Easy over there," a voice spoke over a sound system. "Sit down, inmate."

Donna put her hands together and met his gaze. "Here's how it is, Dean. Your son is going to meet you because he can never be a whole person until he does. He's going to hear the story eventually, and it's astonishing that he hasn't heard it before now. Everybody around him has kept you a secret. He didn't know if you were alive or dead."

"Dead is what I am."

"You're writing songs, working with the prison radio station, you have a jazz ensemble. That doesn't sound dead to me."

"If you bring Thelonious, I won't see him," Dean threatened.

"In which case, I might as well give up, Dean. The state will put your son into foster care until he's a grown man. By the time he finds out about you, he'll detest you with an intensity you'll never overcome."

"Damn you, Donna."

"And damned I may be, Dean, we both are. You are egocentric beyond belief. You claim to have loved Monk's mother so much you killed the man who killed her, and then you turned your back on a piece of her. What kind of love is that?"

"I don't want him to remember me this way."

"He won't remember you at all. He doesn't know you."

She gestured at the people around them. "You know what you have in common with every prisoner in this place? They're selfish. They committed crimes without a thought of anybody who cared about them. You married a black woman and said to hell with the consequences. Then you shut out your family because they didn't approve."

"I didn't shut them out, they shut me out. Mom was always trying to make me into something I didn't want to be. She wanted a concert pianist, for god's sake."

"Well, you showed her," Donna said. "No tuxedos and champagne for you. Your career was set in a smoky bar filled with a noisy beer guzzling audience, uninhibited and nonjudgmental. Even the music is disorganized and freewheeling."

"We call that improvisation," Dean said.

"You took to jazz to defy our parents. The music was just like you wanted your life, no structure and no rules. If you dropped a note who would recognize the error?"

Tattooed men and their overweight women held hands across other tables. A child sat beside his mother, thumb in his mouth, gazing at her man with huge amber eyes. His nose was running, but nobody noticed.

"Abandoning Monk," Donna said more softly, "you denied him his father, stole his education, culture, and security. You killed a pusher that everybody agrees needed to be dead. But at the same time you wounded your own son."

"It's interesting that you see it that way," Dean replied bitterly. "I would expect that reaction from the folks, but not from you. You say I took to jazz to rebel against our parents? Look at you, Donna. You became a teacher only because you knew our parents would approve. When we were children you wanted to be an actress. The moment Mom and Dad criticized the choice, you gave up your dreams and followed the line of least resistance."

"In my case they were right," Donna said. "The chance of success in theater is so slim I would've been a bit player all my life."

"I don't know whether you'd have been a star or not, but you might've enjoyed it. I enjoy jazz. A classic pianist works in a cultured atmosphere, quiet, dignified, and controlled. And that's what I hated about it. Jazz is intuitive, creative, and expressive."

Donna's cheeks felt hot. "You killed a man for purely selfish reasons,

Dean. You tell yourself it was to avenge the death of your wife, but was it? You saw yourself as a hero, and so did everybody else for a while. But the truth is, you couldn't face raising a son on your own. Well, Dean, the time has come for you to take responsibility for the boy."

"What do you think I can do sitting here for the next fourteen years?"

"Write letters," Donna reached for his hand. "Tell Monk about his mother. Show some concern for his future. Call him on holidays. Compose a song for him. Take an interest in what he's interested in."

"Tell him I love him, you mean."

"Show him that you love him."

Dean shook his head, eyes downcast. A young mother at a nearby table bounced a baby on her knee and the toddler squealed.

"Dean, why did you call me to go see about Monk and his grandmother?"

"There was no one else I could turn to."

"You could've asked Quinton Toussaint."

"I called Quinton and he didn't answer. He would never leave New Orleans anyway, and Mrs. James wouldn't go with him if he did. She disapproved of him and the company he kept, including me."

"Do you want me to raise Monk?" Donna asked.

"You know I do."

She presented a release. "Then sign here."

She turned pages. "And here."

"Our parents will never accept him, Donna."

"Then that will be their loss. Although I believe they won't be able to resist if they meet him. This last paper gives me control of your money. It's a power of attorney. You want to think about that before you agree?"

He signed it immediately.

"The truth be known," Donna said, "Monk has incredible appeal. He already plays piano and dances for tourists in Jackson Square. His grandmother has schooled him at home and as soon as I have him tested for proficiency I'll put him into classes somewhere. He's looking forward to learning about computers. For Christmas, I'll see that he gets one."

There were tears in Dean's eyes.

"He's been saving for the day when he could go looking for you," Donna said. "We went by his grandmother's house so he could retrieve a jar full of money he earned before the storm."

"He'll be disappointed in me."

"No, Dean, he'll finally understand. He aches to admire you, so let him."

"He'll want to know why I'm here."

"Then tell him."

He studied a photo of Monk and Donna saw a tear hit the image. "I look at him," Dean said, "and I see Elaine gazing back at me."

"She'd be proud of her son, and I'm sure she'd be devastated by your lack of caring."

"If he doesn't like me, I won't be able to bear it, Donna."

"He'll like you."

Dean twisted away and peered over the heads of other visitors. A child scampered by and a voice on the public address system said, "Children must remain with the approved visitor."

"Oh, God," Dean said. "How will I explain ignoring him all this time?"

"Tell him the truth."

"I'm not sure I know the truth."

"The truth is, Dean, you were afraid."

Donna held his hand and squeezed it.

"Okay," Dean said.

"Okay what, Dean?"

"Okay, I'll think about letting you bring him up. I don't want to do it. But I'll think about it."

On Friday, September 30th, a few days after Hurricane Rita bypassed New Orleans, Mayor Ray Nagin removed roadblocks and cleared the way for the return of residents and merrymakers to the French Quarter. Twenty-four hours later, a dozen bars were in full swing on Bourbon Street. Strip clubs dropped cover charges and threw open their doors. Pedestrians on the banquettes caught a glimpse of feminine fannies as they ambled by. Liquor flowed. Some establishments offered two drinks for the price of one. The carefree aspects of life in the Crescent City resumed.

A month after Hurricane Rita, tap water in the city was still not safe to drink, and in many cases it wasn't suitable for washing hands. Tonight,

Barry was taking Donna and Monk to a bistro near the Probe building. She found sanitizing gel in the rest room beside a stack of hand towels. The walls reverberated with cacophonous sounds of humanity.

Jon refused to come with them this evening. He didn't like going out in public. Crowds made him uneasy. Donna stopped urging him to join them. They left him in his room watching television.

When Donna returned to the table, Monk had moved to sit beside Barry. They observed an impromptu dance by a top-heavy lady wearing mesh stockings and red spike heeled shoes.

"What do you think of that, Monk?" Donna heard Barry ask.

"Jon would like her shoes."

On the streets, people walked around heaps of storm debris amid the wet smell of uncollected garbage. Strolling past the Old Opera House, Donna's hearing was assailed by offensively loud zydeco music. "This place used to be jammed with college kids," Barry shouted to be heard.

Tonight, the clientele was government bureaucrats, construction workers, rescue people, and medical personnel from the navy hospital ship, *Comfort*, where they'd first taken Jon Latour to set his broken bone and put him in a cast. Hospitals in New Orleans were still closed. City services were hit and miss. Barry insisted that a lack of normalcy was normal for New Orleans, and he waxed philosophical about electrical brown outs and mossy stuff oozing from spigots.

Two doctors in green surgical scrubs drank Sazeracs with nurses still wearing professional smocks. The rye whiskey cocktails had a sanguine effect. Buoyant laughter spilled into the street, and Barry said the scene was a microcosm of what the city had been before the storms.

"New Orleans is the most resilient city in the nation," Barry gushed. "I noticed today, people are putting pots of flowers back on balconies. Begonias, jasmine, marigolds, spider plants, and hanging baskets of fern are the flowery lace of civilized man. I saw a musician playing violin to an empty street, but at least he's there, in hopes that an audience will eventually come."

They ate dinner in a small out-of-the-way place whose offerings were posted on a blackboard attached to a wall. Donna never did know the name of the establishment, but the café au lait waitress and portly owner knew Barry. She noticed that they accepted Monk's presence without batting an eye.

"What have you, bro?" the waitress asked Monk, and Monk grinned. "Do you have mudbugs?"

"Just what you see on the board, babe. We got precious little refrigeration these days, so we serve tonight what we could get this morning."

"We'll have a mess of boudin balls," Barry said, "a pitcher of draft beer for the lady and me; a tall root beer for our lad."

"What are boudin balls?" Donna inquired.

"Dey be a local delicacy," the waitress said, "something of an acquired taste for someone out-town like you-self. Boudin balls are the breaded and deep fried testicles of the freshwater boudin, dawlin'."

Suddenly they all burst into laughter, including Monk.

"Dat good line ain't mine," the waitress confessed. "It be spoke by Chuck Taggert on his Jazzfest Log back in '94."

Donna had gumbo so thick there wasn't room left for liquid. The boudin balls were a rice-filled sausage with pork, pork livers, onions, garlic, and loads of spices. Removed from the skins, rolled into balls, breaded, and fried, they were delicious.

"Did your grandmama ever make these?" Barry asked Monk.

"No sir, but Fiona and Earl Thibodeaux did."

"Do you like them?"

"I like them a lot."

"A true Cajun palate," Barry said, and he grabbed Monk by the neck and shook him affectionately.

While Donna was at Angola, Monk had spent the day with Barry at the Probe.

"They took him in like a son," Barry reported that night. "Eddy taught Monk how to handicap a horse race, Tiny showed him a couple of wrestling holds, and he sat in on an editorial meeting where the cover story was decided."

Putting Monk to bed, Donna asked, "Did you enjoy the day?"

"I did, Aunt Donna."

Lamplight fell across his face and she saw herself reflected in dark pools of chocolate eyes. She adjusted the sheet around his shoulders.

"What did you think of the Probe, Monk?"

"I liked it. I'd been there before."

"Oh?" Donna sat on the edge of his bed. "When were you there?"

"Jon and I went there to steal toilet paper one day."

"How did you get in?"

"Through a window at the back."

She bent and kissed him. "Sleep well, baby."

"Aunt Donna, do you think Jon is going to be all right?"

"He's making progress, Monk. The doctor is pleased. The only question now is, can he function in society?"

Jon was in his room down the hall watching television.

"What does he have to do to function?" Monk asked.

Donna pushed back a lock of hair and like a spring it returned to curl over Monk's forehead.

"The judge wants to know," Donna said, "can he make it on his own and hold a job?"

"You think they'll want him to get a job?"

"He has to show some means of support, Monk. He can't pilfer apartments for what he needs. That's not unreasonable is it?"

"If he doesn't get better, what will happen to him?"

"I imagine, at the very worst, they'll put him where other people can look after him," she said. "There'll be a staff to feed and clothe him. It's not like he'd be confined to a cell, Monk. He'll make new friends. There'll be games and activities he'll enjoy. However, for the moment he has been released in my care. When we move to Mr. Toussaint's home I'll pay him an allowance for keeping the yard and maintaining the residence. I think everything is going to be all right."

"Jon can play the piano whenever he wants to?"

"Yes, and I've asked him to continue your piano lessons. He agreed."

Monk thought about it a moment, and then he said, "He still doesn't like to go out in daylight, and he's afraid of people."

Monk's distress was so unsettling, Donna said, "Before we get upset over what might happen, let's wait and see what the doctor says. So far, he's pleased, and so am I. Jon is a good man. If he wants more independence, he can live in Quinton's carriage house when we move over there.

On the other hand, he's welcome to stay in the main house with us."

"The other night I heard him fighting spirits again," Monk admitted.

"But there's less and less of that," Donna said. "His medication is working." She tucked him in and leaving the room she stopped at the door. "He just needs time to get better, Monk."

"Yes ma'am. Good night."

Donna went to bed and lay beside Barry. She touched his hip, and in his slumber he took her hand. This past month she'd seen signs that he could be a good father. He taught Monk to play Scrabble, and helped him use an unabridged dictionary to learn new words. Walking down the street, they linked arms in a gesture so natural neither of them seemed to notice. In Monk, Barry had found an appreciative audience for his corny jokes and they cackled together.

Donna snuggled nearer and kissed his shoulder. Barry snored resonantly and farted in his sleep. The smell of boudin balls and gumbo rose in the room.

{CHAPTER TWENTY-SEVEN}

Today was the day for Grandmama's memorial, and Monk felt bad that he didn't want to go. "The final goodbye," Uncle Barry called it, and the thought of saying goodbye for the last time was heartbreaking. Monk imagined himself standing in an empty building because who else was left to mourn? But the service wasn't for Grandmama alone, Aunt Donna said. It was for everybody who died in Hurricane Katrina.

Aunt Donna had packed a suitcase this morning. It would do them good to get out of town for a while, she said to Uncle Barry. She and Monk needed some time together. It wasn't a vacation. Just a trip for the two of them.

Monk rode quietly in the front seat. The sky was pale blue, the sun a weak and distant star. The world seemed colorless and uncaring.

Riding through Bywater on the way to Baby Jesus Spiritual Church, he saw signs tacked to telephone poles and store fronts. "MEMORIAL SERVICE FOR ALL SOULS LOST IN THE STORM," posters advertised, "BABY JESUS SPIRITUAL CHURCH."

They passed a bar and he heard the voice of Fats Domino singing an old song on a jukebox, "Ain't That a Shame." Outside on the banquette, men smoked cigarettes and sat on a bench playing bourré. Windows of Mr. Benoit's time saver store were covered with sheets of plywood. Gang boys had scrawled their signs across the new wood.

"Since Aunt Bishop Beulah is dead," Monk broke the silence, "who will give the sermon?"

"I didn't think to ask, Monk."

It offended him that people on the street went about their lives as though nothing had happened. Didn't they know Grandmama was dead? Couldn't they sense a void in the world around them? The air felt too heavy to breathe, and after a restless night he woke up feeling exhausted. Even his teeth were sensitive to the touch of tongue. Now, looking out the car window, he saw people laughing. Men leaned against a wall watching a pretty girl on her bicycle. A woman walked by carrying an armload of groceries.

"Where will they bury Grandmama?" Monk asked.

"Remember I told you," Aunt Donna reminded, "they asked for permission to cremate the body and we agreed. They needed to do that for lack of space and for health reasons. Her remains are now ashes."

"I've changed my mind about that," Monk said resentfully. "I don't think Grandmama would like being burned. What happens to the ashes?"

"They'll give them to you," Aunt Donna said. "We'll pick them up at the crematorium when we come back from our trip. You can keep them at home if you wish."

"Grandmama said a grave gives you a place to go when you need to grieve. She went to my granddaddy's grave once in a while."

"We can put her ashes where your grandfather is buried," Donna suggested.

He thought about that for a minute. "I don't want to leave her with somebody I never met."

"In which case, we'll keep her at home until you decide otherwise."

Here and there in the Ninth Ward government house trailers were parked in driveways of homes under repair. By a ring of mud at the high water mark Monk could tell the depth of flooding they'd suffered. Red brick houses were a sickly pink. Board and batten siding pulled away from studs. Blue plastic tarps covered damaged roofs. He'd been on this street many times, but today nothing looked familiar. Trash hung on fences and shrubs like dirty laundry gone to rot. Abandoned toys beckoned children who were no longer available to play.

He recognized one ranch-style masonry house because of ornate burglar bars on the windows. The front door was a heavy iron gate. On the wall was one of those spray-painted X's with the grim notation, "2 dead 3 pets." He could imagine frantic attempts to break through the bars as rising water drove the people and animals to the ceiling where they finally drowned.

He remembered a chow dog at that house, an ugly, heavy beast with a black spotted tongue and a mean disposition. He and Percy rode past here on the bicycle one time, and the chow seemed to charge out of nowhere. Monk thought for sure the animal had them, but suddenly the dog reached the end of his tether and did a back flip. He came up snarling.

Shaking, Percy had said, "I'm going to kill that dog someday."

The storm had taken care of that. In the yard at the end of his chain lay the decomposing body powdered with lime.

Outside the Baby Jesus Spiritual Church, their upright piano sagged under a tree, the veneer warped and ruined. Cars and pickup trucks were parked bumper-to-bumper on the street. People were dressed up as though for Sunday services.

Monk saw Fiona and hurried to her. She towered over him in high heel shoes, her penetrating black eyes framed in long lashes and mascara. She stared down at him as if he were a stranger. Confused, he said, "I'm Monk, Miss Fiona. I saw Randy shoot Uncle Earl."

"Yes," Fiona responded coldly, "the police told me. They said you didn't report it. What's the matter with you, Monk? Why didn't you tell the police?"

He didn't know how to explain, but as it was he didn't have to. Fiona turned away when another adult got her attention.

Alan Benoit sat in a front pew without Cherita and her mother. Now Monk knew for sure they had not survived. He tried to swallow a lump in his throat. His chest ached with the thought that Sister Julianne and sweet baptized Cherita were gone forever.

He scooted next to Aunt Donna in a pew filled with mourners. Strangers stood along the walls from front door to back. Somebody brought in a folding chair for an old woman and another chair for a crippled man. They sat in the aisle. Four men struggled through a side door with a spinet piano. They wrestled it onto the low stage and a moment later, Percy entered and sat down. He looked odd in a pullover turtleneck shirt with a short haircut and shined shoes.

Percy touched the keys to test for tune, and the murmuring congregation fell silent. He did a slow cascade, hand-over-hand, just as Quinton had taught him. Then he played "Amazing Grace."

Monk collapsed into tears and Aunt Donna pulled him under her arm. He couldn't help it. Tears flowed and he sobbed uncontrollably.

He could almost hear Grandmama's voice, singing softly, "… was blind, but now I see … 'Twas grace that taught my heart to fear and grace my fears relieved …"

Percy was never able to resist improvisation. He played a long, slow bridge and worked his way through the last line back to the lead: Amazing Grace, how sweet the sound that saved a wretch like me …

Willy Bouchard preached a sermon as well as anybody could expect from a fruit and vegetable man. He began by thanking a mortuary for the loan of their piano and Percy for providing the music.

Willy thanked God for people spared and begged mercy for souls who perished before they had time to repent for their sins. He reminded everybody that the Bible promised they'd all meet again someday. Then from a long list he called out names of people who died:

"Sister Julianne Benoit survived by her husband, Alan."

Monk saw his hands tremble. "Five-year-old Cherita, their only child."

He read names Monk did not know. Now and then he paused to sip water from a plastic glass.

"Diane James, who played piano for the Blessed Baby Jesus Spiritual Church," Willy continued. "She will be missed by all who knew her. She leaves behind her grandson, Thelonious Monk DeCay."

He recited names of church members and neighbors. From slips of paper submitted by strangers he spoke of victims here and elsewhere. "Over a thousand died in Louisiana and Mississippi," Willy recounted. The audience wept and moaned loudly so the spirits would hear.

When he finished reading the names given to him, Willy Bouchard said, "Is there anyone else?" People from other places stood up to speak of relatives and acquaintances. The lady who raised rabbits and chickens lost her husband when he went out to check the livestock. A nun spoke of a sister caught in a small house where she'd gone to help an invalid. They both died.

Fiona rose to her feet. "My husband Earl Thibodeaux was shot and killed by burglars robbing my store," she said.

"God rest his soul," Willy intoned, and the people replied, "Amen."

After everyone else had spoken, Willy Bouchard said, "To the long list I now add my wife, Bishop Beulah Bouchard, survived by our children, grandchildren, and me. Her heart could not bear the tragedy she came home to find."

Throughout, as mourners spoke, Percy played softly, Amazing grace, how sweet the sound …

The church smelled like too many people in a space too small. The scents of perfumes, lotions, and sweat mixed with a lingering stink from the flood itself. Willie called for the doxology and the congregation linked arms and swayed back and forth, singing. He shouted above the chorus, it was time to let the dead be gone; time to begin their lives anew.

As the crowd filed out of church, Percy came to Monk and hugged him. "I thought you were dead," he said.

"That's what I thought about you." Monk began to cry and Percy held him tighter.

"Your grandmama," Percy choked, and he cried, too.

Monk slumped into a pew and they tearfully recalled people lost. "Cherita and Sister Julianne … Uncle Earl … Aunt Bishop Beulah …"

"Where did you go, Monk? How did you eat? Who were you with?"

Monk explained.

"You lived with the ghost of Vieux Carré?" Percy marveled.

"He's living with us, now," Monk said. He told about going to court with Jon, and Uncle Barry's home near Tulane. He pointed at Aunt Donna standing at the church door talking to Willy Bouchard. "See that woman? She's my father's sister. I'm living with her. We'll be moving into Quinton Toussaint's house in a few weeks."

Percy's lips thinned. "I reckon you'll change," he said.

"No, I won't. What happened to you during the storm, Percy?"

"Uncle Earl wouldn't let me stay here," Percy reported. "He said I had to leave town with my kinfolks. I was stuck in a car with fifteen hundred pounds of people looking for a place to piss. I guess it saved my life. If I'd been here with Uncle Earl, Randy might've shot me, too. Aunt Fiona doesn't understand why you didn't call the cops, Monk, but I do. When is the trial supposed to be?"

"They said at least a year away."

"If there is a trial," Percy concluded. "Don't forget Randy's old man is a cop, and we know what that means. Listen. When you move into Quinton's house, can I come over and play the piano?"

"Sure."

"And meet the ghost of Vieux Carré?"

"Sure, Percy."

When they left church, Aunt Donna drove north. Traffic on the interstate was heavy with army convoys that moved troops and equipment into and out of New Orleans. Along the highway commercial billboards had been twisted and bent by wind. Abandoned cars cluttered the median. The highway was littered with plastic grocery sacks, thermos bottles, Styrofoam ice chests, clothing, and pieces of furniture. An empty Coca-Cola machine lay in a ditch with the lid open.

Monk peered out the car window at snowy egrets stalking insects in fields where motionless humpback Brahman cattle stood like statues of gray stone. The world looked sad.

After miles of silence, he said, "Why didn't Uncle Barry come with us?"

"He's on deadline to write a story for this week's issue."

"Does he have a story?"

"Elvis Attacks Graveyard Thief," Aunt Donna said. "A vandal tried to steal a plaque off the grave of Elvis Presley at Graceland. Going over a wall to escape, the crook fell. He said Elvis pushed him, and it knocked him out."

Aunt Donna drove along Louisiana backwaters where long-legged cranes fed in shallow ponds and swampy bogs. Monk had thought he would get to speak to Grandmama's spirit at the funeral, but it didn't happen. Willie Bouchard said all that was going to be said and very little was about Grandmama. Monk felt mostly left out of the memorial.

They stopped in Baton Rouge for an early lunch, and Monk ate two helpings of banana pudding for dessert. When they were seated again in the car, he said, "Is this the way to Atlanta?

"Atlanta is northeast. We're going northwest."

"Where to?"

"Angola."

"Angola? That's where the prison is."

"Yes," she said.

"Why are we going there?"

She patted him on the knee. "There's somebody I want you to meet."

{CHAPTER TWENTY-EIGHT}

"My father is in prison?" Monk said.

Aunt Donna drove slowly. There was not much traffic on the road to the prison. The whole world seemed to have slowed down.

"What did he do?" Monk asked.

"He killed someone."

"Was he framed?"

"No, Monk. He killed a man."

"It was probably an accident."

"No," Aunt Donna said. "He meant to do it."

He could hardly believe what she was telling him. He listened as she talked about his mother's addiction, and his father's anger. She told him how rage drove Tooth DeCay to murder. "He was overwhelmed by loss and wrath," she said. "He didn't think of the consequences, Monk. He found the man and killed him. It was an awesome error in judgment. Dean didn't want you to know these things, and that was his second error."

He realized she was driving so slowly he could have run alongside the car and kept up. She was giving herself time to tell him what she had to say. He learned that Quinton knew all about this from the very beginning, and so too, Grandmama. Nobody told him, Donna said, because they wanted to protect him. Protect him. He felt deceived and angry.

"Apparently they didn't talk about it to you or anyone else in your presence," Aunt Donna said. "That's how much they respected Dean DeCay."

Suddenly, Monk did not want to meet his father. The thought of it scared him. "Please, let's go home," he said. "I'll write to him first."

"What would you say in a letter?" Aunt Donna reasoned.

"I'd say hello how are you fine I hope."

"You can say that when you meet him."

"I'd say do you want me to come see you?"

"He'd say yes and here you are."

She drove up to the prison gate and guards wanted to know the nature of her business. "Visiting an inmate," she said.

Inmate. His father was an inmate.

In the visitor's center, on a bulletin board were posted facts about Angola. It was the largest prison in the United States with 5,108 inmates and 1,740 staff. A map on the wall showed the prison spread over 18,000 acres located 59 miles northwest of Baton Rouge, surrounded on three sides by the Mississippi River. Interesting facts, the bulletin board advised: blues singer Lead Belly and Tex-Mex artist Freddy Fender had both been pardoned from here.

In the waiting area, Monk found copies of the *Angolite*, a magazine published by prisoners. There were photographs of men riding on bucking bulls and cowboys on horseback chasing calves. It said the prison held a rodeo every year in April and October. Another article reported 84 men and one woman were on death row awaiting execution. Of the inmates in residence, the article said, 86 percent were violent offenders. 52 percent served life sentences and would never be released from prison.

"Is Tooth here for the rest of his life?" Monk questioned.

"No," Aunt Donna replied.

A bus took them to a place called "Camp C" where Tooth was being held. Monk saw prisoners mowing lawns, driving tractors. They looked free enough to him. Most of the visitors riding with him in the bus were black adults. There were a few children, too; all of them strangely quiet as they rode to their destination. Inside the visiting area people went to tables and sat down to wait. Prisoners came in. When Tooth arrived, Aunt Donna stood up.

Monk knew his father was white; Quinton had told him, Grandmama said so, and he'd seen photographs, so he knew Tooth was white. But he never actually thought about his father being white, so it caught him by surprise. Tooth was tall, balding, with blue eyes, unmistakably Caucasian. He was larger than his photographs, of course, and he looked older than Monk expected.

First, Tooth hugged Aunt Donna, and then he turned to gaze at Monk. A cheek muscle pulled his lip as if he were trying to smile, or maybe trying not to smile. Monk thought he seemed nervous. So was he.

"You look like your mother," Tooth said. His voice was not as deep as Monk had imagined it might be.

This was not like any fantasy Monk had ever conjured. They would not be living in a jungle, hunting wild game, camping with nearly naked natives. There was no secret assignment to fulfill. Monk did not have to parachute from an airplane to get here, nor would he be shot from the torpedo tube of a submarine. What he saw around him was all there was. His father had a number on his shirt, and a stenciled reminder that his clothing belonged to LSP—Louisiana State Prison.

Tooth sat on one side of a table, Monk and Aunt Donna on the other. "You look like your mother," his father said again, as though he hadn't said it the first time. "She was the most beautiful woman I ever knew. You have her eyes."

"That's what Grandmama said."

"Your grandmother. Yeah. I'm sorry about your grandmother, Thelonious."

Monk felt like people were listening to them, but he saw that they weren't. At other tables men and women held hands and whispered through nervous smiles. All they heard was one another.

"Do you remember much about your mother?" Tooth asked.

"No sir."

"She had an angel's voice. She was a brilliant performer."

"Yessir."

"When we got married, we thought we were grown up," Tooth said, "but in fact, we were children."

"Yessir."

"Let me see your hands, son."

Monk extended his arms and his father turned up the palms. His touch was electrifying. He had hair on his knuckles and his fingernails were neatly trimmed. "Your mother believed she could tell a person's future by looking at his hands," Tooth said. "When you were first born, she took your hands and studied them. 'This long line is your lifeline,' she said. 'You will live many years.'" He smiled. "She's right so far, isn't she?"

"Yessir."

Tooth pressed flesh with a finger and traced another crease, "This line indicates a happy and successful career. You will marry once, and it will last a lifetime. 'That's good,' she said. She was telling you these things when you were an infant, Thelonious. This was when you were a baby just born. But Elaine looked at these hands like they were pictures of the future yet to come."

Monk could scarcely breathe.

His father bent and kissed the palm of Monk's hand. "Do you remember when we went for a ride on the Delta Queen paddle-wheeler?"

"No sir."

"We had fun that day," Tooth said. He still held Monk's hands. "These lines mean you'll have four children."

Monk stared at the tiny folds that predicted such information.

"We went to the zoo," Tooth murmured. "They had a white tiger."

"Was my mama with us?"

Tooth shot a glance at Aunt Donna. "No," he said. "Your mother was in a hospital trying to get over some bad habits. You and I went to the zoo alone. I taught you to ride a tricycle while she was gone. We fished in a lake and you caught a bream. It was a wee bit of a fish, but the world would've thought it a whale, you were so excited."

Searching for memories of his own, Monk said, "Do you remember playing piano with my hands on top of yours? You played slow songs. I remember that."

By Tooth's expression, Monk didn't think he remembered, but his father said, "That was the day your mother died."

"Oh."

Monk tried again. "I once sang in church with my mother."

"I remember that," Tooth said. "I played piano. You were about three years old. You do recall that, Thelonious?"

"No sir," Monk confessed. "Grandmama told me."

Tooth spread Monk's fingers. "Your Aunt Donna says you play piano."

"Not as well as I want to, but I'm trying."

"You have good hands for it. What kind of music do you like?"

"Boogie-woogie. Jazz."

"Good for you. Play what you enjoy. Don't make yourself miserable trying to create only what others want to hear."

Conversation lapsed and Tooth looked at Aunt Donna. Monk didn't know what to call him—dad, daddy, father, papa, Tooth, Dean, sir ...

"Tell me about when I was born," Monk said.

"You were very young," Tooth replied. Aunt Donna laughed.

"It was Wednesday, August 7, 1996. Your mother wanted to eat before she entered the hospital because she said they wouldn't let her have food once she went into labor. She stuck out so far she looked like a character from *Sesame Street*. Big Bird. You know that character from television?"

"Grandmama didn't have television."

"Taking her to the hospital," Tooth said, "we went to a little place in the Quarter called the Clover Grill."

"I know the Grill," Monk said. "They serve breakfast day and night. Remember, Aunt Donna? We went there."

"I remember." Her eyes were shiny and wet.

"The evening you were about to be born," Tooth said, "a friend of ours took us there; Quinton Toussaint. You know Quinton."

"Yessir."

"The place was a riot, loud music, people shouting. There was a man on the street singing loud as he could. Because Elaine was pregnant, they turned off the music and told people to be quiet. Everybody thought you were about to be born right there in the restaurant."

Monk laughed.

"Elaine said, turn up the music! I want my baby to hear what he's coming to. They plugged in the jukebox, people laughed, and the guy outside began to sing again."

Tooth slipped away from Monk's hands and sat back. "We barely made it to the hospital in time. You were born at eleven o'clock that night. Eight pounds, two ounces. A big, handsome, healthy boy. I'd never seen Elaine so happy. She kissed your fingers. She studied your hands and the soles of your feet. She said, look Tooth! The most beautiful child in the world."

Aunt Donna went to a machine and bought cold sodas. Tooth told about gigs he and Monk's mother had played for huge crowds in cities like New York, Los Angeles, and Chicago.

They did not discuss murder.

The visit was limited to four hours, and ended too quickly. When it came time to leave, Tooth hugged Monk so tightly he couldn't inhale. He kissed Monk on the cheeks and forehead, and finally on the lips.

"I'm sorry we couldn't remember more, Thelonious."

"It's okay," Monk said. "We can make new memories."

"Yeah," Tooth grinned. "That's what we'll do. Make new memories. I'll write to you."

"I'll write you back," Monk promised.

Riding away from the prison in Donna's car, Monk said, "When will Tooth get out?"

"In fourteen years."

They rode past glades and bogs. Egrets were sprinkled through the fields.

"Do you think Tooth will be famous again, Aunt Donna?"

"I don't know."

For a while they rode without speaking, and then Monk asked, "Where're we going now?"

"I thought maybe we could go to Atlanta and meet your grandparents."

"Are they expecting us?"

"No. It will be a surprise."

"I don't want to go, Aunt Donna. Let me write a letter."

"Actually," she said, "that's a good idea. We could send letters and pictures."

"I could make a CD playing piano," Monk suggested.

Aunt Donna nodded. "That's what we'll do."

Back in Baton Rouge, they stopped at the same restaurant where they had lunch earlier. "What did you think of your father?" she asked.

"He's pinker than I thought he'd be. The person he killed was a bad man, wasn't he?"

"Yes, he was. But there's never a good reason for killing somebody. Dean is sorry he didn't let the law take care of the bad guy."

Monk thought about that while he finished a hamburger. He couldn't say this to Aunt Donna, but he didn't blame Tooth for killing the man.

If he'd been old enough, he might have done it himself.

"If Dean had let the law handle the matter," Aunt Donna said, "think how different our lives could have been. Your father would have been there to raise you."

That was true. But Monk wouldn't have lived with Grandmama. He might never have danced with Percy in Jackson Square. Would he have known Quinton Toussaint and Jon Latour? Aunt Donna and Uncle Barry might not have met one another.

Some things had been bad, other things horrible, but Monk wondered what would he change, if it changed everything else?

As they left the restaurant, Monk said, "Grandmama told me one time, to get the good things in life, sometimes we have to put up with the bad."

"It would be nice if we could pick the good to keep and eliminate the bad," Aunt Donna said. She started the car but sat there in the restaurant parking lot with the engine idling.

"Is there someplace else you want to go, Monk?"

He thought about the Lower Ninth struggling through bad times to get back to good again. Willy Bouchard had repaired the Baby Jesus Spiritual Church. Things were broken, but people were trying to fix them. The Saints played football in the Superdome. Big trucks hauled away garbage and workmen cleaned the streets. Here and there soldiers still patrolled, but rifles were slung across their shoulders instead of held at the ready. Monk wanted things right for his father's return. He had fourteen years to get it done.

"I want to go home," he said. "Home to New Orleans."

ACKNOWLEDGMENTS

Writing and publishing a book is an enormous feat that succeeds only when a whole network of talented people put their heads and their backs together to make it happen.

To Kerry Brooks, my publisher, I'm especially grateful for his intellectual energy, enthusiasm for every project, and his creative approach to the old world of publishing which has desperately needed a kick in the butt. Kerry doesn't yet know this, but I've given him the nickname, Batman, because he is my hero, and the hero of many other writers here in the Southeast who are now in the River's Edge Media family. If Kerry is Batman, then Shari Smith is a multi-faceted Wonder Woman, for she is writer, publicist, idea magnet, and nails it every time.

Big hugs and thanks to River's Edge Media staff: Gable White for his brilliant cover design, Paula Guajardo, who created the "special invitation" packets to my book launch; and Robin Miura, speaking in her soft North Carolina accent, as she unerringly enumerated my mistakes. Thank you, Robin, for making me look good.

Most of all, I acknowledge my husband, C. Terry Cline Jr., who left this world in 2013. Terry's creativity, sense of humor, and generous support of every writer he ever met was both sincere and unique. I apologize now, Terry, for all the times I became impatient while you talked for one more hour to a beginning writer who longed for encouragement from a published author. You did the right thing and we all love you for it.

FROM THE AUTHOR

I have loved reading for all of my life, but it was only after marrying a writer that I learned the importance author's place on hearing from their readers. My husband, C. Terry Cline, Jr., would always ask when I finished reading a book, "Was it good? What did you think?" And then he would say, "You should write to the author. Your letter might be received on the very day when that writer most needs acknowledgment or encouragement, no matter how successful he appears."

Some of the best days in my writing life have been those when I received a personal letter from a reader. I realized that every reader comes to a book with a unique perspective, and that he may find meaning in the work I would not have imagined. It is those communications that make the long months of writing worthwhile.

I hope that you will take a moment to comment on "Thelonious Rising" through my website at www.judithrichards.com. In so doing, you'll have made an important contribution to this writer and all the team who made this book possible.

Thank you! I sincerely look forward to hearing from you all. And I'm sending a special thank you to the residents of the Lower Ninth Ward of New Orleans who spoke to me so openly and with great affection for their hometown when I visited there shortly after the devastation caused by Hurricane Katrina.

"Laissez les bon temps rouler!"

Judy